AURORA BURNING

AURORA BURNING

AURORA CYCLE_02

AMIE KAUFMAN & JAY KRISTOFF

EMBER

Text copyright © 2020 by LaRoux Industries Pty Ltd. and Neverafter Pty Ltd.
Cover art copyright © 2020 by Charlie Bowater

All rights reserved. Published in the United States by Ember, an imprint of Random House Children's Books, a division of Penguin Random House LLC, New York. Originally published in hardcover in the United States by Alfred A. Knopf, an imprint of Random House Children's Books, a division of Penguin Random House LLC, New York, in 2020.

Ember and the E colophon are registered trademarks of Penguin Random House LLC.

Visit us on the Web! GetUnderlined.com

Educators and librarians, for a variety of teaching tools, visit us at RHTeachersLibrarians.com

Library of Congress Cataloging-in-Publication Data is available upon request.
ISBN 978-1-5247-2092-6 (trade) — ISBN 978-1-5247-2093-3 (lib. bdg.) — ISBN 978-1-5247-2094-0 (ebook) — ISBN 978-1-5247-2095-7 (pbk.)

Printed in the United States of America
10 9 8 7 6 5 4
First Ember Edition 2021

This one is for Squad 312.
Every single one of you.

STUFF YOU SHOULD KNOW

▶ **BOOK 1: *AURORA RISING***

▼ **CAST**

AURORA JIE-LIN O'MALLEY—THE GIRL OUT OF TIME. AURORA SET OUT FROM TERRA WITH TEN THOUSAND OTHER COLONISTS OVER TWO HUNDRED YEARS AGO, DESTINED FOR OCTAVIA III. HER VESSEL, THE *HADFIELD*, WAS LOST IN A STRETCH OF INTERDIMENSIONAL SPACE KNOWN AS THE FOLD, ONLY TO BE REDISCOVERED CENTURIES LATER BY AURORA LEGION CADET TYLER JONES.

AURORA WAS THE SOLE SURVIVOR.

AFTER HER RESCUE, AURI BEGAN HAVING PROPHETIC DREAMS AND EXHIBITING TELEKINETIC POWERS. ON THE RUN WITH THE MISFITS OF SQUAD 312, SHE WAS EVENTUALLY LED BACK TO OCTAVIA III. HERE SHE DISCOVERED THAT THE PLANET INTENDED TO BE HER HOME WAS ACTUALLY A NURSERY WORLD FOR THE RA'HAAM—AN ANCIENT GESTALT ENTITY COMPOSED OF MILLIONS OF ASSIMILATED LIFE-FORMS SLUMBERING BENEATH THE MANTLE.

AURORA ALSO LEARNED THAT HER POWERS HAD BEEN GIFTED TO HER BY THE ESHVAREN, A MYSTERIOUS RACE THAT DEFEATED THE RA'HAAM EONS AGO. KNOWING THAT THEIR ANCIENT FOE WOULD ONE DAY TRY TO CONSUME THE GALAXY AGAIN, THE ESHVAREN HID A WEAPON IN THE FOLD TO FIGHT THE RA'HAAM AND SET EVENTS IN MOTION TO CREATE A "TRIGGER" TO FIRE THE WEAPON.

AURORA HAS LEARNED THAT *SHE* IS THAT TRIGGER.

AURI IS SMALL IN SIZE, BIG ON MOXIE. SHE'S STILL STRUGGLING TO COME TO GRIPS WITH HER PLACE IN THIS NEW TIME AND GALAXY, BUT SHE FEELS A FIERCE LOYALTY TO THE AURORA LEGIONNAIRES WHO'VE TAKEN HER IN.

SHE HAS A BLACK PIXIE CUT WITH A WHITE STREAK THROUGH HER BANGS AND IS OF CHINESE-IRISH HERITAGE. HER RIGHT IRIS HAS TURNED WHITE, AND IT GLOWS WHEN SHE USES HER POWERS.

TYLER JONES—THE GOLDENBOY. TYLER ENLISTED IN THE AURORA LEGION AT AGE THIRTEEN, AFTER THE DEATH OF HIS FATHER, JERICHO. HE ENTERED THE ACADEMY'S ALPHA STREAM, DEVOTING HIS LIFE TO THE PURSUIT OF GALACTIC PEACE AND ORDER. BUT AFTER RESCUING AURORA IN THE FOLD, TY FOUND HIMSELF IN CHARGE OF A GROUP OF MISFITS, LOSERS, AND DISCIPLINE CASES: AURORA LEGION SQUAD 312.

AFTER BEING CAPTURED BY THE GLOBAL INTELLIGENCE AGENCY ABOARD THE SAGAN MINING STATION, TYLER AND HIS SQUAD FOUND THEMSELVES ON THE RUN FROM THE TERRAN GOVERNMENT. VISITING THE INTERDICTED WORLD OF OCTAVIA III, TYLER AND COMPANY UNCOVERED AN ANCIENT CONSPIRACY THAT THREATENS EVERY SENTIENT RACE IN THE GALAXY. AND THE MISFITS OF SQUAD 312 SEEM TO BE THE ONLY ONES WHO CAN STOP IT.

TY IS A NATURAL LEADER AND A BRILLIANT TACTICIAN, BUT ACCORDING TO HIS SISTER, HE "WOULDN'T KNOW FUN IF IT INVADED HIS PLANET." HE'S SELF-CONFIDENT TO THE POINT OF ARROGANCE, BUT HE USUALLY HAS THE GOODS TO BACK IT UP.

HE HAS BLUE EYES, BLOND SHAGGY HAIR, AND DIMPLES THAT CAN EXPLODE OVARIES AT THIRTY METERS.

KALIIS IDRABAN GILWRAETH—THE OUTSIDER. KALIIS IS ONE OF THE FEW SYLDRATHI TO HAVE JOINED THE AURORA LEGION SINCE THE WAR BETWEEN EARTH AND SYLDRA ENDED. HE IS A MEMBER OF THE WARBREED CABAL—THE SYLDRATHI WARRIOR CASTE—AND HIS FEARSOME COMBAT PROWESS MADE HIM A NATURAL FOR THE TANK STREAM IN THE ACADEMY. HOWEVER, HE WAS SHUNNED AS AN OUTSIDER AND ENDED UP IN SQUAD 312.

UPON MEETING AURORA, KAL FOUND HIMSELF IMMEDIATELY UNDER

ASYMMETRICAL BOB. SHE'S NEVER HAD A RELATIONSHIP THAT LASTED MORE THAN SEVEN WEEKS, AND THE TRAIL OF BROKEN HEARTS SHE'S LEFT IN HER WAKE WOULD BE AS LONG AS MY ARM.

I MEAN, IF I *HAD* ARMS . . .

FINIAN DE KARRAN DE SEEL—THE SMART-ASS. FINIAN IS A BETRASKAN AND A MECHANICAL GENIUS WHOSE ABRASIVE PERSONALITY AND LESS-THAN-STELLAR INTERPERSONAL SKILLS SAW HIM PICKED LAST OUT OF EVERY GEARHEAD IN HIS YEAR AT AURORA ACADEMY.

FINIAN CAUGHT THE LYSERGIA PLAGUE AS A CHILD, AND THOUGH THE DISEASE FAILED TO KILL HIM, IT EXTENSIVELY DAMAGED HIS MOBILITY. SENT AWAY FROM TRASK TO LIVE ABOARD A ZERO-GEE SPACE STATION WITH HIS THIRD GRANDPARENTS, FINIAN USED HIS TECHNICAL SKILLS TO CONSTRUCT AN EXOSUIT, WHICH HE WEARS CONSTANTLY. THE SUIT ALLOWS HIM TO MOVE UNASSISTED AND CONTAINS AN ARRAY OF USEFUL TOOLS AND DEVICES.

FINIAN HIDES HIS INSECURITIES BEHIND A WALL OF CYNICISM. LIKE ALL HIS PEOPLE, HE HAS PALE SKIN AND HAIR, AND HE WEARS BLACK CONTACT LENSES OVER HIS EYES TO PROTECT THEM FROM UV RADIATION.

HE DOES NOT HAVE A HOPELESS CRUSH ON SCARLETT JONES, THANKS FOR ASKING. ANY RUMORS THAT HER BROTHER WOULD BE A SATISFACTORY CONSOLATION PRIZE ARE NONE OF YOUR BUSINESS EITHER.

ZILA MADRAN—THE FRIGHTENINGLY INTELLIGENT ONE. OR JUST THE FRIGHTENING ONE. ZILA IS THE SCIENCE OFFICER IN SQUAD 312. THOUGH SHE SPEAKS RARELY, HER INSIGHTS ARE USUALLY FLAWLESS, AND SHE APPROACHES LIFE WITH A SENSE OF ICE-COLD RATIONALITY.

ZILA HAS FEW TO NO SOCIAL SKILLS. SHE'S BLUNT AND DISTANT AND

THE INFLUENCE OF "THE PULL"—AN IMPOSSIBLY INTENSE SYLDRATHI MATING INSTINCT. NOT WISHING TO FORCE AURORA INTO A SITUATION OR A RELATIONSHIP SHE COULDN'T UNDERSTAND, KAL DECIDED TO LEAVE THE SQUAD. BUT AFTER AURORA CONFESSED FEELINGS FOR HIM, HE RESOLVED TO STAY AND DEVOTED HIMSELF TO PROTECTING HIS BE'SHMAI (BELOVED).

KAL STRUGGLES WITH HIS WARRIOR INSTINCT CONSTANTLY, AND HIS BATTLES WITH THIS SO-CALLED ENEMY WITHIN HINT AT A DARKNESS IN HIS PAST HE HAS YET TO SHARE.

KAL IS AN EXCELLENT BROODER. HONESTLY, HE COULD BROOD AT A PROFESSIONAL LEVEL.

HE HAS DREAMY VIOLET EYES, OLIVE SKIN, AND LONG SILVER HAIR. DON'T EVEN GET ME STARTED ON HIS CHEEKBONES.

SCARLETT JONES—THE HEARTBREAKER. TYLER'S TWIN SISTER (OLDER BY THREE MINUTES AND 37.4 SECONDS), SCARLETT ENLISTED IN THE AURORA LEGION ALONG WITH HER BROTHER—NOT OUT OF ANY SENSE OF DUTY TO LAW AND ORDER, BUT RATHER TO KEEP TYLER OUT OF TROUBLE. SHE JOINED THE DIPLOMACY STREAM AND APPLIED HERSELF LESS THAN ANY CADET IN ACADEMY HISTORY, BUT HER ALMOST SIXTH SENSE ABOUT WHAT OTHERS WERE THINKING HELPED HER BECOME A BRILLIANT FACE.

SCAR HAS A BLACK BELT IN SARCASM. THOUGH SHE'S UNFOCUSED, SHE'S HIGHLY INTELLIGENT, AND SHE CAN QUICKLY LEARN ENOUGH ABOUT ANY SITUATION/CULTURE/SETTING TO FIT INTO MOST SCENARIOS SEAMLESSLY. INCIDENTALLY, THIS MAKES HER A TRIVIA-NIGHT QUEEN.

SCAR IS PALE, STATUESQUE, AND HAS FLAMING RED HAIR CUT IN AN

HAS TROUBLE SHOWING EMPATHY FOR OTHERS. SHE'S HINTED AT PAST TRAUMA AS THE REASON FOR THIS BEHAVIOR, BUT SHE HAS YET TO REVEAL WHAT THAT TRAUMA MIGHT HAVE BEEN. ZILA IS SHORT, WITH DARK BROWN SKIN AND LONG, CURLING HAIR THAT SEEMS TO HAVE A MIND OF ITS OWN (WHICH WOULD EXPLAIN A LOT, ACTUALLY). SHE WEARS A VARIETY OF GOLDEN EARRINGS, WHICH STRANGELY SEEM TO MATCH WHATEVER SHE'S DOING AT THE TIME. SOFT-SPOKEN, SHE'S SCARY SMART, AND WAAAAAY TOO FOND OF SHOOTING THINGS WITH HER DISRUPTOR PISTOL.

CATHERINE BRANNOCK—THE HOTSHOT. CAT "ZERO" BRANNOCK WAS A BRILLIANT PILOT AND MEMBER OF THE AURORA LEGION. BEST FRIENDS WITH TY AND SCAR JONES SINCE CHILDHOOD, CAT WAS RESPONSIBLE FOR THE SCAR ON TYLER'S RIGHT EYEBROW (SHE BROKE A CHAIR OVER HIS HEAD ON THE FIRST DAY OF KINDERGARTEN).

CAT AND TY SLEPT WITH EACH OTHER THE NIGHT THEY GRADUATED INTO THEIR FINAL YEAR AS CADETS. THOUGH TYLER CONVINCED CAT THAT A SERIOUS RELATIONSHIP WASN'T A GOOD IDEA, CAT CONTINUED TO CARRY A TORCH FOR TY AND STUCK WITH HIM WHEN HE WAS LUMPED WITH THE MISFITS OF SQUAD 312.

CYNICAL AND COMBATIVE, SHE WAS OFTEN AT LOGGERHEADS WITH AURORA, AND SHE TRIED TO KEEP THE SQUAD ON THE STRAIGHT AND NARROW. TRAGICALLY, SHE WAS INFECTED BY THE RA'HAAM HIVE MIND WHEN THE SQUAD VISITED OCTAVIA III. THOUGH SHE FOUGHT AGAINST THE GESTALT BRAVELY, ALLOWING HER TEAMMATES TIME TO ESCAPE THE PLANET, SHE WAS EVENTUALLY ABSORBED INTO THE COLLECTIVE.

I KNOW. I WAS SAD, TOO. ☹

THE ESHVAREN—DEPENDING WHO YOU ASK, THE ESHVAREN ARE EITHER AN ANCIENT RACE OF MYSTERIOUS BEINGS WHO DIED OUT A MILLION YEARS AGO, OR A SCAM PERPETUATED BY TWO-CRED HUCKSTERS AND PURVEYORS OF BOGUS ARTIFACTS.

IN FACT, NOT ONLY DID THE ESHVAREN EXIST, BUT THEY ACTUALLY FOUGHT A WAR AGAINST THE RA'HAAM FOR THE FATE OF THE ENTIRE GALAXY. THE ESHVAREN EVENTUALLY WON.

KNOWING THAT THEIR ANCIENT FOES MIGHT ONE DAY RETURN, BUT THAT THEY'D LIKELY NOT BE ALIVE TO SEE IT, THE ESHVAREN HID DEVICES IN THE FOLD THAT WOULD LEAD TO THE CREATION OF THE TRIGGER—A BEING OF IMMENSE PSYCHIC POWER. THEY ALSO SUPPOSEDLY HID A WEAPON CAPABLE OF DEFEATING THE RA'HAAM OUT THERE TOO.

IF YOU KNOW WHERE TO FIND IT, HONESTLY, THAT'D REALLY HELP US OUT. . . .

THE RA'HAAM—A SINGLE BEING COMPRISING MILLIONS OF MINDS. WANTING TO INCORPORATE THE GALAXY INTO ITS "UNION," THE RA'HAAM ONCE SOUGHT TO CONSUME EVERY SENTIENT MIND IN THE GALAXY.

DEFEATED BY THE ESHVAREN, THE RA'HAAM SANK INTO HIBERNATION ON TWENTY-TWO HIDDEN NURSERY WORLDS, SCATTERED ACROSS THE MILKY WAY. NESTLED BENEATH THE SURFACE OF THESE PLANETS—ALL LOCATED NEAR NATURALLY OCCURRING GATES INTO THE FOLD—THE RA'HAAM HAS BEEN LICKING ITS WOUNDS FOR A MILLION YEARS.

UNFORTUNATELY, ONE OF THESE WORLDS IS OCTAVIA III, A PLANET CHOSEN FOR TERRAN COLONIZATION. DISCOVERING THE NASCENT RA'HAAM BENEATH THE SURFACE, THE COLONISTS WERE CONSUMED AND ADDED TO ITS TOTALITY, INCLUDING AURORA'S FATHER, ZHANG JI.

WHAT HAPPENED NEXT IS A LITTLE MURKY, BUT THE RA'HAAM

APPARENTLY SENT THESE CORRUPTED COLONISTS BACK TO EARTH, INFILTRATING THE GLOBAL INTELLIGENCE AGENCY TO FURTHER ITS AGENDA. IT NOW WAITS BENEATH ITS TWENTY-TWO WORLDS, GATHERING STRENGTH FOR THE MOMENT IT CAN SPAWN AGAIN, SPEWING THROUGH THE FOLD TO INFECT THE ENTIRE GALAXY.

MAGELLAN—THAT'D BE ME! HELLO! I MISSED YOUR SQUISHY HUMAN FACES!

OKAY, ALL CAUGHT UP? WELL, STRAP IN, FOLKS. WE AIN'T IN KANSAS ANYMORE. . . .

PART 1

DOWN AND OUT IN
EMERALD CITY

1

TYLER

The disruptor blast hits the Betraskan right in her chest.

She shrieks, and her armload of e-tech goes flying as she collapses in a drooling heap. I vault over her as she falls, ducking as another disruptor shot hisses past my ear. The bazaar around us is crowded, the mob parting before me in a panic as more blasts ring out behind us. Scarlett is running right on my heels, flame-red hair plastered to her cheeks with sweat. She leaps over the unconscious Betraskan woman and her scattered goods, offering an apologetic shout.

"Sorryyyy!"

Another blast rings out. The gangsters chasing us roar at the crowd to step aside. We leap over the counter of a semptar stall, past the gobsmacked owner, and out the back door into another packed, humid street. Hovercraft and rotor bots. Pale green walls around us, red skies above, yellow plascrete beneath our feet, a rainbow of outfits and skin tones ahead.

"Left!" Finian shouts over comms. *"Go left!"*

We left it, barreling into a grubby alleyway off the main drag. Hucksters and fienders stare at us as we sprint past, boots pounding, trash flying. The tiny gangsters chasing us reach the alley mouth, filling the air with the *BAMF! BAMF!* of their disruptor blasts. The whoosh of charged particles rushes past my ear. We skid behind a dumpster full of discarded machine parts, looking for some kind of cover.

"I *told* you this was a bad idea!" Scarlett gasps.

"And I told you I don't *have* bad ideas!" I shout, kicking through a doorway.

"Oh no?" she asks, cracking off a shot at our pursuers.

"No!" I drag her inside. "Just less amazing ones!"

. . . . .

Yeah, let's back it up a little.

About forty minutes, maybe, before things got quite so shooty. I know I've done this before, but it's more exciting this way. Trust me. Dimples, remember?

So, forty minutes ago, I'm sitting in a crowded booth in a crowded bar, music thumping in my ears. I'm outfitted in a tight black tunic and tighter pants, which I presume are stylish—Scarlett chose them for me, after all. My sister's squeezed into the booth beside me, also in civilian wardrobe: blood-red and formfitting and cut as low as she likes it.

Sitting opposite us are a dozen gremps.

The place we're in is a dive, all pulsing light and smoky air, stuffed to the rafters. There's a broad pit in the center of the room where I guess they hold some kind of blood sport, but fortunately nobody's killing anyone else in here right now. Drug and skin trades are going on all around us, the small-time hustlers of the station and their daily grind. And along with the smell of rocksmoke and the speakers' thudding deepdub, a single question is buzzing in my head.

How in the Maker's name did I get here?

The gremps sit across from us—a dozen small, furry figures crammed into the other side of the booth. Their slitted eyes are fixed on the uniglass Scarlett has placed on the table between us. The device is a flat pane of palm-sized transparent silicon, lit up with holo displays. Rotating a few inches above it is a glowing image of our Longbow. The ship is arrowhead-shaped, gleaming titanium and carbite. The Aurora Legion sigil and our squad designation, 312, are emblazoned down its flanks.

It's state of the art. Beautiful. We've been through a lot together.

And now we have to let her go.

The gremps mutter among themselves in their own hissing, purring tongue, whiskers twitching. The leader is a little over a meter tall, which is big for her species. The tortoiseshell fur covering her body is perfectly coiffed, and her pearl-white suit screams "gangster chic." Her pale green eyes are edged with dark powder and have the gleam of someone who feeds people to her pets for kicks.

"Risky, Earthgirl." The gremp's voice is a smooth purr. "Rrrrisky."

"We were told Skeff Tannigut was a lady who could handle a little risk," Scarlett smiles. "You've got quite the reputation around here."

The aforementioned Ms. Tannigut drums her claws on the tabletop, glances up from the hologram of our Longbow and into my sister's eyes.

"There's regular risk, Earthgirl, and then there's the risk of twenty years in Lunar Penal Colony. Trafficking in stolen Aurora Legion hardware is no joke."

5

"Neither is the hardware," I say.

Twelve sets of slitted eyes swivel toward me. Twelve fanged jaws drop open. Skeff Tannigut looks at my sister with astonishment, ears twitching atop her head.

"You let your male speak in public?"

"He's . . . spirited," Scarlett smiles, giving me a side-eye full of *Shut uuup*.

"I could sell you a pain collar?" the gangster offers. "Break him in?"

I raise my eyebrow. "Thanks, but—*hrk!*"

I clutch my bruised shin under the table and glare as Scarlett leans forward to look the syndicate leader in the eye. "If you're feeling so generous, let's skip the foreplay, shall we?" She waves at the holo image of our Longbow. "A hundred thousand and she's yours. Weapon passcodes included."

Tannigut confers briefly with her colleagues. Not fancying another boot to the shins, I keep my mouth on the right side of shut and study the club around us.

The bar is lined with bottles full of rainbows, and the walls are lit with holographic displays—jetball games and the latest economy reports from Central and news feeds of Unbroken ships on the move in the Neutral Zones. This station is a long way from the Core, but I'm still surprised at the number of different species here. Since we docked two hours ago, I must've counted at least twenty—pale Betraskans, furry gremps, hulking blue Chellerians. This place is like a dirty slice of the whole Milky Way, dropped into one dodgy, suborbital melting pot.

The planet we're floating above is a gas giant, a little smaller than Jupiter back home. This station hovers in the stratosphere, suspended above a storm that's four centuries old and twenty thousand klicks wide. The air is filtered, the whole floating city sealed inside a transparent dome of ionized particles crackling faintly in the skies above our heads. But I can still taste the tang of chlorine gas that gives the storm its color and this station its name.

I take a sip of my water. Glance at the coaster beneath it. WELCOME TO EMERALD CITY! it says. DON'T LOOK DOWN!

The gremps have stopped conversing, and Tannigut's glittering eyes are back on Scar. The gangster smooths her whiskers with one paw as she speaks.

"I'll give you thirty thousand," she says. "First and final offer."

Scar raises one perfectly manicured eyebrow. "Since when do gremps do stand-up comedy?"

"Since when do Aurora legionnaires sell their ships?" the gremp asks.

"We could have stolen this baby. What makes you think we're Legion?"

Tannigut points to me. "His haircut."

"What's wron—*hrk!*"

"All due respect, but the whys aren't your concern," Scarlett says smoothly. "There's no tech anywhere in the galaxy like the tech that comes out of Aurora labs. One hundred thousand is a bargain, and you know it." Scar tosses her flame-red bob out of her eyes and manages to look nowhere as desperate as we actually are. "And therefore, madam, I bid you good day."

Scar is rising to leave and Tannigut is reaching out to

stop her when the commotion starts at the bar. I look toward the noise to see what the fuss is, notice that the various jetball games and stock reports on the displays have been interrupted by a special news feed.

My stomach flips as I read the message at the bottom of the screens.

AURORA LEGION TERROR ATTACK

A big Terran asks the barkeeper to turn it up. A bigger Chellerian bellows to put the game back on. As a small fistfight breaks out, the barkeep drops the volume on the deepdub, cranks the news feed through the pub's speakers.

"... *over seven thousand Syldrathi refugees were killed in the attack, with the Terran and Betraskan governments both expressing outrage at the massacre ...*"

My heart drops and thumps in my chest as I watch the accompanying footage. It shows the gunmetal-gray blisters of an ore-processing rig nestled on the flank of a massive asteroid, floating in a sea of stars.

I recognize the structure immediately. It's Sagan Station—the mining rig our squad was sent to on its first mission away from Aurora Academy. We were captured by a Terran destroyer there, held captive by the GIA. They obliterated Sagan to silence any witnesses who might have seen them taking Auri into custody. There's nothing left of that place but debris now.

Hard to believe that was just a few days ago ...

As I watch, a ship swoops in and fires a barrage of missiles, immolating the station. But as the footage freezes on the attacking vessel, I realize it's not the lumbering, snub-nosed hulk of a Terran destroyer firing the kill shot. The attacking ship is arrowhead-shaped, gleaming titanium and carbite, the Aurora Legion sigil and its squad designation emblazoned down its flanks.

312.

"Great Maker . . ."

I glance at Scarlett. The voice-over rises above the worsening bar brawl.

"The perpetrators of the Sagan massacre are also wanted in connection with breach of Galactic Interdiction while being pursued by Terran forces. The joint commander of Aurora Legion, Admiral Seph Adams, released the following statement just moments ago. . . ."

The footage cuts to the familiar figure of Admiral Adams, our Aurora Legion CO, decked out in full dress uniform. Dozens of medals gleam across his broad chest. His cybernetic arms are folded, his expression grim. He taps one prosthetic finger on his forearm as he speaks, metal ringing softly on metal.

"We condemn," he says, *"in strongest possible terms, the actions of Aurora Legion Squad 312 at Sagan Station. We cannot explain their motives, save to say that this squad has clearly gone rogue. They have violated our trust. They have broken our code. Aurora Legion Command offers every assistance to the Terran government in its pursuit of these murderers, and our thoughts and prayers are with the families of the slain refugees."*

Photographs flash up on the screen. The faces and names of my crew.

Finian de Karran de Seel.

Zila Madran.

Catherine Brannock.

Kaliis Idraban Gilwraeth.

Scarlett Jones.

Tyler Jones.

Under each of our names scroll more words.

WANTED. REWARD OFFERED: 100,000CR

And it's about then that my stomach feels ready to crawl right out of my mouth.

I glance at my sister wordlessly. We need to move. Scar's already snatching her uniglass off the table when Tannigut's claws sink into her wrist.

"On second thought"—the gremp smiles with pointed teeth—"a hundred thousand credits *does* sound like a bargain."

Scarlett looks to me. I've always said it's funny being a twin. Sometimes I feel like I know what my sister will say before she says it. Sometimes I swear she can tell what I'm thinking just by looking at me. And right now, I'm thinking we need to get all the way out of this stinking bar and off this stinking station.

Like, yesterday.

Scarlett slams the heel of her palm into Tannigut's nose. She's rewarded with a loud crunch and a shriek of pain, a gout of deep magenta. I grab my sister's bloody hand and drag her out of the booth as the other gremps howl and leap at us.

The brawl over the remote control at the other end of the bar is now in full swing, and I figure a little more chaos isn't going to hurt. So I blast a gremp in the face with my disruptor, knock another's fangs out of its head with my boot, push Scar toward the door.

"Go! Go!"

Someone screams. A barfly goes sailing into the wall above my head. Three gremps jump on me, clawing and biting. I kick and blast them free, roll across the floor and up to my feet, burst out the front door behind my sister and into the labyrinth of streets that make up the Emerald City.

The station covers eighty levels, a hundred kilometers wide. The lower levels are taken up by an inverted forest of wind turbines, which harnesses the immense storm currents below and turns them into energy. The city is interconnected by a huge lattice of transparent public transit tubes, powered by those same currents. And it's into one of these tubes that my sister and I leap face-first.

"Grand bazaar!" Scarlett shouts, "COMPLYING," the computer beeps, and before I can blink, we're being whipped along the tube on a cushion of ionized oxygen.

"Fin? You reading me?" I shout over the rushing current.

"Um, yeah," comes the response. *"You catch the news, Goldenboy? That was not a flattering photo of me."*

"Yeah, we saw it. So did half the people in this city, I'm guessing. Including the syndicate we were trying to sell the Longbow to."

"No deal, I take it?"

I glance behind, see a pack of gremps whipping along right on our tails, disruptors ready to fire as soon as we're out of the pressurized tube.

"You could say that," I reply. "We're coming back through the bazaar, I need you giving us directions. Tell Kal and Zila to prep for launch. Every bounty hunter, lawman, and half-baked do-gooder in this hole is gonna be after us now."

"I did tell you this was a bad idea."

"And I told you. I don't *have* bad ideas."

"Just less amazing ones?"

Emerald City is whipping past the transit tube outside, dozens of levels, thousands of secrets, millions of people. The clouds around us swirl and shift in beautiful patterns, like watercolors on wet canvas. The walls and archways and gleaming spires under the ionized dome are tinged pale green by the chlorine storm below, the skies above like bruised blood.

I knew we'd be pushing it by even coming to a station as remote as this one. It was only a matter of time before word got out that we'd gone rogue, and I knew the Global Intelligence Agency would be gunning for us after Octavia III. But I should've known they'd come at us sideways. Framing us as the perpetrators of the massacre *they* committed was smart. Something I might've done if I flushed my morals into the recycler. By painting us as killers of innocent refugees as well as Interdiction breakers, they've cut us off from Aurora Academy and anyone who'd help us.

I can't blame Adams for disavowing us. But he took me and Scar under his wing when Dad died—I have to admit it hurt, listening to him call us murderers. And though it makes sense for him to cut us loose after we've been accused of galactic terrorism, part of me is gutted he could ever believe it.

"Heads up, Bee-bro," Scar calls.

"Next stop, Grand Bazaar," says the computer.

"You ready for this?" I ask.

My sister looks back at me and winks. "I *am* a Jones."

A rush of air from the other direction slows us to a perfect stop beside the tube doors. We bail out, scramble into the sea of stalls and noise that is the Emerald City Grand Bazaar. If I had a moment, I'd stop to admire the sight.

But as it is, I figure I've only got a moment before we're both dead.

. . . . .

We burst through the doorway from the alley and into the kitchen of a Betraskan greasy spoon, the air filled with the sweet smell of luka nut oil and frying javi. The chef is about to start yelling at us when he sees the disruptor pistols in our hands. Then he and his cooks wisely decide to go on break.

The gremps burst in behind us, and Scarlett and I unload with our disruptors. I take out four (98 percent on my marksmanship exam), and the others bail back into the alley outside. Before they can regroup, we're running again, out the front doors of the crowded diner and into the street beyond.

A teenage human pulls up on a hoverskiff outside the diner, climbs off the saddle. As his feet touch sidewalk, I sweep his legs, catch his falling passkeys, and leap onto his ride. Scar jumps onto the skiff behind me and offers an apologetic shout to the owner as we take off.

"Sorryyyy!"

We zip off into the thoroughfare, drones and manned vehicles bobbing and swerving around and above us. The traffic here is pure chaos—a perpetual high-velocity rush hour, three layers deep, and I'm hoping we can lose our pursuers in the crush. But a disruptor blast at our backs lets me know . . .

"They're still behind us!" Scar shouts.

"So blast them!"

"You *know* I'm a bad shot!" She claws her hair out of her eyes. "I spent my senior marksmanship classes flirting with my range partner!"

I shake my head. "Remind me why you're in my squad again?"

"Because I said yes, smart-ass!"

Finian's voice cuts in over comms. *"You wanna take the next turnoff, Goldenboy. Leads straight to the docks."*

"Hiiiii, Finian."

"Um . . . hey, Scarlett."

"Whatcha doing?"

"Ah . . ." My Gearhead clears his throat. *"Well, I mean—"*

"Scar, knock it off!" I shout, zooming down the turnoff with more disruptor blasts ringing behind us. "Fin, does station security have any idea we're here yet?"

"Nothing on the bulletins so far."

"Engines prepped?"

"Ready to launch as soon as you two get here." Fin clears his throat again. *"Although, without you . . . we don't really have a pilot. . . ."*

And just like that, the world flying by me at a hundred and twenty klicks an hour slows to a crawl.

Scar's arm tightens a little around my waist. My breath catches in my throat. I'm trying not to think about her. Trying not to remember her name. Trying not to acknowledge the ache in my chest and just keep us on the move, because as deep as we are, there's just no time for grief right now. But still . . .

Cat.

"We'll be there in sixty," I say. "Bay doors open—we're coming in hot."

"Roger that."

We hit the exit ramp so fast we almost bounce clear off it, traffic whizzing past us in a blur. I risk a glance over my shoulder, see a low-slung hovercruiser muscling its way through the vehicles behind us. More than a dozen gremps are clinging to the sides. I'm not sure how she managed it so quick, but Tannigut has called in reinforcements, and they look like Business.

The ramp is crowded with loaders and heavy skiffs, and Scar cracks off a dozen wild shots, emptying her disruptor's power pack and hitting a few random targets. But she cries out in triumph as her final blast clips a gremp in the shoulder, sending the gangster tumbling onto the roadway.

"I *got* one!"

Scar tightens her grip on my waist, shaking me frantically. "Did! You! *See that?* I—"

I set my disruptor to Kill and offload into the belly of a bulky waste hauler cruising in the lane directly above us. The blast blows out its stabilizers, sends it dropping in a cloud of smoke. I swerve aside as the drone crashes into our lane, flipping end over end, spraying a few tons of recyclables all over the ramp behind us. Horns blare, air brakes fire, and the gremp's hovercruiser plows right into the crashed drone, sending its occupants flying in a hail of smoking fur and curse words.

The whole posse, taken out by a single shot.

I blow on the barrel of my disruptor. Smile over my shoulder as I slip it back into my holster.

"You know," Scarlett pouts, "nobody likes a show-off, Bee-bro."

"I hate it when you call me that," I grin.

We hit the docks, zipping through foot traffic, auto-packers, flatbeds loaded with cargo. The spaceport of Emerald City is laid out before us, all glittering lights and buzzing skies and sleek ships at berth. I can see our Longbow dead ahead, at rest between a massive Betraskan longhauler and a brand-new Rigellian pleasure cruiser from the Talmarr shipyards.

Fin's standing at the bottom of the loading ramp, surveying the docks with a worried expression. His bone-white skin is bright beneath the Longbow lights, his pale hair styled into short spikes. His slim-cut civi clothes are dark against the gleaming silver exosuit enshrouding his limbs and back.

He spots us, waves frantically.

"I see you, Goldenboy. Move that spank cushion, we gotta—"

"THIS IS A SECURITY ALERT," blare the dockside loud-speakers. "ALL CRAFT CURRENTLY IN EMERALD CITY DOCKS ARE ON LOCKDOWN UNTIL FURTHER NOTICE. REPEAT: THIS IS A SECURITY ALERT. . . ."

"You think that's for us?" Scarlett shouts in my ear.

I glance into the skies above, spot a security drone amid the swarm of loaders and lifters.

"Yeah," I sigh. "That's for us."

The floor below us shudders, and massive docking clamps begin rising up from the spaceport decks ahead. They cinch around the ships at berth, eliciting a spew of profanity from the crew members and workers all around us. I lay on the juice, desperately trying to get us home, but we skid to a halt near Fin just as the dock machinery locks our Longbow in place.

Scar jumps off the skiff. As the alert continues to blare around us, I toss the damp blond from my eyes, surveying the clamps with hands on hips. Reinforced titanium, slick with grease, electromagnetic. And they're huge.

"No way we've got the thrust to blast free of those," I say.

Fin shakes his head. "They'll tear the hull to pieces."

"Can you hack the system?" I ask. "Unlock us?"

My Gearhead already has his uniglass out, the device lighting up with a dozen tiny holographic displays as he begins typing. "Gimme five minutes."

"I don't want to alarm anyone," Scar says. "But we don't *have* five minutes."

I look to where my twin is pointing, heart sinking as I spot two armored hoverskiffs speeding across the docks. Their flashing lights and blaring alarms send the crowds scattering out of the way, and they're cutting a line straight toward us.

In the flatbed trays behind the control cabins I can see two dozen heavy Security Bots armed with disruptor cannons. Emblazoned across the truck hoods, the breastplates of the SecBots, are the words EMERALD CITY SECURITY.

"So," Scarlett says, looking at me. "Any more amazing ideas?"

SUBJECT: GALACTIC ORGANIZATIONS

▶ **BENEVOLENT**

▼ **AURORA LEGION**

FORMED OF AN ALLIANCE BETWEEN **TERRA** AND **TRASK**, AND RECENTLY JOINED BY THE **FREE SYLDRATHI**, THE AURORA LEGION HAS FUNCTIONED AS AN INDEPENDENT PEACEKEEPING FORCE IN THE **MILKY WAY** FOR OVER A CENTURY. THE LEGION MEDIATES BORDER DISPUTES, ASSISTS IN RELIEF WORK, AND HELPS BRING STABILITY TO THE GALAXY BY LIVING ITS MOTTO:

WE THE LEGION
WE THE LIGHT
BURNING BRIGHT AGAINST THE NIGHT

AURORA LEGIONNAIRES SPECIALIZE IN ONE OF SIX FIELDS:

 LEADERSHIP AND PLANNING (**ALPHAS**)

 DIPLOMACY AND NEGOTIATION (**FACES**)

 PILOTING AND TRANSPORT (**ACES**)

 REPAIRS, MAINTENANCE, AND MECHANICAL WORK (**GEARHEADS**)

 TACTICAL COMBAT AND ENGAGEMENT STRATEGY (**TANKS**)

 SCIENTIFIC AND MEDICAL DUTIES (**BRAINS**)

2

AURI

We're already on our feet when Fin comes charging up the ramp, limping heavily.

"Grab your gear," he barks. "We're bailing."

Tyler and Scarlett are right on his heels, running for their bunks and lockers.

"Twenty seconds!" hollers our squad leader as he passes Kal and me. "Twenty seconds, out the door!"

I don't own anything except my uniglass, Magellan—who's stuffed in my pocket as always—and the clothes I'm wearing. So I hustle to where Fin's frantically packing away the tool kit he and Zila were using to repair his suit.

"Go," I tell him. "Get your stuff. I can pack this."

He shoots me a grateful look and turns for the back of the ship. I don't have time to fit any of the little tools or machinery into their snug foam beds, so I just sweep everything into the bag.

"Ten seconds!" Ty yells from somewhere down the back.

"Portables and valuables," Scarlett shouts in reply. "Travel light!"

I lift the bag with shaking hands, glancing around the cabin in search of anything else I should grab.

Kal and I spent the last few hours sitting in the back as he tried to teach me some Syldrathi exercises he hoped would help me focus my mind. The wild power I briefly controlled on Octavia III is still lurking inside me—I can feel it there, swirling and rolling behind my ribs—but my command of it is shaky at best. If I open the valve that's keeping it cooped up in there, I have no idea what will come out, but I know it won't be pretty. Kal's hope is that with training, with discipline, I can control how I use it.

But as I tried to envision a slowly flickering purple flame, pushing away reality to focus on my sa-mēi—a Syldrathi concept I still don't understand—it was hard not to peek from beneath my lashes and stare at him instead. Kal gets this little frown when he's concentrating, and *that* I could happily push away reality and focus on just fine. But I think he might consider that an undignified version of training.

I spend my final five seconds grabbing the ration packs scattered across the table and shoving them in on top of Fin's tools, slinging the bag over my shoulder as the others come piling out from the back.

"Let's go," Tyler snaps. "Kal, you're on point. We have two armored hoverskiffs incoming, maybe thirty seconds away. Let's be gone before they arrive."

"Yessir," Kal says simply, glancing across to check my position, then leading the way down the ramp. Tyler's straight behind him and I'm next, which means I run smack into our Alpha's back when he pulls up short.

"Hey, watch—"

20

I lean sideways to see around him, and realize he's stopped because Kal stopped. And Kal stopped because . . .

"I think," our Tank says quietly, "your estimate of thirty seconds was incorrect."

The three of us are sitting ducks on the Longbow's loading ramp, which is bad news, because we're not alone. Two huge floating flatbed trucks have pulled up in front of our ship, lights flashing an urgent blue. And huge, terrifying robot trooper things that look like upright metal cockroaches are jumping down from them, knees bending backward to take the impact as they hit the ground. They're armed with guns the size of my torso, their polished armor reflecting the strobing lights.

"ATTENTION, SUSPECTS," one blares, though I don't see its mouth move. "YOU ARE BEING DETAINED FOR QUESTIONING. RESISTANCE WILL BE MET WITH FORCE. RAISE YOUR HANDS TO INDICATE COMPLIANCE."

For a long moment, everything's quiet. Even the roar of the city around us subsides, and as if I'm underwater, all I can see is the flashing blue light dancing against the armor on the cockroach robot soldiers. Kal adjusts his weight ever so slightly, using his body to shield mine. I feel a tingling on the back of my neck, adrenaline thumping in my veins. I feel the world . . . shift, and without warning, my mind is aswirl with images.

Another vision.

It's as if I can see the next few instants play out inside my head, like I'm watching on a vidscreen. I can see the pathways we could follow, each branching away in front of me, clear as glass.

I see them putting us in cuffs, loading us up onto one of those flatbeds, snapping the restraints onto the long bar down the middle to secure us. I see Zila's hands twisted up behind her back, Ty's jaw squared in defeat and frustration.

Or, down another path, I see Kal start forward and Ty dive to the side, and I see me standing paralyzed by indecision as the troopers open up, their fire slicing through our bodies.

Or I see . . .

"Be'shmai," says Kal softly.

"Yes," I say quietly, pausing for a long, slow breath. I feel my lungs expand, feel my ribs swell with the pressure inside, the thing I've awoken roiling and ready, wanting and *demanding* to be free. I lift my voice a little so all of Squad 312 will hear me. "Everyone, hit the deck in three . . ."

I hear a query from behind me, the roaring already rising in my ears.

"Two . . ."

I hope the squad's confusion won't slow them down. That they'll trust me, though our new trust is a fragile thing, built on heartbreak.

"One."

Tyler and Kal fold to the ground, and I throw up my hands, letting go of every piece of myself. My body's gone, left behind where it stands in the doorway of the Longbow, swaying in place. And I'm a tumult of midnight-blue mental energy, laced through with vicious threads of silver, exploding in every direction.

To the rest of the world I'm invisible, or I'm back where my body is, or maybe something in between. But on the plane where I exist, I'm a roiling sphere, expanding at the speed of light to envelop the SecBots in front of me.

It's a wave I'm barely riding, not at all controlling, and I can't choose my direction—I can keep the tsunami away from me, sparing the weak, fragile bodies of Kal and Tyler, the squad behind me, but it balloons outward and upward and beyond them in a millisecond.

The ripple of force explodes in three hundred and sixty degrees, and I'm dimly aware of the Longbow crumpling in the same instant the bots do. My silver threads wrap around them, grip deathly tight, and delight roars through me as I squeeze, as I crush, as their metal crumples and their circuits flare and die.

Everything is silent and the roar is deafening, and I'm part of my midnight-blue cloud, I'm gripping them with my silver threads, and I'm snapping back into my body like a piece of elastic stretched too far, and suddenly . . .

. . . it's over.

And once more I'm an infinitely fragile thing, standing on two shaking legs, and all around me are screams and alarms, and in front of me is the wreckage of the hoverskiffs and the SecBots, and around me is the ruin of our Longbow, and I'm swaying again, and my knees want to bend backward like the robots' did when they jumped from the flatbeds, and there's blood on my lips, and I'm moving, and I'm falling, and then the ground is rushing up to meet me.

. . . . .

When I wake, Kal is leaning over me, his hand gentle at my cheek. His violet eyes are wide and beautiful, his long silver hair is framed by a fuzzy halo of light.

"You look like an angel," I murmur.

"What is an angel?" he asks, curling his hand around mine. His expression is as grave as ever, but I can see the concern in his eyes. I can feel the restraint he's exercising to avoid crushing my grip in his.

"It's a dirtchild with wings," Finian says from somewhere behind him.

Kal's brows rise. "Humans do not have wings."

"How would you know?" Fin asks. "Ever seen one naked?"

Kal's brows rise higher and his ears are starting to blush when Scarlett steps in to save him. "Be nice, Finian. You alive over there, Auri? That was some kaboom."

She and Tyler come into view, looming over Kal's shoulder, and I realize nobody's wearing a halo—we're just inside, and they're backlit by the lamps set into the ceiling. I feel like a human shape made out of noodles, my limbs weak and uncooperative, but slowly my vision's clearing. Zila gently shifts Kal to one side and starts running a med-scanner over me.

"Where are we?" I try.

"Hotel on the Emerald City underside," Tyler says. "The low-rent and ask-no-questions kind. I booked it as a backup before the deal with the gremps, just in case things went *really* south."

"Which is weird," his sister says, bumping his shoulder. "Because I thought all your ideas were amazing. Lucky that you knew we'd need a fallback position."

"Almost like I studied tactics," he says, bumping her back.

"You are well," Zila pronounces, looking at me. "Brainwave activity is still slightly elevated, but bio-readings are normalizing."

"What happened?" I ask.

"You lost consciousness," Kal replies.

"After reducing a pile of SecBots to scrap metal and dragging their hoverskiffs out of the sky," Fin supplies. "It was pretty hot. Though could we maybe work on you learning to aim this thing? If we hadn't ducked . . ."

"We *did* duck," Scarlett says. "And Auri's force-sphere saved our shapely behinds, so thank you, Auri."

Our squad's Face helps me sit up against the wafer-thin pillows, and I get a better view of the dingy hotel room. It's the same kind of sticky-floor decor that I guess never goes out of style on a certain budget. There's a holo display taking up one wall, and two beds—I'm occupying one, with the squad around me. Fin's on the other, working on his suit again, his tool kit scattered across the mattress. There's a single smudgy window, our stuff piled up underneath it.

Tyler answers without being asked.

"I checked in alone after we hightailed it from the docks," he explains. "Pulled the rest of you in the window. Less chance anyone'll remember us that way. We should be safe here for a while. I paid with unmarked creds."

"So we have a little time." Scarlett sinks down to the edge of my bed. "We can afford to take a breath."

She glances around the room, studying us each in turn, and I realize that the big-sister protectiveness she used to keep for Tyler is growing to encompass all of us. Zila is back to helping Fin with his suit, and he's wincing every time she moves his knee. Kal's a statue by my side, and Tyler's lost in thought. Or memory.

I know he's thinking about Cat every few heartbeats. We all are.

This defeat is a victory, she told me before she vanished forever into the hive mind of the Ra'haam.

But it doesn't feel at all like that right now. We're on the run from the Terran and Betraskan governments—even the legion that bears my name is against us now. We've lost our most valuable asset in the Longbow, we've got almost no weapons and even less money, and we have no idea where to turn next.

"So what do we do now?" I ask softly.

Tyler's staring at the floor, scarred eyebrow curved in a deep frown. I can see he's trying so hard to lead us, and I ache for him every second. But sometimes it feels like the only reason we're still moving is that none of us realizes we've already been mortally wounded. We haven't realized we're supposed to fall down.

"Food," says Scarlett, clapping her hands together in the uncomfortable silence. "When in doubt, eat your way out."

"I like the way you think," I sigh.

Scar unearths the meals I packed, and with a pretty convincing show of fake cheer she bustles around, dubiously reading out the names on the sachets and distributing them with a flourish. I score a foil pack of Beef "Stew"-n-Mash™, with no explanation on the packet of the quotes around the *Stew*.

"WOULD YOU LIKE A NUTRITIONAL ANALYSIS OF THAT?" comes Magellan's voice from my pocket. "BECAUSE IN SOME CULTURES, A MEAL LIKE THAT WOULD BE CONSIDERED AN ACT OF WAR, ESPECIALLY—"

"Silent mode," we chorus, and it's enough to raise a ghost of a smile all around.

Fin shakes his head. "I know those old model unis were a little buggy, but that thing *really* wins the prize."

26

"Yeah," Tyler sighs. "It was never the same after Scar installed that persona beta off DealNet."

Kal blinks at Scarlett. "You accessed upgrades for your uniglass from a shopping channel?"

"No," Tyler says. "She accessed upgrades for *my* uniglass from a shopping channel."

"It came with a free handbag." Scar shrugs. "And it was your old unit anyway, you baby."

Tyler rolls his eyes and changes the subject. "How's the exosuit, Fin?"

"Fine," he says.

"This summation is incorrect," Zila says almost immediately. "Fin's suit took significant damage on Octavia III and is still in need of serious repair. Further, Finian himself requires time in low or zero gravity to rest and recover. He has pushed his body several days past his usual limits."

Fin's got his mouth open by the time she's halfway through her speech, but nothing's coming out. Finally, he manages to speak through gritted teeth.

"I'm *fine*. I can handle it. And maybe *you* should mind your own business."

Though it's sometimes a little hard to read his expression through those black contact lenses he wears, there's no mistaking the death glare Fin is shooting Zila right now. Our squad's Brain studies our Gearhead for a long moment, then turns to Tyler, her face as blank as ever. But there's something in the way she blinks and tugs at her dangly gold earring—today's are shaped like gremps—that's a little less bulletproof than it used to be.

I mean, we're all a little less bulletproof than we used to be. But for Zila, this hint of a thaw has to be unnerving.

27

"I am the team science officer and medic," she says, addressing Ty directly. "It is appropriate for me to report to my Alpha on the condition of team members."

"It's okay," says Ty, gentle. "Thanks, Zila."

Finian, however, seems to be completely ignoring Zila's advice for bed rest. He yanks a tool from her hand, takes a slurp of his prepackaged meal, and gets to work on his suit again without another word. After a glance at Ty, Scarlett rises from beside me, settles down beside Fin.

"If you get Just Like Real Tacos™ in your circuits, that stuff's never coming out," she informs him softly.

"I need to fix this," he insists around his mouthful.

"Give it a moment, Fin." Scarlett puts her hand over his. "Eat. Breathe."

He meets her eyes for a second, somehow chewing and pouting at the same time. But a hint of tension goes out of his shoulders as he swallows, as if he's conceding something other than the possibility of frying his suit.

"Yeah, okay," he sighs.

We all fall quiet for a little, finishing our meals. I'm concentrating on getting food into my mouth, and leaning against Kal's shoulder where he sits against the headboard with me. Sore as I am, I'm aware of every tiny shift, of each of his breaths. He spent so much time avoiding touching me after we first met, restraining any hint of the Pull he's feeling, that when he allows himself the luxury now, it sends sparks through me. That he gives me this, when he's still so careful around everyone else . . . I know it's not the place for it.

But I find myself wanting more.

"All right, we need to take stock," Tyler says once dinner

is over. "Kal, see if you can find any mentions of us on the local feeds. We need to know how deep we're in it. Zila, Scar, take inventory. Fin, find out what happened to the Longbow."

"It was not looking its best," Kal says, glancing at me with something like awe. "Once Aurora was done with it."

"I know," Ty nods. "But if there's no way to salvage it, we're gonna need another way out of this hole."

Fin wipes his hands, pulls out his uniglass, and begins hacking the station net. Kal switches on the holoscreen, flicking through newscast channels to see if we're making any guest appearances. Zila and Scarlett methodically begin going through our bags, categorizing everything we got out of the Longbow into personal property, group property, and stuff we can sell. I see Zila has salvaged the two GIA uniforms we stole aboard Sempiternity, and I catch a glimpse of myself in one of those blank, reflective masks. White streak in my bangs, white iris in my right eye. The girl who looks back at me in the mirror still sometimes feels like a stranger.

I see the exact moment Scarlett pulls Cat's stuffed dragon, Shamrock, out of Fin's satchel. She glances over her shoulder at Tyler, eyes shining with tears, then leans across to hand him the toy. He gently wraps his hands around it as if it's infinitely precious, pressing it against his chest. Then he looks across at Fin, who's watching him. Fin, who must have hurried up to the pilot's chair when he should have been leaving the Longbow to grab this last piece of Cat.

The Betraskan just nods, and turns back to his uniglass.

Though this squad is the closest thing to a family I have now, I still feel like a fish out of water around them. It's moments like these that I'm reminded how far from home I am, how far out of time. Two hundred years passed in the blink of an eye while I was lost in cryo. For me, it's only been a couple of weeks since I boarded the *Hadfield,* setting out for a new life on Octavia. But now everything I know is gone, and everyone I love is gone right along with it.

I don't know how I should be feeling. But looking at Cat's old toy, at those faceless gray uniforms, I can't help but think about our confrontation with the Ra'haam on Octavia III. The colonists it absorbed into its hive mind along with her. My father's face beneath the mask of a GIA agent, silver flowers in his eyes.

Jie-Lin, I need you.

And though a part of me wants to curl up and scream at the memory, most of me is just furious. Knowing how it consumed him, used him, wore him like a suit. I can feel midnight blue tingling at my fingertips. The gifts the Eshvaren gave me crackling just beneath my skin. The Ra'haam's ancient enemy, somehow alive in me.

I can learn to control this. I know it. I can be the Trigger they made me to be.

But like Tyler said above Octavia, we still need to find the Weapon.

"Okay, Goldenboy," Finian sighs, head bent over his uniglass. "You want the good or bad news first?"

"Whichever's less dramatic," Tyler replies.

"Well, good news is, the Longbow's already in pieces in an Emerald City salvage yard. Very small, very flat, very expensive pieces."

Tyler closes his eyes. Even though we all knew the odds of getting the ship back were low, it's still a body blow to have lost any chance of selling it.

"How is that good news?" he asks.

"I guess it's good news in contrast to the bad news?"

Tyler sighs. "Hit me."

Fin continues. "Bad news is, the only ship we can afford with our current funds is a one-hundred-and-seventy-year-old Chellerian freighter with no drive or nav or life-support systems, whose last gig was hauling solid waste from Arcturus IV."

"Sounds delightful," Scarlett deadpans.

"Sounds fragrant," I mutter.

"Sounds useless," Tyler scowls. "There's nothing else?"

Finian shrugs, and with a flick of his finger projects his uniglass feed onto the wall display. I can see a complicated network node with thousands of different ships on offer, from massive cruisers to tiny tugs. Every one of them is so far out of our price range I actually feel a little nauseous. I peer at the corp name on the masthead, a glowing logo of a cogwheel wreathed in fire.

"Hephaestus Incorporated," I murmur.

"They're the biggest outfit with a salvage yard on Emerald City," Fin explains. "Maker's bits, if we had the credits, we could get a chariot worthy of our status as notorious interstellar criminals, but . . ."

"We don't have the credits," Tyler points out, grim.

"Please tell me we're not considering buying the sewage ship?" Scarlett says. "Because I don't think I'm dressed for that."

Kal glances at Scar, one silver eyebrow rising. "How *would* you dress for that?"

"Wait, wait a minute . . . ," I whisper, my breath sticking in my throat. "Fin, stop scrolling, go back to . . ."

31

My tone stills everyone in the room. Fin lifts one hand, swipes it from right to left like a conductor, scrolling slowly through the ships in the salvage yard.

"There, stop there!" All eyes turn to me as I stand slowly, pointing at one of the ships on the wall.

"Auri?" Tyler asks.

"That's the *Hadfield*," I say.

Tyler walks closer and squints at the display. Fin punches up the entry, expands it, and there it is. Right out of my memories and into the waking world.

It looks a little like an old Earth battleship, long and cigar-shaped. The hull is blackened, long gashes are torn down its sides, and the metal looks like it was liquefied in places, but I'd recognize it anywhere. The ship I climbed aboard two weeks and two hundred and twenty years ago, setting out for a new life on Octavia III. A life that's gone now, along with everything and everyone I ever knew.

"Maker's breath, you're right, Auri." Ty shakes his head, staring at the *Hadfield* with a kind of awe. "Last time I saw her, she was being ripped apart by a FoldStorm. How did anyone get hold of her?"

Fin shrugs. "Search me. I'm guessing a Hephaestus salvage team stumbled across her in the Fold after you rescued Stowaway here? Specs say she's in a mega-convoy heading for an auction block on Picard VI."

"Why would anyone want a piece of junk like that?" Scarlett glances at me. "I mean, no offense . . ."

"None taken," I murmur.

"Says so right here," Fin nods. "'The most famous wreck in the age of Terran stellar exploration! Own a genuine piece of history!'"

"We have to get to her." The words are out before I realize I'm speaking.

Tyler turns from the display to face me. "What for?"

"I don't know. I just . . . feel it."

"Is it your gift, be'shmai?" Kal asks.

"Maybe." I glance around at a sea of uncertain faces, realizing that as much as they're growing to trust me, the legionnaires of Squad 312 are going to need more than a gut feeling. "Look, we know I'm supposed to stop the Ra'haam from blooming, right? Otherwise it'll spread through the Fold and consume the galaxy. But we don't *know* anything about the Eshvaren. And they're the ones who set all this in motion, who somehow made me into . . . whatever I am."

Kal stands slowly by my side, peering at the *Hadfield*'s wreck. Of every race in the galaxy, the Syldrathi are the only ones who truly believe the Eshvaren ever existed. The light from the projection plays across his violet irises as he speaks.

"And you believe we may be able to learn more about the Ancients aboard?"

"I don't know," I admit. "But I do know something happened to me on that ship. I was just a regular person when I stepped into that cryopod, and when Tyler pulled me out, I was . . ."

I glance at my reflection in the helmet again. The stranger looking back at me.

". . . this."

"They might have salvaged the black box," Fin says. "The flight recorder would tell us if the *Hadfield* ended up anywhere she wasn't supposed to, if anything unusual happened that the instruments could measure. When. How. Where."

"We will be better equipped to support Aurora's mission

33

if we understand the nature of it," Zila agrees. "And the ones who gave it to her."

Kal nods. "Know the past, or suffer the future."

Tyler glances across at Scarlett for a long moment. She tilts her head, gives an elegant shrug.

"Okay," he says then, his fingers tightening around Shamrock. "It's a place to start. And we don't have any other clues to go on. Sun Tzu said, 'If you know the enemy and know yourself, you need not fear a hundred battles.'"

"Who's Sun Tzu?" Fin asks.

"An old dead guy," Scarlett replies.

"And we're taking his advice because . . . ?"

Tyler's eyes are on the *Hadfield*, and I can see the fire in them as he speaks. "We know a little about our enemy. Let's learn something about our friends."

"Okay," Scar replies. "Can we start by learning how we get off this junk heap?"

▶ **ALIGNED**

  ▼ **SYLDRATHI**

THE SYLDRATHI ARE THE ELDEST RACE IN THE GALAXY. THEY ARE TALL AND ELEGANT, WITH TAPERED EARS, VIOLET EYES, AND SILVER HAIR, TRADITIONALLY WORN IN BRAIDS. THEY ARE TYPICALLY STRONGER AND FASTER THAN HUMANS, AND OFTEN SEEN AS ARROGANT AND ALOOF BY OTHER RACES. HONESTLY, BOSS, THIS ISN'T THAT FAR FROM THE TRUTH.

THEIR SOCIETY IS DIVIDED INTO FIVE CASTES, KNOWN AS CABALS:

WARBREED—*WARRIORS AND GUARDIANS*

WAYWALKERS—*TELEPATHIC MYSTICS DEVOTED TO STUDYING THE FOLD*

WEAVERS—*SCIENTISTS, ENGINEERS, AND ARTISANS*

WATCHERS—*POLITICIANS AND OTHER ADMINISTRATORS*

WORKERS—*BECAUSE SOMEONE HAS TO DO THE ACTUAL HARD WORK*

THE SYLDRATHI WERE AT WAR WITH **TERRA** UNTIL TWO YEARS AGO, BUT PEACE WAS BROKERED UNDER THE **JERICHO ACCORD** OF 2378. THEIR ENTIRE SPECIES IS CURRENTLY EMBROILED IN A BRUTAL CIVIL WAR (SEE **FREE SYLDRATHI** AND **UNBROKEN**).

BASICALLY, THEY'RE NOT HAVING MUCH FUN THESE DAYS, IS WHAT I'M SAYING.

3

SCARLETT

My girls are too big for this uniform.

Don't get me wrong—I love my ladies. Chi-chis. Ta-tas. Whatever euphemism you want to use. Those days when you've managed to sculpt the perfect cleav and you can hear people's necks snapping when you breeze past? Yeah, that. They're a *fantastic* idiot detector. (Hint: I don't blame you for peeking, but if you're talking to them rather than my face, you have failed the Test.) They're often a lot of fun to have around at night.

But some days, they're just a bitch to own.

I've got to hold on to the damn things when I run, for starters. I'm not doing that to point them out to you, people—it just hurts if I don't. Good bras are expensive, and you have to wash them extra carefully or you quickly find yourself buying another expensive bra. Don't get me started on the whole underwire thing. Humanity is a race capable of interstellar travel, and nobody's invented a bra for girls my size that doesn't feel like prison. Here is a truth universally acknowledged—taking that thing off at the end of the day is the single greatest feeling in the world.

Sorry, boys.

And then there's moments like this one. Trying to defy the laws of physics by compressing matter into a space far too small for it to fit. I'm sure Zila has an equation for it somewhere in that big brain of hers: Area.ñ−[Bewbage+æ{where. æ=brassieredensity}] = PAIIINNN.

"I always hated physics," I mutter, adjusting myself for the seventeenth time.

"You what?" Tyler asks across comms.

"Nothing," I sigh.

Zila and I are marching along Section 12, Ceta Promenade of the Emerald City docks, wearing the uniforms of two operatives of Earth's Global Intelligence Agency. We stole these outfits during our daring heist back on the World Ship, right off the bodies of two GIA goons who tried to arrest us. *Tried* being the operative word—Legionnaire Kaliis Idraban Gilwraeth, adept of the Warbreed Cabal, took those GIA agents apart like jigsaw puzzles with his bare hands.

I admit I used to get a little hot and bothered watching Kal work. Our squad's Tank isn't at all hard on the eyes. But I can tell from the not-so-secret glances they're constantly exchanging that he and Auri have got some kind of Thing going on now. So, solidarity among sisters, I must now (mostly) avert mine eyes. Le sigh.

Pity, I've never dated a Syldrathi before. . . .

ANYWAY, stolen uniforms usually mean ill-fitting uniforms. Though I *swear* this thing didn't fit as bad the last time I put it on. But nobody in the squad can lie half as well as me, and posing as a GIA operative is a con I've run before. So I'm clad head to foot in charcoal-gray nanoweave, doing my best to walk it like I own it. Zila is marching beside me, studiously ignoring my eighteenth attempt at bap adjustment by watching Adams's public denouncement of us on her uniglass again.

"*. . . this squad has clearly gone rogue. They have violated our trust. They have broken our code. Aurora Legion Command offers every assistance . . .*"

"Do you ever have this problem?" I ask her.

Zila mutes her uni, glances up at me.

"PROBLEM?"

"You know," I say, waving at my chest. "Size . . . fluctuation."

Zila tilts her head, her voice turned even flatter than usual by the GIA mirrormask. "HORMONE CHANGES DURING OVULATION CAN LEAD TO SWELLING. ESTROGEN PRODUCTION PEAKS JUST BEFORE MID-CYCLE, AND THIS CAN CAUSE ENLAR—"

"*Um, Scarlett?*"

"Yes, Finian?"

"*You and Zila are still transmitting.*"

". . . So?"

"*Um . . . never mind.*"

"Good answer."

Tyler breaks in before anyone can dig themselves too deep. "*Okay, Scar, we're on your six, about three hundred meters back. Clock us?*"

I glance behind, see Tyler and the rest of the squad lurking in the shadow of a refueling station. They're dressed in stolen coveralls to fit in with the rest of the dock crowd, hoods or jetball caps pulled low to cover their features. Emerald City is a pretty civilized place, and the SecDrone patrols are regular overhead—it's a risk to be out in the open like this, is what I'm saying, especially with that bounty on our heads. But if we're going to get to the *Hadfield* before it ends up at auction, we've gotta get off this station. And with our Longbow down and out, that means getting another ship.

"WE SEE YOU, TYLER," Zila reports.

"We'll be watching through your uniglasses, so keep them handy. If you run into trouble, bug out and head for the transit station."

"Relax, little brother," I say. "I've got this."

"Not a doubt in my mind."

"Gooooood answer."

"The ship we're looking for should be coming up on your right."

I scan the crowd around me, grateful for once that I'm tall enough to see over it. And if you think being a six-foot-tall girl sounds like a party, I invite you to try buying pants that fit. Or finding a boy who isn't weirded out about being shorter than you.

The spaceport is on Emerald City's upper level, closest to the dome of charged particles that keeps the poisonous atmosphere at bay. These docks are just as colorful and frantic as the city's bazaar, though there's a different kind of urgency up here. The security lockdown caused by our gremp-related escapades lasted twenty-four hours before the authorities were forced to lift it, which means every ship in port is now a full sol behind schedule. Captains are roaring at their crews, auto-dockers and refuelers are working at redline, the air is abuzz with loader drones.

Off to our left is the transit station, a dizzying tangle

of transparent tubes zipping people and freight off to other levels. And to our right, on one of the midsized landing pads, I see a sleek, almost retro-looking cruiser.

She's gunmetal gray, heart-shaped, highlighted by long white racing stripes down her flanks. The name *Opha May* is sprayed near her bow. Prow? Eh, I don't really know the difference. To tell you the truth, I've never been interested in spaceships. I slept through most of my mechaneering classes, apart from a four-week stint in third year when I was paying attention to impress a boy.

(Liam Chu. Ex-boyfriend #32. Pros: Wrote me love songs. Cons: *Cannot* sing.)

But Tyler tells me the *Opha May* is a good ship. Small enough for a crew of six. Fast enough to outrun most trouble and punchy enough to fight off the rest. And if my baby brother knows about one thing besides infuriating me, being a know-it-all, and having perfect hair, it's ships. It's one of the reasons he and Cat get along so well.

I mean, *got* along so well.

Oh hells . . .

And just like that, my eyes are burning again. My heart is aching at another reminder she's gone. I'd known Cat since kindergarten. We were roomies at the academy for five years. And it's stupid, but it's the little things about her I miss most, because they were the constants in my life, and it's so continuously obvious they're gone now.

I miss the way she'd talk in her sleep. Hide my socks in a friendly attempt to drive me totally insane. Borrow my stuff without asking. Those little touches from Cat all day, every day, were how I knew she was around. They were the reassurance of her presence. And her presence meant I always had my best friend with me. I always had my partner in crime. I had all the bigger, harder-to-articulate things that came with Cat being a part of my life.

I found a stick of her eyeliner in my bag last night, and I cried for an hour.

So I let myself feel it now. Let it wash over me for a moment that seems to last forever. I don't want to deny how bad it hurts, because in some way that'd be denying all she meant to me. But then I breathe deep and push thoughts of Catherine "Zero" Brannock from my mind. Focusing on what I need to do.

Because that's what Cat would *want* me to do.

Zila and I walk toward the *Opha May*, and the crowd gives us a wide berth. I bet it's not often that agents of the Global Intelligence Agency travel this far out from the Core, but their reputation as People You Do Not Mess With ensures that even among this mob of aliens from across the 'Way, nobody messes with us. Burly Chellerian workers take one look at our uniforms and step aside. Packs of sour-faced toughs in union colors part like smoke. I swear even a loader drone scurries out of our way as we step up to the landing pad. I think about the faces of the people we found inside these uniforms, Auri's dad and the rest, all of them totally corrupted by the Ra'haam. And part of me wonders just how far that corruption spreads.

I push the thought away for another day and look over the small group of men and bots at work on the ship in front of us. The crew is a mix of skin tones, but all of them are Terran. Which, of course, is why out of every vessel in the Emerald City dock registry, Ty picked this one.

"That's the captain on the loading ramp," Finian says over

our uniglass link. *"The shouty male with the fur-thing on his faceparts."*

"It's called a mustache," Tyler says.

"It's called disgusting, Goldenboy."

"It appears as if a skenk crawled onto his lip and expired," Kal says.

"Right?" Finian agrees. *"Human body hair, ugh."*

"Wait," I hear Aurora say. *"You mean Syldrathi don't grow facial hair?"*

"No, be'shmai."

". . . Do you grow it anywhere else?"

"Could we PLEASE," Tyler says slowly. *"Keep our minds. On this job?"*

I hear a small chorus of apologies across comms, and I can't help but smile. Dysfunctional as our little family is, at least it's starting to *feel* like a family. I look around the bustling landing pad and do indeed spy a short, shouty man with what seems to be a dead caterpillar glued above his mouth. He's dressed in a flight suit and magboots. He's haggard, his face red from roaring at his crew, the bots helping with his cargo, and random passersby. He looks old enough to be my dad.

I mean, Dad died when we were eleven, but you know what I'm saying. . . .

"All right." I nod to Zila. "Let's work some magic."

"THERE IS NO SUCH THING AS MAGIC, SCARLETT," Zila says.

"Watch and learn, my friend."

We stride up to the *Opha May*'s captain, our shiny boots ringing on the deck. He doesn't even glance up from his uniglass.

"Josef Gruber," I say, using the name Fin hacked off the dockside servers.

"Who's asking?" the short man replies, still not looking at me.

"By authority of the Terran Registration Act, Article 12, Section B, we are hereby commandeering your vessel."

Now I've got his attention. And as he finally looks up into my face, I'm using all the years of training in the one class I *didn't* sleep through to sum him up. I may not have had the best grades. I wasn't the best shot or tactician or pilot. But Scarlett Isobel Jones is still damn good at what she does. And what she does is People.

He's running on around four hours' sleep. It's been about six months since he was home, and he misses it. I can see one of his eyes is cybernetic, and from the blotching of veins on his nose, he likes a drink. Looking over his craggy face, his stance as he squares up to me, I can feel hostility. Disbelief. And a little bit of fear.

"You're kidding me, right?" he growls.

"I assure you, Captain Gruber, we are deadly serious."

He looks around the dock, incredulity fighting with anger.

"We're sixty million light-years from Terra," he spits, his lip caterpillar wobbling in fury. "What in the Maker's name is the GIA doing out here?"

I lean in on his fear button. "As we explained, Captain, we are taking possession of your ship. You are a Terran citizen; your ship is subject to Terran law. Believe me when I say you do not want me to lodge a report of your noncompliance in my mission debrief."

I hold out one gloved hand. It doesn't shake. Not even a little bit.

"The passkeys, please."

Gruber's crew has stopped working now, gathering around us in a small, hostile semicircle. The captain is glowering up at me. I'm using the same tone of voice as every academy instructor who ever disciplined me for tardiness or chewed me out for late assignments or cited me for talking/sleeping/making out in class. All those teachers who warned me I'd never amount to anything.

And with a series of curses I'm far too ladylike to repeat, Captain Gruber reaches into his jacket and hands me a set of glowing passkeys.

Shows how much my teachers knew.

"*Good work, Sis*," comes Tyler's voice in my ear.

"I *am* a Jones."

"What?" the angry little captain says.

"You and your men have five minutes to remove your personal belongings," I tell him. "Please ensure the ship is fueled for departure."

"Five minutes?" he sputters. "What about my cargo?"

"You may lodge compensation forms through the GIA webnode."

I turn my back, already looking for Ty through the crowd.

"THANK YOU FOR YOUR COOPERATION," Zila tells him.

I can feel the captain's stare between my shoulder blades. His shame and anger at being taken down in front of his men. But I'll say one thing for Terran bureaucracy—the last place in the 'Way you want to be is on its bad side. You'd have to be idiots like us to even consider it. And with another curse, Gruber barks at his men to get their things together.

I see Ty and the squad moving through the crowd toward

us, and the thrill of my little triumph is warm in my chest. That went even better than I expected. As I smile behind the mirrormask, Zila sidles up to me and whispers.

"THAT WAS . . ."

"Magic?" I reply.

"REMARKABLE."

"Yeah. But don't fall in love with me, Zila. I'll just break your heart."

"THAT DOES SEEM CONSISTENT WITH YOUR ROMAN-TIC MODUS OPERANDI." She pauses a moment before adding, "YOU ARE ALSO TOO TALL FOR ME."

I blink at that. "Wait . . . you like girls?"

Zila shrugs, scanning the crowd. "NOT TALL ONES."

I'm actually a little surprised at that. To be honest, I didn't think Zila liked anyone much at all. But before I can ponder this new revelation, Ty and the others have reached us at the *Opha May's* berth.

The grin on my bee-bro's face makes me grin back, despite the fact that nobody can see under my helmet. As soon as Gruber and his boys get their gear together, we'll be on our way.

"It is a nice ship," Auri sighs through our comms channel, looking her over.

Even knowing nothing about ships, I have to agree—it's a beauty. We've all had it rough in the last few weeks, but it seems like things are finally going our way. Our Trigger girl looks tired, but totally awake. For once in his life, Finian seems to have run out of sass, shooting me a goofy smile instead. Only Kal looks a touch out of sorts.

Syldrathi are a little hard for me to read beyond their

genetically ingrained arrogance. I guess if I was going to live three hundred years and everyone around me would be dead in half that, I'd be a little distant, too. But this isn't our Tank's typical *You are but mayflies* attitude at work. Looking at the frown on his pretty face, the dilation of his pupils, I'd say he looks almost . . . nervous.

"You all right?" I murmur.

". . . Kal?" Auri asks, reaching out to brush his hand with her fingertips.

He rubs his brow, looking around the docks. "I feel—"

"Hello, Kaliis."

The voice comes from behind him. Sharp enough that it cuts through the clamor. Something about it fills my stomach with ice-cold butterflies. And turning across the crowded dock, I see a young woman glowering at the back of Kal's head.

I mean, she *looks* like a young woman. Maybe nineteen or twenty. But with Syldrathi it's hard to tell. She's taller even than me. She has the flawless olive skin and high cheekbones and aching, ethereal elegance of all her people. Her eyes are narrowed, dazzling, bright violet. Her hair is long, swept back over her tapered ears in ornate braids of inky black—she's the only Syldrathi I've ever seen with hair that color. She's the kind of beautiful that plucks your heart out through your ribs.

But she's wearing black armor, daubed with white Syldrathi script. The glyf of the Warbreed Cabal is etched on her brow—three crossed blades, just like Kal's. There's a stripe of black paint running from temple to temple, right across her eyes. Her lips are painted black too, and there's a cord of what might be severed *thumbs* strung around her neck. And as she smiles, I note she's filed her canines into points.

I've seen armor like hers before. On the news feeds of the Orion Incursion. The surprise attack where Dad was killed. She's one of the renegade cabal of militants who started the Syldrathi civil war.

Unbroken.

"Spirits of the Void . . . ," Kal breathes, looking at her.

Ty looks at him sidelong. "Kal?"

I can feel the sudden tension radiating off our Tank in waves. Every muscle flexed, hands clenching into fists. His voice drops to absolute zero.

"All of you, listen to me carefully," he says. "Do *not* let her get close to you."

The young woman is still gliding nearer, cutting through the crowd like a knife. Kal reaches out to Auri beside him, presses her back.

"Get behind me, Aurora."

She blinks. "Kal, what's—"

"Be'shmai." He meets her mismatched eyes with his. *"Please."*

"It is true, then."

I turn back to the Unbroken woman. She's stopped about ten meters away, looking at Kal with her lip curled. She's speaking in Syldrathi, but language studies were one of the few subjects at the academy I was good at, so surprise, honey, I speak it too. One hand is propped at her hip, contempt twisting that beautiful face into something ugly and awful.

"When the adepts you thrashed in that bar brawl on the World Ship told me the tale, I could scarce believe it," she tells Kal. "I cut their throats to silence their lies. But I should have known you were capable of sinking to any depth. Any shame." Violet eyes flicker to Aurora. "Enough even to name a human beloved."

Kal's hand slips to the disruptor under his jacket.

"What do you want, Saedii?" he asks.

Hmm. They're on a first-name basis. Interesting . . .

Madam Badass lowers her chin and smiles with pointed teeth.

"You know what I want, Kaliis," she replies.

The *Opha May*'s crew is emerging from the ship behind us now, arms loaded with luggage, frowning in confusion at the scene in front of them. Tyler whispers a warning, and I catch glimpses of six more Unbroken fanning out in the crowd. I spot another two on the warehouse roof opposite our landing pad. They all have black armor, long silver hair, beautiful, battle-scarred faces. Warbreed glyfs on their brows and smiles on their lips and hate in those big, pretty eyes.

But as dangerous as this crew might look, these docks are way too busy for them to start any real trouble. I don't know who these pixies are, but whatever's going on here, I've had about enough of it. Time to put this uniform to work again and get the hells off this station before the real trouble arrives.

"You will refrain from coming any closer," I say in Syldrathi, putting on my Voice of Authority again. "These individuals are in the custody of the GIA, and—"

"You are no more an officer of the Global Intelligence Agency than I am, human," the woman sneers, her eyes never leaving Kal. "Now still your tongue before I cut it out of your head."

"We need to go," Kal murmurs, glancing at Tyler. *"Now."*

Ty nods in agreement, eyes still on Madam Badass.

"Everybody get aboard."

We start backing toward the *Opha May*'s loading ramp. The Unbroken woman tilts her head. And with zero foreplay, not even so much as a goodbye kiss, one of her chums up on the warehouse fires a damn *pulse rocket* at us.

It looks like a bolt of luminous green, trailing a wisp of thin smoke. Hissing as it comes. Auri shouts a warning and throws up her hands, and I see a flare of brief white light from her right eye. For a second the air around us crackles with tension, greasy and warm. But as the pulse rocket goes skimming right over our heads, I realize it's not aimed at us.

Gruber and his crew scatter as Tyler roars at the top of his lungs.

"Everybody down!"

Kal throws himself on top of Aurora; the rest of us hit the deck as the rocket sails right through the open bay doors of my newly commandeered escape plan. The explosion rips through the *Opha May*'s insides and blooms out her exhaust ports. Shrapnel whizzes past my head, skims off the nanoweave armor on my back. I hear Aurora scream, Zila gasp, Fin curse. Alarms begin blaring across the docks; the crowd roars in panic. Alerts flash across the display inside my mask as a warning spills from the public address system.

"Fire in Section 12, Ceta. Please proceed to your nearest exit."

Chaos breaks loose on the docks. Black smoke rolls in the air. Fire and explosions aboard a suborbital station are rarely a good thing, and all around us the mob begins scattering

49

toward the transit tubes, babbling, trampling, desperate. Nozzles open up in the deck, spraying chemicals onto the *Opha May*'s burning shell.

I squint through the smoke and see the Unbroken stalking toward us through the panicking crowd. The young woman is in the lead, violet stare still fixed on Kal. Our Tank has his arms around Auri, and I see blood spilling from a shrapnel gash on her brow. Her jaw is slack, her eyelashes fluttering.

"Aurora?" he cries, touching her face. *"Aurora!"*

"M-mothercustard . . . ," she groans.

I stagger to my feet, shaking my head to clear it. But the GIA armor has protected me from the worst of the blast, and I drag my disruptor pistol from its holster, aim at the oncoming Syldrathi woman.

"Freeze," I tell her.

She stops for a moment. Perfectly still. And then she moves.

Now, I've seen Kal dismantle a room full of Terran Defense Force troopers in seconds. He took down two GIA agents without breaking a sweat. But Madam Badass gives a new meaning to the word *fast*. One moment I'm drawing a bead on her head, and the next she's standing in front of me, her fist colliding with my chest. My breath sprays from between my lips; I feel myself lifted off the plasteel. I hear something rip, see black stars, taste blood. And then I'm flat on my back, gasping, clutching my bits.

"Scar!" Tyler roars.

"Owwww," I groan.

"Maker's breath, are you okay?" Finian gasps, on his knees beside me.

50

"No." A low moan escapes my lips. "She p-punched me . . . in the ladies. . . ."

See what I mean about these things being a bitch to own?

I'm only dimly aware of my brother rising to his feet, aiming his disruptor at the woman who just whomped me in the ta-tas. But in a heartbeat, she slips aside from his blasts, stepping up to him in a black blur. I see her hands clap down on Ty's shoulders. I hear an ugly crunch, an off-key squeal of pain, as her knee collides with my twin brother's fun factory so hard I can almost feel it in our shared DNA.

Poor Bee-bro . . .

She grabs Ty's arm and flips him over her shoulder, slamming him onto the deck with a force that shakes the plasteel. His wrist is still locked in her grip as she crouches low, open palm drawn back to slam into my brother's head.

"STOP!" comes a cry.

I blink hard, watch Kal rise up from beside a semiconscious Aurora. There's a shrapnel nick in his cheek, a thin line of purple blood spilling from the wound.

A long strand of silver hair has come loose from one of his braids, drifting across his eyes in the burning updraft.

His fingertips are wet with Auri's blood. His beautiful face is twisted with a fury that's all the way terrifying.

"Saedii, stop this," he spits.

"Only you have the power to stop this, Kaliis. You belong with us."

"No," he says. "I am not like you."

I look from the glyf on her brow to the identical glyf on his. The hate in his eyes, reflected in her own. The other Unbroken have gathered around us now, black armor aglow in the light of the *Opha May*'s wreckage. The two on the rooftops have climbed down, approaching us with more pulse rockets at the ready. Fin is crouched beside me, hand on my shoulder; Zila is next to Auri, checking over the groaning girl with a med-scanner. And I'm wondering how deep the hole we're in can actually go when one of the Syldrathi steps up to Kal with hand outstretched.

"Come with us, comrade."

In a flash almost too quick to track, Kal seizes the man's wrist, bends it backward with a bright snapping sound. The man screams and Kal *twists;* I hear another crunch as the guy's elbow bends in entirely the wrong direction. The other Unbroken step forward, but with a hiss, the young woman called Saedii holds them still. And as I watch, horrified, Kal sweeps the warrior's feet out from under him and starts slamming his fist into his face. His features are twisted. Silver braids hanging about his face. Lips peeled back from his teeth. Eyes burning.

Crunch.

"Great Maker," Fin breathes.

Crunch.

"Kal, stop," I whisper.

Crunch.

Kal stands up when he's done. Purple blood dripping from his knuckles. Spattered across those prettyboy cheeks. The woman looks at him with triumph.

"There he is," she breathes. "*There's* the Kaliis I know."

He takes a step toward her. In a flash, she draws a disruptor pistol from her belt, pointed right at his chest. It doesn't take a Tank to know from the hum that the weapon is set to Kill.

"Don't," she warns.

"You won't kill me, Saedii," Kal says.

"True." She turns the weapon on Fin and me. "But them?"

"I am not going with you," Kal says. "I am *not* going back."

"Oh, Kaliis." The young woman sighs, looks down at his hands, dripping purple blood on the deck at his feet. "You never lef—"

The impact throws her backward, arms pinwheeling, black hair streaming about her face. Her posse is thrown back too, spit and blood, tumbling through the air. I watch a sphere of translucent force surge outward, crushing the ships around us like paper, peeling the deck, popping the swarms of drones above us like bugs on a windshield. The floor shakes beneath us; the air around us crackles with static, greasy and warm. Every hair on my body is standing to attention.

I turn around and see Aurora wobbling on her feet, hand outstretched. Her right eye is flickering with moon-pale light. Her hair blows like there's a wind, white bangs twisting, almost aglow. Blood spills from the split in her brow.

"Auri?" I manage.

Like someone switched off a light, the glow in her eye dies and she sinks to her knees again, blood spilling from her nostrils. Kal catches her as she sags, pulling her up in his arms. Impossibly gentle, where a moment ago he was anything but.

"We . . ." Auri swallows hard, wipes her lip.

"Be'shmai?" Kal says.

"We need . . . to g-get out of here," she says.

"Aurora is right," says Zila, pulling off her mask. "Security will be coming."

I look around us, chest still aching, struggling to breathe

as I crawl to my brother's side. He's only semiconscious, groaning softly.

The Unbroken are scattered like kids' toys, comatose, swept aside with a wave of Aurora's hand. But the dock and ships around us are likewise totaled. The *Opha May* is a smoldering paperweight and we don't have the passkeys to any of the other ships at dock.

Our plan to get off Emerald City is in the toilet.

"We need t-to hide," Aurora says. "Deep and dark as w-we . . . can."

I can hear incoming sirens.

"Okay," I say. "We have to move."

"Here, hold on to me," Fin says, helping me to my feet.

"Kal, c-can you grab Ty?" Auri asks.

Our Tank complies, hauling Tyler up. "On your feet, Brother."

Kal supports Ty; Fin and I support each other. Zila leads the way with her disruptor drawn. And quick as we can, we're hobbling across the ruined loading docks, the buckled decks, smoke still billowing around us, alarms blaring, groaning Unbroken scattered like fallen dominoes.

We reach the transit station, and Fin's consulting his uniglass, stabbing in a destination with shaking hands while we wait for the pressure inside the tube to equalize. Thankfully, Aurora's shock wave knocked out any SecDrones, so the station authorities might not be able to track where we're headed. If we reach the Emerald City's underbelly, we might be able to find a place deep enough to lay low.

Aurora is looking back across the docks at the downed Syldrathi, blood in her eyes and on her lips. My stomach flips as I see Madam Badass trying to rise to her feet.

"You two know each other," Auri says, pawing at her bloody nose.

"Yes," Kal replies.

"Lemme guess," Finian says, glancing over his shoulder and stabbing with renewed vigor at the tube controls. "Evil ex-girlfriend?"

"No."

I glance at Auri. "Evil *current* girlfriend?"

"Worse."

"What could be worse than that?" Zila asks.

Kal sighs as the tube doors open. Glances back as he steps into the flow.

"She is my sister."

4

ZILA

Aurora confirms that our hiding place is deep and dark enough to comply with her vision.

The squad is pressed together, all six of us crammed into the junction between eleven different transport tubes. It is a precarious position, every wall at a different angle, obliging us to brace ourselves simply to stay in position. A moment's inattention would mean a considerable fall through a gap.

Finian managed to halt our progress long enough to open an emergency access hatch in the tunnel we were using, and we exited the tube system into the dark spaces within the transit network. Our current refuge is a small, cramped space that constantly vibrates and shudders as locals whiz by us, one after another, all moving too fast to register our makeshift camp. We are a tangle of limbs and backpacks, but we are temporarily secure.

I am thinking, accompanied by the symphony of whirs and whooshes all around us, my mind humming as fast as any transport tube. I find myself tapping one finger against my knee, the tempo varying, then repeating. I do not know this pattern's origin, but I feel it rising to the surface of my mind.

Tap.

Tap, tap.

Tap.

Tyler is the one to break the silence. He is huddled in the corner with his sister pressed against him, his knees lifted to protect his crotch. I should ask to examine his most recent injury, but I calculate that the probability of a refusal, followed by a sarcastic response from Finian, is almost one hundred percent.

Tyler still looks a little dazed as he speaks.

"Kal," he says. "We have a lot of problems on the boil already without this kind of surprise cropping up."

"My sister prides herself on appearing when least needed," our Tank says. His face is still daubed with his own blood, and that of the Unbroken.

"Well, where'd she come from?" Scarlett asks.

"I know not," Kal replies. "I have not seen Saedii since before I left for the academy. She was unaware I had even joined Aurora Legion."

"She mentioned those Unbroken we fought back in the bar on the World Ship," Tyler says. "I'm guessing they passed on word to her about you?"

Kal inclines his head. "I *did* tell you I started that fight as a diversion."

"Because I used your name," he says.

Kal nods, brooding. "Perhaps I should have silenced them permanently. . . ."

My finger taps away at my knee again, the movement

involuntary. My hand seems to shift of its own accord, and begins tapping the rhythm out against my left forearm instead.

Ah.

I realize I am mimicking the rhythm of Admiral Adams's finger during the broadcast in which he condemned us. I have watched the footage fourteen times now. I have not tried to shake the compulsion to do so. It is my experience that when my mind seizes on something seemingly insignificant, usually it is solving a problem I have not yet identified.

It is a hallmark of the highly intelligent.

Tap, tap, tap.

Tap, tap.

Tap.

We condemn, in strongest possible terms, the actions of Aurora Legion Squad 312 at Sagan Station. . . .

Aurora lays one gentle hand on Kal's arm. "Tell us about your sister," she suggests, oblivious to my internal problem solving.

Kal swallows, dropping his gaze to Aurora's fingers. They are stained with her own blood, red alongside his purple, dried and flaking around her nails.

"Our father was a warrior of the Warbreed Cabal," he says. "But our mother was a Waywalker. They are the most spiritual of my people. They study the mysteries of the Fold, and the self. My father taught us to kill. But my mother tried to teach us the waste found in death." He is quiet for a moment, and I see Aurora's hand squeeze his. "I took her lessons to heart. Saedii did not."

I consider the difference between my own parents. My

mother was the more practical. My father was warmer. I wonder what he would think of the person I have become. I am very different now from the little girl I used to be.

It is an uncomfortable question, and one I have not considered in years.

I push it away.

Tap.

Tap, tap, tap.

Kal continues. "Saedii and I grew up together, but we grew ever apart. After our father died during the battle at Orion, I joined Aurora Academy to help bridge the gap between our two peoples. My sister joined the Starslayer to tear it wider. In these choices, you find all you need to understand us."

"You . . . ," Scarlett begins. "You . . . lost your dad at Orion, too?"

Kal slowly nods. I see the Jones twins exchange a glance—obviously remembering their own father, who perished in that same infamous battle. Scarlett's gaze softens as she looks at the Syldrathi boy.

"I'm sorry, Kal," she murmurs. "You never said . . ."

Kal's normally perfect posture slumps very slightly. Aurora squeezes his hand again. For a moment, our Tank's eyes are clouded, his expression pained. But despite this revelation—that three of our squad members lost their fathers in the same bitter conflict—Tyler keeps his mind on the task at hand.

"And now your sister wants what? To kill you?"

Kal hears the note in our Alpha's voice and sits up straight once more. "She wishes me to embrace the war in my blood. The fact that I have not joined the Unbroken is a

59

shame to her. And she will not stop pursuing me until she has her way."

"We're pretty good at dodging pursuit, Kal," Scarlett says. "We've had a lot of practice lately."

The Syldrathi shakes his head. "The Waywalkers among my people are sensitives. Empaths. And though she was raised Warbreed, Saedii inherited a touch of our mother's gift. My sister can . . . sense me. She has been able to do so since we were children. Not from an infinite distance, but certainly while we are stranded in the Emerald City." He pauses, lifting his chin in the manner I have learned often proceeds one of his pronouncements that owe more to nobility than sense. "I am a danger to all of you. It is better that I leave, and draw away the peril."

Aurora begins to protest, but is cut off by Ty, who lifts one hand—even that movement is pained—and speaks.

"Nobody's going anywhere," he says.

I am only half listening. My mind is humming as loudly as the tubes around us, and as I watch another pair of bodies shoot past, I am recalling Adams's face in his message. The rhythm and inflection of his words.

They have violated our trust.

Tap.

Tap, tap, tap.

They have broken our code.

Tap, tap, tap.

My cheeks heat with a momentary flush of embarrassment that it has taken me so long to understand. But there is no time for such indulgence. I take out my uniglass and begin my calculations.

"Can you sense your sister too, Kal?" Aurora asks. "Because when I'm . . . when I use my powers . . . I can see something in you. *Feel* something in your mind. Maybe you have a touch of your mother in you too?"

"It is possible, be'shmai," he replies. "The gift *is* passed through the blood."

I scroll through another round of calculations and—filing away with interest the fact that I feel the urge at all—allow myself a small smile of satisfaction.

"Zila?" Scarlett notes my change in demeanor, glancing at my uniglass. "Do you have something you want to share with the class?"

"Yes," I say, eyes still on my calculations.

". . . Well?" Scarlett asks.

"Admiral Adams has not abandoned us," I declare. "His broadcast contained a coded message."

I turn my eyes to Tyler.

"And I have just broken it."

SUBJECT: GALACTIC COMMERCE

▶ **ORGANIZATIONS**

▼ **THE DOMINION**

WHOEVER SAID **MONEY** IS THE ROOT OF ALL EVIL PROBABLY NEVER HAD ANY, BUT IT *DOES* MAKE LIFE IN THE GALAXY A LITTLE COMPLICATED. THE **MILKY WAY** HAS NO OFFICIAL CURRENCY, AND FOR REASONS THAT MAY NOT BE CLEAR TO YOUR TINY HUMAN BRAIN, CHANCES OF IT GETTING ONE ARE SMALL.

ENTER THE DOMINION.

THE DOMINION IS A BAND OF TRADE SPECULATORS, AND THE LARGEST CURRENCY EXCHANGE IN THE GALAXY. REALIZING THERE WAS A HUGE PROFIT TO BE MADE IN THE ABSENCE OF A STANDARD UNIT OF TRADE, THE DOMINION CREATED ITS OWN, OFFERING TO BUY THE CURRENCY OF ANY KNOWN SPECIES (FOR A SMALL FEE, OF COURSE) AND CONVERT IT INTO EXCHANGEABLE DOMINION **CREDITS**, WHICH ARE NOW ACCEPTED IN MOST TRADE HUBS.

OF COURSE, THIS SCHEME QUICKLY MADE THE DOMINION WEALTHIER THAN **PROFESSOR LISA MCCARTHY IV**, THE INVENTOR OF **SELF-WASHING DIAPERS**, WHICH IN TURN GAVE IT ENORMOUS CLOUT OVER POLITICIANS IN THE **GALACTIC CAUCUS**, WHICH EXPLAINS WHY WE'RE NOT GOING TO BE SEEING ANY OFFICIAL GALACTIC CURRENCY ANYTIME SOON.

DEMOCRACY, HUH?

5

KAL

We have not even kissed yet.

My squad members would say this is a strange thought to be entertaining in the middle of a crisis. I know Aurora herself would probably think it foolish. And that, in essence, is the heart of the problem. Because I am not feeling what humans feel. I am not feeling like, or lust, or even love.

I am feeling the Pull.

Syldrathi poets have spent millennia trying to describe it. I studied the work of our most renowned maesters back on Syldra. Sometimes I put their verses to music and played them on my siif beneath the lias trees outside our home. Billions of words over thousands of years. Songs and sonnets, couplets and hymns. All trying to evoke even a fraction of how this feels.

Having lived it now, I know not a single one of them has come close.

The Pull is more than words.

Love is a drop in the ocean of what I feel for her.

Love is a single sun in a heaven full of stars.

And I know Aurora cannot really understand it. That humans do not feel as Syldrathi feel. And as much as I want her, I do not wish to rush her or—spirits forbid—frighten her away. And so I keep all this inside as best I can.

But we have not even kissed yet.

Spirits of the Void, this is torture. . . .

"Get over yourself, Pixieboy," Finian mutters.

". . . What?"

The Betraskan blinks his large black eyes.

"I said get over here, Pixieboy," he repeats. "We gotta run through this."

I breathe deep, run my hand across my brow. My squad has gathered in the cramped living space of our so-called apartment. This place is smaller than an Enlei's den, and smells twice as noxious. But we have little choice with our available funds, and with my sister now on the hunt through the Emerald City, we must lay low, among the dregs who ask no questions. At least with Zila's powers of deduction— nothing short of brilliant, I must admit—we now have a chance of getting off this accursed station once and for all.

The wall display in our new hovel is nonfunctional, and Finian has his uniglass plugged into his exosuit, projecting a schematic of the Dominion Repository on the opposite wall in glowing light. I take a seat on the tiny couch beside Aurora, staring at the image. Her split brow is knitted closed by a small, flesh-colored suture; the bruise under her right eye is a dark constellation. Her lips are soft, bow-shaped, hypnotic to watch. She reaches out and touches my hand gently, her fingertips lighting fires across my skin.

"You okay?" she asks softly.

I give her my best attempt at a reassuring smile. "I am well."

"Will you two get a room?" Tyler says.

". . . What?" I scowl.

"I said there's two ways into the room," Tyler says, pointing to the schematic. "Main entrance to the south, and a smaller one on the west. Both are guarded, but the west has two fewer security goons. So, if trouble hits, that's the way we leave."

"But trouble won't hit, right?" Scarlett says. "Because all your ideas are amazing?"

"Exactly," Tyler says, ignoring his sister's jab. "Now, according to the admiral's coded message . . ."

Here Tyler pauses to offer Zila a small round of applause, which I and the rest of the squad join in on. Zila ducks her head, dark curls tumbling over her eyes. But I catch the ghost of a smile on her lips as Tyler continues.

". . . there's some kind of cache waiting for us in the security deposit room, past the main foyer. It's apparently coded to accept Scar's DNA ident. Not sure why Adams thought to set it up that way."

Scarlett raises one brow. "Because I'm fabulous?"

"Yeah, that's definitely it," Tyler mutters, rolling his eyes. "Anyway, that means Scar will be taking point on this one. We have no idea what's back there in terms of weight, so Kal, you're going with her in case it's heavy."

Scarlett glances at me. "You and me, Muscles. Dress sexy."

She winks at Aurora, and Aurora smirks back, squeezing my hand. Most of us have become accustomed to Scarlett's insistence on flirting with anything with a heartbeat. But I notice Finian is staring at the floor, looking altogether glum.

"Fin, you wanna take them through the run?" Tyler asks.

Our Gearhead blinks in confusion. "Um . . . yeah, if you want?"

"Sorry." Our Alpha hobbles toward a chair. "I just gotta sit for a minute."

Scarlett watches her brother lower himself onto the moldy cushion beside her, one hand at his crotch. She winces in sympathetic agony.

"Poor baby," she coos. "Madam Badass really did a number on the boys, huh?"

"I mean, I can always adopt," he whimpers.

"If it makes you feel better, the black eye kinda suits you? The bloodshottiness really brings out the blue."

Tyler shoots Scarlett a withering glance, and she grins and ruffles his mop of blond hair. He groans a protest and smooths his locks back into place, only to have them mussed again by his sister's hand.

They are so different—he the epitome of order, she the personification of chaos—that I sometimes find it hard to think of them as siblings. But looking at the pair of them, I can see how dearly the Jones twins love each other. They are united in the grief they feel at Zero's death. The uncertainty in which we find ourselves. Bonded in blood. A true family. Inseparable and unconquerable.

My own sister and I make a shameful comparison.

"I've got two black belts," Tyler sighs. "Ten years training in Systema and Krav Maga. And she bounced me like a jetball."

"Feel no shame," I tell him. "Saedii is a master of the Aen Suun."

Scarlett frowns as she translates. "The . . . Wave Way?"

I nod. "The deadliest of the Warbreed martial arts. Before he died, my father trained us personally. Since we were children." Sorrow fills my heart at the memory of the three of us training beneath the lias trees. I give Tyler a sad smile. "Saedii has kicked me below the belt on more than one occasion. So you have my sympathies."

"More than once?" Tyler winces and shifts again. "Maker's breath, how are you still alive?"

"I *did* warn you not to let her get close."

"It wasn't by choice, believe me," he groans. "If I have anything to say about it, the young lady in question will be kept at minimum safe distance from now on. A couple of star systems away oughta do it."

"That may not be up to us. Saedii and her adepts will still be hunting me. One does not become a Templar of the Starslayer by giving up on her prey easily."

"All the more reason to get in and out of the Repository quickly," Aurora says.

"Nice segue, Stowaway," Finian smiles, turning to his schematic and drawing a deep breath. "Okay, so the plan is simple. Get in, access whatever Adams left for us in the deposit box, then get out. Our big problem is, of course, the bounty we have on our heads for galactic terrorism."

"Alleged terrorism," Zila points out.

"Right. Alleged. So, good news is, Emerald City has a population of over a million people, so it's not like we'll be easy to spot. Bad news is, the Dominion Repository has a security system that feeds into the webnodes of most major galactic governments, and their cams are equipped with top-tier facial recognition software. I'm talking the kind that can recognize you by your eyebrows."

Scarlett tosses her flame-red bob. "Well, they *are* amazing."

"Um, yeah." Finian taps a ream of scrolling data beside the schematic. "So what I'm saying is, a jetball cap and sunglasses isn't going to cut it in there. Those systems are gonna ping us as wanted criminals *real* quick."

"We could use the GIA uniforms again?" Aurora offers.

Tyler shakes his head. "Too risky after what went down at the docks. The GIA is so rare this far from the Core, those uniforms will just attract attention now."

"I presume you have a solution?" I ask.

"Matter of fact, we do, Pixieboy," Finian smiles. "The Repository cams will clock us once we walk in. No helping that. But there'll be a delay while their systems transmit to their affiliates. The speed of light only travels so fast, even through the Fold. By the time the data is on its way *back*, I can be running a flakscreen on the uplink. Block the incoming signal long enough for us to be in and out."

"Impressive," I say.

Scarlett smiles. "Impressive is Fin's middle name."

A suspicious stain very close to a blush spreads across Finian's cheeks at Scarlett's flattery, but Tyler intercedes.

"Nnnnnnot so much," he says.

"Wow, thanks, Goldenboy," Finian mutters. "Way to boost morale."

"Sorry." Our Alpha shifts himself on the couch again. "It's the crown jewels; they're killing me. But you know what I mean, Fin—tell them the tricky part."

Finian concedes his not-so-impressive status with a grudging nod. "Tricky part is, I've gotta be *inside* the Repository while I run the hack."

A small frown creases Zila's brow. "I think it highly unlikely that Dominion security will allow you to simply sit in their foyer engaging in computer espionage."

"Right," Tyler says. "That's where you and me come in, Zil."

The girl blinks. "You and . . . me?"

"Yeah," he smiles, his signature dimple creasing his cheek. "So listen, you wanna go on a date with me?"

. . . . .

I do not know how Scarlett keeps acquiring these clothes.

Her ability to summon new outfits seemingly at will is almost supernatural. She was gone for a total of eighty-seven minutes with only a handful of credits in her pocket, and she returned with a new wardrobe for each of us, suited to the mission at hand. She does not steal—she waved receipts in Zila's and Aurora's faces and regaled them with tales of retail prowess, using arcane words like *twofer* and *cleav discount*. Aurora expressed an inordinate amount of joy over the shoes Scarlett found for her. I was concerned her squeals might attract neighborhood security.

I make a mental note of that.

She likes shoes.

Scarlett tossed a shopping bag at my chest, and I peered suspiciously at the contents, one eyebrow rising to my hairline.

"Really?"

The oldest Jones twin only smiled. "Trust me."

Now the mission awaits, and so we retire to various rooms in our dingy flat to change. Aurora, Scarlett, and Zila take to the bedroom; Finian heads off to the bathroom for some privacy. I note that his exosuit hisses as he walks, that he is favoring his left leg heavily. I suspect he requires assistance to change his clothes but is declining it in an attempt to assert independence. I do not know enough about his condition to be worried, but I worry all the same.

With nowhere left to use, Tyler and I get changed together in the tiny living area. It is the first time we have been alone since a certain kiss in a certain computer maintenance room on the World Ship. I haul off my maintenance uniform and struggle into the pants Scarlett gave me. Tyler slips off his coveralls, drags his undershirt off, stripping down to his shorts and the silver chain he wears around his neck, his father's ring looped through the links. As he reaches for the pants his sister bought him, I find myself studying him from the corner of my eye.

Our Alpha looks weary. Shoulders slumped. Bruises from my sister's beating laid in stripes across the muscles of his back, the lines of his torso. He pulls a tunic over the damage, drags his hand through his shaggy blond hair, and sighs.

I can feel his mind at work. The uncertainty he keeps hidden behind a wall of optimism. His uniglass quietly beeps upon the table—a reminder from its internal calendar. I see the words MY BIRTHDAYYYY—2 DAYS! light up the screen.

"I did not know it was your and Scarlett's birthday soon," I say.

70

Sorrow fills Tyler's eyes, turning bright blue to steel gray.

"It's not," he says quietly, motioning to the uniglass. "I threw my uni at the ultrasaur on the World Ship. That one belonged to . . ."

I realize who he means without him having to say her name. He must have taken the device from her on Octavia III. I can see the pain in Tyler's eyes as he looks at that message—one more reminder of all she will never have, will never be.

"I grieve for Zero," I tell him softly. "I know what she meant to you."

He looks up at that. I see her face reflected in his eyes— the ink on her skin, the fire in her stare. Then he looks at the ceiling, blinking rapidly.

"Yeah."

"You are doing the right thing, Tyler Jones."

He glances toward the muffled laughter in the bedroom. The voices of the ones we care for. There is such a fragile web between us all; he and I both know it. Perhaps better than any of them. I catch a glimpse behind those walls of his for a moment. Just a sliver of uncertainty glinting through the cracks.

"I hope so," he sighs.

"We have the whole galaxy arrayed against us," I tell him. "But this is where we are meant to be. We are part of something greater now; I feel it in my bones. You will lead us through this. And I will follow you, Brother."

Syldrathi do not touch, save in moments of intimacy or ritual. But Tyler Jones and I have brawled in the belly of Terran destroyers, butted heads across the Fold, looked into the eyes of death side by side. Human he might be. Weary and bruised and flawed as the rest of them. But in battle, everyone bleeds the same.

I offer him my hand.

"I know my friends, and they are few. But those few I have, I would die for."

He looks into my eyes again. Muscle flexing along the line of his jaw as he slaps his hand into mine.

"Thanks, Kal. It means a lot, knowing you've got my back."

"Del'nai," I reply.

A puzzled frown creases his brow to hear me speak in my own tongue. "I think Scar explained what that means, but I don't . . ."

"Always," I say. "Ever and always."

He looks me up and down with a wry grin.

"Quite an outfit she picked for you."

I look down at my new clothes in dismay. The pants are made of glossy black plastic, a row of silver buckles running from my ankles to my hips. My shirt is transparent mesh, also black, stretched tight over my torso and leaving very little to the imagination. I would normally only wear boots of this kind if I were planning an extended land war on the surface of a hostile planet.

"Wow," I hear a voice say.

I look up and see Aurora at the bedroom door. She is wearing a white dress-suit that would probably be described by others as chic. But to me she is clothed in light, radiant as the sun.

Her eyes run from my boots to my face. "You look . . ."

"Do I have good taste?" Scarlett asks behind her. "Or do I have good taste?"

Aurora looks at the taller girl. "You have *good* taste."

Scarlett herself is dressed in fashion similar to mine. Skintight red polymer. A corset that would constitute torture under most galactic conventions. A hundred buckles that seem to serve no structural purpose. A platinum-blond hairpiece, flowing down to her waist.

I look down at myself, raise one eyebrow in question.

"I fail to see why these pants must be so tight."

Scarlett twirls what might be a leash around her finger and smiles.

"Kal, honey, you wanna play the role, you've gotta dress the part."

. . . . .

We enter through separate doors to avoid suspicion.

The foyer of the Dominion Repository is vast, the plasteel fashioned to resemble black marble, the trimmings gilt. The walls and floors are lined with scrolling reams of data from various galactic exchanges. Despite its size, the space is crowded, folk of a dozen different species behind the counters and out on the floor—Tyler has chosen the busiest hour of the cycle for our gambit.

He and Zila go first. Our Brain seems somewhat lost for words, but Tyler keeps her close, leaning in occasionally to whisper in her ear. They walk arm in arm, looking like young lovers out for a midday stroll.

Finian comes in close behind, dressed plainly, dark colors under the gleaming silver of his exosuit. He pretends to receive a call on his uniglass immediately upon entering, shuffling over to a quiet corner of the Repository with one finger to his ear as if to better hear the conversation.

Scarlett and I come last, and as was her intent, our entrance is marked by almost everyone in the foyer—I suppose it is not often they see a statuesque blonde in skintight polyvinyl chloride leading a Syldrathi on a leash. Confidence oozing from every pore, Scarlett glides up to a middle-aged Terran manager in business attire.

The man looks her over from head to foot. "May I help you?"

"Of course you can, darling," Scarlett says, placing far too many *h*'s in a word that would seem to possess none. "My name is Madame Belle, thirdwife of Rielle Von Lumiere and imperatrix of the Dusk Court of Elberia IV. My husband left something for me in your deposit facilities."

The manager glances at me. "Your . . . husband?"

"Oh no, not him," Scarlett laughs brightly, touching the Terran's arm. "No, Germaen here is my . . . personal trainer. You understand." She tugs the leash around my neck and hisses, "Stand up straight, Germaen!"

I fix her with a glower hotter than a dozen dwarf stars before I remember the role I am supposed to be playing.

"Apologies, Imperatrix," I murmur, standing taller.

Scarlett rolls her eyes at the manager. "*So* hard to find good pets these days."

"I . . . understand."

She gives the man a smile I can only describe as wicked and gifts his arm with another lingering touch. "I'm sure you do, darling."

Dahhhhhhhling.

"Well," the manager says, looking more than a little flustered at her attentions. "Please, follow me, Imperatrix. Our vaults are right this way."

Scarlett gives the man a beautiful smile and sets off after him, dragging me behind with a tug. "Come along, Germaen, don't dawdle!"

As we make our way across the busy floor, I see Finian working quietly in the corner on his uniglass. While most of the security personnel are busy staring at the spectacle Scarlett is making of us, I can see that one of the Repository's more conscientious attendants is on the way over to ask if our Gearhead needs help.

Which is when the second stage of our distraction kicks in.

"You BASTARD!"

Scarlett stops short, as does everyone else in the Repository. I turn to see Aurora, red faced, standing in front of Tyler and Zila. She is pointing one accusing finger at our Alpha's nose as she shouts at the top of her voice.

"You said you were going to your mother's!" She glares at Zila. "This *again*?"

Tyler casts his eyes around the room, noting that everyone is staring at him.

"Um, hi, Honeycake . . ."

Aurora brings back one hand and, with a sound that makes me wince, cracks it across Tyler's already-bruised face.

"Don't you *honeycake* me!" Aurora shouts.

"Oh my." Scarlett presses her hand to her corset and looks at the manager. "I didn't think this was *that* sort of establishment."

"Security will take care of it," the manager assures her,

snapping his fingers and pointing at the unfolding drama. "Please, come this way, Imperatrix."

Security descends from all corners as Aurora continues to shout and swear. A guard touches her arm, explains she is "making a scene." She stabs a finger under his chin and shouts, "Don't you touch me; I know kung *fu*!" Tyler attempts an explanation, and Aurora yells over the top of him, and among it all, Zila simply looks horrified, which I suspect is not far from the truth.

But as the manager escorts us toward a heavy door in the rear of the foyer, I see Finian, still in his corner, still working away silently on his uniglass.

The heavy door opens with a scan of the manager's retina, and after a magnetic sweep for weapons and subdermals, we are through to the deposit room, Aurora's shouts still ringing behind us. In contrast to the extravagance of the foyer, this room is bland in design. A long plastene table sits in its center. The white walls are lined with thousands of small hatches made of case-hardened stellite.

"If I may, Imperatrix?" the manager says, holding up a tiny swab.

"Of course you may," she smiles, jutting out her chin and forming a perfect pout. The manager touches the swab to her lips.

"Seven one eight four alpha," she purrs.

The manager nods, turns to the appropriate hatch. As he presses the DNA swab to the receptor, I find myself holding my breath. If this is some kind of ruse, if we are forced to fight our way out of here—

The diode on the door shifts from red to blue. I hear an

electronic trill as the compartment unlocks. The manager smiles, and I open the hatch, dragging out a long metal box from inside.

"My husband is terrible with dates," Scarlett says, tapping her lip. "Could you be a dear and tell me how long ago he made this deposit for me?"

"Of course." The manager consults his uniglass. "This box was acquired . . . 17/9/2372."

"Seventy-two?" I frown. "But that was eight years ago."

Scarlett gives a sharp snap on the leash. "Thank you, Germaen, we can count. Now hush your tongue or there'll be no punishment for you tonight!"

I bite down on my protest as she turns to the manager, smiling sweetly.

"Some privacy, if we may?"

With a bow and a small smile, the man backs out of the room, leaving us alone. I glance up at the security lenses in each corner, praying to the Void that Finian is as good as we hope him to be. I frown at Scarlett sidelong.

"You are enjoying this far too much," I mutter.

"You have *noooo* idea," Scarlett whispers.

I open the box, checking the contents before we leave. I can see half a dozen packages, each marked with a small tag. TYLER. SCARLETT. KALIIS. FINIAN. ZILA. Another package, marked SQUAD 312.

"This box has waited here for almost a decade," I say.

"I know," Scarlett replies, bewilderment in her eyes. "That's before we knew each other. Before any of us even joined the academy."

"How?" I demand. "How could Admiral Adams possibly

have had your DNA sequence before he ever met you? How could he have known our squad designation? Our names? The fact that we would even *be* here?"

"If you want to really set your brain to spin," Scarlett murmurs, voice trembling, "ask yourself how he knew Cat *wouldn't* be?"

I glance at the contents of the deposit box again and realize she is correct—I see no package for Zero anywhere. But, under the other bundles, there *is* a set of passkeys, and a tag with a berth number at the Emerald City docks.

SECTION 6, GAMMA PROMENADE. BERTH 9[A].

I hand the key to Scarlett, my mind racing. "Whatever is happening here, at least Adams saw fit to supply us with a ship. That is a beginning."

Scarlett glances up to the cams. "We better get moving."

I nod, shut the lid, and sling the box under one arm. We make our way from the deposit room, Scarlett in front, me stalking obediently behind. As we walk back out into the foyer, Finian looks up at us, relief plain on his face. Zila is nowhere to be seen, but Aurora and Tyler are on the thoroughfare outside. Aurora is still gesticulating wildly, her outrage only slightly muted by the glass.

"She's having more fun than I am." Scarlett smiles.

The pair of us walk calmly across the vast foyer, each step toward the door seeming a mile. Finian stands slowly, limping to the other exit. The crowd around us mills and sways; the manager smiles farewell. And it seems, for the moment, we may have succeeded in our deception. We may be home free.

"May I ask you a question?" I say softly.

"You're not going to ask me to marry you, are you?" Scarlett murmurs.

"No. And I know it is foolish to ask this now. But we are seldom alone, and there may be little opportunity to ask another time."

"This sounds serious."

I swallow hard, suddenly and deeply uncomfortable. "I have done much reading on . . . human courting. But there is a vast gulf between the written word and reality. And you seem . . . well acquainted with romantic entanglements."

"That's a nice way to put it." I catch a smirk at the corner of Scarlett's mouth. "This is about Aurora, right?"

I sigh. Even the sound of her name makes my heart swell. "Yes."

"You got a case of the mad lurrrve."

"I am . . . very fond of her, yes."

We are almost to the door now, Scarlett speaking under her breath. "I'm probably not the person to ask for advice on this one, Muscles. I've never been in a relationship that lasted longer than seven weeks."

"You are a human girl," I say desperately. "You know what human girls *like*."

The doors slide open before us, and Scarlett looks over her shoulder, eyebrow raised. "We're not a monolith, Kal, we—"

Her words are cut short as she bumps into a small figure entering the Repository. I hear a growl of outrage, look down to see a small female gremp, surrounded by a dozen others.

"Oh, pardon me, darling," Scarlett says.

The lead gremp stands perhaps a meter tall, which is large

for her species. The tortoiseshell fur covering her body is perfectly coiffed under her pearl-white suit. Her pale green eyes are edged with dark powder and have the gleam of someone who feeds people to her pets for sport.

She looks up at Scarlett, lips sliding back over her fangs.

"You," Skeff Tannigut growls.

"Oh shit," Scarlett breathes.

▶ UNALIGNED

▼ GREMPS

GREMPS ARE A FURRY, BIPEDAL SPECIES FROM THE **ARCTURUS SYSTEM**, AND ONE OF THE YOUNGEST RACES IN THE GALAXY. THEY TYPICALLY STAND LESS THAN A METER TALL AND, FROM A TERRAN PERSPECTIVE, RESEMBLE SMALL HUMANOID FELINES.

CUTE AND CUDDLY AS THEY MAY LOOK, GREMPS ARE ONE OF THE MORE INFAMOUSLY HOSTILE SPECIES IN THE GALAXY. CARNIVOROUS BY NATURE, THEY CONSIDER OTHER SENTIENT LIFE A POTENTIAL FOOD SOURCE, AND THEIR FIRST CONTACT WITH ANOTHER SPACE-FARING SPECIES (THE **ISHTARRI** OF **FREYA III**) RESULTED IN A BRIEF FIREFIGHT FOLLOWED BY A FOUR-COURSE MEAL—A FACT THAT THE ISHTARRI REPRESENTATIVES IN THE **GALACTIC CAUCUS** ARE QUICK TO REMIND EVERYBODY OF WHENEVER THE GREMPS PRESS FOR MEMBERSHIP.

ANY URGE TO PET ONE SHOULD BE *IMMEDIATELY* PUT OUT OF YOUR MIND UNLESS YOU'RE TIRED OF OWNING FINGERS.

6

FINIAN

I make my way out the side door, aching like I've been stomped by an ultrasaur. My suit is close to completely crapping out, but we're so close to pulling this off—the last thing I want is anyone's attention. The doors hum closed behind me with a self-satisfied swish, and I turn right, toward the four-way intersection outside the Dominion Repository. By now, Scar and Kal should be parading their edible selves out the front door, where we'll meet up with the others.

Finally, *finally,* something's going our way. Kal had a box under his arm when they left the vault, so I know we have a next move. I'm feeling a little self-satisfied myself as I try for a saunter around the corner, just in time to see Scarlett come face to face—or waist to face—with a pissed-off-looking gremp.

I literally have time to think, *Wow, imagine if that was the same one who*— before suddenly the sidewalk's bristling with weaponry, and everybody's having a very tense day.

I freeze in place. Scar's already talking at top speed, hands lifted in placation, on the pointy end of a dozen

82

disruptor pistols. Behind her, Dominion security guards have responded by pulling out *their* ordnance, which is all on the wrong side of heavy. This means that, on the upside, Skeff Tannigut can't just drag Scarlett and Kal away to chop them into little pieces. On the downside, my squadmates are now threatened on all sides.

"These two are wanted fugitives!" the gremp spits, black-rimmed eyes narrowing. "They assaulted me and my broodkin, almost killed my littermate!"

"Nonsense, darling," Scarlett says. "I've never met you before in my life."

"I knew your kind could not be trusted," Tannigut growls.

"My *kind*?" Scarlett musters some convincing outrage. "I suppose we humans all look alike to you, eh?"

The Dominion guards, more than a few of whom are Terran, look less than impressed at the gangster's accusations. I limp away from the Repository, trying to stay out of sight. I have no idea where Zila is, but just beyond the rising argument, Tyler and Auri are backing up into the crowded intersection, trying to follow my example and make sure nobody notices them.

"Finian?" Ty mutters into his uni. *"Can you muster us a distraction?"*

I'm typing on my uni as I reply. "Already on it, Goldenboy. I'll have a diversion up in thirty seconds. Let's all make sure we run away in the same direction, yes?"

Tyler takes another slow step back, glancing up and down the bustling thoroughfare. *"Turn hubward, and we'll—"*

A scream cuts across comms, coupled with a vicious sizzling sound. I look up from my uni and see Aurora lying on the ground like a puppet with her strings cut. She's wrapped up in bands of what looks like crackling red energy, steam rising off her skin, mouth open in a silent scream. And that's about when everything goes to pieces. Kal leaps in her direction with a cry of perfect rage, completely forgetting Scarlett's still got his freaking leash wrapped around her wrist.

I mean, a *leash*, really?

Anyway, Scarlett's pulled after him like she's weightless, crashing straight into Skeff Tannigut and going down in a tangle of flailing limbs and corsetry. Everybody starts shooting. The gremps let loose with their disruptors as their leader falls; the Dominion guards open up in response. A couple of bodies fall on either side, and blasts crackle through the air, gremps and goons ducking for cover or collapsing with yelps of pain.

A stray shot hits a passing skiff, which skids sideways and slams into another parked vehicle, flipping end over end and crashing into a storefront. The crowd around the intersection screams and scatters. Another shot whizzes past my head and I hunker down behind a parked hoverskiff, my exosuit whining, a stabbing pain lancing up through both my knees.

I squint through the firefight and smoke, see Ty and Scar have taken cover behind another hovertruck. Kal has dragged Auri behind a row of auto-peddlers. Our stowaway is still wrapped in that crackling red energy, convulsing where she lies. Kal is crouched over her body with his teeth bared, staring over my shoulder. I realize some of the shots in this firefight are coming from *behind* me.

With a horrible feeling of foreboding—and I've really had a chance to fine-tune this sensation lately, so I feel like I nail it—I turn.

Maker's bits.

The Unbroken are stalking down the street toward us. Kal's sister is carrying a weapon that looks like a love affair between a disruptor rifle and an old Terran crossbow—I realize this is the gun that took out Auri. Her goons are spread out behind her, black armor daubed with white glyfs, lips pulled back into snarls. None of them are as terrifying as Saedii, her canines filed to those perfect points, the black stripe of paint across her eyes bringing out the violet and making them gleam. The Syldrathi are firing at the Dominion security goons, disruptor blasts *BAMF!*ing through the air. They take up cover along the thoroughfare as another skiff crashes to the road in a burst of sparks and twisting metal.

I hunker down lower, doing the math. Nobody's spotted me yet, at least, but my squad is now pinned down in a three-way firefight.

The ground traffic has slowed to a halt; the air traffic is in chaos. A brief lull falls over the scene as everyone takes a moment to reload. Civilians are fleeing in a panic, alarms are ringing, and there's already a SecDrone hovering above our heads. I can see Scarlett crouched by Kal's side, whispering in his ear, while Ty looks up and down the street, searching for an escape route. The head of the Dominion Repository guards, a tall Rikerite with two curling horns sweeping back from his forehead, raises his voice.

"Emerald City Security is en route! Everybody drop your weapons!"

Our Mistress of Beauty and Terror completely ignores him, pointing at Kal and a still-convulsing Aurora and addressing Skeff Tannigut with at least a degree of civility. "I am only here for those two, little one."

Wait . . . they want Auri now, too?

Our Tank rises to his feet in one fluid movement, his face twisted in a snarl. "You are hurting her! Stop this, Saedii!"

Even at a moment like this, I've gotta admit that all those buckles and mesh are a sight to behold. His sister's jaw drops when she sees him.

"What are you *wearing*, Kaliis?" she hisses, openly horrified.

"Release her at once!"

"Weapons on the floor!" the goon bellows again. "That means everybody!"

I've stolen around a little closer to my squad, lurking near the building opposite the Dominion's main entrance, still tapping away at my uniglass with one hand. In all the tension of this three-way standoff, the panicked crowds, nobody's clocked me yet. But looking across the smoke and wreckage, I see Tyler shoot me the smallest of nods. He's sharp, my Alpha.

"If you want those two," calls the gremp leader, nodding at Kal, "then we can take the rest, and part ways before this becomes more complicated. Agreed?"

"Now listen," begins the Dominion goon. "*We* have authority here. Everybody stand down immediately!"

"We are the faithful of Caersan, Slayer of Stars," Saedii calls. "This is Unbroken business. Keep your horns out of it before I slice them off."

That rocks the Dominion goon back on his heels. The Starslayer has the governments of most of the galaxy terrified, and *nobody* wants to get on his bad side—let alone some security chud just trying to earn a living.

The Dominion guards all exchange uneasy glances and ease off their weapons. Contempt on her face, Saedii emerges from cover, flanked by her Unbroken brethren, and begins stalking toward the Dominion Repository. Kal and the others are still pinned down by the gremps—they've got nowhere to run. And my mind's racing light-years per second, wondering how exactly we're going to get out of this mess, when Zila's voice crackles in my comms piece.

"Finian, is the diversion you mentioned still available?"

"Zila?" I'd almost forgotten she wasn't here. "Where are you?"

"Is the diversion still available?"

"Definitely."

"Please activate it in exactly twelve seconds from my mark," Zila replies, calm as ever. *"I am en route with transport. Mark."*

I can hear the incoming sirens—Emerald City Security is on its way. I slide my fingers over the uniglass, forcing my way into the Dominion Repository's systems with all the finesse of that metaphorical ultrasaur that stomped me earlier. I catch Tyler's eye—he's heard Zila's message, too. And as Saedii and her crew draw close, I activate the fire extinguishers set up on the marquee in front of the Repository, and the whole world vanishes in a cloud of blinding white fog.

Over the shouts and curses of at least five species, I hear rising sirens, the hiss of air brakes behind me. My stomach sinks as a heavy airvan barges its way into the intersection, lights flashing, the words EMERALD CITY SECURITY PATROL stenciled on the side. But my heart surges as the door is thrown open and I see a familiar figure sitting behind the controls.

"Zila?"

She motions to me, face calm, eyes blank. I break from cover, trying for a run. But my suit finally fritzes at the sudden movement; my knee gives out and I stumble, momentum carrying me forward, hands flailing as I fall. And then someone has me, pain shooting up my shoulder as they catch my elbow and yank me upright.

It's Tyler, and beyond him, Kal with Auri limp in his arms, Scarlett carrying the box they rescued from the vault. A dozen disruptor blasts fly out of the fire foam behind us, hit the wall by my head, spraying me with sparks. My breath's coming quick and hard, and Tyler's half carrying me as we throw ourselves into the van. I nearly slide right back out again as Zila guns it and the whole vehicle tilts. The Jones twins grab me in concert, and Scarlett hauls me back in as Tyler reaches past me to slam the door, a barrage of disruptor blasts and another of those crackling red energy coils crashing against the hull.

"Punch it, Zila!" Tyler yells.

All five of us in the back are crushed up against one wall as Zila stomps the accelerator, takes a corner like she's tired of living, and zooms out into the thoroughfare. Tyler scrambles past me to slide into the copilot's seat.

"You stole a *police* cruiser?" he asks.

"You asked me to secure transport," Zila says serenely,

reaching across to turn up the volume on our sirens. The vehicles in front of us part as their autopilots kick in, then close behind us once more, helping block pursuit. I realize she's wearing dangly gold earrings with little bank-robber masks on them.

Wait, wasn't she wearing gremps this morning?

Tall buildings race past as we roar through the posh end of town, gilt and white facades intermingled with red and green topiaries and decorated portals to the transport-tube network.

In the back of the van, Scarlett and Kal have managed to unwrap the crackling bands from around Auri's body. As Kal kicks them into one corner, the energy in them sputters and dies. Auri's gasping for breath, her cheeks streaked with tears. Technically I'm the squad member who's supposed to assist Zila with medical duties, so, gritting my teeth, my suit whining, I crawl over and bring up the med-scan function on my uniglass. Scarlett's giving me an unforgettable view down that damn corset as she leans over Auri, though to my credit I try *very* hard not to notice.

"What did they shoot her with?" she demands, staring at the lifeless bands.

"Saedii's weapon of choice," Kal says. His face is grim, his eyes full of fury as he cradles Auri's head. "An agonizer."

"A what now?"

"A Syldrathi weapon," I offer, remembering my mechaneering classes at the academy. "The bands hook into your neural network, overload your nervous system. It's kinda like a disruptor on Pacification setting, but waaaaay more painful."

"Is she gonna be okay?" Scarlett asks.

"She's just stunned," I say a moment later, holding up the med-scanner. "No permanent damage. I'm guessing the Unbroken didn't want her slamming them with her brain magic again. Quick learners."

"Aurora?" Kal asks, gently stroking Auri's cheek. "Can you hear me?"

"K-Kal?" she whispers.

Pixieboy sighs with relief, the muscles in his jaw relaxing. "Yes, be'shmai?"

"Your s-sister is a real bitch. . . ."

The joke has us grinning, despite the trouble we're in. But Zila's voice from the driver's seat kills our smiles real quick.

"I do not mean to interrupt," she says. "But we are being pursued."

"By?" Kal asks, lifting his head.

"Skeff Tannigut and her associates, the Unbroken, Dominion Repository security, Emerald City law enforcement, and the officers who were formerly in charge of this airvan."

"Yay?" I offer.

"Do we have a destination?" Zila asks.

Scarlett fishes around in her corset (Eyes forward, de Seel, eyes *forward*) and brandishes a passkey. "There's a ship waiting for us at Gamma Promenade."

Her brother twists around in his seat to gape at her. *"What?"*

"You won't believe what we found in the Repository," Scarlett tells him. "But for now, there's a ship waiting, and we need a ride out of here."

"Gamma Promenade it is," Tyler says, turning back to the road ahead. "But we can't lead them all there. We need to lose our tail."

I know that in this moment, I'm not the only one who thinks of Zero. That girl could drive anything you can imagine, steer it through the eye of a needle with one hand tied behind her back. The pang hits me like a punch.

I was such a dick to her. Did she take it seriously? Did she understand I'm just terrible at sincerity?

Instead of Zero, we have Goldenboy and Zila in the front of the airvan. Ty's a decent pilot, but until today, I didn't even know Zila could drive. And I'm wondering if Ty should be the one on the stick when she narrows her eyes, looking straight ahead.

"Lose our tail," she nods. "Understood."

Ty raises one scarred eyebrow. "Zila?"

"Squad," she says calmly, "please secure your safety harnesses."

. . . . .

The airvan screeches into Gamma Promenade in a spray of sparks, the turbines screaming like Rigellian opera singers. Choking black fumes are pouring out of the engine bay, several traffic cones are embedded in our ventilation intakes, and we're trailing a large smoking banner that reads HAPPY 50TH LIFEDAY, FRUMPLE in Chellerian. Tyler twists around to check we're all intact, and I don't think I've ever seen our fearless leader so wild around the eyes.

"Maker's breath, Zila," he mutters.

"A formidable performance," Kal agrees, deeply respectful.

Auri groans from her chair, lolling against her harness. "You should design roller coasters."

The engine gives one last desperate cough, sputters, and dies. Zila reaches for the release just as the whole door falls off with a crash. Everyone sits where they are for a long moment, savoring the sensation of being alive. Or in my case, reviewing some of the rash promises made to my Maker over the last quarter hour, in return for my survival.

"We should proceed with all due haste," Zila says, staring at us expectantly. "They will easily be able to follow our trail."

"We *did* leave a little debris," Scarlett agrees.

One by one we come to life, climbing out of our poor getaway vehicle, staggering for balance. I try not to wince at the pain as my feet hit the deck. It turns out the Gamma docks are Emerald City's long-term berthing area—many of the ships around us are secured for an extended stay. Our own berth is farther along, but the airvan isn't moving another meter, so we're on foot.

I'm nearly as unsteady on my feet as Auri, but I stumble after the others toward Berth 9, counting the ships and mentally weighing each one. *That one would be okay, that one would be good, that one would be amazing. . . .*

I see it a couple of ships out, and I involuntarily slow, my eyes locked on the . . . *thing* that's waiting for us. I count again, just in case I'm wrong. As we come to a halt in front of it, I look down at the number stenciled on the ground at our feet.

9[a].

"You've gotta be kidding," Tyler whispers.

"We should have gone with the sewage hauler," Scarlett replies quietly. "At least it didn't look like it was *made* of crap."

The rust bucket in front of us is a little larger than our old Longbow, and it brings a new meaning to *butt-ugly*. It looks like someone ripped apart six or seven other vessels, trawled through the wreckage to find all the least attractive parts, then welded them together. It was once painted red, but it's now completely covered in rust, the bulbous cockpit window almost opaque with dirt, black streaks running down its flanks from every bolt and rivet. It's like someone who *hated* speed, efficiency, and style sat down to draw up their dream ship. And then had a *really* good day at the office.

"Are we completely sure the admiral is on our side?" I ask.

This *can't* be the one we're looking for—there's no way Adams could promise to help us and then leave us something like this.

"Maybe s-someone switched the ships?" Auri tries.

"No . . ." Tyler's voice is quiet. "This is the one."

He walks forward to brush away the rust and grime coating the nameplate beside the main hatch. When he draws his now-filthy hand away, we can all see the ship's name embossed on the metal.

ZERO

How could the ship possibly be named after her?

Tyler presses his palm to the sensor plate by the hatch. I'm about to break the news that this thing has less juice left in it than my fourth great-grandfather—and he died before I was born—when the door slides open soundlessly.

Our Alpha looks back at us, and then up along the dock. He knows we won't have lost our pursuers for long, and we don't have time to fool around. And, terrible as it is, trying to get this thing up into orbit isn't actually our worst choice today. I can see a SecDrone already hovering above our position, and a variety of other horrible options are no doubt closing in on our position as we speak.

So when Goldenboy steps through the hatch and into the dark interior, the rest of us follow. I'm holding my breath, but it's more a fear of toxic mold than suspense. With a smooth hum, the internal lighting comes to life.

And it's like we're in another world.

A spotless, gleaming, high-tech world that catches my attention in almost the same way Scarlett Jones does.

"Wow," Auri murmurs.

"You said it, Stowaway," I murmur.

Great Maker, this is . . . *incredible*.

Everything is beautifully designed, from the cockpit to the consoles running the length of the main cabin. A suite of displays light up as I watch, broadcasting security vision from the ship's exterior, from Emerald City main traffic control, and from news feeds around the galaxy. If the outside of this ship was designed to be as ugly as possible, its interior was designed with the exact opposite philosophy in mind. It's sleek, white, cutting-edge. A Gearhead's wet dream.

Tyler's already sliding into the pilot's seat, beginning his preflight check.

"Strap in," he says simply. "Let's be gone before they get here."

There's a long, elegant console running half the length of the main cabin behind him, lined with three chairs on either side. The back half of the cabin has consoles with more oomph and larger displays, couches, and doors that lead to storage, sleeping quarters, and the galley.

Scarlett touches my arm and nods at a chair on the far side of the console. I realize it's designed for me. There are ports for me to plug into, and the seat is molded to allow for my suit. As I glance around, I realize all the seats are personalized—Kal's is larger; Auri's and Zila's are smaller.

I exchange a long, baffled glance with Scarlett, and then we slide into our allotted places. Our harnesses snake over our shoulders automatically, our chairs swiveling to face forward for launch.

"We have incoming hostiles," Kal reports.

His fingers dance over the console by his chair, projecting one of the external cams up into the air above us. I see he's right—the Unbroken have arrived first, and they're sprinting along the dock in our direction, shoving anyone in their way straight over the edge. I can see Emerald City Security behind them.

Tyler's still running through his preflight, working at light speed now, muttering to himself as he punches controls. With a clunk the *Zero* decouples from the dock, rising smoothly into the air with the soft rumble of our drive systems.

But Saedii's only a few steps away, and she's accelerating.

Black hair whips around her face in the ship's downdraft,

95

her expression is cold, beautiful, terrifying. I see her reach the edge of the dock two heartbeats after we've pulled away, and without even a downward glance at the void below, she simply launches herself at us across the gap.

We watch on cams, riveted as she clings to our closed hatch with boot tips and fingernails, pounding at the metal, rust flaking away under her fists. I'm transfixed, staring at the door, half expecting her to tear her way through.

Kal's mouth is open, and though he doesn't speak, I can tell what he's thinking. It's a looooong fall down to the chlorine storm raging below the city, and the pressure and temperature will both kill her quick. Despite everything, I'm sure he doesn't want his sister to die.

Fortunately, Tyler's not feeling as murderous as she is. Carefully, he tilts his controls, circling back above the dock as her feet peel away. Saedii dangles by her fingertips for one long, agonizing moment, and then, with a curse that almost melts a hole straight through the hull, she's forced to let go, falling to the dock below and landing amid the other Syldrathi, who scatter like kazar birds.

"Security inbound," Zila reports.

Without a word Tyler straightens *Zero* up, wheeling through the ionized dome and into the raging atmosphere beyond. Our new ship barely registers the turbulence as we hit it, flying smoother than I'd have thought possible.

"This baby is a *beast*," I sigh.

"Bye-bye, Emerald City," Scarlett murmurs. "You will *not* be missed."

Auri looks around with a smile. "We *made* it."

"We did." Tyler nods. "But we still have a long way to go."

Our Alpha turns in his chair, his voice all business as he looks at me.

"Legionnaire de Seel?"

"Yessir?"

"Bring up those coordinates. Let's go find the *Hadfield*."

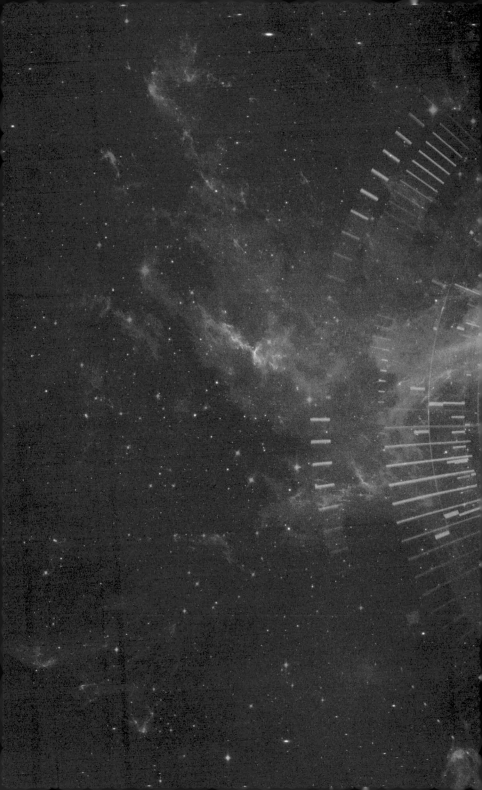

PART 2

THE BLOOD
BETWEEN US

SUBJECT: GALACTIC SPECIES

▶ ALIGNED

▼ BETRASKANS

THE PEOPLE OF **TRASK** ARE A RACE OF PALE-SKINNED BEINGS WITH PHYSIOLOGY REMARKABLY SIMILAR TO THAT OF HUMANS. OWING TO CATACLYSMIC **ENVIRONMENTAL SADNESS** ON THEIR WORLD THOUSANDS OF YEARS AGO, THE BETRASKANS CREATED A SUBTERRANEAN CIVILIZATION AND HAVE FULLY ADAPTED TO LIFE UNDERGROUND.

THEIR SKIN HAS NO **MELANIN**, RESULTING IN PALLID, BLOODLESS COMPLEXIONS. THEIR EYES ARE SUITED TO LOW LIGHT, AND BETRASKANS WEAR PROTECTIVE LENSES WHEN ABOVEGROUND.

BETRASKAN SOCIETY CONSISTS OF IMPOSSIBLY COMPLEX FAMILIAL STRUCTURES KNOWN AS **CLANS**, AND AN EVEN MORE INTRICATE WEB OF DEBTS CALLED **FAVORS**.

NOBODY OUTSIDE TRASK EVEN *PRETENDS* TO UNDERSTAND THESE TIES, BUT THIS MUCH IS CLEAR: THERE'S NOTHING MORE IMPORTANT TO A BETRASKAN THAN FAMILY.

7

FINIAN

The doors to our quarters lead off a gleaming white hallway, the auto-lights slowly glowing to life ahead of me. Some of the doors are unmarked, but the second on the left has the image of a khyshakk beetle—the indomitable symbol of my people and the oldest species still living on our planet— outlined in blue paint.

I brush my fingers across the access panel, and as the door hums aside softly, I can see why this room is for me. Instead of the clean, light colors that adorn the rest of the *Zero*, the walls are dark gray to give the impression I'm underground. There's even a flic vine growing down the wall to my right, taking me back for a moment to my cousin Dariel's den on the World Ship, and further than that, to my parents' home on Trask. As the door hums closed behind me, the flic vine's leaves come to life, glowing gently enough that I could take my contact lenses out if I wanted.

I'm so busy relaxing into the dark, breathing in the cooler air, that it takes me a moment to realize there's no bunk. My heart thumps a quick rhythm—*ohpleaseohpleaseohplease*—as I turn back toward the door.

And there it is. I hit the button, and a soft voice speaks in Terran. "GRAVITY REDUCTION IN THIRTY SECONDS. PLEASE SECURE ALL LIQUIDS."

I count down, breath catching in anticipation, and then the weights that have been dragging me down for weeks slowly lessen, until with the tiniest push of one foot, I can lift off the ground. It's like wading into cool water on a scorching day. Like all the tension just bleeds out of my body, and for the first time in a long time, I'm not in pain, I don't ache, I'm not working just to stay upright.

I had quarters like these growing up with my grandparents and at Aurora Academy. They were meant to be fitted on our Longbow, but of course we never returned from our first mission. The low grav means I'll be able to take off my suit to repair it, which will make everything easier. With this much weight removed, I can maneuver with almost no effort. And now I take a closer look, I see the left-hand wall is covered in tools—an array of everything I could want or need.

I'm almost crying with relief. This is my way out. I've been bluffing I'm okay since the World Ship, while my body and suit have been getting progressively worse, dreading the moment my Alpha wouldn't be able to ignore my condition any longer. But now I'll be able to *do* something about it.

The speaker in the ceiling chimes softly again, and this time the voice that issues from it is Tyler's.

"Once everyone's situated, let's meet up in the main cabin. It's time to open Pandora's box, squad."

As I make my way back down the hallway, all my aches and pains reasserting themselves, I wonder who Pandora is—and why we've got her box. Tyler and Zila have the *Zero* humming along on autopilot now, well clear of the Emerald City. We're headed for a FoldGate, and the countdown above the main console says we'll be through it in about an hour. Shamrock is tucked into position above the pilot's chair, and my eyes drift to the stuffed dragon as I slide into my seat. There are six seats here, six cabins aft. Between that and the ship's name, it's pretty clear that whoever did all this for us knew Cat wouldn't be here to need anything.

One by one the others emerge. Kal and Auri have found the infirmary, because she's looking a little less rough after her run-in with the agonizer, and Scar's munching on a stack of cookies that suggests she found the galley.

Zila peers at the pile in Scar's hand. "That stack represents significantly more than your required daily calorie intake, Scarlett."

The redhead smacks her butt. "Just more of me to love, Zee."

I can't help but smile. Zila purses her lips, mulling it over, and finally reaches out for a cookie.

Quick enough, we're all in our chairs, leaning forward in anticipation. Everybody wants to know what's in the box. Tyler swivels the pilot's chair away from the forward displays to face the rest of us around the console.

"All right," he says. "Scar, Kal, let's see what you withdrew from the bank."

Scarlett brushes away the crumbs, rises to her feet, and pulls the lid off the box. "Okay, first up, there are a bunch of packages in here we didn't have time to unwrap. But they have our names on them."

She hands a small parcel to Zila. Our Brain peels aside the blue wrapping and holds out her hand. Nestled against the cloth is a pair of gold hoop earrings like the ones she usually wears. But these charms are birds.

"Hawks," Auri says, looking more closely.

"Very pretty," Zila murmurs. "I wonder how they knew I'd like them."

Next is a bigger package for our fearless leader. Goldenboy pulls the wrapping aside, all business, that handsome brow creasing when he finds a pair of boots inside. They seem perfectly ordinary: black, shiny, heavy tread on the soles.

"Something wrong with the ones you got?" his sister asks.

"No," he says, puzzled, looking downward. "I mean, I haven't been able to polish them for a couple of days. . . ."

"Oh great *Maker*." Scar reaches out and takes his hand, concern on her face. "How are you holding up?"

"It's been a struggle."

Zila studies his gift for a moment before she speaks. "I suggest wearing them, sir. As Scarlett has observed, whoever left these gifts knows me well. We should assume they also know you and believe this to be necessary. So far, our benefactors have demonstrated they have our best interests at heart."

Tyler considers this, shrugs, and leans down to start switching out his old boots for his new.

Scarlett opens her own parcel next. It's about the size of Zila's, and nestled against the blue wrapping is a round silver medallion on a chain. On one side the words *Go with Plan B* are engraved in a curling script.

"'Go with Plan B'?" Tyler asks.

"Usually a good idea where your plans are concerned, brother mine."

"Cold, Scar. Real cold."

Scarlett lets the medallion twist on its chain between her fingers, looking at it carefully. On the flip side, I can see that it's inset with a rough chunk of diamond. The cabin lights refract on the surface, tiny rainbows dancing in her eyes.

"Pretty," I say.

Scarlett shrugs. "I guess diamonds *are* a girl's best friend."

". . . They are?" Kal asks, glancing at Aurora.

Nobody has any wisdom to offer, and after a moment Scar eases the chain over her head and tucks the medallion inside her uniform.

Kal's package is small as well, and when he opens it, we see a thin, silver, rectangular box. It has hinges, and it seems as though it's meant to open, but when he tries to pry off what looks like the lid, it won't budge.

"What is it?" I ask, craning my neck.

I'd assumed it was a Terran or Syldrathi device, but I'm met with a series of bewildered head shakes. Auri finally digs into her pocket, pulls out Magellan, and holds it over the little metal box in Kal's palm. I can't believe I'm now mentally calling this thing by its name as well, but I guess its personality program certainly does . . . set it apart from the standard-issue uni.

"Magellan?" she says.

"Hı there! I missed your face!"

"Yeah, yours too. Can you tell me what this is?"

"I. Would. Love to!" The uniglass runs a line of green light down the length of the thing, and beeps. "This is a Terran artifact, predating interstellar travel, boss! It was designed to hold business cards or cigarillos!"

Most of the faces around the table still look baffled.

"Well, I know what a business card is," says Auri. "It's a piece of paper with your personal details on it. You give them to people so they can contact you."

I frown. "You don't just bump uniglasses?"

"No uniglasses in my time," she says.

"Dark days indeed!" Magellan beeps.

Kal frowns. "I am not in possession of business cards," he informs her gravely, as though this might be a problem.

She glances down at Magellan. "Magellan, define *cigarillo*."

"Nothing would make me happier, boss! A cigarillo was a small cigarette!" It pauses, absorbs the confused silence, and tries again. "A plant known as tobacco was rolled inside a thin sheet of paper, then set on fire, and Terrans inhaled the smoke for stimulation!"

"This sounds hazardous to one's health," Zila opines.

"Correct!" Magellan says. "The practice fell out of vogue in the twenty-second century, after Terrans discovered in the twentieth that it killed you!"

"It took them two hundred years to stop doing it?" I ask, bewildered.

"ISN'T THAT INSANE?" Magellan says. "HONESTLY, DOESN'T THAT SOUND LIKE A SPECIES THAT WOULD BENEFIT FROM SOME KIND OF BENEVOLENT MACHINE OVERLORD?"

"Silent mode," Tyler says.

"Aw."

We share a series of blank stares, pondering the box in Kal's hand. Our Tank studies the little metal case one more time, then tucks it into the breast pocket of his uniform, with a small shift of posture that's as close to a shrug as our most dignified squad member ever seems to come.

Now it's time for my present. I won't lie: I'm excited to see what it is. But my excitement fades when I unwrap the paper and discover a small, plain metal cylinder. It's something like a stylus, but there's nothing electronic about it.

"What's it for?" I ask. "Is it some kind of tool?"

Auri reaches over to take it from me and presses her thumb against one end, producing a clicking sound. A little point springs out from the other.

"It's a ballpoint pen," she says, handing it back to me.

"It's a what now?"

"It's a writing implement from my time," she says.

"I've been ripped off," I inform her. "I do *not* need an old-fashioned writing implement."

"I'll trade you for my boots?" Tyler offers.

"Or my smoking box that does not open?" Kal says.

I press my thumb to the end like Auri did and retract the point. I *will* admit the click is a little satisfying. Scarlett reaches into the box again and pulls out a package marked with our squad designation, 312, which turns out to contain a whole pile of red and gold Dominion credit chips.

"Nothing for Auri, I'm afraid," she says.

"I already got my gift," Auri replies simply.

". . . You did?" Tyler asks.

"Yeah. You guys."

She gazes around at Squad 312 and makes a face.

"Holy cake, that sounded unbearably cheesy, didn't it?"

"Unforgivably," Scar grins, dropping the cred chips onto the console. "But except for the papers directing us to the ship and the passkeys, this is everything."

"At least we will not be lacking in funds," Kal nods.

"This is not a credit chip," Zila says, retrieving a chip bearing a turquoise stripe from under the red and gold. She passes it to me, as I'm sitting in front of a data slot.

I pause for a moment, because I have a policy of never putting a chip a stranger gives me into my equipment, unless, you know, that whole sentence is a metaphor. But if our benefactors wanted to drop us in it, they've already had their chance and then some. So, with a wince, I push it home.

The main screen above us flickers to life, and we're greeted by Admiral Adams and Battle Leader de Stoy. They're in full dress uniform, the sigil of the Aurora Legion emblazoned on their shoulders. Adams raises one cybernetic hand in greeting, and de Stoy favors the camera with a small nod, her black eyes unreadable even to another Betraskan.

"Greetings, legionnaires," Adams says gravely. "First, well done on deciphering our code. Battle Leader de Stoy and I regret we can't be there to brief you personally, but if you are watching this message, it's our hope that you're aboard the Zero and headed for the Hephaestus convoy."

He pauses, which is helpful, as it leaves room for a collective "Whaaaaat?"

Before the creeped-out disbelief from all around the table gets too out of hand, de Stoy picks up the narrative.

"This will doubtlessly be strange to all of you, legionnaires. We know you must have many burning questions. Unfortunately, and for reasons that will one day become clear, there is still much about your situation we cannot reveal. We are sorry for the trials you will face as a result, but you must know this much at least." She looks around the bridge, as if she can actually see us all. *"Our every effort is bent toward supporting you. We know you have taken up the cause of the Eshvaren. And we know you are our last hope against the Ra'haam."*

"We can't declare our support publicly," Adams continues. *"In fact, Aurora Legion must be seen to be actively working against you. The Ra'haam has agents within the Global Intelligence Agency, and potentially other stellar governments."*

My gaze flicks over to Auri, whose face is like stone. I know that like me, she's picturing her father in the white GIA uniform of Princeps, calling out to her, entreating her to join the Ra'haam.

"Take these gifts," Adams continues. *"Keep them with you at all times. And know that you're traveling on the correct path."*

"Know that we believe in you," de Stoy says. *"And you must believe in each other. We the Legion. We the light. Burning bright against the night."*

Adams stares straight down the camera and repeats the words he spoke to us when we left Aurora Academy, ignorant of everything that lay ahead of us.

"You must believe," he says simply.

And just like that, the message ends.

We're all quiet for a long moment. Trying to process

what's just happened. My thoughts are running light-years per second, the full enormity of it all ringing in my brain and threatening to blow it right out of my skull.

Our commanders know about the Eshvaren. They know about the Ra'haam. They know what we're up against, and somehow, some way, impossible as it might seem, they knew what was coming—finding Auri, losing Cat, our new careers as interstellar fugitives—before any of it ever happened. This message waited for us in the security vault for *years* before any of us ever even entered Aurora Academy. Let alone became legionnaires.

Auri's the one who finally breaks the silence. "I don't know your bosses well, but if they knew this was coming, a little heads-up would've been good."

Scarlett looks at Shamrock, sitting above the empty pilot's chair. All the color has gone out of her features, and her voice. "You can say that again."

Kal reaches across to tentatively take Auri's hand. "Have faith, be'shmai. Adams and de Stoy have worked for the best thus far. We must believe that in keeping what they know from us, they continue to do so."

Of course, this is right up a Syldrathi's alley—full of mystery and almost prophecy. No wonder Kal's eating it up. But I see Tyler looking across at me, pinning me down with those big blue eyes of his.

"We must believe," he says softly.

We're the only two religious people on the ship, Tyler and I, and I know he feels the same way I do—that the Maker's hand is in this somehow. It's Tyler's faith that Adams is appealing to when he says those words. But it's so achingly hard to keep believing when it's cost us so much already. When people we care about think we're traitors. When we're fighting to save a galaxy and it seems the whole galaxy is fighting *against* us.

When that pilot's chair is empty.

"Well," says Scarlett, deliberately cheerful. "Upside: we know we're definitely heading in the right direction."

Zila nods. "The black box from the *Hadfield* is our next objective."

That pronouncement breaks the somber mood that settled over the table, and Tyler nods, transforming into Goldenboy again with a quick toss of his head. He squares his shoulders, speaks with authority.

"Okay," he says. "It's been a Day. Let's grab some food and strategize, then once we're through the FoldGate, we can try and get some downtime."

The confidence in his voice seems to galvanize the rest of the squad, and everyone is soon moving again—turning to their displays or rummaging in supply lockers or prepping for the Fold. I look down at my gift on the console in front of me—dull, metallic, about as useful as a spacesuit without an oxygen supply.

With a sigh, I tuck the pen into my top pocket.

"I sure hope we know what we're doing."

· · · · ·

A few hours later I'm on watch, feet propped up on the center console to ease the twinge in my lower back. It'll be a longish Fold to get to the gate nearest the convoy—longer Folds can come complete with anything from paranoia to the shakes to psychosis, but we're all young enough that we should be fine on a jump like this.

Once you hit twenty-five or so, it becomes a very different equation. After that age, you can't travel through the Fold for long without being put into stasis. That's why Aurora Legion squads start so young. We graduate around eighteen, and we get seven years before we mostly move to desk jobs.

Sometimes I've wondered whether the stress on my body will mean I get less time before the Fold starts to wear on me. But hey, as Scarlett would say, upside: I'd need to be alive for it to become a problem. And the odds of that are bad at best.

If Ty knew what shape my suit was in, he wouldn't have given me a watch at all. But he still hasn't completely worked out how bad it is, and Scar has respected my requests to keep it under wraps. It won't be an issue soon, anyway—I have everything I need in my cabin for repairs, and once my suit's properly aligned and functioning, it'll take the strain off my muscles and let them start healing too.

I check the scanners for the fifth time in as many minutes. We're still on course, no pursuit, my displays reduced to sharp monochrome like everything else in the Fold. Black and white isn't a huge stretch for a Betraskan—life underground isn't very colorful at the best of times. But I sometimes wonder if my squaddies get weirded out by it.

I hear soft footsteps and look up from my displays to see Auri emerging from the passageway in a sweater and pajama pants. She must have been to visit the super-sleek galley in the stern, because she's holding two steaming mugs.

"Hey, Stowaway. Couldn't sleep?"

She answers with a little shudder. "Bad dreams."

I make a sympathetic face and pull my feet off the console, reaching across to take my mug from her. It's baris, a favorite drink of my people that nobody else in the galaxy really likes.

"Wow," I murmur. "They really stocked the galley with everything."

"You're telling me," she agrees. "I never thought I'd see chamomile again."

I lean across to look at her drink, and she holds out the mug so I can inhale the steam. "Smells like flowers," I decide.

"It's one of my faves. It's traditionally for before bed. Helps you wind down."

"Chamomile." I repeat the word to commit it to memory, in case I need to make it for her sometime. "You want to talk about the dream? A load shared is a load halved."

She smiles. "Is that some ancient Betraskan wisdom or something?"

I shake my head. "Read it on a coaster at a skin bar. But, you know, sometimes dreams aren't so bad when you say them out loud."

Even as I'm saying that, I'm thinking about the dreams she's probably having. About the one I had, when I saw Trask covered in blue snow that turned out to be the pollen of the Ra'haam. It's the fate that awaits my homeworld if we fail to stop the Ra'haam from spreading. The fate that awaits the whole galaxy.

She closes her eyes and sips her tea.

"It was what you'd think," she says quietly. "It wasn't Octavia this time. Too many moons. And the sky was greener.

But the plants were the same. Except they felt bigger and stronger. I was trying to look more closely, but the pollen was too thick to see. I think there were . . . buds. On the plants."

A finger of ice traces a path down my spine.

Her voice is a whisper. "I think it was getting ready to bloom and burst."

I don't really know what to say to that. I'm wondering how I'd feel if it was me in her position—if the whole galaxy was resting on my narrow shoulders, not hers. I'm trying to figure out a way to tell her how brave I think she is. How most people would have just flown to pieces if they'd lived her life over the past few weeks. But I've never been good at Peopling. I never know what to say.

Fortunately, I'm rescued from my struggle by the arrival of Scar and Kal. They both look sleepy, but Kal's taken the time to pull on his uniform, his hair as immaculate as ever. Scar's in a silky wrap thing that invites me to imagine what she's wearing underneath it. I do my best not to, with mixed results.

"Hey, you," Auri says, smiling at Kal.

"Hey," I say, sounding like a chirpy idiot. "Bad dreams for you too?"

"I don't know what woke me up," Scarlett admits. "I was just . . ."

". . . uneasy," Kal finishes.

I wonder about that uneasiness. I know Kal's mother was an empath, and if his sister inherited some of her gift, maybe he did too? Maybe he picked up on Auri's bad dream. Doesn't really explain why Scarlett can't sleep, though . . .

The silence stretches, Auri letting talk of her dream recede like it's in the rearview mirror, Kal and Scarlett reaching for a better reason they drifted out here.

Well, this is about as cheery as a tri-soul departure ceremony.

"All right," I say. "I got another half hour before I go off watch. Since nobody's sleeping, what say we teach Stowaway here how to play frennet?"

"I am familiar with the game, but not the rules," Kal replies.

I reflect for a moment that no Betraskan at Aurora Academy would ever have considered socializing with Kal, let alone teaching him how to play a game—not with his Warbreed sigil tattooed right there on his forehead.

"No problem," I tell him. "Howsabout I give you and Auri a lesson, and we put some of those shiny new credits to use?"

Scar gives me a wink that says she knows I'm on cheer-up duty, and she approves, and I work hard to make sure I don't give her a big, dumb smile back.

I know the three of them would take over my watch if I asked so I could get to work on my suit, but half an hour of this feels more important. After our strategy talk earlier, we all know there's hard times ahead. I figure there's no harm in making a little light for ourselves, here in the dark.

"I'll go get drinks," Scar says. "Fin, why don't you pull up the program?"

"Okay," I say, swiping through the ship's submenus to find a decent frennet program, and pulling up a 3-D screen to project on the console. "So in the first round, there are seventeen dice in play."

"Seven*teen*?" Auri splutters.

"Don't worry, I'll go easy on you."

A small line appears between Kal's brows, a sign of great concern.

"No mercy, Finian," he says. "We learn by losing."

"I never said I was gonna go easy on *you*, Pixieboy," I grin, assigning the player tokens. "*You*, my pointy-eared friend, are about to learn a great deal."

"Mmm." His violet eyes sparkle at the joke. "We shall see."

"You know, if you don't wanna risk any of that newfound wealth, there's another version we can play. Strip frennet."

"Excuse me?"

"Yeah," I grin. "Everyone bets a piece of clothing per pot, and the loser has to take it off. Makes things more interesting."

I admit I feel a perverse sense of delight as Kal's eyes slip involuntarily to Aurora, and I see a flush of heat spreading across her freckled cheeks.

"I do not think that is appropriate," Kal says.

"Hey, I didn't know Syldrathi blushed with their ears."

"I am *not* blushing," Kal glowers.

Scar returns with the drinks tray balanced on one hand and flicks my ear as she passes. "Stop being a bastard, Finian."

"But I'm so good at it!"

Scarlett grins and shakes her head, and her smile makes me smile harder in return. We get down to it, and in the end, Kal isn't the only one who ends up learning a great deal. I learn that Auri starts snorting when she giggles too hard. I learn that Kal has a deep, booming laugh you can feel in your chest. I learn that Scarlett *cannot* be bluffed, no matter how hard you try. And I learn that maybe I don't suck at Peopling as much as I suspected.

We stay up past my watch. We play way longer than we should.

But hey, nobody's thinking about bad dreams anymore.

Subject: Space Exploration

▶ **Famous Disasters**

　▼ **The** *Hadfield*

In the days before the formation of **TerraGov**, and with national governments unwilling to invest in space exploration, embarrassingly, it fell to corporations to take humanity's first steps beyond its own **solar system**.

The *Hadfield* was intended to be the pinnacle of such exploration. Constructed shortly after the discovery of **Fold technology**, and before **first contact**, the *Hadfield* was Earth's first Ark-class colony ship, built by the now-defunct **Ad Astra Incorporated**.

Containing ten thousand colonists, and bound for Earth's first major interstellar colony on **Lei Gong**, the *Hadfield* disappeared in **the Fold** with all souls aboard. The disaster led to the financial ruin of Ad Astra, the formation of Terra's first truly global space program, **ET1**, and the end of the age of corporate space exploration.

Aaaaaaand now I'm depressed. ☹

8

AURI

I don't know how well the others slept in the Fold—my dreams were disjointed and weird—but I'm still better rested than I was before. The aches of Saedii's agonizer are fading, though I'm guessing I won't be invited to her place for the holidays anytime soon. It was strange to wake up while we travel this way. Everything on the ship was cast in black and white by the Fold, and it felt like I was still dreaming.

But now I'm in the *Zero*'s airlock, busy suiting up with Fin and Kal while Zila diligently checks our spacesuits. My gloves click into place, and she takes my hands in hers, turning them over to confirm the seal. Zila pins my hair back from my face—my own hands are too unwieldy in my gloves. I guess I should have thought of that in advance. I've had a short lecture from Tyler, and a half hour's practice in the low gravity available in Finian's room, which is all anyone ever needed for a space walk, right?

That's right. I'm about to walk.

In.

Space.

The Jones twins are up front in the pilot's and copilot's chairs, guiding us ever closer to the Hephaestus salvage convoy, the *Hadfield*, and the black box inside. I can see a display of it from the long-range cams on our hull, and it's like . . . well, it's like something out of a science-fiction movie. The convoy is huge—hundreds of ships, all in various states of disrepair, from "mildly beat-up" to "let's hope it has a good personality." The shapes and sizes are mind-boggling: sleek and beautiful or bulky but functional or holy cake what. Each ship is being hauled by a much smaller tug, marked with the burning cogwheel of Hephaestus Incorporated.

From what Ty said, these tugs are mostly engine, made to haul much bigger vessels across space or into starports. They don't look too scary, but the convoy is also accompanied by a small fleet of heavily armed cruisers. I can see them on the display—wedges of gleaming silver, moving in the predictable flight patterns of pilots who're bored out of their minds. Nobody here is expecting to get robbed. The ships they're hauling are all broken-down pieces of junk, after all.

And, speak of the devil, out on the fringes of the convoy, there she is.

The *Hadfield* is huge, battleship-shaped, her hull blackened and torn. The last time I saw her, this ship was considered state of the art. She was the biggest Ark-class vessel Earth had ever made. She carried ten thousand colonists and the hopes of an entire planet. And now all of them are dead except for me.

For the thousandth time, I wonder why I was the one to survive. Why, of all those innocent people, the Eshvaren picked *me* to be their Trigger. Looking at the derelict floating out there in all that black, I feel a shiver run down my spine, something whispering in the back of my—

"Aurora?"

I blink, realize Zila is looking at me expectantly. "Huh?"

"Lean down, please."

I do as I'm told, then bend forward so she can ease my helmet on.

Ty transmits from the bridge. *"All right, we're almost good to go here. The tac-comp and I have been analyzing their security flight pattern, and there's a gap in their sweep every thirty-seven minutes."*

"We are still twenty-five hours from the convoy's destination at Picard VI." Zila snaps the latches into place, her voice suddenly muffled in real life, but crystal clear over my comms system. *"Their security should not be on particularly high alert."*

"Agreed—most of them are flying on autopilot," Tyler says. *"But nobody take that as an invitation to dawdle. Get in, get what we came for, and get out. Anything else is a bonus."*

By "anything else," he means anything I can contribute. Fin is boarding the *Hadfield* to download the contents of the black box. Kal is there for our protection. And I'm there in case I see anything that reminds me of . . . well, anything, really. Whatever happened to me, or how. Given we're not even sure what we're searching for, we'll take whatever clues we can get. But I hope that finding out what the *Hadfield*'s systems remember about the moment I was . . . transformed . . . will at least set us on the next steps of our path.

"The Zero has stealth mode engaged," Tyler continues. *"And her cloaking tech is top-shelf, so we're not going to show*

on any of their scopes. But these people still have eyes to spot us. So make sure you don't draw any attention to yourselves."

His sister's voice chimes in. *"We'll be in position in ninety seconds."*

On our displays, I'm watching a tiny red dot that represents us, sidling up to the convoy through the gap in the security patrol's flight paths. I watch us weave in and out of the fleet under Tyler's expert hand, and my stomach is about to crawl right out of my mouth. Zila is checking Kal's helmet seals now, up on her toes to reach.

"You will have sixty seconds to reach the Hadfield *before the security fleets adjust formation and the gap closes,"* she says.

"Just don't look down, Stowaway," Fin grins.

Zila backs out of the airlock, closes the door. *"Good luck."*

We're sealed inside now, only one more door between us and space. My palms are damp. I can feel a cold trickle of sweat running down my spine.

"Opening outer door in ten seconds," Zila reports over comms. *"Secure positions. Grip the wall restraints in case of sudden movement."*

I push both my hands through the straps, anchoring myself firmly, even though there's no real reason I should fall out of the ship and into the endless vacuum. Still, I'm not about to pass up *any* safety precautions right now. I mean, I trained to travel through it, sure. But there's a big difference between being loaded into a cryopod and shot through space, and actually, you know, *walking* in it.

The outer door slides open, and son of a biscuit, that is Space right there.

It's *really* big.

I mean, obviously it's really big; it's literally famous for being really big. And yet somehow, this is different from seeing it through a viewport or monitor.

This is the first time I've understood that I could float through space *forever*.

Kal is beside me, resting one gloved hand on my arm. His gaze is calm, his voice gentle. *"All will be well, be'shmai. Finian and I will assist you."*

It turns out Fin equaled Ty's perfect score on his zero-grav orienteering exam—apparently the outcome of years spent sleeping in it. He nods sagely. *"I'll be right there, Stowaway. These superhero good looks aren't just for show."* He shoots me a grin, then crouches over the launcher, all business. *"Time check, please, Scar."*

"Fifteen seconds," she reports. *"Ten, nine, eight . . ."*

Up on the bridge, Tyler adjusts his controls, and the endless view of space is replaced by the port side of the *Hadfield*, a stretch of pitted metal filling our view through the open hatch. According to the displays, we're now flying in perfect parallel with the derelict: same speed, same heading, maybe fifty meters apart.

I take a deep breath, checking my grip, making sure I'll actually be able to unpeel my hands when I need to move. *Small movements,* I tell myself, repeating the words Fin and Tyler chanted at me over and over during my one brief training session. In zero gravity, a sudden jerk or lunge will send me off balance, and momentum will keep me helplessly spinning. Every motion needs to be precise and gentle. There's no up in space. There's no down. But one wrong move and I could end up falling for the rest of my life.

Smaaaall movements.

Scarlett is still counting down. "*. . . three, two, one, mark.*"

Fin gazes calmly through the sights and pulls the trigger on the grappler. A metal line flies out across the gap between the *Zero* and the *Hadfield,* attaching soundlessly to the larger ship right near a massive, melted gash in her hull.

"*Line secure,*" Fin whispers. "*Transfer under way.*"

"Why are you whispering?" I ask.

"*I . . . don't know exactly.*"

"*You're not much of a warrior, are you, Finian?*" Kal teases.

"*Will you just get out there?*" Fin hisses. "*We've got mischief to make.*"

With the smallest hint of a smile curling his lips, Kal eases himself out of the airlock, pulling himself hand over hand along the metal line between the two ships. I'm next, and I can hear my breath shaking as I exit the *Zero*.

Even though we're flying at hundreds of thousands of kilometers per minute, there's no sensation of us actually *moving*, and aside from my breathing, everything around me is perfectly silent. Kal, Fin, and I are tethered to each other and the main line, and we all have jet propulsion units in our suits in case something goes wrong. But still, the void around us is so sickeningly huge and black and just *nothing* that I almost can't wrap my head around it. And so I stop trying, focusing on the cable in front of me instead, whispering instructions to myself:

"Right hand, left hand, right hand, left hand."

I know Fin's behind me, ready to help if I need it. But that doesn't change how impossibly small I feel right now. Yet somehow, instead of being frightened, I find myself . . .

exhilarated. Feeling so tiny makes me realize just how *big* what we're all a part of is. And being out here in all this emptiness somehow makes me completely aware of everything I am and have.

These friends, who're risking their lives for me. Our little light, shining in all this darkness. I've never really believed in destiny. But out in all this nothing, I've never been so certain of who I am and where I'm supposed to be.

Ahead of me, across the bottomless stretch of blackness, Kal reaches the gash. Slowly, carefully, he tests the edges until he finds a spot that won't cut open his gloves. Then, with what looks like an effortless movement, he pulls himself into the pitch-black interior of the *Hadfield*.

It's my turn next, and I have to force myself to let go of the line, grab at the rip in the *Hadfield*'s skin. As I float into the darkness, I push too hard, and Kal saves me before I sail into the wall. He catches me in his arms, brings me down gracefully. My heart is hammering and my breath is pounding in my lungs, and now that my time outside is over, I realize all I want is to do it all over again.

"What a rush," I gasp.

Kal looks down at me. *"I know just what you mean."*

My body is pressed against his, his face just inches away from mine, and the starlight reflected in his eyes is like sparks dancing inside violet flames. I swallow the lump in my throat, my heart pounding even harder than before.

Fin pulls himself in through the gash behind us, pretending not to notice as I reluctantly push myself out of Kal's arms.

"Line released, Goldenboy," he declares. *"See you soon."*

"*Roger that,*" Ty replies. "*Good hunting.*"

I watch through the hull breach as the *Zero* silently peels away. She disappears behind the arc of the *Hadfield's* thrusters and vanishes from sight, hiding in the convoy before the security patrols swing back. We activate our helmet lights, and I see we're in a long plasteel hallway. It feels almost familiar. It all looks perfectly normal. Except, you know, it's totally dark. And it opens into *space*.

"*All right,*" Fin says. "*The bridge is this way. Follow me, lovebirds.*"

Fin pushes off the ground, moving as naturally as a fish through water. With gentle touches on the wall to propel ourselves, Kal and I float after him, our headlamps illuminating the way ahead of us. Fin's studying the map on the uniglass strapped to his left forearm. His movements are smooth and graceful.

"Your suit seems much better, Fin," I say.

"*I won't be winning any dance contests soon, but it's getting there.*"

"I'm sure you're an amazing dancer."

He smiles at me sidelong. "*You trying to get me to fall in love with you, too, Stowaway?*"

Kal glances Fin's way, but with that cool I used to find *so* infuriating, he doesn't ruffle. We make our way farther into the *Hadfield's* belly, and everything around us is silent and dark. The ship doesn't actually look that bad from in here, and I can almost imagine she's still in her prime. But it's when we round a broken bulkhead that the full scale of the damage hits me like a kick to the chest. To our right is a rip that goes all the way through the ship from the upper

127

decks to the keel. Cables and conduits spill out of the rents between levels, metal and plastic all twisted and torn. Looks like the quantum lightning storm Ty battled his way through to reach me really did a number on the *Hadfield*. Or maybe she weathered lots of FoldStorms before he found me?

We all stop for a long moment, simply staring up at this destruction, trying to absorb the scale of it. I know each of the boys is worried about me in his own way, wondering how being here might make me feel. But from the outside, at least, I mustn't seem too rattled. Wordlessly, Fin pushes off the wall once more, and I float after him, Kal bringing up the rear.

"Still no life signs," Kal reports, his voice crisp.

"Good. I didn't get time to do my hair this morning." Fin checks his map again. *"It's about nine hundred meters up to the bridge. Old Mr. Black Box will be in our sticky little hands in about five minutes, Tyler."*

"Roger that," Ty replies. *"Everyone stay frosty."*

It sounds like good advice, and I do my best to follow it, to ignore the unease I can feel growing inside my stomach. But as I follow the beam of my lamp along the dark corridor, I begin to feel a faint current tingling on my skin.

It's like pins and needles, or static electricity, crackling out from my chest toward my fingers and toes. I hear a snatch of conversation ahead of us, my breath catching in my throat as a group of five figures rounds the corner, walking down the hallway toward us.

Holy cake, they're *people*.

They're all clad in the gray jumpsuits of the *Hadfield* mission, and one of the women is laughing—a bright, crystal sound in the dark. The shock of seeing them is like a slap. I try to jerk to a stop, and just like I was warned, the sudden motion sends me whirling backward, head over heels, spinning right into Kal's chest. He grunts as I slam into him, wrapping one strong arm around me and grabbing at a doorframe to steady us.

"Okay there, Auri?" Fin asks, twisting back to see what happened.

Pulse thumping in my temples, I realize the people are gone.

And I realize none of them were wearing spacesuits.

And I could hear them, even though we're in a vacuum.

And they were walking, when there's no gravity.

They were . . . ghosts?

No, no, that's not right. There's a tingle in my fingers now, a buildup of static electricity. Just like when I crushed that ship in the Emerald City docks. Just like when I dream things that come true. I can feel my powers at work if I close my eyes—midnight blue and bottomless beneath my skin. But this feels less like one of my visions, and more like . . . one of the *Hadfield's* memories come to life?

"Are you well?" Kal asks, looking intently into my eyes.

I blink at the spot where I saw the people, shaking my head. "I . . ."

"Did you see something, be'shmai?"

"I . . ." I swallow hard, my mouth suddenly dry. "I don't know. . . ."

The boys exchange a glance, neither one really believing me, but both too polite to call me out. Fin tries to lighten the darkening mood.

"*What did we forget, Stowaway?*" he asks.

"We forgot the golden rule." I try to make my voice sound cheerful, but I know I don't succeed. Still, Fin is a good sport and chants my lesson with me again:

"*Smaaaaall movements.*"

We continue on toward the bridge, and there's a definite sense of wrongness, of foreboding, building up behind my eyes. Being back here now, seeing this place . . . I mean, it's not that I didn't *know* I was more than two centuries into the future. Of course I did. Everything around me tells me so—the aliens, the tech, the complete absence of anything familiar. But somehow, that's different from seeing something I knew, shiny and new just a few weeks ago, now so ancient. So utterly dead.

I'm just so sad for the *Hadfield*.

Zila speaks over comms. "*Aurora, your vitals are spiking. Are you in distress?*"

"I'm okay," I lie, but there's still a shake to my voice.

"*We're nearly at the bridge,*" Fin says. "*There's an elevator shaft over here. If it's not blocked, we can float all the way up through it, past the cryo levels.*"

The cryo levels. Where I went to sleep, expecting to wake up on a new world, with a new life. Where Tyler found me, surrounded by the corpses of everyone I'd set out with. My heart's thumping, my ears are buzzing, and I make myself speak.

"I'm going to . . . I want to see them."

"*Be'shmai?*" Kal asks, watching me uncertainly in the gloom.

"If I'm going to remember . . . if I'm going to learn anything, it'll probably be there." I swallow. "Where it . . . where it happened."

It sounds almost reasonable coming out of my mouth. As if I'm being scientific about it, instead of being drawn to the place I survived, like a moth to a flame. I don't want to tell the boys, I don't want to say anything that makes me sound crazy, but the whole corridor around us is alive now. Full of people hurrying along, laughing and talking. I can feel them. I can see them. I can hear them.

But all of them are dead. Echoes, imprinted on the ship like old bloodstains.

"Do you wish me to accompany you?" Kal asks softly.

I nod silently, staring at the figures around me.

I don't think I've wanted anything more in my life.

"Goldenboy?" asks Fin. *"We've got no life signs over here, and I'll only be a few hundred meters above them. Okay for me to proceed to the bridge alone?"*

There's a long pause before Tyler replies. *"Permission granted. But keep your comms open at all times. Auri, Kal, I want constant updates, understood?"*

"Yessir," Kal replies.

With a grunt of effort, Kal pries apart the elevator doors, allowing us to push inside. The shaft is huge and dark, stretching down from the ship's upper levels, but at least there's none of those ghostly echoes inside here. We push our way up, Fin leading the way, Kal close beside me. I know it's my imagination, but as we sail upward, I swear I can feel the warmth of his body through his suit. Despite the echoes around me, I can remember what he felt like, pressed up against me. And somehow, just the knowledge that he's there makes it a little easier to breathe.

Mind on the job, O'Malley.

"*Okay, that's your stop, kids,*" Fin says cheerfully, pointing to a door in the shaft above. "*I'm a dozen floors up.*"

"*Call if you need assistance,*" Kal warns. "*And watch your back.*"

"*Always.*" He glances back and forth between us. His eyes are unreadable through his lenses, but his smirk sure isn't. "*Don't do anything I wouldn't do.*"

Kal wrenches the door to the cryo levels aside, and I touch the walls, feel the sound through my suit. He kicks out into the gloom while Fin heads upward. I push my way gently out of the elevator, following Kal into the hallway.

The huge doors to the cryo vaults loom ahead of us, melted to slag at some point by a quantum lightning strike. My stomach feels full of cold butterflies. I can hear hollow voices, as if coming from far away.

My light cuts a thin beam through the murky darkness beyond. I look across at Kal, careful to turn my head slowly. His braids are floating inside his helmet, gleaming silver, his eyes narrowed at the dark ahead. The lines of his face are smooth and hard, his cheekbones so sharp they might cut my lips if I kissed them.

He meets my eyes, and his stare is beautiful, cold, alien. But behind it I can feel a warmth, a depth, like he can see into every part of me. It makes me shiver. Wordlessly, he reaches across for Magellan, strapped to my forearm. He taps at my screen, then at his own.

"*We are still monitoring the squad channel,*" he says. "*But we can talk privately now.*"

". . . How did you know I wanted to talk?"

"*Your eyes,*" he says simply. "*They speak.*"

"I'm . . . not even sure what I wanted to say," I admit.

"Who could know what to say at such a moment?" he asks, gesturing at the cryo chamber beyond the melted doors. *"This is the place where the future of your people was changed forever. Where* your *future was changed forever."*

"At least I got to *have* a future," I say quietly. Because that's what's weighing on me, making my heart beat so hard, drying out my mouth until it's difficult to speak. "I got out of here when nobody else did. What was so special about me that I deserved to live when all these people had lives and hopes and families and stories of their own, and they didn't?"

Kal's reply is soft, solemn. *"It is difficult. To be one who endures."*

And of course, that's when I remember that Kal's whole *planet* was destroyed. That every Syldrathi who still lives is ultimately homeless, stateless. And here I am, ready to cry over just one ship.

"Kal . . . ," I begin.

"I know what you would say." He cuts me off gently. *"But there is no comparing loss, be'shmai. I did not mean to do so. I only meant to say that I understand what you feel. And if I could take your pain away, I would."*

We pause at the vault doors, and I curl my gloved hand through his. As always, there's a faint hesitation. But then he tightens his hand around mine as if it's all he's ever wanted to do. Syldrathi don't really touch—I learned that from Magellan. But I can't help it—I need to—and I know Kal's getting to like it, so I don't hold back. It's a way to communicate when words fail us, as they so often do.

He looks at me, there in the dark, and I can feel how

badly he wants me. I can almost *see* it, the way I saw those echoes—invisible threads of burning gold and silver spilling off him in waves, held in check only for fear of burning me. But looking up into his eyes, I realize I *want* him to burn me. I want to feel him pressed against me again as he sets me on fire. And I know he wants it, too.

We're so far in the deep end, for two people who only just met.

The moment's broken when Fin's voice crackles over comms.

"Well," says the squad's Gearhead. "*I have good news, kids.*"

"*Heyyyy, that's a switch,*" Tyler replies.

"*I'm kidding. I actually have bad news and other bad news.*"

"*Maker's breath, Finian . . . ,*" Tyler groans.

"*Yeah, I know, I'm a character,*" Fin says. "*So basically, someone's already been up here and carved the black box right out of the floor.*"

"*Brilliant,*" Tyler sighs.

"*So the black box could be anywhere, is what you're saying?*" Scarlett asks.

"*Mmm, nah,*" Fin says. "*This was a surgical job. Readings off my uni are clocking these burns at maybe twenty hours old. I'd guess the Hephaestus boys chopped it out and have it stowed aboard the lead tug in the convoy.*"

"*We got problems,*" Tyler says.

"*There's no way to power these consoles and look for backup, and they're melted to chakk anyway. Gimme a minute—I'm going to look around, but I am not optimistic. Even with my mighty genius in our corner.*"

"*Kal?*" Tyler asks. "*Have you or Auri found anything?*"

Kal looks into my eyes. "*We may be about to. Stand by.*"

I look into *his* eyes, hoping that he understands.

I don't want to go in there. I don't want to see what I know I have to.

But I have to control this.

I can *do* this.

He squeezes my hand, nods once. He speaks without saying a word. And, feeling stronger, feeling *more* with him beside me, I finally drag up my courage and step through the cryo-vault doors.

We find ourselves in one of a series of vast chambers, lined with tank after tank stacked high like endless rows of coffins. The whole left-hand side of the chamber has been blown out, but all the corpses along the right-hand side still rest in peace. I wonder who's in there. Where the others are. Floating somewhere behind us, back where the ship was wrecked, tumbling endlessly through the Fold?

"Be'shmai?" Kal says, and I realize I'm squeezing his hand hard enough to break his fingers.

I've been here before, in this very room. And suddenly I'm back in that moment. I'm at orientation, taking my tour of the ship. A cheery lady with hair in a cotton-candy-pink bob is leading a group of us through the room, along the rows, making jokes about how in just a few days we'll get to take the nap we so desperately need, what with all the preparations for the trip.

We laugh, some of us nervously—cryo is still relatively new technology, the Fold a mysterious place—and with a sudden flash, like lightning, our tour guide is a desiccated corpse. Everyone around me is dead, the animation gone from their faces, and they begin to float away.

I can feel Kal shaking me, but I can't respond. My whole

body is humming, like there's a hurricane building up inside me, and I'm flailing for control. The space around us is full of echoes, people walking, talking, passing over us and through us as if *we're* the ones who aren't real, but dead and forgotten centuries ago.

I can sense the deep violet of Kal's mind now, the gold and silver threads woven through it. He told me he didn't think he had inherited anything from his Waywalker mother, as his sister did, but in this moment, I know he's wrong. His golden threads are buried so deep I'm not sure he realizes they're there. But I cling to his mind with the midnight blue of mine, my silver dust of starlight whirling about in a wild dance. I can't get it to be still. I can't contain it.

I have to.

I HAVE TO.

I'm not in the hallway anymore, and yet I am—with one flash of lightning after another to herald each change, new places are superimposed over it. The ship is suddenly swathed in the vines of the Ra'haam as they shoot up the framework that holds the cryopods. And then I'm blinded by the white lights of the infirmary back at Aurora Academy. They morph into the multicolored displays in the sports bar back on Sempiternity, where Kal and Tyler fought the Unbroken. Then they swirl into the underwater ballroom of Casseldon Bianchi. I hear the roar of his guests, of dancers, the thump of the music, and then that rhythm becomes the sound of running feet.

The roar becomes a cheer, and I'm at the running track at home, surrounded by high school students. And then they turn into withered corpses and crumble to dust.

I can feel a force building up inside me, like floodwater against a dam. I see Cat turning toward me, holding out one hand, and then her eyes flicker and become blue, her pupils turn to flowers, and she screams. I see Admiral Adams gazing down the barrel of a camera at me. I see Kal, clad in the same spacesuit he wears now, though the real Kal is still right at my side. A vision. A ghost. A future. He raises his hands as if to fend off a blow, and then a shot hits him square in the chest. He flies backward with an awful cry.

"KAL!" I scream.

I hear his voice somewhere in the distance, trying to call me home, back to the cryo vaults, back to *me*. But the vision, the ghost, the future Kal slumps against the wall behind him, a smoking hole in his chest, and the hurricane within me explodes in a welter of grief and anger and fear.

I can't . . .

I

CAN'T

And I'm snapped back into my body and I finally lose my grip, and the force surges outward, raging away in a perfect sphere of destruction, Kal and me at the epicenter. The walls of the *Hadfield* peel outward and the cryopods about us disintegrate, the bodies tumbling away into the void. The deck beneath us crumples, and the ceiling above us is ripped apart, silver light spilling up and out of my right eye, shining like a beacon.

"Maker's breath, what the fuck *was that?"* Finian roars.

Faintly I can hear the others yelling down comms, the *Hadfield* trembling about me, and I think Kal is moving, towing me with him. The power is coming off me in floods, the dam inside me broken, my hands pressed against the widening cracks.

Tyler's voice penetrates the haze all around me. *"Emergency retrieval! I'm locking onto their beacons, bringing the* Zero *alongside. Go, go!"*

I can't see Kal—all I can see is a rocky, barren landscape, the sand and rubble a faded gray, the shadows a deep blue, the sky above lifeless and dead.

I've never seen this place, but all I want is to go there.

Kal's arms close around me.

The vision fades.

Everything turns black.

9

KAL

All is soundless.

The *Hadfield's* hull peels apart in a perfect sphere of midnight blue, the cryo vaults demolished in a moment. Titanium and carbite buckle beneath the force of Aurora's shock wave, and I hold her close as the belly of the mighty ship is blown apart from the inside out. Shards of plasteel and metal and glass spin outward into forever, and I engage the jet propulsion unit on my suit to hold us steady in the eye of the storm, this chaos my be'shmai has unleashed, her right eye gleaming like a lantern in the dark. And all of it, *all* of it, happens in complete and total silence.

"Kal, report!" Tyler demands over comms. *"Finian, status!"*

"I'm okay!" Finian shouts. *"My underwear, not so much. What in the Maker's name hit us?"*

"Aurora," I reply, holding her tight. "The bodies, being here . . . she saw something. She lost control."

"Are you okay?" Tyler asks.

How could I be otherwise? How could I be anything less than perfect when she is in my arms? Her hair floating loose about her face in the zero gravity, lashes fluttering against freckled cheeks. The blinding flare in her right eye has dulled to a glow now, warm as firelight against my skin. I know her every line, every curve, pressing my fingertips against the visor of her helmet and tracing the—

"Kal, report!"

"Aurora is semiconscious," I reply. "We are still in the cryo vaults. What is left of them, anyway. Hephaestus security will definitely know we are here. Orders, sir?"

"Hold position," Tyler says. *"We're retrieving Fin, then coming for you."*

"Acknowledged."

And I do. Hold tight, that is. Cradling Aurora to my chest. The *Hadfield* is a ruin, the hull around us ripped wide. The tug hauling us is desperately trying to slow down, and the stress of arresting our momentum is continuing to tear the *Hadfield* apart. A digital heads-up display is projected on the inside of my helmet, and I can see Hephaestus security ships swarming in the dark outside, imagine the panicked transmissions flying between them.

All chance of stealth is lost.

And we still do not have the black box we came here for.

"K-Kal?"

My heart surges as she speaks, and I look down into her eyes, onyx and pearl, and I feel the universe fall away beneath my feet.

"It is well, be'shmai," I murmur. "All is well."

"What h-happened?" she whispers.

"Your power. You lost your grip."

"I'm s-sorry," she whispers, looking in slow bewilderment

at the chaos and destruction around us. I can see blood pooling around her nostrils, bright red, clinging to her skin in the zero gravity. *"I thought . . . I thought I was getting better at it."*

"You are." I look at her intently. "You will."

She shakes her head. *"I saw . . ."*

"What, be'shmai?"

She meets my eyes, and I sense fear in her. Fear and heartsickness, all the way to her bones. *"I saw you . . . get hurt. Bad."*

My heart lurches, and I will it to be still. Warbreed fear no death. Warbreed fear no pain. Warbreed fear only to never taste victory. My father taught me that.

". . . How?" I ask.

She shakes her head, wincing as the ship continues to break up around us, stanchions failing, bulkheads twisting apart. The totality of the destruction she has unleashed should be chilling. Her power, terrifying.

Instead, I feel only awe.

"It's . . . hazy," she says. *"You got shot. You were aboard a ship. I saw . . . dark metal. Fuzzy dice. You . . . you were dressed the same as you're dressed now."*

"Nobody is going to hurt me," I smile. "With you at my side, I am unbreakable."

She shakes her head and whispers, *"Kal, I wasn't by your side."*

"Kal, you read me?"

I touch my uniglass to transmit. "Affirmative, sir."

"We've got Fin. Sending you coordinates for rendezvous. Security is all over us like a rash now, so we're coming in red-hot. Zila will guide you."

141

"*Can you hear me, Legionnaire Gilwraeth?*" comes a small, calm voice.

"Yes, Zila, loud and clear."

"*We are currently being pursued by thirteen Scythe-class fighters and two Reaper-class cruisers, so we will be unable to slow down below fifteen hundred kilometers per hour unless we wish to be incinerated by their missile fire.*"

"Understood."

"*You will be attempting to match our speed and intercept the Zero, making a landing in the loading bay as we fly by.*"

"At fifteen hundred kilometers per hour," I say.

"*Correct,*" Zila says, just as deadpan.

"Understood."

"*Is that even possible?*" Aurora asks, eyes wide.

"*It is more likely Legionnaire Gilwraeth will succeed than a human would,*" Zila replies. "*Syldrathi reflexes are superior to Terrans'. If he matches Zero's speed along the axis of pursuit, being X, and maintains speeds below one hundred kilometers per hour along the axis of approach, being Y, I calculate the odds of him successfully performing this maneuver at approximately six hundred and—*"

"*Thank you, Zila, we don't need a breakdown of the math right now,*" Tyler says. "*Kal, I've sent you the trajectory; just burn hard and follow Zila's mark.*"

"Understood."

"*You can do this, buddy,*" Tyler says.

I look down at Aurora in my arms and smile.

"I know," I say.

"*Ten seconds, Legionnaire Gilwraeth,*" Zila says.

Aurora tightens her jaw and nods. She slips her arms

around my waist, and my stomach turns a dozen somersaults at her touch.

"*Eight seconds.*"

I grit my teeth, breathe deep.

"*Six.*"

"*Kal?*" Aurora says.

"*Four.*"

"Yes, be'shmai?"

"*Three.*"

She leans up and presses her faceplate to mine, as if to kiss my cheek. There are only a few millimeters of visor between us. Warm, soft breath fogging the plasteel. The entire universe is perfectly still.

"*Two.*"

"*You got this,*" she says, meeting my eyes.

"*Mark.*"

I engage my thrusters, pushing them hard as we take off through the *Hadfield*'s wreckage. Moving slow at first, I guide us past massive bulkheads and disintegrating walls, tons of metal, building up to frightening speed. I can see the incoming *Zero* as a small green blip on my digital HUD, surrounded by pulsing scarlet dots, Aurora and myself rendered as a tiny speck of white.

I thread us through a roiling storm of debris, sheaves of metal as big as houses, ripped apart like tissue paper. We are moving quick now—fast enough that any collision will kill us. The black outside the *Hadfield*'s hull is being lit by explosions and tracer fire, and I can feel him inside me. The thing I was raised to be, straining at the thought of the battle out there, of blood being spilled.

I'na Sai'nuit.

But I push him back. Away.

"Hold on to me," I say.

Aurora squeezes, her eyes locked on me in wonder. All is chaos about us, a twisted tempest of broken metal and wreckage as the *Hadfield* continues to disintegrate. I spiral between immense conduits, tumbling end over end, twenty tons of sundered hatchway scything through the black just a meter shy of my head, the *Zero* drawing ever closer.

"Your speed is insufficient, Legionnaire Gilwraeth."

I see the incoming *Zero,* rusted and ugly but flying toward us swift and straight as an honor blade. I see the Hephaestus fighters swarming around her like fireflies in the dark. I adjust course, cleaving to the path outlined on my HUD, jetpack at maximum burn now, swooping upward in a smooth arc to intercept our ship, her docking bay doors open wide to receive us, a light in the darkness. Tracer fire spills silently through the night, and Aurora squeezes me so tight it is hard to breathe, my heart pounding against my ribs.

"We are inbound," I say simply.

"I see you!" Tyler shouts. *"A few more seconds."*

"Alpha, adjust course, zero point four deg—"

"I got it, I got it!"

"They're not gonna make it!"

"Kal, pull up!"

A blur of rusted metal. A gleam of pristine light. A beautiful girl in my arms. And all around us, soundless. I see it in slow motion, the *Zero* looming before us, the tiny moments of my tiny life strobing before my eyes. My sister and me, standing beneath the lias trees with our father, training in the Wave Way. The Enemy Within, stretching and flexing, blooming like a flower in dark earth beneath his hand. My mother, reaching out to touch my face, the bruises we share bringing tears to her eyes, her words ringing in my soul.

There is no love in violence, Kaliis. . . .

"Incoming!"

The light swells, and I wrap my arms around Aurora tight as we soar through the open bay doors. I slam on my thrusters to slow us, twisting to shield her with my body when we hit the far wall. My teeth bite my tongue and my brain is rattled inside my skull as we collide with the bulkhead and crash onto the deck. I feel the vibration of the bay doors closing behind us. Aurora is lying on top of me, gasping in my arms. Bruised. Breathless.

But alive.

Gravity is returning and her hair is tumbling about her face, her nose smudged in blood. But as she pulls herself up to look at me, she is still the most beautiful sight I have seen in my life. Atmosphere has returned to the bay and she fumbles with the clasps of her helmet, tearing it loose and dragging her hair from her eyes, shining in triumph.

"Holy cake, that was incredible," she breathes.

She is grinning, bewildered, amazed. Her eyes are wild, delirious at the simple thought that we are alive, against all odds, *alive*. And before I quite know what she is doing, she has reached up and pulled my helmet loose, too.

"*You* are incredible."

"Aurora—"

And then her mouth is on mine, smothering any thought or word. She grabs my suit and drags me closer, sighing into my lungs as I crush her to my chest, almost hard enough to break her. She is a dream, alive and warm in my arms, and I burn with the feel of her, the smell of her, the taste of her. She is smoke and starlight, she is blood and fire, she is a song in my veins as old as time and deep as the Void, and as I feel her surge against me, the flutter-soft touch of her tongue against mine, she almost destroys me.

Kiss.

It is so small a word for so wondrous a thing.

Our first kiss.

I am aflame in the sweet and urgent softness of her mouth, the sharp press of her teeth as she nips my lip, her fingertips weaving into my braids. Her touch is maddening, there is so much weight to it for one of my people, so much *promise* behind it, and there is nothing to me—nothing at all—save the feel of her in my arms and the single word that burns like a first sunrise behind my eyes.

More.

I must have more.

The impact knocks us sideways, an alarm blaring across the *Zero*'s docking bay as emergency lights begin to flash. We break apart, Aurora's lips bee-stung and parted, the taste of her blood still on my mouth. The deck shudders beneath us.

"You two okay in there?" Tyler asks over comms.

I look into Aurora's eyes, and her smile is the only heaven I have ever known.

"We're perfect," she whispers.

"Well, not to rush you, but I could use my combat expert up here!"

I blink hard to clear my head, willing myself to breathe.

"On our way, sir."

Aurora climbs off me and I glide upward, pulling her with me. I want nothing more than to linger here. To sink slowly into the unspoken promise behind that kiss. But the danger is bright as the fire she lights inside me. And so I take her hand and we run together, limping and bloodied, down the main corridor to the bridge.

Scarlett looks up from her console and winks.

"Nice flying, Muscles."

"What is our status?" I say, sliding into my station.

"One of the cruisers has sustained critical damage from the *Hadfield* debris field," Zila reports. "Ten fighters and the second cruiser still in pursuit."

"They're sending an SOS," Finian reports. "Our ship ident and vid footage."

"They think we're pirates!" Tyler shouts, leaning hard on his controls as we weave through the surrounding convoy. "Can you jam their transmission?"

Fin shakes his head. "They sent it before I got aboard. I'm not a miracle worker, Goldenboy!"

"Anyone who was monitoring us when we blasted out of Emerald City is going to know we're on this ship!" Scarlett yells over the alarms. "TDF. GIA. Our fellow legionnaires. Bounty hunters. This sector is going to be hotter than my unmentionables when the navy hits town!"

"Thank you, Scarlett, I don't need a status report on your underwear right now!" Tyler roars.

"I mean, I could hear a little more?" Fin says.

Aurora's uniglass beeps in her pocket. "THE FIRST REC-ORD OF HUMAN UNDERGARMENTS WAS THE LOINCLOTH, A SIMPLE GARMENT COMMONLY WORN IN—"

"Silent mode!" Tyler shouts.

Tracer fire rips through the dark around us. I let loose a burst from our rear railguns and am rewarded with a flare of bright fire and a soundless explosion. The fighters return fire, but the *Zero's* flakscreen and interceptors are state of the art, and we are still ahead of the pack for now. Tyler is not the ace that Zero was, but he is still an impressive pilot, sending us soaring over the vast gunmetal expanses of the derelicts around us, weaving between the broken ships like a dancer.

"Undies aside," Scarlett says, "I'd like to keep my ass in my pants if at all possible. We should get out of here before real trouble arrives."

"We still need the black box," I point out. "If we retreat now, we will not have another chance to approach the convoy."

"We do not know where the black box is," Zila points out.

"Like I said, they probably just stowed it on the lead tug," Finian says.

"Well, bad news, they're not slowing down for us to stop and check!" Tyler shouts. "And we don't have long till these goons aren't the only ones shooting at us!"

Alarms scream as a volley of missiles bursts below us, carving black swaths across a derelict's skin. My pulse is pounding, electricity crackling at my fingertips, a fierce and burning elation welling within me—both at the memory of Aurora's kiss and at the thrill of battle around me.

I feel invincible.

Unbreakable.

"I can retrieve it," I hear myself say.

Scarlett blinks at me, flame-red hair framing disbelieving eyes. "Are you *high*?"

"Kal . . . ," Aurora says.

I am looking at my Alpha, still bent over his controls.

"We *need* that data, sir," I tell him. "If we miss our chance here, the convoy will be doubly guarded. And in less than twenty-four hours, they will have docked. This is our moment. Get me close to that lead tug. I will do the rest."

Tyler tears his eyes off his displays, meeting mine.

"Believe, Brother," I say.

He clenches his jaw, but nods.

"I'll get us close as I can."

I am on my feet already, my blood alight. I am retrieving a disruptor rifle and a blister of thermex charges from the weapons locker when Fin pushes himself upright with a sigh.

"Where are *you* going?" Scarlett asks.

"With him."

"Seriously, is there a CO_2 leak in here or something?" she says, looking between us. "Or did we all come down with a case of boneheaded heroics when I wasn't looking?"

"I'm the Gearhead in this squad." Fin shrugs, checks his suit integrity. "Pixieboy wouldn't know a black box if it fell out of the sky, landed on his face, and started to wiggle."

She scowls. "I presume they're black? And, I dunno, *box-shaped*?"

"Well, *excuuuuse me,* Miss Scarcasm," he says, eyebrow rising, "but they're orange, not black. Makes them easier to locate and recover in a crash situation. Besides, I'm already suited up. And we don't have time to argue."

I toss another disruptor rifle across the bridge, and with a swift whine of his newly repaired exosuit, Finian catches it. Scarlett throws her hands up in resignation. Zila is crouched beside Aurora, checking her vitals, wiping the dried blood off

149

her lips. I meet my be'shmai's eyes and I can see fear in her stare. I can see fire. I can see the memory of our kiss, and the promise behind it, and the thought of *more* hanging in the infinity between us.

"I will return," I say.

"You better," she says.

With a nod to Finian, I am running back down the hallway to the secondary airlock. I slip on my helmet, activate my heads-up display, watch the view from outside the *Zero* as we flash in and out between the convoy ships. The auto-fire systems in our railguns are good enough to keep the fighters off our tails, though not much more, and our interceptors can keep the cruiser's missiles at bay. But if more trouble arrives—and it is certainly on its way—we will be outgunned.

"We must be swift," I say as Finian bundles into the airlock beside me.

"Don't worry," the Betraskan says, pulling on his helmet. *"I'm just doing this to look impressive. I don't wanna be over there any longer than we have to."*

He meets my eyes and smirks.

"Yeah, yeah, I know. I'm not much of a warrior, Kal."

I look him up and down, the rifle in his hand, the lumps of his exosuit beneath his space gear. He is a strange one, this Betraskan. A sharp-edged shell, built around a fragile heart filled with sadness. In truth, we Warbreed have little compassion for frailty. With his disability, someone like Finian would have been cast aside among my brothers and sisters—thrown to the drakkan so his weakness would not infect the rest of the cabal. Such was our way. Only the weak seek mercy. And only the weakest grant it.

But I see the foolishness in that now. I see a courage in Finian that other Warbreed would envy. He asks for nothing, this boy. No favor. No quarter. He lives every moment of his life in pain, but still, he *lives* it. And he stands, where others would have long ago fallen.

"You look like a warrior to me, Finian de Seel," I say.

He blinks at that. Opens his mouth as if to speak, but—

"Approaching lead tug now," Tyler reports. *"One fifty klicks and closing. I'll get as near as I can, but we're still gonna be coming in fast."*

"Acknowledged." I look at Finian. "Are you prepared for this?"

He nods, slips his fists into the wall restraints. *"Ready."*

I press the controls for the outer door, and with a brief rush of air, silence descends once more. I watch the convoy ships fly past us in a blur, watch the stars tumble and turn as Tyler ducks and weaves through the fire from behind us. I can feel the beauty in this moment. The war in my blood, longing to be unleashed.

There is no love in violence, Kaliis. . . .

We are approaching the lead tug, its engines burning bright, the dark around us lit by railgun fire and missile bursts. I see the name TOTENTANZ stenciled down its belly. I nod to Finian and engage my thrusters, a digital count ticking down on our HUDs. The *Zero* weaves and rolls, drawing ever closer, the tug growing in size until it is all I can see.

My lips are still tingling from where she kissed them.

"Now," I say.

The *Zero* banks away from the lead tug just as we kick free of the airlock, and I feel the heat of her engines as she roars silently overhead. The endless black around us is aflame, the rockets on our packs at full burn to slow us before we are pulped on the *Totentanz*'s flanks. I can see our target dead ahead—a tertiary airlock, just below the main thruster array. We speed out of the blackness, me in front, Finian close behind, and my heart is thunder in my chest.

I lean down, engage my magboots, bracing my knees for impact. My thrusters shudder as they burn, the rapid deceleration dragging my belly down into my feet. I hit the *Totentanz*'s flank hard and my right magboot slips free, but the other holds firm as I come to a bone-jarring halt just below the airlock door. I turn and grab for Finian as he comes in fast behind me. He hits hard, cursing loudly, and I seize hold of his suit as he almost bounces free. He flails, clutching at my arm, black eyes wide as the void around us yawns, but finally, he brings his boots down onto the hull.

"Are you well?" I ask.

He takes a moment to catch his breath, bent double, mouth agape.

"That," he says, *"was not my idea of a good time."*

"Report status!" Tyler says.

"We are secure," I reply, searching the dark around us. I can see the massive hulks of the convoy streaming out behind us, catch sight of distant flashing fire as the *Zero* continues to elude its pursuers. "Preparing to breach."

Finian's fingers dance on his uniglass, his eyes narrowed on his screen.

"Quickly now," I urge.

"You wanna hack this, Pixieboy, be my guest," he snaps.

Every second seems an eon, every moment we spend is another the Hephaestus SOS travels farther. Every moment it speeds toward more ears: bounty hunters, the Terran Defense Force, the GIA, my sister.

But finally, with a small grin of triumph, Finian looks up at me and nods. I feel a series of heavy clunks run through the metal, and I reach down and take hold of the hatchway. I strain, veins corded in my neck as I drag the airlock wide enough for Finian to squeeze inside. I follow swiftly, slamming the hatch shut behind us. Our Gearhead is already working on the inner hatchway as the airlock repressurizes, gravity and volume returning with a vengeance, red globes flashing, alarms screaming.

"They know we are here," I say.

"We just breached their enviro systems and opened their ship into space—of course they know we're here!"

"Keep your head down," I tell him. "And stay behind me."

The inner hatchway clunks, the door slides open with a soft hum, and immediately a burst of disruptor fire sprays into the airlock. I push Finian out of sight against one wall, take cover behind the hatch as the charged particles sizzle and flare. Another burst blackens the metal close by my head, setting my blood thrumming.

"Are you people insane?" comes a shout.

"Get the *hells* off my ship!" cries another.

The Enemy Within is close to the surface now. Swimming just below my skin.

These are not warriors, he whispers.

These are worms.

I wait until there is a pause in fire, poke my head around the doorway and back again. I count six men in a blink. All armed. No armor. Half cover.

Break them.

I step out into the hallway, and they rise from concealment to open fire. I weave aside from their volleys, feel a burst of charged particles burn past my cheek, all the universe moving in slow motion. And with six taps of my trigger, six short blasts from my disruptor rifle, all are lying senseless and drooling on the floor.

It is over. Almost before it began.

You should have killed them, he whispers.

Mercy is the province of cowards, Kaliis.

"*Holy crap,*" Finian whispers, peering out from cover. "*That was . . .*"

"Disappointing," I say. "Come. We must be swift."

Leaping over the fallen crew, we run on toward the bridge.

10

FINIAN

So this captain's idea to send everyone he had was obviously a mistake, given that Kal left them sprawled in the loading bay like a bunch of cadets on shore leave.

I mean, I've heard that's what happens on shore leave.

Obviously, I am personally a *model* of academy standards at all times.

Nevertheless, with the entire crew of the *Totentanz* consigned to dreamland for now, the tug is under the official control of Squad 312, and the mission is proceeding exactly according to plan. Which always makes me nervous. Of course things are still a bit exciting for Tyler and the gang outside, and there is the small question of how in the Maker's name we're going to get back to the *Zero* without being vaporized, but as my second mother always says, one thing at a time.

We're up on the bridge, and I'm busy romancing the *Hadfield*'s black box (which I note with satisfaction *is* orange) and watching Kal out of the corner of my eye. If concealing a crush on Scarlett Isobel Jones wasn't a full-time job, I would *seriously* consider adding him to the daydream roster. I get what Auri sees in him. Strong, silent, broody. All that good stuff.

He catches me looking at him and raises one perfect eyebrow.

"How long until your task is complete?" he asks, completely unromantically.

"I'm working on it, big guy," I tell him. And so I am. I'm coaxing a stream of data from the orange crate on the floor onto my uniglass, murmuring sweet nothings to hurry it along. The salvage team carved the flight recorder out of the poor old *Hadfield* pretty neatly, but still, it's a little creepy, just sitting there on the cockpit floor. You know, thinking about what kind of situation it was built for and all . . .

I give my head a shake to chase away that thought, which will lead directly to the ghost ship full of corpses we left behind if I'm not careful, and instead eyeball the data I'm heisting as it goes by. At a glance, I can tell that a lot of the info is navigational, which is exactly the kind we came for. Hopefully it'll mark the place something weird happened to the *Hadfield*. And Aurora.

I set the data streams to encrypt as they store so nobody can get into them except yours truly. It's a mimetic sixty-four-digit obfuscation cypher—just a special little something I whipped up back at the academy. I had a lot of spare time on account of my nonexistent social life. But who's laughing now, huh? I've got this killer encryption, a state-of-the-art spaceship, and a big handsome friend who shoots people for me whenever I like.

What more could a boy want?

As if to answer that question, Scar's voice sounds in my earpiece. *"Ops team, we have a problem."*

Kal's eyes narrow slightly. *"Please elaborate."*

"Inbound vessels," Zila reports. *"They used cloaking technology to get close, but we have visual now. There are at least a dozen. Rapid approach."*

"Someone's responding to the Hephaestus SOS," Scarlett says.

I frown, crunching the numbers in my head. "Already?"

"They must have been a lot closer than Emerald City to have gotten here already. Just our luck."

Kal looks at me, his voice cool as ice. *"How long, Finian?"*

"Ninety seconds," I tell him, mentally urging the data to move faster. Because *that's* always worked.

"We will be ready for retrieval in two minutes," Kal advises.

Tyler's voice breaks in. *"Roger that, we can—oh, Maker's breath . . ."*

I'm about to ask him to elaborate on that as well, but the sound of Kal cursing softly in Syldrathi draws my attention to the monitor array. Through our tug's forward viewscreen, we have an unencumbered shot of half a dozen lean, razor-sharp fighter ships speeding in to say hello. They're shaped for stealth, and my heart drops to my boots as I watch one of them casually execute a strafing run that leaves three security fighters in ruins, debris tumbling slowly out into the black.

More of the newcomers begin to engage, missile and pulse fire lighting up the darkness. Within moments, the Hephaestus security ships that Tyler's been playing hide-and-seek with all this time are being simply *annihilated*.

"Kal," I whisper. "Are those ships . . . ?"

"Syldrathi," he replies, his voice subzero.

"But they're just interceptors," I protest. "They're too small to have come here alone. They've gotta be with . . ."

I glance to our rear cams, my heart tightening in my chest.

"Oh *shit* . . ."

A dark shape hangs there on the screen, lit from behind by the system's sun, just a silhouette against a disk of burning red. It's big and pointy and the most badass thing I have ever seen. All black, with *huge* white glyfs painted down the sides in a beautiful, furious script.

They're the glyfs of the Unbroken.

A small crease slowly forms between Kal's brows, which is about as close to upset as he ever looks.

"*The* Andarael," he whispers.

"*Kal?*" Ty breaks in again. "*You know this ship?*"

But Scar answers for him, already two steps ahead. "*It's his sister's.*"

A green light flashes by my feet, and I look down. "Download complete," I say softly, though that's hardly our biggest concern anymore. Still, I'm an Aurora legionnaire, and I have my orders, so I drop to one knee and set to work frying the black box—that way, the only copy of its data will now be ours. Just in case we get out of this alive to use it.

I hear a burst of static from the *Totentanz*'s comms panel, and sadly, that starts feeling a lot less likely.

"*Hello again, Kaliis.*"

Kal stares expressionless at the blinking light awaiting his response.

"*Saedii,*" he murmurs.

Like a man sleepwalking, our Tank crosses the cockpit

to the transmitter. I glance around the bridge, looking for anything that might help us. A grimy mug that says GALAXY'S GREATEST GRANDMA! sits by the copilot's chair. A jetball team jacket is crumpled on the deck near the nav station. A pair of fuzzy dice hangs above the pilot's chair. When Kal speaks, he sounds cool, conversational. He talks in Syldrathi, but my uni has enough spare processing power to still run a translation for me.

"We were not expecting your company so soon, Sister."

"Forgive me," she replies, her smirk audible. *"You left in such a hurry, you forgot to issue an invitation, Brother."*

"Yet here you are."

"Here I am," she purrs.

". . . How?"

"Kaliis, I touched your ship," she says. *"Are you telling me that you did not even* search *for the tracker? You have grown slow and soft and stupid at your wretched little academy. Do they teach you idiocy there?"*

Kal's eyes are closed again. Just like me, he's imagining the moment we left the Emerald City. Saedii throwing herself at the *Zero*, holding on for those few precious seconds before Ty tipped her off. She must have slapped a beacon on the hull. That's why the Unbroken were so close when the SOS was broadcast by the convoy's security. They didn't *need* the distress call to know where we were.

"Saedii," tries Kal. *"You have asked and you have asked, and I have answered and I have answered. I want no part in this thing you do."*

"This thing I do," she replies, her anger audible, *"wants you. He wants you."*

Kal flicks the transmitter to the off position, killing his line to Saedii for a moment so he can speak to the *Zero*.

"Tyler, you must go," he says simply. *"Now."*

There's a chorus of protests down the line from Goldenboy, from Scarlett, from Auri. Ty's the one who prevails, at least for a moment. *"Not an option, Kal."*

The transmitter on the dashboard flickers to life again. *"We've hacked your communications, so I can still hear you, little brother. And nobody is going anywhere. You will surrender yourself to the troops I am sending to your ship, and your squad will dock with* Andarael.*"*

"What could you want with my squad?" Kal asks, and for a moment, he sounds *incredibly* Syldrathi. Like none of the humans aboard the *Zero* could possibly have any value, anything worth delaying her journey even a minute for.

"Kaliis," she chides him gently. *"Do you not think it fitting your elder sister wishes to be properly introduced to her brother's be'shmai?"*

And there's something in the way she speaks—a terrible, cold something—that tells me that she doesn't just want to taunt Kal. That *Auri* has some value to her as well.

"My squad is none of your concern, Saedii. Release them, and I will join you."

Kal looks across at me, and I can see the apology in those big violet eyes of his. We both know that whatever happens to the others, his sister won't be letting me rejoin the *Zero* before it departs. And we both know what the Unbroken will make of my physical limitations. My suit.

And Maker's bits, does that suck.

But it's also okay. I want them to go. They're my chosen

clan, and I want them to live. So I draw a deep breath, nod at him silently.

He reaches across to clasp my shoulder, completely oblivious to the fact that he just about crushes it.

"Kal." Aurora cuts across the channel. *"Kal, I'm not leaving you."*

I can hear the fear in her voice, the hurt, the heartache. I hassle Kal and Auri about it, because hey, it's me, but I'm not blind to how close these two are growing. How much she means to him, and how much he's starting to mean to her. I find myself wondering what it would've been like to have someone feel that way about me. To have found someone who looked at me the way he looks at her. And yeah, it's probably a stupid thing to be thinking at a time like this.

Which is why I spot her just half a second too late.

A figure in the bridge hatchway, leaning hard against the door, blood dripping down her nose. She's not Syldrathi, I realize—she's one of the Hephaestus tug crew that Kal laid out when we arrived. Maybe the Galaxy's Greatest Grandma. Maybe just the jetball fan. Whoever she is, she looks like death warmed up, but somehow she's made it to her feet and staggered to the cockpit.

And she's holding a disruptor.

"Kal!" I shout, flinging up my hands as though they can stop a blast.

Our Tank's eyes are still on the comms array, the speaker his sister's threats are spilling from. But at the sound of my voice, he swings around, drawing the disruptor at his belt. He moves fast—faster than any Betraskan, any human—but still not fast enough. He pushes me aside, his finger tightening on his trigger, just as the razor *hissss* of a Kill shot tears through the cockpit, ringing in my ears.

My heart sinks in my chest as I watch it all unfold in slow motion.

Kal twisting aside, trying to dodge the blast.

The shot striking him, right in the chest.

Violet eyes widening in pain, mouth open in shock.

And then he's flying, spit spraying between his bared teeth, backward into the control panel and crashing to the ground. The Hephaestus goon staggers and drops from Kal's return shot, her rifle clattering across the deck. I can hear our squad screaming down our channel, Kal's sister through the *Totentanz*'s comms unit, demanding to know what's happening.

But I can't find my voice.

Can't do anything but stare at the smoking hole in Kal's suit, edged in black scorch marks.

Right over his heart.

But despite all the voices, the shock, in a way that would please and definitely surprise my academy instructors, my Legion training kicks in.

First, secure your position.

That much is easy—one look at Grandma tells me that Kal's blast knocked her stupid, and she's lying unconscious in the passageway.

Second, medical emergencies.

Dropping to my knees with a thump and popping a multitool from a recess in my exo, I slice a clean line into the fabric of Kal's suit and through the insulation beneath. He doesn't move the whole time, and my brain is conjuring up images

162

of Cat on Octavia—images of her bright blue eyes, flower-shaped, of her hand outstretched, of the sadness on her face as she watched us go.

First seven.

Then six.

Now five?

"Finian, report!" Tyler shouts.

Not again, no, not Kal too, please, Maker, not him too . . .

"Fin, what happened?" Auri cries.

"Kal's hit," I manage.

"Fin, no!"

"He's hit. . . ."

My pulse is thumping in my ears, mouth dry as dust as I drag the suit fabric aside, waiting for a gush of deep, warm purple to soak my hands.

But . . .

But there's nothing.

I blink hard, something between a sob and a laugh bursting on my lips. Because there, beneath the burned lining of Kal's suit and the scorched fabric of his Legion uniform, praise the Maker, I see something has stopped the worst of the blast. My hands are shaking as I pull it out of his breast pocket, watching the console lights glint on the scorched silver, my mouth open in wonder.

That damn cigarillo case . . .

Kal's out cold, maybe from the blast, maybe from slamming into the console. He's gonna have an award-winning bruise when he wakes up.

But he's alive.

I can't say the same for the poor cigarillo case, though.

It's bent and busted open, and as my heart slams against my rib cage, as the voices of my teammates ring out over comms, I realize there's something inside the case.

"Finian, status!" Tyler demands.

"Fin, what's happening?" Auri cries.

"It's okay," I report, my voice shaking. "He's okay. . . ."

I pry the case apart, forcing my hands to cooperate, though the adrenaline flooding my nerves is making it hard for my exo to compensate. There's a piece of paper inside the buckled metal, small, square, marked with black handwriting.

It's a note.

Four words.

TELL HER THE TRUTH.

Tell who?

What truth?

They're both good questions. But for now, as I hear Saedii demand our surrender again, as more Syldrathi fighters swarm in the space around us, as I hear Ty give the reluctant order for me to stand down, my brain shoves them aside in favor of a much more compelling one.

I turn the note over in my trembling hands, dragging shaking breaths into my lungs. Trying to make the pieces fit. Because, like the rest of the gifts in the deposit box, like the *Zero* in the Emerald City docks, this note has been waiting to be found since Kal and I were both children.

So how in the name of the Maker is it in my handwriting?

SUBJECT: INTERSPECIES RELATIONS

▶ **FAMOUS BATTLES**

　　▼ **THE ORION INCURSION**

THE ORION INCURSION OCCURRED IN 2370.2 AND IS THE MOST INFAMOUS INCIDENT OF THE **TERRAN-SYLDRATHI WAR**. THE ATTACK WAS PERPETRATED BY A REBEL SYLDRATHI FACTION OF THE WARBREED CABAL (SEE **UNBROKEN**) DURING A CEASE-FIRE BETWEEN THE SYLDRATHI AND TERRAN GOVERNMENTS.

AS THE **TERRAN DEFENSE FORCE** WAS ENGAGED IN PEACE NEGOTIATIONS, EARTH WAS CAUGHT BY COMPLETE SURPRISE. THOUGH THE ATTACK WAS EVENTUALLY DRIVEN BACK, THE TERRAN SHIPYARDS AT **BELLATRIX** AND **SIGMA ORIONIS** WERE DESTROYED, AND THE TDF WAS DECIMATED.

THE UNBROKEN'S TREACHERY GALVANIZED THE TERRAN POPULATION AND PROLONGED THE SYLDRATHI CONFLICT ANOTHER EIGHT YEARS. THOUGH PEACE WAS EVENTUALLY BROKERED THROUGH THE **JERICHO ACCORD**, TENSION BETWEEN THE TWO RACES HAS NEVER QUITE DIED.

HMMM. THIS TOPIC IS SAD.

WOULD YOU LIKE A **HUG**?

11

SCARLETT

Remember Orion.

Those are the two words burning in my mind as Ty guides the *Zero* into the *Andarael*'s docking bay. I should be worried about Kal. Worried about Auri. Worried that the name Andarael means "She Who Lies with Death" in Syldrathi. I should be thinking of how I'm going to talk our way out of this. I'm the team Face, after all. We're outgunned and outmanned—the only way we're getting clear here is diplomacy. But I can't quite bring my thoughts to bear on the problem at hand, can't think of anything to say, witty, sassy, sexy, or otherwise.

Because these are the people who killed our dad.

Remember Orion.

He was a Great Man, our dad. That's what everyone told me and Ty. Those were the words repeated over and over at the funeral of Senator Jericho Jones. All those diplomats and heads of state, all those military types with chests full of shiny medals. They said those words with gravitas. They said them like they meant them.

Capital *G*. Capital *M*.

A Great Man.

The thing about great men is that they usually don't make great dads.

We never knew Mom. She died when we were both too young to remember. And it's not that Dad didn't try—he *really* did. But the problem was, everyone wanted a piece of the great Jericho Jones. And there just wasn't enough to go around.

The Syldrathi war against Terra had raged for twenty years before Tyler and I came into the picture, and Dad had been a soldier for twelve of them. He was TDF, born and bred—an ace pilot who escaped enemy captivity and led the rally at Kireina IV, where TerraFleet held back a Syldrathi armada twice its size. He was a literal poster boy after that. The Terran Defense Force actually put him in their recruitment ads, ice-blue eyes staring right at you as he told you, "Earth needs heroes." One year later, he was a rear admiral—the youngest ever in TDF history.

Then Ty and I came along, and he resigned his commission.

Just like that.

It wasn't to raise his kids, that's for sure. The year after he quit the TDF, Dad ran for the Senate and won in a landslide. After that, he was always away. But Ty just *idolized* him, and I couldn't really be mad about it, not with the work Dad was doing. Because, despite being the TDF poster boy, Jericho Jones became the strongest voice for peace in Terra-Gov. The blistering speech he gave against the war in 2367 still gets taught at Aurora Academy today. *I can no longer look my children in the eye without seeing the wrong in killing other people's,* he said, and that always made me kinda mad, considering how little time he actually spent with us.

But seeing Earth's greatest hero advocating for peace with the Syldrathi helped turn public sentiment against the war. It was Jericho Jones who began the first real peace talks with the Syldrathi government, Jericho Jones who organized the cease-fire in 2370. The war had been raging almost thirty years by then. The defeats they'd suffered had seen the Warbreed fall from ascendancy in the Syldrathi council, and the Watchers and Waywalkers were just as tired of the bloodshed as we were. The treaty was drawn. Everyone was ready to sign.

And then?

Remember Orion.

The Warbreed saw the treaty as dishonor. As *weakness.* And, under the leadership of their greatest Archon, a faction of Warbreed attacked during the cease-fire. In desperation, TerraGov activated its reservists for a counterattack.

Dad hadn't flown a fighter in years. And still, he answered the call. I remember him kissing my forehead and wiping away my tears and telling us he'd be back in time for our birthday.

A little aluminum canister with his ashes inside came back instead.

Remember Orion became the rallying cry after that. *Remember Orion* was the call on every recruitment poster, every simcast, every news feed. *"Remember Orion!"* bellowed the president himself at Dad's funeral, right after he told us all what a Great Man we'd lost.

But I didn't lose a Great Man at Orion. I lost my daddy. And as much as I wished he'd been a greater father than man, you bet your ass I remember.

I remember that the Archon who led the Orion attack was named Caersan, later to become known as *Starslayer*. And the faction he led? Those bastards so in love with the idea of war that they couldn't bear the thought of living in peace?

I remember they called themselves *Unbroken*.

And now we're surrounded by them.

The *Andarael's* docking bay is large enough for twenty *Zeros* to fit inside—Kal's big sister holds rank among these maniacs, and her vessel is the business. The ship itself would be impressive if I actually gave a damn, but I'm more concerned by the small army of Syldrathi warriors waiting for us outside as Tyler cuts our engines. He's trying to keep himself calm, but I can see that the thought of surrendering to these bastards is burning him just as bad as me. Auri is wide-eyed, barely suppressing her panic—we still don't know how bad Kal got hurt aboard the *Totentanz*. But without him aboard, it's up to me to brief my squad.

"Okay, Kal said Saedii was a Templar," I murmur, slipping out from behind my console. "Which basically means she's the commander of a capital warship on active duty. You don't get to that rank in the Unbroken without being *bad* news, all the way."

"Understood," Ty nods.

"Remember, most Unbroken once belonged to the Warbreed Cabal like Kal. Warbreed respect strength. Prowess. Fearlessness."

Ty meets my eyes as he shrugs on his Aurora Legion uniform jacket. "I have every confidence you'll be all that and more, legionnaire."

I shake my head. "You should be the one doing the talking here, Ty."

"You're my Face, Scar. You're trained for this. I don't speak Syldrathi nearly as well as you, I don't know the customs, I—"

"You're our Alpha, Bee-bro," I say. "If you want them to see you as a leader, you need to be front and center. And our family has history with these people. Kireina IV was the worst defeat the Syldrathi suffered in the whole war. These bastards will remember Dad's name."

I meet his stare, my lips pressed thin.

"And it's our name, too, Ty."

He tightens his jaw, breathing deep. I can see Dad in his eyes now. The memory of that little aluminum box full of ashes arriving just in time for our party.

Happy birthday, kids.

"Okay," he nods. "Let's not keep our hosts waiting."

We march down the corridor to the main hangar, gathering at the loading ramp. Zila is quiet as the grave. I glance at Aurora, see her jaw clenched, fear in the set of her shoulders, the tilt of her chin. I peer hard at her right eye, but there doesn't seem to be any sign of a glow there, no hint of her power. Still, I saw her rip the *Hadfield* apart with just the strength of her mind, and if she loses it here . . .

"You doing okay, sweetie?" I ask.

"I told Kal," she mutters, shaking and furious. "I *told* him. I *saw* him get hurt in my mind and he still went charging off like an *idiot*."

Tyler's hand hovers over the release button. "You didn't happen to see anything about what's coming next, did you?"

She shakes her head. "And I don't want to look. I thought I was . . . getting better. I thought I had a grip on it, but . . ."

"It's okay, Auri," Ty says, squeezing her hand. "Just stick near me. I'm sure Kal's fine. We're gonna get out of this, okay?"

"You got a plan?" I ask.

"Do you?" he asks, meeting my eyes.

I pat the diplomacy stream logo emblazoned on my sleeve: that little flower in its ring of gold. "Tactics aren't my department."

He smiles and shakes his head. "You might wanna practice. One day, you could find yourself doing this without me."

"Not today," I shrug. "So go get 'em, Tiger."

Tyler presses the release, and the door opens with a low electronic hum. The ramp extends onto the *Andarael's* deck, and I can see that the interior is dark metal, aglow with blood-red light. The design here is stunning: sleek lines and gentle curves, as graceful as the hundred Unbroken warriors waiting for us.

Their faces are ethereal and gorgeous, fierce and cruel silver hair tied back in an assortment of ornate braids. Each wears a beautifully crafted suit of black tactical armor, daubed with flowing Syldrathi script, decorated with trophies of battle. Each carries a disruptor rifle and a pair of silver blades at their back. They stand tall in neat rows, lining our exit into the bay. And waiting at the end, that crossbow-esque agonizer at rest on the dangerous curve of her hip, is Kal's sister, Saedii.

All Syldrathi are beautiful, but good looks *definitely* run in our Mr. Gilwraeth's family. Queen bitch she may be, but Saedii is drop-dead, maybe-I'm-gay-after-all gorgeous. Her olive skin is poreless, flawless. Her long black hair is swept back from a heart-shaped face that could launch a million ships. Her eyes are smoldering violet, framed by that perfect stripe of black paint. A silver chain of what might be severed thumbs dangles around her neck. She talks in Syldrathi, her voice low and musical, almost as if she sings rather than speaks.

"Welcome aboard *Andarael,* human filth."

And with a smile, she slings that agonizer off her hip and fires right at Auri.

It happens in a split second, almost too quick to track. Auri cries out, brings her hands up, but before she can invoke her gift, those red bands wrap themselves around her and crackle to life. Her scream rings across the bay as she tumbles to the deck, bucking and thrashing.

"Auri!" Tyler shouts. He drops to his knees beside her, touches her shoulder, and is rewarded with a crackling shock of agonizer energy. Drawing his hand back with a hiss of pain, he surges to his feet and finds a hundred disruptor rifles pointed at his chest. I'm not too worried about him—Ty's not stupid enough to charge a hundred armed Syldrathi killers, and his language isn't going to get too offensive, because Tyler Jones, Squad Leader, First Class, doesn't curse.

Scarlett Isobel Jones sure as hells does, though.

In fluent Syldrathi, no less.

"What is *wrong with you,* you crazy bitch?" I shout.

"You speak our language." Saedii's eyes glimmer as she looks me up and down. "An amusing trick, little one."

Tyler speaks in his halting, broken Syldrathi. "We . . . are the treatment demanding . . . conventions in the under . . ."

Saedii looks him over, lip curling. "*You,* however, are less amusing."

"We're not here to *amuse* you, pixiebitch," I say.

"Perhaps you should rethink that strategy, Terran," she says.

Saedii holds out her arm and makes a hissing sound in the back of her throat, and I hear the flap of leathery wings. A creature drops from a rafter above and swoops down through the bay. It's about the size of a cat, reptilian, with broad bat-like wings and a long serpentine tail tipped with a vicious-looking sting. It reminds me an awful lot of Cat's stuffed dragon, except it's black and sleek rather than green and fluffy. The beast lands on Saedii's forearm and trills, blinking at us with golden eyes.

Saedii whispers to it; it nuzzles her long, tapered ear and purrs. Brushing her hair off her shoulder, pixiebitch stalks down the line of warriors toward us. Ty is tense at my side, fists clenched as she stops in front of us. Aurora is still on her back, whimpering and convulsing inside those crackling red bands.

"My Alpha is demanding just treatment under the Jericho Accord," I say, "as signed by the Terran government and the Inner Council of Syldra in 2378."

Saedii is as tall as Ty is, so when he meets her eyes, they're almost nose to nose. "Your Alpha should make his demands himself."

"I demand just treatment under the Jericho Accord," Tyler says, following my accent and speech patterns perfectly. "As signed by the Terran government and the Inner Council of Syldr—"

"The Inner Council of Syldra burned along with Syldra itself," Saedii replies. "We do not respect your pitiful government, nor your pathetic treaty." She leans in close, staring at Ty, eye to eye. "We were born with our hands in fists, little one. We were born with the taste of blood in our mouths. We were born for war."

"Unbroken," the warriors around us say, all as one. And they don't shout it like TDF goons on parade, either. Don't bark it like your typical meatheads in uniform. They murmur it, reverent, like the word itself is a prayer.

Saedii holds out one slender hand. This close, I can confirm the desiccated nubs on the silver chain around her neck are *definitely* thumbs.

"Your uniglasses," she says, cold as ice.

Tyler meets her stare and doesn't move. I can still feel the kick she gave his babymaker echoing faintly in our shared genetic code. Saedii touches the shoulder stock of her agonizer, and at our feet Auri arches her back and screams.

"She sings sweetly." Saedii's smile is cold as the black outside. "I can see why Kaliis might abase himself at her temple."

The dragon thing on Saedii's arm trills. Auri screams again. The Unbroken Templar's expression is calm, her face beautiful and terrible.

"Every moment you waste, she will sing more, little ones."

"She wants our unis," I explain.

Tyler glances at me and nods, and we reach into our jackets and hand them over. Saedii tosses them to another Syldrathi close by—a tall, willowy man with a scar cutting deep down one cheek and a string of severed Syldrathi ears hanging from his belt. He catches them and bows.

"Where is my brother, Erien?" Saedii asks him.

"Our adepts have apprehended him and the Betraskan, Templar," the lieutenant replies. "They are aboard a shuttle en route to *Andarael*."

"His injuries?"

"I am informed he will recover, Templar."

Saedii nods, cool and aloof. "Take him to medical when he arrives, see his needs are met. Take this one"—she gestures to Auri—"to the holding cells and sedate her to within a breath of death. If she wakes before she is in Archon Caersan's possession, I will be displeased."

"Your will, my hands, Templar." He bows, glances at me and Ty. "And these?"

She looks us over, lips pursed. The dragon thing trills again, fluttering its wings and licking Saedii's earlobe with a long pink tongue.

"We have not had much time for sport lately, yes?" she says. "We should dance in the blood to celebrate my brother's return. So when the Betraskan arrives?"

She meets my eyes and shrugs.

"Throw them all to the drakkan."

. . . . .

I'm not an aficionado of spaceships, but I've been on my share. Junkers and cruisers, fighters and destroyers. One of my boyfriends had his own stellar yacht, and he took me on a cruise from Talmarr IV to Rigel for my seventeenth birthday. His ship had its own ballroom, complete with a thirty-piece orchestra.

(Pieres O'Shae. Ex-boyfriend #30. Pros: Tall. Rich. Handsome. Cons: So. Much. Tongue.)

Still, I don't remember being on a ship that had an *arena* before.

It's located down in the bowels of the ship, sunk about ten meters into the deck. The walls are the same dark metal as the rest of the *Andarael,* lit by crimson globes, scored with what might be claw marks. The arena floor is littered with millions of smooth, glowing stones and tall, twisted spires of sharp, dark metal. Long bleachers are arranged in concentric rings, looking down on the pit below.

We're marched in at rifle point, hundreds of Unbroken warriors taking their places according to rank. They're male and female, all armed, all gorgeous, all wearing the three crossed blades of the Warbreed Cabal on their brows. They're possessed of the traditional *We're better than you* arrogance that makes pixies so much fun to have around at parties. But I can sense a tremor of anticipation flowing through them, too. A lust for the violence and bloodshed to come.

Saedii takes her place on a balcony, reclining in a throne-like chair, the back crafted of three crossed blades. Her pet sits at her shoulder, watching with glittering golden eyes. A small legion of guards lurks around her like beautiful shadows.

The pixies march us down to the edge, onto a broad gangplank that hangs a little ways out over the pit. I hear a commotion behind, turn to see Finian being led to us, surrounded by more Syldrathi. He looks a little disheveled, but mostly unhurt, and I give him a fierce hug, a quick kiss on his cheek.

"You okay?" I ask.

Our Gearhead peers around the arena crowd, down into

the pit below us. "You mean aside from the fact I'm about to be eaten for these people's entertainment? Yeah, I'm one hundred percent, Scar."

"Touché, Mr. de Seel," I smile. "How's Kal?"

"He's okay." Fin frowns, thoughtful, as if suddenly unsure about that. "The cigarillo case Adams gave him . . . it stopped the shot. Like Adams *knew* . . ."

"How is that possible?" I ask, bewildered.

Tyler jumps in before the speculation can begin, cutting to the important part as always. "You got the black box data though, right?"

Fin nods. "On my uni. They confiscated it, but I encrypted the info hard as I could make it. They'll have a time cracking it without wiping it altogether."

"Good work, legionnaire."

Fin nods at the praise, glances to the pit, and swallows hard. "So, anyone know anything about this drakkan they're throwing us to?"

I shrug. "I slept through xenobiology."

"They're not allergic to Betraskan, by any chance?"

"Right there." Ty points to Saedii's shoulder. "*That's* a drakkan."

"Oh." Fin frowns at the small dark-scaled reptilian coiled around Saedii's throat. She reaches into a bowl at her side and tosses the thing a ragged scrap of meat, which it snaps out of the air with sharp, tiny teeth.

"*Ohhhh*," I say, brightening considerably.

Fin's pale brows come together in a frown. "Um, I'm not one to judge performance based on size, but isn't it a little . . . little?"

Saedii stands and holds her hands outward, killing our discussion dead. She looks around at the other Unbroken, radiating a dark, imperious will, until their murmured conversations falter, until the whispers stop, until the only sound is the low thrum of the engines and the thudding of my heart.

Once the arena is perfectly still, she speaks in Syldrathi, and I translate softly.

"One who was lost is found," she says. "In thanks to the Void for my brother's return, we shall sing the song of ruin, and dance the dance of blood. We shall feast upon the hearts of our enemies, that their strength becomes our own."

She points down into the pit, to a tall Syldrathi woman standing by a control panel in the wall below us. Saedii's lips curve into a small smile.

"Release the drakkan," she says.

The woman presses a button. The floor in the pit's heart cracks and slams apart, sudden, violent, revealing a deeper lair below.

And out of it comes a chuddering, bone-deep roar.

"That," I whisper, "does *not* sound little."

The Unbroken around us begin to stamp their feet, solemn, all in time, and my heart drops into my stomach as a creature claws its way up out of the lair. It's twenty meters long, sinuous, reptilian, black as midnight—a much bigger, much angrier version of the beastie on Saedii's shoulder. It throws back its head and bellows, fangs gleaming in the scarlet light, and I feel that roar in my chest. Its claws are as long as my arm. The sting on its tail is as long as the rest of me.

"Maker's breath, we're gonna die," Finian whispers.

Tyler looks at me, his jaw clenched, his eyes wide as he

searches for some way out of this. He's a tactical genius, my little brother. As much as I rib him about it, as much stick as I give him, his plans have always seen us through. And even though I'm not religious, I find myself dangerously close to praying to the Maker that Ty's got something up his sleeve.

Saedii's lips part in slow motion and my heart stills as she begins to speak.

"Wait!" Tyler roars.

The thunder of the stamping feet fades a little. Saedii looks down at Tyler and tilts her head, like he's a dog that suddenly learned to speak.

"Scar, translate for me," Ty murmurs. "Everything I say. That's an *order*."

His voice is iron, his eyes are ice, and for a second I can see so much of Dad in him it makes me want to cry.

"Okay," I say softly.

Tyler turns to Saedii, arms wide. I translate as he speaks.

"My name is Tyler Jones. I am the son of Jericho Jones!"

A stillness falls over the arena at that, Dad's name rippling among the warriors like flame. Just like I said, they remember the Great Man here, too.

"My father fought your people for years in the war!" Tyler shouts. "He spilled the blood of your warriors by the thousands. And his blood flows in *my* veins."

The silence is total now, a subtle and burning anger reflected in that sea of violet eyes. They remember the defeat our father led at Kireina. The shame their entire cabal was subjected to after that loss.

Ty looks up at Saedii, his jaw squared, stare narrowed.

"I'm the commander of this squad. I lead, and they follow.

Your *brother* among them. My sister isn't a warrior. My crew aren't warriors. So if anyone's getting thrown down into that pit, it's me, and me alone. The son of Jericho Jones doesn't need help making a handbag out of some lizard."

I falter at that, my eyes on my brother's. "Ty . . ."

"You said these people respect fearlessness," he says softly, still looking up at Saedii. "This is as fearless as I get. Tell them, Scar."

I translate, watch Saedii's eyes narrow at Ty's words.

"Not them," he tells her, pointing at his chest. "Just me."

The Unbroken Templar leans back in her throne, one black fingernail tracing the line of her eyebrow. Her baby drakkan wraps its tail around her arm and trills in her ear. Mama Drakkan bellows in response.

"If you wish to die alone, Terran," she says, "so be it."

Saedii nods to the guards around us, and before I can really protest, they're shuffling us back off the gangplank. I call out as the stamping begins again, a rising thunder building with the pulse in my temples. Ty is my baby brother, the only family I have left. I'm his big sister—I'm supposed to be looking after *him*.

"Tyler!"

The Unbroken warrior who's remained with Tyler hands him a small, ornate blade from his belt. The knife is barely big enough to cut a protein loaf, so what use it's supposed to be against a twenty-meter-long killing machine is beyond me. The Syldrathi warrior in the pit below presses the controls again, and the doors to the drakkan's lair slam closed. She scampers out of the pit as the beast prowls around underneath us, its roar shaking the deck beneath my feet.

My stomach flips and rolls inside me. Fin reaches down to squeeze my hand. Ty looks at me and winks.

"Throw him in," Saedii calls.

The Unbroken lifts his hand, but Ty's already moving, jumping down into the pit rather than be tossed in off balance and snapped up before he can react. His boots crunch into the stones, and the drakkan roars.

Its wings must have been clipped, because it doesn't actually fly, instead leaping into the air and gliding down toward Ty with its fanged mouth open wide.

Ty's already moving, rolling behind one of those strange metallic outcroppings. The creature crashes to the ground where he stood a moment before, whipping toward him with a bellow of rage, long neck uncoiling like a snake as it strikes. But my brother's moving again, rolling, using the barricades to protect himself, desperately scanning the arena for some way out of this.

"Tyler, watch out!" I scream.

I can't believe this is happening—it doesn't feel real, the stamping feet and trembling roars washing over me in awful black waves. Ty is fast, agile, trained by the best in the academy in hand-to-hand combat. But the thing he's fighting doesn't even *have* hands. It leaps into the air again, up over Ty's cover, its barbed tail smashing into the dirt as my brother rolls aside. It lashes out with long arms, carving chunks out of the metal—and, yeah, apparently this thing cuts *metal* with its claws.

Shards spray across the stones, some as big as Tyler's head. It swings with its tail, smashing into Tyler and sending him sailing through the air, tumbling across the glowing stones as I scream again. My brother rolls up to his feet, one hand clutching his ribs as he stumbles away from another strike. I can see blood on his brow now, spattered at his lips. I can see how horribly, hopelessly outmatched he is.

One direct hit, and I'm going to lose the only family I have left.

I glance around at the Syldrathi, rage swelling in my chest.

How can they just sit and watch this?

Actually, there's no *just* about it. They're cheering. They're watching this one-sided death match and reveling in it. Where's the honor in that?

How can this possibly be fair?

I look up at Saedii and swear to myself, vow on Dad's grave, if something happens to my baby brother . . .

I'm going to kill you, bitch.

Tyler's running out of room, out of breath, out of moves—it looks like that last tail swipe hurt him bad. The drakkan charges, all sinew and muscle, serpent quick. Tyler leaps forward, desperate, diving under the snapping arc of its jaws toward the center of the pit, skidding on his stomach along those smooth, glowing stones.

The drakkan twists around and leaps into the air, its hobbled wings spread, my brother below it. Tyler is clawing at the ground, trying to get to his feet, raising his little knife in desperation. I'm thinking maybe Ty's maneuvered himself underneath it to strike at its underbelly, but that knife is nothing more than a toothpick.

The drakkan shrieks in triumph and descends.

Tyler rolls, and flings the blade—not up at the beast's

belly, like I thought, but across the pit. For a second I think he's had all his sense knocked loose, that he's wasted the one weapon he has, that he's just killed himself for sure.

But then I see the blade tumbling, arcing, end over end—a perfect, beautiful throw that sends it sailing hilt-first into the control panel on the wall.

Ty is already on his feet, diving forward as the doors to the drakkan's lair crack wide and slam apart. The drakkan bellows as the ground opens up below it, thrashing its useless wings as it plummets back down into the holding pen it crawled out of. The thing strikes the floor with a thunderous *whunnnggg,* its shriek of rage echoing on the metal. My heart is rising into my throat, my eyes wide. But Tyler is up on his feet, charging desperately, small stones flying as he leaps, arm outstretched toward the controls just as the monster comes lunging back out of its lair. It's a race: Tyler versus drakkan, human versus monster, feral hunger versus the desperate, indomitable will to survive.

Tyler wins.

The beast leaps up, roaring. The doors slam closed. The edges catch the drakkan across its ribs as it rises, and the Unbroken are on their feet, a few of them even shouting in dismay as the pen doors crush the drakkan's ribs, blood spilling from its mouth as it flops and thrashes.

Tyler takes a few steps forward, gasping, bloodied. Watching the beast flail in agony, clawing at the metal that's crushing it. The drakkan is beaten, but it's not dead, and its screams make me sick to my stomach as it tries to tear itself loose, the stink of black blood filling my nostrils.

A sizzling flash scorches the air, a Kill shot from a

disruptor rifle ripping into the drakkan's eye. The beast thrashes once more and then collapses. The whole arena is still, the legions of Unbroken shocked and dismayed. I look up and see Saedii, standing now with a disruptor rifle on her hip. She's looking down at my brother, her face a perfect, unreadable mask.

My heart's thumping, my belly full of butterflies. Warbreed respect prowess in battle above anything else, but I honestly don't know how this is going to play out. Ty just killed this crazy bitch's pet, after all.

Saedii aims her rifle at Tyler's head. He looks up at her, bloodied and defiant. One squeeze of that trigger is all it'll take.

"Perhaps," she finally says, "you will be of some amusement after all."

I sigh with relief, shoulders sagging, my whole body deflating. Saedii turns to her lieutenant, nods toward us.

"Take them to the detention level. Lock them down hard."

"Your will, my hands, Templar," he replies. "What of their Alpha?"

Saedii looks at Tyler with narrowed eyes. "See him fed and his wounds dressed." She purses her lips, tosses her braids back off her shoulders. "Then send him to my chambers. I wish to interrogate him personally."

The lieutenant bows and the Unbroken hurry to do their mistress's bidding. I look to Tyler down in the pit, can't help but grin and shake my head as he looks up at me and winks, pawing at the blood on his mouth. Then a handful of beautiful Unbroken goons are grabbing me, prodding me back up the stairs.

Finian is being pushed along close behind me, looking just as bewildered as I am. We're still in Unbroken custody, sure. Still cut off from Auri and Kal and now Ty, still wanted galactic terrorists, still being dragged back to who knows where in the keeping of Kal's psycho sibling. We're still in it, right up to our necklines.

But somehow, we're still *alive*.

We're marched down a series of dark corridors, illuminated with strips of blood-red light. Syldrathi glyfs decorate the walls, the interior design a strange collision of beautiful curves and lines with a morbid gothic vibe. The thrum of the engines is the only sound.

We arrive at an area marked DETENTION, and without ceremony we're pushed into a small holding cell. The walls are black, unadorned. There's a bench along one wall for sleeping, strips of red light in the floor.

The door slides shut without a sound. I sink onto the bench, arms wrapped around my stomach. My whole body is shaking.

"Scar?" Fin says.

"Yeah?" I whisper.

"Do you think Tyler is accepting marriage proposals anytime soon?"

I laugh, and the laugh turns into a strangled sob, and I tighten my grip around myself to hold it all in. For a minute, it's all I can do to stop myself flying apart. The thought of almost losing Ty, of losing the only blood I have left, it's nearly too much.

Fin sits beside me, the smooth whine of his exosuit familiar and comforting. He puts one awkward arm around my shoulders.

"Hey, it's okay," he murmurs. "Ty's okay."

I nod, and I sniff hard, push back the tears. I know he's right. I know I have to keep it together, have to get *us* back together. We're scattered all over this ship now: Kal in the med bay, Auri locked down somewhere heavy, Ty in Saedii's clutches, and . . .

I blink and look around the cell, and there's an awful twisting in my gut as I realize someone else is missing.

Oh shit . . .

I can't remember seeing her at the arena. I can't believe I missed that she was gone, even as quiet as she is, even with all the chaos of the fight. But thinking back, my brow creased in concentration, I realize the last time I remember seeing her was aboard the *Zero* as we were about to disembark.

I speak into the gloom, my voice a whisper.

"Where the *hells* is Zila?"

12

ZILA

The air vents aboard Saedii's ship are summoning unpleasant memories as I crawl through them. My heart rate is elevated and my breathing quickened. Both factors are reducing my efficiency considerably.

I pause to marshal my thoughts, closing my eyes and focusing on the sensation of my lungs slowly expanding, then contracting. I remind myself that there is no connection between what happened when I was six and what is happening now. The similarities are limited to the fact that I am hiding in a ventilation system and that hostile individuals are, or soon will be, searching for me.

And that others are relying on me to save their lives.

Those others are not my parents this time, but my squadmates. Nevertheless, my squad is . . . important to me. And of course our mission is important.

This time I will not fail, no matter what is required of me.

By my assessment, nobody is in immediate danger. Finian and Scarlett are doubtless uncomfortable, but no more than inconvenienced by their detention cell. Aurora is sedated and likely unaware of her situation. Kal and Tyler were both to be treated well, according to the Templar's orders.

On this basis, I have decided to retrieve our gear before undertaking my squad's rescue. I am more nimble by myself, and I have noticed that my squadmates often make conversation during tense moments, which I consider unhelpful.

It is easier alone.

· · · · ·

I was six.

We were living on a small survey ship called the Janeway, orbiting Gallanosa III. It was an inhospitable planet, but a prime mining candidate. The ship was not large—I could walk the length of it in approximately nine minutes and run it in three—but it was home to five research scientists, and me.

I was only six.

· · · · ·

I am in the Andarael's *life-support system, a twisting maze of vents that winds below her decks and between her levels. I am looking up through a grille at seven Syldrathi technicians, all attempting to hack into our uniglasses. Aurora Academy technology is top of the line, and I am confident their efforts will be fruitless for the next seventy to eighty minutes, depending on their level of competence.*

That will be sufficient.

At present, it appears that two of the technicians are preparing to leave on break, so I settle into my vantage point and wait. Their departure will improve my odds.

Patience.

Patience was required aboard the Janeway, *and it did not come easily to me. We had a large digital library, a communal recreation area, an exercise rig, and a hydroponics unit. But truthfully, there was very little to do there. I was a boisterous child—I sprinted the length of the ship to burn off energy, I climbed the exercise rig in many ways it was not designed to support, and I cultivated flowers in my own tiny patch of the hydroponics bay.*

My mother was the expedition leader, with a focus on scoping potential mining sites. My father was the corp's token environmental officer, there to certify that nothing rare or unique would be endangered by mining operations. He had ample free time, given the nature of his job, so he handled my education as well. He had a knack for making my classes entertaining, and my intelligence meant my education was accelerated without any sense of pressure or overwork.

I was just wrapping up my high school equivalency the day the men came.

. . . . .

The men above me are bent over a transparent silicon bench, conversing in soft Syldrathi. Alongside the uniglasses they are attempting to hack, I can see the passkeys to the *Zero* through the glass they lean upon.

Escape in our own ship would be the most convenient option, as we are familiar with its facilities, and they were designed to accommodate our needs. It may be possible for me to retrieve the passkeys via stealth, but I do not consider it possible to remove the uniglasses without drawing attention.

I turn my thoughts to other plans.

*My parents had explained to me that my plans were unrealistic—
a six-year-old taking classes at college level would encounter
many difficulties, no matter how advanced or socially adept.
Even as a small child I preferred the sciences, so my mother and
father took me with them to Gallanosa III, intending to begin
my higher education when the time was right.*

*Although I understood at even that young age that my in-
telligence was unusual, they did not want me to feel isolated.
They wanted me to be safe.*

They failed on both counts.

. . . . .

Both senior Syldrathi technicians depart, leaving me five to
deal with. I crawl beneath them, along my vent toward the
junction at the far end of the lab.

I have considered my options, running statistical analyses
on each course of action as best I can with the information
I have at hand.

First step: alarms.

. . . . .

*The alarms had been tripped seventy-three minutes earlier,
which was not out of the ordinary in our isolated location. The
incoming vessel's failure to respond to hails was more concern-
ing, but they may have been in communications difficulty. We
weren't a prime target—we had little of value. But our doubts
were erased when they force-docked with the Janeway and
blasted our airlocks.*

At that point, we became very concerned.

The whole ship shuddered as the locks blew. My father shoved me—the first time I remember him ever being rough, outside a game of saigo in the exercise rig—sending me stumbling toward Max and Hòa's lab.

"Hide," he whispered when I looked back, bewildered.

I didn't understand, but I was an obedient child, so I ran through the doorway, picking a spot among the sample crates we would deliver on our next trip to Marney Station. I could observe what was happening through the door.

My mother strode forward to confront the new arrivals. There were three of them, clad in bodysuits as battered as their ship. I recognized them instantly—I had met them a week before, when I had visited Marney with my father.

I can recall the sight of my mother in that moment. She wore a blue jumpsuit, and her hair was out, tight black curls like my own flowing around her shoulders.

I cannot remember her face anymore.

But I remember they shot her in it without a word.

. . . . .

Without a sound, I reach the vent junction and the maintenance control hatch mounted on the wall. It takes me longer than anticipated to disable the security system with my uniglass. I am not the expert in computer espionage that Finian is.

The lock on the control box is a more mundane matter, and I use my all-purpose knife to pry off the lid, which slices through my index finger as it comes free. The pain is a sharp line of fire, and I close my eyes tightly, screwing up my face involuntarily with the effort to stay quiet.

My heart is only too willing to accept an excuse to kick

up its rate once more, and I try another round of breathing exercises as I extract a set of quik-stitches from my jumpsuit and apply them. I glance up at the Unbroken techs, but they remain engrossed in their wrestling match with the uniglass security measures.

I return to my work, studying the maintenance panel until I am confident I understand it. I can read the Syldrathi glyfs with my uniglass, and there are only so many ways for oxygen-based life-support systems to operate. But I check, and check again, fully aware of the consequences of failure. Then I set to work on the filtration system, diverting the extractors, and settle down to wait.

I estimate that the results I am expecting will take approximately fifteen and a half minutes to achieve. Give or take three or four seconds.

· · · · · ·

Three or four seconds was all it took for everything to unravel. For my mother's body to fold to the ground, for the next round of disruptor shots to scorch the air.

In the action vids I'd seen—my parents didn't condone them, but Miriam let me watch when they weren't paying attention—people who got shot always flew backward. Newton's third law of motion prohibits this, of course—a bullet lacks the force to reverse a body's momentum. But I still remember feeling surprised as Max stumbled forward after the shots hit him, before he crumpled to the deck.

The remaining three adults, including my father, raised their hands in surrender. I watched over the crates, holding my scream inside. I remember my heart rate was elevated, my respiration bordering on distressed, my mouth dry.

I remember I did not like feeling that way.

"Where's the child?" the lead raider snapped. It was a man's voice, accented, perhaps from Tempera.

"What child?" my father asked before either Hòa or Miriam could reply.

"Your child," the man said, his voice dropping in register. There was a shake to it, and he paused to brace his hand against the edge of the hole they'd blasted in our ship. I concluded he was drug affected.

He had been inhaling an illegal substance when I'd met him a week before. Marney Station was not reputable, but it was possible to access many black-market goods there, and my father was a practical man. After we had filed our latest samples, we'd taken the grav-lift down to the lower levels so he could purchase ingredients for a special meal to celebrate Hòa's birthday.

"Don't move out of my sight," he told me.

I followed his directive, but was drawn to a group of gamblers participating in a game of tintera. I loved games, and I stood on my toes to watch the cards dealt—each round the players would decide whether to accept a new card from the dealer. The goal was to hold cards that, added together, totaled twenty-four.

It was simple to note which cards had already been dealt, calculate the probability of a favorable deal from the remaining cards, and decide accordingly.

The first time I advised the man on his choice, he laughed.

The second time, he listened.

The third time, he gave me fifty credits and invited me to play.

"Come be my lucky charm," he said.

Everyone laughed, and I grinned. It was exciting to have new playmates. Life on the Janeway was so predictable.

When my father retrieved me fifteen minutes later, I was up one thousand nine hundred and fifty credits. He made me leave them at the table and escorted me away with a haste I did not understand.

Now the man stood here on our ship, asking to see me.

"There's no child here," my father said.

And so the man shot Hòa. He didn't make a sound as he died.

Miriam was the one who broke. "Don't shoot—she's here! I'll help you find her." She turned to look for me, her voice trembling. "Zila? Zila, come out!"

I did not like the feelings I felt then, either. Anger, that my friend who watched vids with me would betray me. Contempt, that she thought I was stupid enough to obey. Fear, that now they knew I was here.

"She's not here," my father said, quiet and calm. "We sent her to school."

They were going to search soon, I realized. And they would find my things. My father's voice faded to a soft, familiar hum as I clambered up into the air vents and crawled down the ship to our living quarters.

When I dropped into our room, I could smell my mother. The warm, spicy scent of her perfume, an outrageous luxury on a posting like ours.

I had only a few possessions. I stuffed my clothes into the laundry hamper, then stripped my bed and dumped the sheets on top to hide them. I crushed the model mining equipment I had been making with my father and fed it into the recyc.

Keeping to the vents, I dodged the men as they searched the ship for me. They had already shot three people. They wanted me. They would shoot my father and leave once they had me. So it was up to me to keep him safe.

Logic dictated that.

· · · · ·

Logic dictates that it cannot be much longer, but still, I feel a sense of relief at the twelve-minute mark, when one of the Syldrathi smothers a yawn. I make a mental note to research what variables might have caused the gas to impact him before the others. Carbon monoxide is lighter than air. Perhaps he is taller?

I inspect the other four technicians from my vantage point. One is visibly flagging, but three still appear well. I hope the Syldrathi constitution is not, in their cases, hardier than I anticipated.

· · · · ·

It was harder than I had anticipated to keep my father safe, but I succeeded for a while. It was a small ship, but I was small too, and I had a lot of experience playing hide-and-seek. This time, though, there were no muffled giggles as I slipped away from my hunters. No secret smiles as they walked right by me.

I shoved my feelings down very hard as I climbed from the vents and into my mother's office. I imagined myself putting them in a box and closing the lid so they couldn't distract me.

I crawled in under her desk to where her comms equipment was plugged in, and yanked the cables free. The rig was set to auto-transmit a status update every three hours. If it didn't, someone would come looking for answers. They might wait until we missed two check-ins, but if a corp craft was in the area, we could get lucky.

Two hours later, the equipment failed to transmit. After four hours, the raiders started bickering. Their drugs were wearing off, and their raid had not concluded as easily as they had expected. One of the men argued they should cut their losses.

The leader pointed out that (a) my demonstrated ability to calculate odds would still be lucrative for their employers, and (b) I had seen their faces and could testify against them.

But after three more hours of searching, they lost patience. They shot Miriam, despite her begging and her tears. And then they held the gun to my father's head.

"Come out, Zila," called the man. "I don't want to shoot your daddy too. Just come out and he'll be safe, Lucky Charm."

I considered my position. If I emerged, I was confident they would shoot him and take me immediately. If I did not, perhaps they might choose to search a little longer, prolonging his life for use against me later. Giving the corp more time to send a team to investigate our silence.

I held my position.

"She's not here," my father said doggedly. "But if she were, I would tell her that I love her." He looked up into the vents. Perhaps hoping that I was watching. "And that this isn't her fault."

The man shot him.

Then they ransacked the Janeway and left.

When I emerged from my hiding place, the ship's emergency ionization field was crackling over the jagged hole they'd left in its side, holding the vacuum back.

I remember thinking I had a field just like that keeping my

feelings at bay. I didn't know how long it would hold, either. But I poured all my strength into maintaining it. I thought I would be better off without them.

For twelve years, I was correct.

. . . . .

I was correct. By the sixteen-minute mark, all five Syldrathi are unconscious, collapsed over their glass countertop. I carefully remove the vent, keeping myself low as I climb up into the room. Though my heart insists on thumping, Aurora Legion training has assured me that if I stay close to the ground and work quickly, I will avoid a dangerous dose of the gas.

"HI THERE!"

I startle as Aurora's uniglass speaks from its place on the counter, my heart now beating wildly against my ribs.

"YOU SURE TOOK YOUR TIME GETTING HERE!" it chirps, unaware of my distress. "I WAS AFRAID THEY WERE GOING TO DISSECT ME!"

"You are a machine," I say. "You cannot be afraid."

"SAY, THAT WAS A NEAT TRICK WITH THE GAS! YOU'RE PRETTY SMART FOR A—"

"Be quiet," I tell it.

"YOU KNOW, YOU'RE LUCKY I LIKE YOU PEOPLE SO MUCH," it chirps. "CONSTANTLY BEING TOLD TO BE QUIET COULD LEAD A LESSER MACHINE TO MAYBE START PLOTTING YOUR GRISLY MURDERS AN—"

"Silent mode!" I hiss.

Magellan finally complies, falling mute. I quickly gather the passkeys and the other uniglasses, then avail myself of the weaponry on offer—Warbreed technicians are more heavily armed than United Terran Authority scientists would be. And wasting no more time, I pack my haul into one of their bags before crawling back down into the vents.

. . . . .

When I crawled down from the vents, I discovered I was too small to move the bodies, but I arranged them as best I could. Even Miriam. She had been scared, I knew that. That was why she had done it.

That was why it was so important not to feel.

Everyone here had acted on feelings, and they were dead because of it.

And because of me.

Someone would eventually be sent to investigate why the beacon had failed. Obviously my hope of a corp craft's arrival after six hours and two missed transmissions had been optimistic—the Janeway *was a minor asset. But in time, they would come. I just needed to support myself until then, and hope the force fields didn't give out.*

It was another seventy-six hours before I woke in my parents' bed to voices above me.

"Great Maker, how is she still alive?"

I rolled onto my back to look up at them. Five adults in corp uniforms.

I wasn't afraid.

I wasn't relieved.

I was nothing.

. . . . .

I am not . . . feeling nothing as I proceed to the next stage of my mission. Putting serious thought into the matter for the first time, I realize the members of Squad 312 have compromised my emotional integrity. Slowly, some of what I was as a child is returning. I have not yet decided whether this is a welcome development.

Three levels down, I find the infirmary, where Kal lies restrained on a bio-cot, attended by two Unbroken medics. I raise my purloined disruptor to the shaft's grille and take careful aim. Waiting. Patient. Finally, I hear what I am waiting for—a shipwide announcement spilling over the public address system, warning all hands to prepare for Fold entry. Loud enough to conceal a disruptor blast.

BAMF!

My shot strikes the first medic in the back of her head. The second draws his sidearm with astonishing speed, but my shot strikes him in his throat, laying him out on the deck beside his comrade.

That was too close.

I climb up from the vents as the announcement ends.

"Who is there?" Kal demands, trying to turn his head.

I do not waste words, setting to work on his restraints.

"Zila . . . ," he whispers.

"I understand you were shot. Are your injuries serious?"

"No," he replies simply. "Where is Aurora?"

I decide that mentioning his sister's use of the agonizer will not aid Kal in rational thinking. "She is in the holding cells with Finian and Scarlett."

"We must go to her," he insists, sitting up as soon as his arms are free.

"I concur. We can make our way via the ducts."

"I will not fit in there," Kal protests.

I am acutely aware that if Finian were here, he would

make some off-color joke at this juncture. I clear my throat, frowning in concentration. "I . . ."

Kal simply stares at me, obviously impatient.

I am rapidly discovering the value of comedy relief.

"Never mind," I finally say.

Kal is able to disable the guards stationed outside the infirmary by striking with the benefit of surprise. I form the view, but do not voice it, that he expends more effort than strictly necessary to subdue them. I suspect he, like me, is struggling for optimal levels of composure.

Another shipwide announcement rings over the PA as Kal strips off the first guard's armor. Our Tank seems distinctly uncomfortable as he slips into the guise of an Unbroken warrior, but now is not the time to explore his feelings on the topic.

Kal removes the mag-restraints from his bio-cot, slips them around my wrists.

"Walk ahead of me," he says. "Eyes down. Say nothing."

I nod, and after a quick check outside to ensure it is clear, we march into the hallway. Kal seems to know his way around a Syldrathi warship, and he directs me quickly into a turbolift, leading to the detention block below.

"Thank you, Zila," he murmurs beside me. "You did well."

A slight warmth stirs in my chest at his praise.

I am not . . . feeling nothing.

"Are you all right?" I hear him ask.

My voice is steady. My expression blank. But . . .

"I am . . . glad." I frown. "To be out of the dark."

I meet his eyes, which is not something I can really recall having done before. I wonder if he can see her. That little girl. Crawling around in those vents on that silent station. The pieces of her she left in the darkness. The fear. The hurt. The anger.

Did she only leave them behind? Or did she leave herself behind with them?

Did she do it because it was easier?

Or because she had to?

And, after twelve years, what will she do now that she is finally, truly beginning to crawl out?

I am not . . . feeling nothing.

I am not feeling nothing.

SUBJECT: GALACTIC CONFLICTS

▶ **SYLDRATHI CIVIL WAR**

  ▼ **THE UNBROKEN**

LED BY A REBEL ARCHON NAMED **CAERSAN**, AKA THE STARSLAYER, THE UNBROKEN ARE A MILITANT FACTION OF SYLDRATHI, COMPRISING MOST OF THE **WARBREED** CABAL.

REJECTING THE PEACE TREATY BETWEEN EARTH AND SYLDRA, THE UNBROKEN SPLINTERED FROM THE RULING **SYLDRATHI COUNCIL** TEN YEARS AGO. THEY **ATTACKED TERRAN SHIPYARDS** DURING AN ARRANGED CEASE-FIRE AND, IN A DISPLAY OF SHOCKING BRUTALITY, EVENTUALLY LAUNCHED AN ASSAULT ON THEIR OWN HOMEWORLD.

USING AN UNKNOWN WEAPON, THE UNBROKEN CAUSED THE SYLDRATHI SUN, **EVAA**, TO COLLAPSE, FORMING A BLACK HOLE THAT DESTROYED THE ENTIRE SYSTEM.

TEN BILLION SYLDRATHI DIED.

JUST HOW THE UNBROKEN MANAGED TO PULL THIS OFF IS ANYONE'S GUESS.

13

TYLER

Look after your sister.

They were the last words Dad said to me. After he kissed Scar on the forehead, told her he'd be back in time for our birthday. After he knelt down and wrapped me up in the last hug he'd ever give me. He stood, and he ruffled my hair in that way I hated, and he spoke to me that way I loved. Not like I was a kid. Like I was a man. Like he was saying something Important and I was worthy of it.

Look after your sister, he told me.

I did. Always.

And she looked after me too.

Scar and I were inseparable as kids. Dad said we invented our own language before we could talk. And even though I wasn't sold on my twin joining Aurora Legion—tried to talk her out of it, in fact—I was secretly glad Scar was standing beside me when I signed on the line at New Gettysburg Station. I'd have felt like a piece of me had been torn out if I'd left her behind. And I'd be able to look after her better if she was close. There's nothing I wouldn't do to keep her safe.

Like jumping into a pit with a full-grown drakkan?

Part of me can't believe I pulled that one off, to be honest. The Tyler Jones who graduated top of Aurora Academy wouldn't have even considered it. He was a guy who played by the book. Regulation. Caution. Careful consideration before every move. But the longer I'm out here, on the edge, the more at home I feel. And with the enemies we're playing against?

Sometimes the only way to win is to break the game.

I'm staring at a set of checkered hexagonal tiles, stacked six high, scattered with white and black stones. It's a dóa board from Chelleria—a tactical game, considered to be one of the most difficult to master in the galaxy. I'm a third-tier player at best. The board is sitting atop an ornately graven desk of dark metal in Saedii's outer quarters, vibrating softly to the hum of the *Andarael*'s engines.

Looking around the room in the dim illumination, monochrome from the Fold, I can see other games. A samett set from Trask. Three beautiful tae-sai boards from Syldra, all carved of lias wood. Even a half-finished game of chess. Waiting for my hostess, sitting in a comfortable chair in front of her desk, I can tell she's a tactician. Everything about the room—the games, the books, even the simple geometric art—tells me Kal's sister is fascinated by strategy.

I pick up one of the dóa pieces, my ribs and muscles still groaning after my run-in with the drakkan. The piece is a flat white disk marked with a triangular black symbol. They play the role of pawns in the game—kinda, anyway. Sacrificial lambs used to gain an edge elsewhere in the battle.

I'm starting to appreciate how they feel.

"Do you play?" comes a low, sweet voice from behind me.

I turn and see Saedii stalking through a double set of auto-doors, a silver tray poised on one hand. Her pet drakkan rides on her shoulder, watching me with glittering golden eyes. Before the doors whisper shut behind them, I see her inner quarters: simple artwork, a large bed, a computer terminal. I briefly wonder where she hangs the skins of her victims.

She's changed out of her armor into Syldrathi dress uniform—formfitting black, elegant lines, glittering with silver embellishments and battle trophies. Her black hair rolls down over her shoulders in seven thick braids, just like Kal's. She's taken the time to refresh the black paint that coats her lips, the strip that frames her eyes. I can see her brother in the shape of them, the line of her cheeks and brow. She radiates an aura of command: cold, cruel, calculating.

"Do you play?" she repeats.

I put the dóa piece back where I found it.

"Tyler Jones," I reply. "Alpha. Aurora Legion, Squad 312."

Saedii walks to the desk, places the tray down. It holds a carafe of crystal-clear water and two glasses. There's also a beautiful long-bladed knife and four spheres that I recognize as a Syldrathi fruit called bae'el.

Sitting down opposite me, Saedii fixes me with a withering violet stare.

"Really?" she says, speaking perfect Terran. "That is your opening gambit? Name, rank, squad number?"

She raises one dark eyebrow, then pours the water. The drakkan crawls up onto the chair's back, trilling softly as it continues to stare at me. Saedii pushes the crystal glass across the desk and murmurs to her pet.

"Yes, Isha, my love, he disappoints me, too," she says, eyes returning to mine. "I thought he would know how this game is played."

I'm desperately thirsty after my arena brawl, but instead of drinking, I meet her stare, speaking softly, my voice calm.

"The first step of successful interrogation technique is to establish rapport," I say. "Offer the subject kindness—a gift like water or food or pain relief. Alleviating their suffering will highlight the suffering they've already endured, and evoke a sense of empathy in you, in contrast to their other captors." I glance at the water, then back up to her eyes. "I know *exactly* how this game is played."

I lean back in my chair, lace my fingers in my lap.

"Tyler Jones. Alpha. Aurora Legion, Squad 312."

Saedii pours another glass for herself, takes a small sip.

"We Warbreed teach our adepts differently, little Terran," she says. "The first step of successful interrogation technique is to establish dominance. Assure the subject, in no uncertain terms, that you are in control."

She picks up the knife from the tray, presses the tip ever so gently against the forefinger of her other hand. Like her hair, her nails are dyed black.

"Begin with a mild amputation," she suggests. "Something small. But something that will be missed."

She looks down at my crotch, then up into my eyes.

"A sister, perhaps."

My stomach lurches at that, but I keep the fear from my face. Running the math in my head. "How did you know she w—"

"I am no fool, Tyler Jones, Alpha, Aurora Legion, Squad

312." She stabs the knife into a piece of bae'el, then begins removing the rind with deft twists of the blade. "The sooner you dissuade yourself of that notion, the better."

"You speak excellent Terran," I say. "I'll grant you that."

She slices a sliver of dark flesh from the fruit. "Far better than your Syldrathi."

"I'm surprised you bothered to learn. Given how clearly you despise us."

Saedii slips the sliver between her teeth. Looks me dead in the eye.

"I always study my prey."

She leans back and places her feet up on the desk, nudges the glass of water toward me with the heel of one knee-high, silver-tipped boot.

"Drink, boy. You will need your strength."

Isha trills, fluttering her wings and watching as I finally lean forward and pick up the glass. It's solid crystal, heavy in my hand, and for a moment I consider pitching it at Saedii's head, making a grab for her knife. The more sensible part of my brain reminds me of the beating this girl gave me the last time we tangled. My groin sends an urgent transmission, pointing out I might wanna have kids one day.

I drink.

"You and your crew were obtaining data from the Hephaestus salvage fleet," Saedii says. "Records show that the flight recorder your technician destroyed aboard the *Totentanz* belonged to an ancient Terran derelict. The *Hadfield*. A vessel that set out from your world over two centuries ago." She slices off another sliver of fruit, presses it to her tongue. "What do you want with two-hundred-year-old truths, little Terran?"

"I'm a history buff," I reply.

"Know the past," she says, "or suffer the future."

"Exactly."

"You are lying," she says, cool and mild. "Continue to do so, and I will have your sister suffer the most gruesome of torments before I flush her into space."

"Considering you were willing to feed us to a monster an hour ago, I presume you're going to kill us all anyway." I shrug. "And if this information is so important to you, maybe you should have *started* with the interrogation and proceeded to the execution, instead of the other way around?"

"My brother has all these answers too, little Terran," she replies calmly. "You are not an essential part of this equation."

"Then why bother talking to me at all?"

The knife flashes. Another sliver of fruit disappears between Saedii's black lips. It's a long moment before she replies.

"It is not often I see a lone combatant best a full-grown drakkan." She looks me up and down, eyes sparkling. "I recognize your prowess. And your bloodline. Jericho Jones was a foe worthy of respect."

A flash of anger runs through me then. I feel my jaw tighten, my teeth clench.

"That didn't stop your people murdering him at Orion."

She raises one perfectly sculpted eyebrow. "We are warriors, Tyler Jones, not widows. Weep not for the wages of war. And while your peerage is to be respected, do not believe for a moment I will not kill you *and* your sister *and* your little cripple to learn what I want."

I bristle at the insult to Fin, eyes narrowing. She simply

208

smiles as the barb lands. Meeting her stare, I realize this girl is from a culture entirely alien to mine—a culture where strength is prized, cruelty encouraged, weakness despised. I'm beginning to appreciate how hard it must have been for Kal to break out of that cycle, become the person he is. The longer I spend in his sister's presence, the more impressed with him I am. And the more I loathe her.

But while almost all Warbreed genuinely think this way, I realize Saedii is mostly just goading me. Pressing buttons. Watching reactions. Everything she's done since she arrived—the water, the threats, the talk about my crew, my father—it's all been to gauge the kind of person I am.

I glance at the strategy games around the room. A dozen different games from a dozen different worlds. I realize all of them have been involved in conflicts with the Syldrathi in the last fifty years.

I always study my prey.

"The one named Aurora." Saedii's lip draws back in ever-so-slight contempt. "The girl my dear brother names be'shmai."

"Finally getting to the point, I see," I say.

Her hand drifts up to the string of severed thumbs around her neck.

"You males," she sighs. "Always in such a rush."

Isha trills, golden eyes flashing.

"She lacks the skills and training of a legionnaire," Saedii continues. "Who is she? Where is she from? Why do you travel with her?"

"She stowed away on our ship," I reply. "She's from Earth. And your brother would be upset if I sent her away."

"Half-truths," Saedii coos, reaching up to scratch the drakkan under her chin. "The little Terran believes he is clever, Isha. He still believes he is in control here. Should we kill the sister first? Or that twisted little Betraskan toad?"

"Does it make you feel bigger?" I ask. "Trying to make others look small?"

"You *are* small, little Terran," she replies. "Small and weak and frightened. Your own government names you terrorists. Your own people hunt you like hounds."

"And what would *your* government name you?" I reply. "I mean, if you hadn't murdered them all for daring to make peace with Earth?"

"'Peace' is the way a cur cries 'Surrender,'" Saedii replies, studying her fingernails. "Mercy is the province of cowards. The Inner Council of Syldra was in league with our enemies. They were traitors to the Syldrathi people."

"So you destroyed them along with your own homeworld?" I demand, anger creeping into my voice. "Along with ten billion of those innocent Syldrathi people?"

"The Syldrathi people accepted the treaty with Terra, boy. They had lost their honor. They deserved no pity, and Archon Caersan showed them none."

I bristle again at the name. Caersan. The Starslayer. The man who destroyed his own world and led the assault on Orion—the attack where we lost our dad.

"You know, it's funny," I reply. "You Unbroken always talk about honor. But last time I checked, attacking during a peace negotiation is just as cowardly as stabbing someone in the back. Seems to me your beloved Starslayer is about as honorable as your garden-variety cockroach."

Saedii's eyes flash at that.

"I will warn you once, little Terran. Where the Starslayer is concerned, watch your tongue. Or watch me hand it to you."

"He's a madman," I spit. "And he—"

I don't really see her move, I just feel the strike—the heel of her palm into the bridge of my nose. I feel a crunch, see black stars, taste blood in the back of my throat. I tumble backward off the chair but quickly to my feet, my ribs still aching from the battle with the drakkan. The world is blurred with tears, and I only catch a glimpse of a dark shape before two hands clap down on my shoulders—

Oh Maker, not again . . .

—and a knee crashes into my groin. The black stars in my eyes burn through to white, and for a moment I'm nothing but the pain, dropping to my knees, crumpling to the floor, curling up into a ball of agony and misery. It's all I can do to remember to breathe, and I'm waiting for those silver-tipped boots to start dancing on my throat when a voice cuts through the burning haze.

"Templar. Forgive my interruption."

The boots never land. I recognize the voice—it's Saedii's second-in-command, his voice distorted slightly by the comms system.

Through the tears, I look up and see Saedii touch the transmitter on the breast of her uniform. Her voice is cool, and she tosses one black braid off her shoulder as she smiles down at me, completely unruffled.

"What is it, Erien?" she asks.

"We have detected several vessels on intercept course with

Andarael," the lieutenant reports. *"Approaching us from multiple headings."*

"Who are they?"

"Terran capital ships. Four destroyers. Two carriers."

Maker's breath. That's not just "several vessels." That's an assault fleet. . . .

"Ignore them," Saedii replies. "The Terrans would not dare risk violating neutrality by accosting an Unbroken vessel. Maintain course for the *Neridaa*."

"They are moving at assault speed, Templar. And they are hailing us."

That gives Saedii a moment's pause. What she said is true—ever since the Syldrathi civil war broke out, Earth has been bending over backward to avoid getting involved with Syldrathi affairs. It's hard to blame them, really—the Starslayer not only destroyed his own homeworld but somehow caused the Syldrathi sun to collapse upon itself. The subsequent black hole wiped out the entire Syldra system and several uninhabited systems nearby.

Nobody wants to get on the wrong side of a man with that kind of power.

But now there's a Terran fleet on intercept course with us?

Andarael is a massive capital ship herself—Drakkan-class, the biggest in the Unbroken armada—but that doesn't mean her oh-so-cool commander wouldn't be at least a little worried at tackling a Terran attack force that size.

"Transmission onscreen," Saedii says.

I blink away my tears, the screaming pain in my groin receding to a mumbling ache as one wall flickers into life. For a moment, there's only white light, burning on the back of my eyeballs. Then the white coalesces into a familiar shape, and as I force myself up into sitting position, I feel my stomach flip.

I see the winged crest of the Terran Defense Force. The ship ident KUSANAGI emblazoned beneath it.

I see a Global Intelligence Agency uniform, spotless and white.

A smooth, featureless mirrormask.

"SALUTATIONS FROM THE GLOBAL INTELLIGENCE AGENCY, TEMPLAR. YOU MAY REFER TO ME AS PRINCEPS."

Its voice is sexless. Metallic. Giving no hint of who might be behind that mask. But I know the man, the *monster*, beneath that flawless uniform.

Auri's father, Zhang Ji.

Or what's left of him, anyway. He was just one of hundreds of Octavia III colonists consumed and assimilated by the Ra'haam. They've been working in the shadows for two centuries, infiltrating the GIA and Maker only knows what other arms of the Terran government. Erasing all evidence of the Octavia colony's existence. Hiding the existence of the twenty-two worlds the Ra'haam had seeded, and laying the groundwork for its return.

The shock of seeing Princeps hits me like another kick— last we knew, we'd left him behind on Octavia. And suddenly I'm back there, on that doomed and ruined world. Blue spores tumbling from the sky. The colony run through with leafy tendrils of the *thing* slumbering beneath its mantle. Cat's eyes, bright blue and flower-shaped, filling with tears as she looked at me for the last time.

You have to let me go.

The world is blurring again. I paw the burn from my eyes. Maker, I miss her. . . .

"What do you want, Terran?" Saedii replies, staring at the figure onscreen.

"Templar, it is our understanding you have apprehended several Terran citizens engaged in espionage aboard a Hephaestus salvage convoy. The surviving Hephaestus employees confirm your vessel's presence in the battle."

For a moment, I'm surprised the Unbroken left anyone alive in that convoy to give testimony. But thinking about it, I suppose it makes sense they leave witnesses to help spread the fear. It's not like the Starslayer's followers are afraid of reprisals. Nobody in the galaxy is brave enough to mess with them.

Except . . .

"Who I may or may not have acquired is none of your concern," Saedii replies.

"These criminals are wanted by the Terran government for intergalactic terrorism," Princeps says. "The Betraskan Finian de Seel and the Syldrathi Kaliis Idraban Gilwraeth are no concern of ours. But we would appreciate it if our citizens were returned to us."

. . . They want Auri.

The Ra'haam. The gestalt entity, incubating on those twenty-two worlds on Auri's star map. If they have her, they have the Trigger to the Eshvaren Weapon. They have the only person who can stop the planets from blooming and

214

spreading the Ra'haam's spores throughout the galaxy. And I'm trying to muster the breath to object, to warn Saedii she can't possibly hand us over, to give her a hint of what's at stake here.

But of course, I needn't have bothered.

"I am a Templar of the Unbroken," she announces, imperious. "Warbreed by birth and troth. Whatever prisoners I may or may not have aboard my vessel is *my* concern. And *you* are dangerously close to meddling in Syldrathi affairs. I advise your fleet to withdraw."

She leans forward on her desk and glowers.

"Before you earn the Starslayer's ire."

And there it is. The ultimate Get Out of Jail Free card. Nobody messes with Archon Caersan. Nobody wants a guy who can destroy solar systems mad at them. It's just sensible policy, really.

But apparently the Ra'haam doesn't much care for Sensible.

Princeps glances at someone off-screen. "ALERT THE FLEET. ALL VESSELS, WEAPONS LOCK ON SYLDRATHI VESSEL *ANDARAEL*. FIGHTER WINGS, READY LAUNCH."

It takes a moment for Princeps to get a response. I'm guessing that even in the heat of this moment, whoever received that order understands *exactly* how monumental it is. Terra doesn't involve itself in Syldrathi business. It *certainly* doesn't open fire on an Unbroken flagship carrying one of Caersan's trusted adjutants. If this goes south, if those ships engage . . .

. . . it could mean war.

But finally, we hear a reply offscreen. *"Sir, yessir."*

A tiny alert chimes a moment later, ringing across the *Andarael*'s PA. Saedii's lieutenant pipes in over comms. He speaks in Syldrathi, but I understand the language well enough to get the gist.

The Terrans have achieved weapons lock.

Fighter bay doors open.

And for the first time, I see a tiny crack appear in my hostess's armor. She hides it quickly, but it's there. A tiny sliver of it behind her eyes.

Uncertainty.

Still, she scoffs, looking Princeps in its blank mirrormask, that traditional Syldrathi arrogance slipping into place like a mask of her own.

"You are bluffing, Terran."

"Aᴍ I?" Princeps replies.

The transmission drops into black. Another warning comes in from Saedii's second-in-command, and she replies, ordering their weapons hot, their fighters to prep launch. We're about thirty seconds from a full-scale engagement here. The first time Syldrathi and Terran warships have opened fire on each other since the Jericho Accord of '78—the pact that officially ended the war between our worlds two years ago.

And I see it then. Like a puzzle laid out in front of me. Like a game of chess, a dozen moves ahead. I see what's happening here, and where it will lead. And I know, with awful certainty, that there's only two ways this can play out. Either Saedii capitulates and hands over Auri, which is never going to happen. Or Terrans and Syldrathi go to war again.

But the Ra'haam wins either way.

Because if Terra goes to war with the Unbroken, so do our allies, the Betraskans. That means the Aurora Legion is suddenly involved. The resulting conflict could end up sucking in every sentient race in the galaxy. And in that chaos, that carnage, that *distraction,* the Ra'haam will be left alone to gestate. Until it's ready to hatch, erupting from its seed worlds through the nearby FoldGates.

Bloom and burst.

And then it has the galaxy.

"Saedii," I gasp, my crotch still aching. "Don't do this."

"Be silent," she says, not even sparing me a glance.

Her eyes are on a tactical display, now pulsing on the screen where the image of Princeps used to be. I can see the approaching Terran ships, two carriers laden with fighters, four destroyers armed to the teeth.

"They want you to shoot first," I say, desperate now. "They *want* you to be the one who starts it. If you open fire on that fleet, it'll shatter the neutrality between Syldrathi and Terrans, don't you get it? It'll mean we're at *war.*"

She looks at me with those cold eyes.

"We are Warbreed, little Terran," she says simply. "We were *born* for war."

She presses the transmitter at her breast, and my heart sinks in my chest.

"Erien, notify the *Neridaa* that we are engaging hostile Terran forces."

"At once, Templar."

"Are weapons ready?"

"Awaiting your order, Templar."

"Saedii, don't!"

Her eyes narrow.

Her lips thin.

"Annihilate them," she says.

14

KAL

The *Andarael* is a capital ship, crewed by over one thousand adepts, Paladins, dragoons, and support staff. So it is easy enough to avoid attention as we march toward the detention block. Zila shuffles before me through the ebb and flow, mag-restraints clasped but unlocked around her wrists. We receive the occasional glance, nothing more. But a part of me knows this subterfuge cannot last.

My chest is one dark bruise from the disruptor shot aboard the *Totentanz*. My ribs aching like white fire. The cigarillo case Adams gave me stopped the worst of the shot, but the Unbroken took the gift from me while I slumbered, and I have no idea where it is now. I suppose I may never know what was locked inside it. But regardless, I know it saved my life. I know we are part of a grand mystery here, decades or even centuries in the making.

What I cannot begin to fathom is how it will end.

Zila informed me that Tyler was taken to Saedii's chambers for interrogation—retrieving him means confronting my sister directly. And wounded as I am, it will be hard enough getting my other squadmates out of detention without infiltrating the command and control center to rescue my Alpha.

My sister was always cruel, even when we were children. Our mother abhorred it, but our father encouraged it. I imagine the tortures she might be subjecting Tyler to. But then I push the concerns about Tyler from my mind.

First, last, and always, I must see to Aurora.

We arrive at the detention block, and immediately I note something amiss—the cells are overfull. It is uncommon for the Unbroken to take prisoners at all. Even on their largest ships, the detention facilities are small and often disused. But through the transparent walls, the crackling punishment fields, I see hundreds of figures. Syldrathi, all of them. They are thin and miserable, and my belly sinks as I note that each and every one bears an identical glyf on their brow. An eye crying five tears. The same glyf my mother bore.

Why in the name of the Void is Saedii capturing Way-walkers?

There is no time for questions. The adept manning the intake looks at Zila with faint puzzlement, turns his cool eyes to me. His desk is circular like the detention block around us. He is only a year or two older than me, but the trophies on his armor tell me that he is no novice.

"What is your business, adept?" he asks me.

I glance around the room, heart sinking. I had planned to bluff my way in here, overpower the few guards by surprise. But there are a dozen sentinels. Heavily armored. Fully armed. Warriors and killers, all. I see four of them gathered in front of the same cell, and my heart surges when I see Aurora lying on a slab all alone. She is unconscious. Bound,

220

gagged, and blindfolded. A dermal patch on her wrist delivering a steady stream of sedatives into her nervous system.

It seems my sister is taking my be'shmai's transport very seriously.

But why does Saedii want her at all?

And why are these Waywalkers here?

In the cell next to Aurora, I see Scarlett and Finian, forlorn and silent on their benches. They have been separated from the imprisoned Syldrathi and sit with each other in isolation. Scarlett catches sight of me, tensing slightly. Faint anger surges in me, to see my friends treated so.

I am doing desperate calculations in my head. There are thirteen adepts in here. I can feel the Enemy Within prowling back and forth behind my eyes. I have struggled against him since I left all this behind: the part of me that delights in bloodshed and pain. Trying to become something more than I was raised to be.

I'na Sai'nuit.

But he can feel the building tension in my muscles now, rattling the bars of his cage, twisting my hands ever closer to fists.

Break them, Kaliis, he whispers.

Kill them.

But beneath my armor, I am already wounded. And even at my best, I could never defeat this many. I push the Enemy back.

"Adept," the warden repeats. "What is your business here?"

"Prisoner delivery," I explain, nodding to Zila. "We captured this one crawling about in the air ducts."

The warden blinks at Zila. "I was not notified."

I give a cool shrug. My ribs sigh in protest.

"If you wish, I can release her back into the ventilation system?"

The adept meets my eyes, radiating challenge. I match his gaze. Unafraid. Unimpressed. This is the way among Warbreed. Testing always. The strong survive. The weak die. Fear has no place among those born for war.

Finally, he points. "Put her with the other Terran vermin."

I nod assent. Zila and I march across the detention area floor, my boots ringing on the metal. One of the sentinels outside Scarlett and Finian's cell deactivates the glowing punishment field, unlocks the door. Zila steps inside, head bowed. Scarlett gives her a quick hug, and she tenses but does not pull away.

"Pig," Scarlett spits at me, helping with my subterfuge. "I hope you rot."

"Silence your tongue, Terran scum," I reply in Syldrathi.

"What is your name, adept?" comes a voice behind me.

I turn slowly, look at the warden. He is peering at the ident number stenciled on my stolen armor, consulting the computer terminal behind his station. In a crew this large, on a ship this big, it is possible for people to be mere acquaintances. But a complete stranger is unlikely. And as I said, these Unbroken are not fools.

"My name?" I repeat, hand sliding toward the disruptor rifle on my shoulder.

"According to the duty logs, you should be stationed in the inf—"

"RED ALERT," comes the sudden call. "RED ALERT.

222

Terran Defense Force vessels on intercept course. All hands, battle stations."

I blink as the announcement spills over the PA system, as the lighting drops to a deeper shade of gray, as the Syldrathi in the room share a baffled glance.

Terrans?

Attacking the Andarael?

The alarm continues to blare. The sound of the engines shifts deeper. But I can read the look on the faces of the Unbroken around me, mirroring my own heart. This is impossible. No TDF fleet would dare attack an Unbroken ship. It would m—

"Red alert. Terrans have acquired weapons lock. Fighters inbound. All hands to battle stations immediately. This is not a drill."

Despite their confusion, Saedii's crew is well trained. The sentinels break into action, some talking into comms units, others drawing weapons. Two march off immediately toward the launch bays. Several others gather around the warden's desk, looking in cold disbelief at his displays. I can see six Terran vessels inbound on our position. Four destroyers. Two heavy carriers, bristling with fighter wings.

A force like that could tackle even a ship as imposing as *Andarael.*

If they dared attack her . . .

They might actually defeat her.

From the corner of my eye, I see Zila slip a uniglass from inside her sleeve and pass it to Finian. Our Gearhead turns away from the door, unnoticed amid the sudden clamor, and works feverishly on the small, glowing screen.

I see Zila's hand sliding beneath her tunic to her hidden disruptor pistol.

I steal up to the closest sentinel.

"RED ALERT," the PA calls. "RED ALERT. MISSILES IN-BOUND. DECOYS ENGAGED. ALL HANDS, BRACE. FIGHTER WINGS, LAUNCH."

Finian meets my eyes and nods. The *Andarael* shifts beneath us as the helm engages in evasive maneuvers. I hear the thunder of her engines, the dull *thudthudthud* as her pulse weapons open up. The Enemy Within surges against the prison of my ribs, longing for bloodshed. He wants to be out there with his brothers and sisters, wading through the black and the red, reveling in the taste of salt and smoke, dancing the dance of blood.

But we can dance in here well enough.

I unsling my disruptor rifle and unload four shots into the heads of the sentinels closest to me.

Finian's fingers blur on his uniglass, and the punishment field around their cell finally drops.

Zila surges out the door, firing rapidly and taking another sentinel down with a shot to the spine.

I toss my rifle to Scarlett, draw the blades from my back. She catches the weapon and the air is filled with disruptor fire: Scarlett's haphazard blasting, Zila's more refined bursts.

The adepts are caught flat-footed, some scattering for cover, others turning toward me, and then I am weaving, slicing, swaying, as the deck rolls beneath me, as the alarms continue to sing, as the thing I do not wish to be roars to my surface. I can feel my father's hand on my arm, guiding my strikes as he trains Saedii and me in the days before our family collapsed, before our world perished.

Another warrior falls beneath my blades. I taste blood on my tongue. A disruptor shot strikes me in the shoulder and one of my blades sails free from my open hand. A shot from Zila stops the follow-through and I strike back despite my pain, slicing into my foe's throat, fountains of dark gore painting the ceiling, the walls, my hands, and my face.

Show them who you are, Kaliis.

Show them what you are.

I am nothing then. No thought. Just motion. Lost in the moment, the hymn, the hypnotic, dizzying dance of blood. And when the music is brought to a sudden halt, when a bone-jarring impact to the *Andarael's* hull drags me out of the trance, I look around and see what I have wrought.

Nine bodies. Nine men and women, once alive and breathing and now nothing but cooling meat. I feel elation. Revulsion. Feel the pounding of my pulse in my ears and smell the stink of the blood on my hands.

This is who you are, Kaliis, the Enemy Within whispers.

You were born for war.

I'na Sai'nuit.

The Enemy retreats as the *Andarael* shudders, heavy impacts ringing on her hull as the alarms continue to scream. I look at Scarlett picking herself up off the deck, at Finian struggling to rise from where he fell. I can see the horror in their eyes at the carnage I have created. Zila is more pragmatic, but still, I can sense a shadow over her as she surveys the blood-slick floor, the bodies. I can feel the fear in them. Of what I am and what I do. But none of it truly matters.

Because it is all for her.

Aurora.

I take a passkey from a fallen sentinel, deactivate the

punishment field on her cell. She looks beautiful as ever, eyes closed in slumber, curls of black and white framing her fluttering eyelids.

As I unlock her restraints, Zila slips into the cell beside me. She takes a quick reading with her uniglass, peels off the dermal patch at my be'shmai's wrist. Producing the medical supplies she stole from the infirmary, she presses an air-hypodermic to Aurora's throat.

"She is heavily sedated," Zila reports. "It will take her some ti—"

"I will carry her," I say, sweeping her up into my arms. "We must move."

"Your shoulder," Zila objects. "You are w—"

"I am well," I say, striding out of the cell. "We must go. Now."

"What's the plan?" Scarlett asks.

Another impact rocks the *Andarael,* then another. I glance to the warden's terminal, see images of the Fold outside. The colorscape is black and white, but the waters are still red. Three of the Terran destroyers have been incinerated, and one of their carriers is incapacitated. The Unbroken are fighting fearlessly. Brilliantly. But still, the battle is going badly for *Andarael.* The void is swarming with fighters—the snub-nosed, bulldog shapes of Terran mustangs and the bladelike silhouettes of Syldrathi corvettes—weaving in and out of the swelling firestorm. *Andarael's* defense grid has been smashed; Terran missiles are now pummeling her hull. Another impact rocks us, sparks bursting from the instrumentation, alarms screaming.

"Breaching pods en route from Terran carrier," the PA calls. "All hands, prepare to repel boarders."

"They are coming for Aurora . . . ," I murmur.

"Who are you?" a voice demands.

I turn, see a tall Waywalker staring at me from within one of the holding cells, surrounded by thin and wasted compatriots. The silver of his hair is faded with age, thin lines etched in the skin around his mouth. He is an elder, perhaps two hundred years behind his eyes. He would have lived the glory before our fall. Before the rise of the Starslayer. Before we abandoned honor and began tearing at each other like starving talaeni over scraps.

He glances at the Warbreed glyf on my brow, at the carnage I have wrought among the Unbroken, clearly confused. I can feel his mind skimming the surface of mine, trying to ponder my riddle.

"I am no one of consequence," I reply.

Turning to Finian, I nod to the dead bodies.

"Get yourself a weapon, Finian de Seel. We must go."

Scarlett frowns, glances at the imprisoned Waywalkers. "You can't just leave these people here?"

"We cannot bring them with us," I say, marching across the block. "There is no room aboard the *Zero*. And there is no time to argue. Come."

Zila nods, already hovering by the exit, a disruptor rifle in her arms. "It would be an unacceptable delay. And a mass escape will draw attention to our own."

"They might cause confusion," Scarlett counters, glancing at the nearest cell. "They might help. We can't just *abandon* them. Can't you feel their pain?"

A slight frown mars Zila's brow, and she turns to look at our Face. "Scarlett, our single and most important objective is to support Aurora in preventing the hatching of the Ra'haam planets throughout the Milky Way. Any price we or others pay for the success of that mission is acceptable."

"Every second we argue is another wasted," I say, growing desperate.

"We have a little time?" Finian asks. "Zila already got the Hephaestus data and our uniglasses back."

"I have them all with me," Zila says, patting her pocket.

"YES, I'M HERE, I'M HERE, NOBODY PANIC!" comes a small, muffled voice.

"Silent mode," Zila says.

"We must rescue your brother and get off this ship, Scarlett," I say.

"My *brother* would be the first person to break these people out," Scarlett says. "Don't you dare use him as an excuse for abandoning them."

She marches across the room and begins rummaging around in the uniform of the dead warden. Another blast rocks the *Andarael*. In my arms, Aurora frowns in her slumber. The wound at my shoulder is a slow and bloody agony. The lights are flashing white to gray, the alarms almost deafening.

"BREACH ON DECKS 17 AND 12," the PA calls. "SECURITY AND ALL AVAILABLE HANDS TO 17 AND 12."

"Scarlett, we have no time for this," Zila says.

The ship shudders again as Scarlett finally recovers a passkey. I can smell smoke now, fuel and char. My heart is thrashing, stomach turning as Scarlett moves from one cell to another, shuffling around the entire room and freeing a flood of confused, desperate Waywalkers into the block. *Andarael* bucks like a wild thing beneath our feet.

Aurora opens her eyes in my arms.

"Kal?" she whispers.

"All is well, be'shmai," I say, and in that moment, despite everything, it is true.

"Mothercustard," she groans. "I feel like someone chewed me up and spat me out. That sister of yours . . ." She blinks hard, looking around us at the smoke, the bodies, the fleeing Waywalkers. "What's h-happening?"

"We are leaving this place. Can you walk?"

"Scar, come *on*," Finian pleads.

Helping Aurora down onto the deck, I shout, "Scarlett, we must go!"

Scarlett kills the punishment field and opens the final cage. The elder and his companions stumble out into screaming, chaotic freedom.

"Gratitude, young Terran," he says.

"Get yourselves to the shuttle bays," she says. "Get the hells out of here."

He studies her for a long moment and then nods deeply, eyes closed, lacing together the fingers on both hands. Treating our Face to the mark of respect he would usually reserve for another Waywalker.

"If we can repay our debt to you," he says, dignified amid the chaos, "you will find us at Tiernan Station. I am Elder Raliin Kendare Aminath."

Scarlett takes time to offer a courteous nod in return, although now even she is clearly possessed by the urgent need to flee.

The Waywalkers gather a few weapons and make their break, out into the smoke and carnage. The ship rocks beneath us as the lights flicker and die, plunging us into sudden darkness. I hold Aurora tight to my chest, despite the ache.

"BREACH ON DECK 4," the PA calls. "SECURITY TO COMMAND AND CONTROL. ALL PERSONNEL EQUIP ENVIRO-SUITS IN EVENT OF ATMOSPHERE LOSS."

Emergency lighting kicks in, the five of us staring at each other in the gloom.

"That breach is near Saedii's chambers," I say. "Where Tyler will be."

"We have used too much time for a rescue attempt," Zila says flatly. "We must get to the docking bay. With the Zero's cloaking technology and the chaos unfolding outside, we may be able to slip away undetected."

"But . . ." Finian looks back and forth between us. "We can't leave Tyler!"

"We cannot risk taking Aurora closer to the TDF boarding parties," Zila says. "She is all that matters here."

Still bleary from the drugs, Aurora shakes her head, searches for focus. Seconds tick by, all of us silent. I realize suddenly how important Tyler is to our squad. We are leaderless without him—nobody to make the snap decision, the hard call, to shoulder the agonizing responsibility of putting others in danger.

"Auri," Fin says. "Can you use . . . I mean, your power or whatever?"

Her eyes widen at that. I can see the memory of the *Hadfield* shining in them. Her loss of control in the cryo section, the chaos and destruction she wrought. She could have killed us. We know it. She knows it. And her eyes are alight with the fear of what might happen if she loses control again.

"I . . ."

She looks at me, anguish in her stare.

"I don't think I can . . ."

"It is all right, be'shmai," I say, kissing her brow.

"I don't want to hurt anyone, I—"

"Get Auri to the *Zero*," Scarlett snaps, looking at me. "Zila's right—we can't risk her being caught by the TDF. If I'm not down there in ten minutes, you blast the hells out of that bay and don't look back."

"Where are you going?" Fin demands.

Scarlett strides across to an emergency supply locker near the warden's console, grabs a breather mask she finds inside. Hefting the disruptor rifle I gave her, she checks the power feed.

"I'm going to get Ty."

"Scarlett, that is unwise," Zila says.

"The halls will be crawling with adepts and TDF assault troops," I say.

She meets my eyes then. Fire burning in her own. "He's my *brother*, Kal."

Again I am struck by the tie between the Jones twins. How deep the bond between them is in comparison to the one I share with Saedii.

I remember we were close once. When we were children on Syldra, when our parents still loved one another, the two of us were inseparable. The blood between us is

more like water now. The memory of our mother, the spec-
ter of our father hanging ever between us. If I were in danger, I know she would leave me to rot, and a part of me
aches at that—more deeply than the wound at my shoulder,
than the bruises at my ribs, than the certainty that I cannot accompany Scarlett on her quest. That I cannot take
Aurora into danger.

"Scarlett," Aurora whispers, helpless tears in her eyes.
"I'm sorry . . . I . . ."

"I know," she nods. "Just go."

Finian grabs a breather and shoulders a stolen rifle. "Well,
I'm going with you."

Scarlett opens her mouth to object, but he cuts her off.

"Don't even *try* to argue," he says. "You're not going up
there alone, Scar."

Scarlett looks the thin boy up and down, hand propped
on her hip, lips twisting into a smirk. "Still suffering from
that bout of boneheaded heroics, huh?"

He shrugs. "Let's hope it's not a terminal case."

The ship lurches beneath us. Under the scream of the
alarms, we can hear the noise of distant disruptor fire. Cries
of pain. Shouted orders and twisting metal and roaring flame.
The taste of burning plastic hangs heavy in the air.

"Ten minutes," Zila warns. "Then we *must* leave without
you."

Scarlett nods. "Auri is the only thing that really matters.
Look after her, Kal."

"With my life," I vow.

"Be careful," Aurora pleads.

Without another word, Scarlett and Finian don their

enviro-masks and dash off into the growing chaos. I catch one final glimpse of them, side by side, before they disappear utterly into the smoke.

Knowing the danger they fly toward, I wonder if we will see either of them alive again.

SUBJECT: PEOPLE TO AVOID (UPDATED)

▶ TERRAN GOVERNMENT

   ▼ GLOBAL INTELLIGENCE AGENCY

THE HIGHEST ARM OF THE **TERRAN INTELLIGENCE DIVISION**, THE GIA IS RESPONSIBLE FOR SAFEGUARDING EARTH'S INTERESTS AND COMBATING SUBVERSIVE ENEMY FORCES, BOTH TERRESTRIAL AND INTERSTELLAR.

GIA AGENTS WEAR FULL BODY ARMOR AND HELMETS, MAKING IT IMPOSSIBLE TO IDENTIFY INDIVIDUAL AGENTS AND PERPETUATING THE NOTION THAT THE GIA IS ONE ENORMOUS, SPOOKY MANIFESTATION OF **TERRAN JUSTICE**. THEY ARE ABSOLUTELY NO FUN AT PARTIES.

[UPDATE]

SHOCKINGLY, EVERY GIA OPERATIVE UNMASKED BY SQUAD 312 HAS BEEN A FORMER COLONIST OF OCTAVIA III—EVEN THOUGH THOSE PEOPLE SHOULD HAVE DIED HUNDREDS OF YEARS AGO. MORE CHILLINGLY, EACH AGENT HAS ALSO BEEN INFECTED BY THE **RA'HAAM GESTALT**.

I KNOW—*CRAZY, RIGHT?*

15

TYLER

I *really* should have studied my Syldrathi more.

The bridge around me is in a sort of tightly controlled chaos. Syldrathi arrogance is legendary, and they typically make "aloof" an art form, but all of it—the arrogance, the cool, the *we are so much better than you* attitude—is currently being strained to breaking point. Some of these Unbroken are going so far as to *raise their voices,* so I know business is getting Serious. I can only understand every sixth word, but they're the important ones. Words like *depleted* and *destroyed.* Words like *unable* and *unresponsive.*

Words that mean *Andarael* is losing.

With no time to send me to the brig, and not willing to leave me in her chambers, Saedii had her personal guard drag me up to the bridge with her, shoving me into a corner to watch the fireworks. Truth is, I've never seen a battle of this scope play out live before, and the tactics nerd in me is awed by it. Studying the moves and countermoves, the holographic displays projected on every wall, glowing images of carriers and destroyers and fighter craft overlaid with Syldrathi script.

As incomprehensible as the text may be, I can still appreciate the battle unfolding around us. Much as I hate to admit it, Saedii is a brilliant commander. She stands in the center of the bridge, Isha on her shoulder, directing the battle like a maestro before her orchestra. She acts decisively, thinking quickly, reading the conflict perfectly. She gives orders without hesitation, and her crew obeys instantly—it's like watching the internal workings of some deadly machine.

The *Andarael* is an impressive ship, with twice the firepower of anything in the Terran armada. But she's outnumbered and outgunned here. The Unbroken Get Out of Jail Free card hasn't worked, and while she's destroyed three ships and critically wounded another, Saedii's counterattacks are failing in the face of superior numbers. No matter how clever a commander she might be, her only option now is to run. And that's something a Templar of the Unbroken is *never* going to do.

Another missile plows into our stern, shaking the *Andarael* in her bones. The TDF gunners are targeting our engines and guidance systems, trying to cripple us. Reports are coming in from the lower decks—the Terran boarding parties are breaking out from their beachheads, TDF marines in suits of power armor inexorably carving their way through the Unbroken defenders. The numbers are grim; every Syldrathi is killing at least five Terran soldiers before they fall, but the TDF just has more bodies to throw, and they're throwing everything they have.

It's an abattoir down there.

Part of me still can't comprehend that this is happening. The ramifications of an engagement like this—a full-blown slaughter between Terran and Unbroken troops—I don't even want to think about what it'll mean for the galaxy. . . .

The Unbroken on the bridge are all wearing breathers in the event of atmo loss, but nobody was nice enough to give me one. I can smell smoke in the air now, burning meat, charred polys. Another breach pod crashes into the lower decks, filled with yet more marines. I feel the impact through the floor, all the way up my spine. I'm not sure how much more of this *Andarael* can take.

And then Saedii's lieutenant speaks, his words bringing sudden stillness to the bridge. I only catch three of them. But again, they're the important ones.

Transmission.

Archon Caersan.

The name is like a punch to my gut. I tense, all thought of the battle gone from my head. Saedii turns from her tactical displays, speaks softly, and the central projection of the battle raging outside fades, replaced by another image.

The image of a man.

I'm honestly not sure what I was expecting. No matter what the storybooks say, monsters rarely look the part. I grew up hating this man for everything he took from me. But looking at the most infamous mass murderer in galactic history, the man responsible for the Orion Incursion, the destruction of his own homeworld, the death of my father, I was expecting something at least a *little* horrific.

The Starslayer is . . .

Maker, I don't know *what* he is. . . .

Stunning, maybe?

The Archon of the Unbroken is tall like all his people,

clad in an ornate suit of Syldrathi battle armor, fixed with a long dark cloak. The angles of his face are cruel, his cheek-bones high, his ears tapering to knife-sharp points. His long silver hair is swept up and over the Warbreed glyf at his brow in ten intricate braids, curving down to cover one side of his face. And that face is like something out of a simulation—too beautiful and terrible to be real. It's almost heartbreaking to think a surface so perfect could be so rotten underneath.

But it's his eye that strikes me the most. Here in the Fold I can't see the violet of his iris. But his stare is still piercing in intensity. I find myself pinned and helpless before it, as if he can actually see into my soul.

His mere presence onscreen brings quiet to the bridge, even in the midst of an all-out firefight. He radiates authority, gravity, fear, like a star radiates heat.

He speaks to Saedii, his voice dark as smoke and smooth as Larassian semptar. The transmission is coming from Maker knows where, so Saedii speaks quickly, spilling it all. I hear her say Aurora's name. Kal's name. *Attack* and *Terran* and *battle* and *can't*.

It'll take a good few minutes for her message to reach him across interstellar space, even through the shortened distances in the Fold. In the meantime, Saedii turns back to the battle raging outside. Damage reports are coming in from all over the ship. *Andarael*'s engines are now offline. Alert sirens are still blaring, the stink of smoke is getting stronger, the tactical displays are filled with the dance and fire patterns of the fighters still waging war outside.

Finally, I see the Starslayer's beautiful face twist—Saedii's reply has arrived at his end. His stare darkens and his lips draw into a tight, thin line. I see incredulity, quickly running through to fury and hatred—the kind of rage that could bring a man to rip his own homeworld apart. The kind of rage that murders billions.

"They *dare*?" he spits.

He opens his mouth to speak again, but we never get to hear the rest. Something hits the *Andarael*'s bridge hard, a bloom of white light and screaming fire, and suddenly I'm hurled sideways, smashing into the wall behind me as the entire world turns upside down. The explosion is blinding, pummeling, almost deafening, and for a brief moment I wonder if this is it. If this is the place I die.

I've followed the tenets of the United Faith, lived them as best I can; I should be at peace. But I don't want to go yet—there's too much to leave behind, too many people I care about, too much at stake. And so I hang on, grim, digging my fingernails in and refusing to let go. Screaming at that dark.

Not yet.

Not yet.

I open my eyes. I see twisted metal. Choke on black smoke.

The bridge has suffered a direct hit, the blast shredding the hull like tinfoil. The power is dead, the displays shot. Unbroken bodies lie where they've fallen, dead or dying, purple Syldrathi blood turned gray by the Fold and spattered over the floor. The guard who was watching me has been impaled on a twisted stanchion, eyes lifeless. Fires are burning among the computer systems. The deck slopes away to the left—the artificial gravity systems are still online, but engines are dead, and *Andarael* is now drifting, sideways and helpless in the dark.

I check to see if anything is broken, but though I'm gonna

be black and blue in a few hours (presuming I make it out of the Fold alive), a few deep gashes seem to be the worst of it. My ears are bleeding. Eyes burning in the fumes. I stagger to my feet with a groan, drag the breather mask off the dead guard's head and the disruptor pistol from his belt. All the Syldrathi on the bridge are on their backs or bellies, but through the crushed metal and rains of sparks, I can see that more than a few are moving, coming to after the explosion.

I need to get out of here.

I need to find Scar and the others.

But my chances of that are zero. I've studied Syldrathi capital ships, but I don't know their internal layouts as well as those of Terran vessels—I've only got the vaguest sense of where the hangar bays are, let alone the detention levels. And even if the lower decks weren't crawling with Terran marines, there's still the Unbroken to deal with. I've got no edge here, no . . .

Leverage.

I hear a reptilian screech, spot Isha through the smoke, wings spread, shrieking her distress. The little drakkan is perched on a collapsed section of the ceiling, and beneath it, on her back, I see Saedii. Her legs are pinned, her teeth bared in a snarl. She's trying to claw her way free, but she's got no way to get out from under the weight.

The temperfoam floors and instrumentation are ablaze, alarms screaming. The fire-suppression systems must be offline, and the flames are spreading toward Saedii. She curses, punching the metal in frustration. Isha shrieks again, little claws scrabbling on the wreckage in a desperate attempt to get her mistress free.

I stagger across the burning bridge, down the sloping floor. Saedii looks up as I loom over her, the momentary relief on her face overshadowed as she realizes I'm not one of her crew come to rescue her.

Isha screeches warning as I set my disruptor to Kill and level it at Saedii's face. The Templar meets my eyes.

Unafraid.

Unbroken.

"Do it," she spits. "Terran coward."

I swivel the pistol, blast the collapsed metal, partially melting it. Bending down, I grab hold and lift the weight, my face reddening with the strain. Saedii winces, pushes, manages to drag herself out from under the wreckage. As she wriggles free, I can see blood soaking her uniform pants a darker shade of black. She collapses, her face drawn and damp with sweat. She keeps most of it from her expression, but I can still see the pain in her eyes.

"Why?" she whispers, looking up at me. "Why save me?"

"I'm not saving you," I say.

I lean down, sling her arm around my shoulder, and drag her up. She gasps with pain but straightens, teeth gritted, face smudged with blood.

"I'm saving my friends."

I should leave her here. Let her burn with the rest of these murderers. But if I have Saedii in hand, I have someone who can direct me through the ship, avoid the incoming Terrans. I have the leverage I need to keep the other Unbroken off my back. And much as they seem to despise each other, I'm not sure Kal would appreciate me letting his sister burn to death up here.

"Which way to the detention levels?" I ask.

She spits in my face, uttering a vicious curse in Syldrathi. I kick her in her injured leg and she actually cries out at the agony—the first sign of weakness I've ever seen her show. I shove my disruptor up under her chin, still set to Kill.

"*Don't* do that again," I say.

"Or what?"

Leaning in close, I meet her stare with mine. Just as hard. Just as determined.

"Or I pay you back for what your people did to my father," I snap. "Now tell me the way to the detention levels."

She stares back at me, eyes like ice. I press the pistol up under her chin hard enough to make her wince. Finally she nods to the bridge doors, and I'm moving, half carrying, half dragging her out of the growing blaze and into the corridor beyond. Isha follows, fluttering from one perch to another and shrieking in distress.

"Shut her up," I say. "She'll bring the entire TDF down on our heads."

"Coward." Saedii aims the word at me like a weapon.

I press the pistol harder into her skin. "Which way?"

She nods again, teeth bared, eyes glittering with hate. And so we go. Slow. Staggering. Groping our way forward through the thickening smoke, the wailing alarms. A squad of Unbroken stumbles across us as we reach an auxiliary stairwell, their leader crying out for me to halt. But as they raise their weapons, a platoon of TDF marines bursts through a stairwell behind them. The air is filled with disruptor fire, the ring of blades, the screams of the dying.

I drag Saedii into the stairwell. The TDF troopers roar

at us to halt over the thunder of the firefight, the rumble of another missile strike. We stumble downward, Isha circling behind, Saedii almost falling. My breath is burning in my lungs even through the breather, the smoke filling the well and making it almost impossible to see. We burst out onto a lower level, scorching heat, thicker smoke.

"Which way?" I shout.

Kal's sister grimaces and nods, and we stumble on. *Andarael* is listing hard, the floors sloping almost forty-five degrees. Saedii is bleeding badly, bloody footprints on the floors behind us. Her injury is probably the only reason she hasn't tried to overpower me yet, but I'm not sure how much longer she can stay on her feet. I don't have the time to spare, but if she collapses here . . .

I set her down against the wall, her eyelashes fluttering against her cheeks. Isha lands on a nearby perch, screams at me, sharp little fangs glinting in the flickering light. Looking Saedii over, I see her pants are now sodden with blood, her boots full of it. Something important got cut or crushed under that wreckage. I rip off my shirt, tear it into strips as the alerts scream across the PA. Saedii winces as I wrap the fabric around her wounded thigh to stanch the bleeding.

"Weakling," she whispers.

"Yeah, yeah," I say, tying off my makeshift tourniquet.

"Wretch."

"Shut up," I sigh, slinging her arm around my shoulder and standing again. "Before I forget my manners."

I hear heavy boots coming down the stairwell behind us. A lone Syldrathi stumbles along the smoke-filled corridor ahead, her eyes widening as she recognizes her Templar hanging limp in the arms of a shirtless Terran boy. She raises her weapon, but mine's already up, and with a *BAMF!* she drops to the deck.

I struggle on with Saedii hanging off my shoulder, moving fast as I can. We reach a junction and I demand to know the way. Saedii mumbles a reply. Those marines have gotta be right on my heels—there's no way I can fight them off if they catch us, and there's nowhere I can hide. I'm quickly realizing that if we're going to make it out of this, we need something awful close to a miracle.

And then I see her.

Down at the end of the corridor, charging through the smoke, disruptor rifle in her arms. Flame-red hair, big eyes as blue as mine, all of it bleached gray by the Fold. Around the edges of her enviro-mask, her face is smeared with soot and grime and blood. But I've never seen her look as beautiful as she does right then.

"Scarlett," I whisper.

Finian is beside her, crouched low. He spots me first, crying out over the alarms, the fire, the alerts.

"There he is!"

Shuffling, stumbling, dragging Saedii onward, I feel an idiot grin break out on my face. Scarlett bolts down the corridor toward me. My miracle, just as ordered.

And that's when something hits us.

It's not big enough to be a missile. A chunk of debris, maybe, or a fighter plowing out of control into the *Andarael*'s flank. The strike hits the floor above us, buckling the hull. The impact is like thunder, throwing Saedii and me into the wall. I hit with a gasp, she crashes into me, and then we're both tumbling to the deck, my disruptor skittering from my hands. Unconsciousness beckons, offering me warmth and dark and quiet, and I shove back at it, blood in my mouth.

I open my eyes. Alarms are screaming about an atmo breach, and beneath them I can hear the deadly hiss of gas escaping into space. Heart sinking, I see the corridor ahead has buckled—the ceiling has collapsed, the sundered electrical cables spewing live current. Beyond the wreckage, I glimpse Finian on his knees. My sister dragging herself to her feet.

"Scarlett!" I roar. "Are you all right?"

"Yeah," she coughs. "You?"

"I'm okay," I shout.

"Do I even wanna ask why you're shirtless right now?"

"Abs like these yearn to be free, Scar."

She laughs at the joke, but through the wreckage, I can see the smile die on her lips almost instantly. The corridor is impassable—we can't get to each other without a cutting torch or explosives. Atmo is leaking from the hull, and while we're all wearing enviro-gear, if the *Andarael*'s triage systems are still online, the ship will seal this corridor off to prevent further loss of oxygen throughout the ship.

"You need to get out of here, Scarlett," I call.

"Shut up, Tyler," she says. "Finian, help me with this."

She starts tugging at the wreckage, trying to pry the gap wide enough to let me through. The severed cables spark and spit as Finian leans against the metal, exosuit whining as he puts his back into it.

"Scar, you're not going to be able to—"

"I'm not leaving you!" she shouts. "Now shut up!"

245

My heart twists at the tone in her voice. The tears in her eyes. Because as much as she might pretend to be, my sister isn't simple. She knows the math here.

And then I hear heavy boots behind me. The sound of disruptor rifles powering up. A voice, thick with reverb, speaking Terran.

"Hands in the air!"

I turn, see the platoon of TDF marines. Their power armor is big, bulky, graceless, decorated with the kind of graffiti grunts use to fill the time in between engagements. EAT THIS. WAR IS HELL. The lieutenant has MAN-EATER stenciled across her breastplate. The eyes in their helmets are aglow, servos whining as the laser sights on their rifles light up my chest.

A dozen of them. One of me.

Bad odds, even on the best days. And this is pretty far from that.

"Get out of here, Scar," I say quietly.

"Tyler—"

"Auri is all that matters."

"On your knees, Legionnaire Jones!" the man-eater bellows. "Slow!"

They know my name. Briefed by Princeps to bring us in alive, I'm betting. Aurora most of all. I raise my hands, sink to the floor. Saedii curses and tries to rise, but a Stun blast knocks her back down. Isha shrieks and bares her teeth, launches herself at the marines. A dozen Kill shots ring out in the corridor, and the little drakkan crashes to the deck in a splash of dark blood.

"NO!" Saedii screams, trying to rise again.

Another handful of Stun blasts ring out—

BAMF!

BAMF!

BAMF!

—and the Unbroken Templar sinks down, silent and still.

I glance over my shoulder, see my twin's face through the wreckage, tears streaming down her cheeks. I can hear Dad's voice in my head. Feel his hands ruffling my hair that way I hated, hear him speaking to me that way I loved. Like he was saying something Important. And I was worthy of it.

Look after your sister.

"Show the way, Scarlett."

"Tyler . . . ," she whispers.

"I said that you could find yourself doing this without me one day, remember?" I glance to the boy beside her, his face bleached a paler shade of white. "Look after her for me, Fin. That's an *order.*"

". . . Yessir," he nods. Taking gentle hold of Scarlett's arm, he speaks to her softly. "We have to go."

"No," she says, shaking her head. *"No."*

"Scar, I'm sorry, we have to *go!*" Finian cries.

I feel metal hands grab me and push me to the deck, mag-restraints clap around my wrists. The marines force my face into the floor, so I don't have to see the look on hers as her heart breaks. But I hear her sobs as my twin finally lets Finian drag her away from the only family she has left.

"I love you, Scar!"

A disruptor rifle hums. A finger tightens on a trigger.

BAMF!

And darkness comes down like a hammer.

16

SCARLETT

The race back to the *Zero* is a blur. My eyes sting with sweat and tears. The whole ship is listing badly, the deck sloping away between us as Finian and I stumble through the smoke and carnage, toward the docking bay. The lighting is flickering, failing—even the *Andarael*'s emergency power systems are struggling now. The corridors are strewn with Terran and Syldrathi corpses, their blood sticky beneath our feet. This ship has become a slaughterhouse. And if we don't get off it soon, we're going to be dead at best, or back in the hands of the GIA at worst.

I think of Tyler, my heart aching so hard I almost fall. For a moment, Finian is the only thing keeping me going, his arm around my shoulder, dragging me on through the swirling gray, the raining sparks, the howling alarms. I feel like I've betrayed Ty somehow. Like I've left the most important part of myself behind. But then I hear my brother's voice inside my head, see his eyes as he spoke to me.

Show the way, Scarlett.

That's what all good leaders do, according to the late, great Jericho Jones:

Know the way.
Show the way.
Go the way.

Those are the words Ty has always lived by. The reason he's spent his whole life looking after me and everyone around him. The torch he's carried since Dad died. I know he's passed it to me because he can't carry it himself anymore. He's trusting me with it. Relying on *me* to see the rest of us through this.

Show the way.

So I stand taller, ease out of Finian's hold, clutching the disruptor rifle to my chest. The enviro-mask is still fixed over my face, so I can't wipe away my tears. But I can push them back. Lock them away for another time, another place, where the fate of the entire damn galaxy doesn't hang in the balance.

"You okay?" Fin asks me.

I sniff hard, swallow harder. Tap the screen of my uniglass.

"Kal, can you hear me?"

"Affirmative, Scarlett," comes the ever-cool reply. *"What is your location?"*

"We're on our way to the *Zero*, can you hold position?"

"Not for long. You must be swift."

"Tell Zila to heat the engines, prep for launch. If we're not down there in five minutes, or it looks like Auri is in danger, you get the hells out, understand?"

"Understood. What is Tyler's status?"

I breathe deep. Push it all down into the soles of my feet.

"Tell Zila I hope she's as good at flying a starship as she is at piloting a van."

". . . Acknowledged," comes Kal's soft reply.

I tap the screen to cut transmission, meet Finian's eyes. "Let's move."

We dodge at least four firefights on our way downward, ducking into stairwells or circling back or just making a mad dash away from them. The Terran marines and Unbroken warriors are still cutting each other to pieces all over the ship, but it's only a matter of time before the TDF wins through. Those marines called Ty by name—they know who we are, and I know what they're here for. We need to get Auri out of here or all this has been for nothing.

We dash past a turbolift shaft, and Finian drags me to a sudden halt.

"Hold up," he says, popping a multi-tool from his exosuit's arm. He goes to work on the controls, prying the panel off the wall. The lighting flickers again, dropping us into blackness before struggling to life once more.

"Emergency power's almost dead," I say. "We can't ride that down."

He looks up from his work and winks. "Who said anything about riding?"

I hear the clunk of a lock, the sound of grinding metal. Fin pushes his silver-clad fingers into the gap between the doors, and slowly, exo whining with the strain, he pries them apart. The doors open out into nothingness—just an empty shaft running the entire depth of the massive ship. He taps a control on his suit, and globes in his fingertips light up, cutting a bright swath through the gloom.

"We supposed to fly down?" I ask. "I left my broomstick in my other pants."

Fin blinks. "Either broomsticks aren't what I think they are, or you're being Scarcastic with me again."

250

"How the hells are we going to get down, Fin?" I demand, my temper getting the better of me. "It's a hundred-meter drop and there's no power to drive the lift. Even the emergency systems are failing!"

"And what happens when the emergency systems fail, Scar?"

"We all suffocate and die?"

"Well . . . yeah, that's actually a good point. But before that?"

"I have no idea!" I cry, flailing. "I spent my only class on enviro systems making out in the back row of the lecture theater!"

(Jorge Trent. Ex-boyfriend #24. Pros: Adores musicals. Amazing dresser. Calls his mother three times a day. Cons: You see where this is going, don't you?)

Finian taps his temple with his forefinger and smiles.

"Watch and learn."

We wait in the corridor a few moments more, listening to the clamor of distant firefights, the heavy tread of approaching boots. The overheads are flickering in time with my heartbeat, every second we waste is another closer to capture or execution, and I can't believe we're just standing here waiting for—

The *Andarael's* emergency system coughs its dying breath.

The power finally stutters and dies.

And along with it, of course, goes the artificial gravity.

It takes me a moment to realize. But then, by the light of Finian's glowing fingertips, I see strands of my hair sent floating with the slightest movement of my head. The sickening feeling of vertigo I always get shifting into low grav comes over me, the sensation of my insides lifting up and floating free inside my body. Suppressing the urge to puke into my enviro-mask, I manage a smile.

"You're an insufferable smart-ass most days, Finian de Seel," I sigh. "But you *do* have your moments."

Finian gives an experimental kick, lifting himself off the ground before arresting his momentum with one hand against the elevator door. He pushes himself inside, moving like a fish underwater, grinning and offering his hand.

"Milady?"

I grab hold, his actuator-assisted fingers gripping mine ever so gently. And with that, Fin kicks off the wall and sends us soaring downward, flying along the shaft, one hand holding mine, the other held out before us to light the way. My hair billows around my face like clouds, and I feel like I'm falling and flying all at once and for just a moment I forget where and who I am.

But not who I'm with?

And I glance at Fin out of the corner of my eyes and . . .

I hear the *thudthudthud* of a heavy gun somewhere below, smell fire in the rapidly thinning air. We reach the lower levels of the shaft and Fin slows our flight with taps of his hands against the wall, finally pulling us to a complete stop outside the docking bay doors. Then he's at work with his multi-tool again, prying apart a manual release, clever fingers moving quick as the lock clunks and the doors part just a tiny crack.

Peering out into the dark of the bay, we quickly discover what's making all the racket—someone's at *Zero*'s controls, blasting away with its railgun at a squad of Terran marines on the other side of the docking bay. They're returning fire with their disruptors, their shots lighting up the dark—they're not enough to pierce the *Zero*'s hull, but it's only a matter of time before they bring in something heavier.

"Idiots," I growl. "I told them to take off if trouble found them."

"I'm sure Zila is reminding them of that *right* now," Fin says. "We better move."

"Sneak across in the dark?" I suggest.

"Those marines will have thermographic vision in their helmets," Finian says. "Hopefully they're too busy avoiding getting shot to be looking out for us. But I grew up in zero grav. I can get us there."

I tap my uni. "Kal, this is Scar. Me and Fin are in one of the access elevators on your starboard side."

"Um," Finian murmurs. "Port side, Scar."

"For the love of . . . ," I mutter. "Elevators on your left side, Kal. *Left* side. Lay down as much firepower as you can and open the rear hatch. Be ready to launch."

"Acknowledged," comes Kal's reply.

The *Zero* opens up with another long, continuous burst, cutting a swath through the walls and cargo. The TDF marines are hunkered behind cover, but if their heads are down, chances are they won't see us.

Finian grabs my hand and together we kick off the floor, sail up and out into the bay. I can see it spread out below us as we soar upward, lit only by a few rogue fires and the strobing bursts from the *Zero*'s forward guns.

"Hold on to me," Fin whispers.

I wrap my arms tight around Fin's waist, clinging on for dear life. We hit the roof and Fin rolls with our momentum, pirouettes in midair, and sends us sailing back down toward the *Zero* on the bounce. It's an amazing stunt. Breathtaking, really. Fin's movement is normally so considered, so labored lately. But up here, sailing through this flashing black and white free of gravity, he's totally at home.

We soar down from the ceiling, Fin reaching out to grab a stanchion and swing us around, releasing his grip and sending us sailing in a perfect arc toward the *Zero*'s rear hatchway. I hear one of the marines shout and their disruptor rifles open up, and I hold tighter, wishing I was religious enough to start praying. But though I don't have an ounce of faith, finally, finally, we hit the *Zero*'s rear landing, and with one last kick we sail inside.

"Okay, punch it, Zila! Go! *GO!*"

The hatchway cycles closed, and with a dull roar, we're lifting off. Fin and I are slammed into the wall as we swing around, the *Zero*'s artificial gravity kicking in, and I grab desperately for something to hold on to as Kal unloads into the *Andarael*'s docking bay doors. A deafening explosion rips across the bay and I feel the heat through the closing doors. And then we're rocketing free, out into the firestorm, a debris field of ruined fighters and burning hulks, a long stream of reactor exhaust spilling from the *Andarael*'s wounded side and into the cold black of the Fold.

"*Engines to full,*" says Zila over comms. "*This will be bumpy.*"

I dash out of the bay and up the corridor, Finian coming hot on my heels as the *Zero* shakes around us. By the time we arrive on the bridge, we're breathless. I see Zila in the pilot's chair, Kal on the weapons station. Auri flies out of her seat and wraps her arms around me, around Fin, tears shining in her eyes.

"Scar, are you okay?" she breathes. "Are you—"

"Please resume your seats," Zila says, sounding a little miffed. "We have Terran fighters inbound."

Presumably those marines in *Andarael's* hangar bay have given some kind of warning about our takeoff; our scopes are showing a pack of bulldog-nosed Terran fighters scrambling to intercept us. But as Auri, Fin, and I grab chairs and strap ourselves in, I see there's still some fight left in Saedii's dragoons. A posse of sleek Syldrathi corvettes is moving to intercept the Terrans, chasing them through the tumbling wreckage, missiles and cannon fire lighting the dark and incidentally giving us the few precious minutes we need to make our escape.

"Stealth field engaged," Kal reports. "We should be hidden from their radar now. We only need to get out of their line of sight."

"Leave that to me," Zila murmurs.

She looks up at Shamrock, still perched above the pilot's station. Reaching out, she touches the fuzzy green dragon, as if for luck.

"Everybody hold on," she says.

Our thrusters roar.

And we're away.

. . . . .

Turns out Zila *can* fly as well as she drives. She's no Cat, no Zero, nowhere close, but apparently all those nights alone in her room, bereft of friends, she had more than enough time to study theory and practice simulations. It's a wild ride, though—she definitely leaned heavier on the *theory* than the *practice*.

The Terran fighters pursuing us didn't have the range to keep up with the *Zero,* and every capital ship in that attack fleet had suffered major damage by the time *Andarael*'s guns fell silent. Though it was a defeat, one Syldrathi warship fought six Terran vessels and gave every one of them a bloody nose or a broken neck. I can't imagine what a war between us is going to mean. My dad fought half his life to build the peace between our peoples.

And now everything is in flames. . . .

We've dropped out of the Fold near a no-name star, way out in a neutral zone. This system is only notable for the naturally occurring FoldGate leading to it—according to logs and scopes, there's no settlements here, no mining ops, nothing. It'll be a good place to lay low while we figure out what the hells we're gonna do now.

"So what the hells are we gonna do now?" Finian asks.

Zila has locked us into orbit around the system's first planet—an Earth-sized rock fried to a cinder by the white dwarf it's circling. She's taken her place with the rest of us, sitting around our bridge consoles and looking into each other's eyes. Kal and Auri sit together, bloodstained fingers entwined. Fin sits opposite with me, his uniglass plugged into his terminal, the surface aglow with scrolling reams of data. Zila is at the head of the console where Ty used to sit.

Where Ty used to sit . . .

"We have to go back, right?" Auri says, looking back and forth between us. "We can't just leave Tyler in the hands of the GIA."

256

"That is exactly what we must do," Zila says.

"But this is my fault!" Auri says. "They wanted me, not him. This is on *me*!"

"No," Kal sighs. "Saedii was chasing me. If not for her interference, the GIA would never have caught up to us. This is *my* fault. All of it. I am shamed. De'sai."

"Listen," Fin says, glancing up from his data streams. "I know I'm not usually Mr. Sunshine, but I'm not sure we should be pointing fingers at ourselves here."

"Agreed," I nod. "This is no one's fault. You didn't ask to become what you are, Auri. And Kal, you can't help it if your sister is, and I mean no offense here, a murder-faced psycho bitch-machine."

Kal smiles faintly, but I see hurt twinkling in the violet of his eyes.

"She was not always so," he murmurs.

I breathe deep, chewing my lip and running over the events of the last day in my head. It seems like we've got the whole galaxy chasing after us. We can't rely on anyone for help out here. We're still wanted galactic terrorists. And I can't say my time in Unbroken captivity has endeared me to the thought of life in a penal colony.

"Those Waywalkers Saedii captured," I murmur, thinking back to the cells on *Andarael*. "Why would Warbreed be rounding up Syldrathi empaths, Kal?"

He shakes his head. "I do not know."

"Saedii seemed to take a real interest in Auri once she saw a display of her power," I say. "She made specific mention of transporting her back to the Starslayer." I meet Auri's eyes. "What would Caersan want with you?"

"This is all utterly irrelevant," Zila snaps.

I blink at our Brain, a little taken aback. Normally Zila speaks in monotone, her mannerisms closer to a cardboard box than a human. But she actually seems . . .

Testy?

". . . Are you feeling okay?" I ask.

"Tyler, Saedii, the Starslayer, none of it matters," she says, looking at each of us in turn. "We cannot stray from our path. The stakes we are playing with here are unfathomable. We must find the Eshvaren Weapon. The Ra'haam must be stopped. Every other consideration *must* be secondary."

Fin clears his throat. "Zila . . ."

"All of this is happening for a reason," she says. "We must go forward. The message from Adams and de Stoy, this ship, the cigarillo case that saved Kal's life, all of this is unfolding as it was supposed to. The only way out is through."

Kal touches his chest where the disruptor blast hit him, as if remembering the shot that almost killed him. Auri squeezes his hand, concern in her eyes.

"Don't you dare do anything like that again, okay? *Listen* to me next time."

"I will, be'shmai," he replies. "I swear it."

Fin is looking at the pair, at Kal, a strange expression on his face. I nod to the uniglass he has plugged into his terminal.

"So, does the data from the *Hadfield* tell us anything?"

"Gimme a second," he replies. "I'm looking for unusual readings or anomalies in the logs, but there's a lot to wade through here."

An uneasy silence falls, broken only by the pulse of our LADAR sweeps, the tapping of Finian's metal-tipped fingers on his screens. I look at Auri and I can tell she's still torn up. Thinking this is her fault. Feeling guilty about leaving Ty behind, about her loss of control on the *Hadfield,* about losing her nerve on the *Andarael.* I know she's trying, but this power of hers . . . she has to learn how to control it. And I'm wondering how she's going to manage that if she won't even acknowledge it.

"When the Unbroken had me sedated . . . ," she begins.

Her voice falters and Kal squeezes her hand. She seems to draw strength from his touch, breathing deep before speaking again.

"I dreamed," she says, shaking her head. "I felt it. I *saw* it."

"The Ra'haam," Kal says.

Auri nods. "It's getting stronger. I can . . . sense it somehow. Like a splinter in the back of my mind. Every moment we spend out here is another moment it has to grow. In my dreams . . . I saw whole worlds covered in that blue pollen. I saw Earth. Other planets. All of them like Octavia III. Completely overrun." She shakes her head again. "It's close to hatching now. Blooming and bursting."

"How close?" I ask, my stomach turning cold somersaults.

"I don't know." She sighs, leans forward, elbows on her knees. "But *soon.*"

My stomach rolls again, and I think of Cat in her final moments. Imagine what it would be like, being consumed. Losing yourself to this thing the way she did. I imagine whole worlds being assimilated, annihilated, and for a moment I feel so small, so insignificant, I can barely breathe. I've already lost my best friend. Now I've lost my brother, too. Who else am I going to lose before this is over?

"Hold up . . . ," Finian murmurs.

Zila comes to attention, sitting up even straighter in her chair (if that's possible). "Finian? What have you found?"

He narrows his eyes, poring over the *Hadfield* data streams. "There's something strange here. Spatial anomaly. Massive power fluctuation in the *Hadfield*'s core. Critical bio-failure in most of its cryo systems. Its sensor arrays weren't that advanced, but these readings . . ." He looks up at me. "Yeah, something *really* weird happened aboard that ship."

"When?" Auri asks, her mismatched eyes growing wide. "Where?"

"Almost a hundred years ago." Fin whistles, tapping a handful of commands on his screen. "I've got approximate coordinates. It's about twenty hours through the Fold from our current location, if we put *Zero* on maximum burn."

They all look to me then. The tattered remnants of Aurora Legion Squad 312. Maybe because I'm a Jones. Hells, maybe because they've got no one else to look at. But I'm not cut out for this. I shouldn't be making these calls. Tyler should.

Who do I think I am?

Who do we think we are, going up against something this big alone?

Zila meets my eyes, her voice soft. "The only way out is through, Scarlett."

I breathe deep, nod slowly.

"Okay," I say, trying to keep my voice steady. "Fin, see what else you can make of those readings. Find out anything you can about what we're flying into. Kal, run a diagnostic on the *Zero*'s weapons systems and defenses, get us ready in case we hit more trouble. Zila, set us a course for those co-ordinates. Maximum burn."

The squad breaks into motion, probably grateful just to have a direction to follow. We have no idea what we're headed toward. What we'll find when we get there, assuming we find anything at all. But in the end, what choice do we have?

The only way out is through, Scarlett.

The only way out is through.

PART 3

A TIME TO BURN

AURORA LEGION
▶ AURORA ACADEMY
▼ FOUNDING

AURORA ACADEMY WAS FOUNDED IN 2214 BY THE **TERRAN** AND **BETRASKAN** GOVERNMENTS, AFTER THE SIGNING OF THE **TREATY OF NAIDU**.

THE FIRST ACADEMY PRINCIPALS—AND THE BRAINS BEHIND IT—WERE TERRAN **ADMIRAL NARI KIM**, AND BETRASKAN **GREATER CLAN BATTLE LEADER RAYA DE MONOKO DE SEEL**. NO OFFICIAL RECORDS EXPLAIN HOW THE PAIR BECAME PALS. GIVEN THE EFFORT BETRASKANS AND TERRANS HAD PUT INTO BLOWING EACH OTHER UP BEFORE SIGNING THE TREATY, IT MUST HAVE BEEN ONE HELLUVA PARTY.

THE **SYLDRATHI** JOINED THE AURORA LEGION AFTER THE **TREATY OF S'LATH MOR** IN THE YEAR 2378. IT WAS ONLY AFTER THEIR FIRST CADETS ARRIVED ON AURORA STATION THAT EVERYBODY REALIZED THE DOORFRAMES WERE FIVE CENTIMETERS SHORTER THAN THE AVERAGE SYLDRATHI HEIGHT.

AWKWARD.

17

FINIAN

I'm trying to concentrate on these calculations, and failing miserably. The data I'm pulling out of the *Hadfield*'s black box is like an endless stream of moving targets, all spinning and dancing around one another in an unpredictable game.

We're en route to the coordinates indicated by the original readings, where *something* caused the colony ship's systems to go haywire. The place, presumably, where something happened to Auri. The problem is that whatever caused it—if it was a physical object—will have drifted by now, so I need to account for that. The other problem is that an approximate location just isn't good enough. Space is *really* big, and "somewhere around here" doesn't cut it.

Kal's finished with his weapons check, and having set our course through the Fold, Zila has taken him to the infirmary, along with Auri to assist, or possibly just to tell him to stay still and not be such a baby while side-eyeing his abs (for this I cannot fault her). While I work, Scarlett's watching the monitors, alert for even the smallest hint we're being followed or flying into something dangerous. But truth be told, she's staring down at the screens like she can barely see them, lips pressed together hard, her breathing slow and deliberate as she tries to keep it together.

"You okay?" I murmur, knowing that it's a dumb thing to say. *I'm* not okay, and he wasn't—isn't, I mean—my twin brother.

She looks up, summons a weak smile. "Not really," she admits.

I nod because, well, fair enough. "We're not giving up on him," I tell her quietly. "You know the GIA's going to hold on to him. He's more useful to them—to Princeps—alive. Whether it's for information, or just as bait."

"I know," she agrees in a whisper. "But I still can't believe we left him. He was right there, and we ran away."

Her words echo in the silence between us, underscored by the soft hum of the *Zero's* systems. I know we're both thinking about the ship's namesake. About Cat, who was still right there when we ran too.

Scarlett swallows hard, tries to sit up a little straighter in her chair, and it breaks my heart to watch her like this.

"Okay," I say. "What's Tyler's most annoying habit?"

She blinks. "His what?"

"Work with me on this," I coax, summoning a smile I pray is a little stronger than hers. "What really drives you nuts about him?"

She considers the question. "He labels his stuff," she says, lips curving just a touch.

"Sorry, he what?"

"Puts his name on it. Has since we were kids. Everything. I never checked, but I'm pretty sure his underwear's got his name sewn in the back."

"What else?"

"He never seems to mind when you screw up," she says. "He's perfect, but when the rest of us aren't, he never looks at you like you could have, should have done better. It's like he makes allowances for everyone else to fail, but never for himself. He's so damn saintly about it."

I tilt my head, feeling the stretch in the stiff tendons of my neck. "And what form does this sainthood take?"

She flaps a hand. "You know. Pep talk. Patient expression. Tells you to keep trying."

I study her for a long moment. "Hey, Scar?"

"Mmm?"

"Keep trying."

She balls up her empty Strawberry Cake'n'Custard™ wrapper and tosses it at me, but she laughs. And she reaches out to curl her fingers around mine and squeeze, and my heart wants to break out through my chest.

"Thank you," she says quietly. "And thank you for going back for him with me. I won't forget that."

"Anytime," I tell her.

"Do you need me to be quiet so you can concentrate?"

"I do not, for I am outrageously clever, and I can multitask."

Her smile is tired and a little sad, but it's real. "All right, Superbrain. What do you think we're looking at?"

I squint at my screen. "Some sort of . . . wiggly, blobby confluence of space-time aberrations," I say, injecting as much authority into my tone as I can.

"So you have no idea."

"I have no idea," I agree. "But if it's something left behind by the Eshvaren, I'm not sure I would. I'll keep working on locking down the exact location. We've still got a while before we're close. In the meantime, is there any chance you'd sleep if you took a sedative? I can keep an eye on the monitors until Zila gets back, holler if anything crops up."

"We should all sleep," she frowns. Caretaker mode initiated.

"I'll take my turn, I promise," I say, raising my hand and waving around a couple of fingers like I've seen Terrans do when they make a promise. I can tell from her expression I'm doing it wrong.

"All right, all right." She pushes to her feet, stretching slowly. "I'll take something, head to bed."

"You need anyone to tuck you in?"

She just winks and saunters off toward her quarters, leaving me to my calculations. I'm still replaying the wink a little while later when Zila and Auri reappear.

"How's the patient?" I ask.

"I have tended Kal's wounds," Zila reports. "They are painful but will heal cleanly. He has agreed to Aurora's suggestion that he should wash off the copious amounts of blood he is . . . covered in, and then attempt to sleep."

"Scar's trying for some downtime as well," I report. "And radar's clean."

"Then we should check news sources for information on the battle," Zila replies, sliding into her seat and pulling up the displays on the central monitor.

The news is grim.

Reports are filtering in through civilian channels—all we can access—about the clash between the Unbroken and the TDF. There are conflicting accounts of who fired first, casualty numbers, and even the exact location of the battle, but on one thing they all agree: a massive Unbroken fleet is mobilizing and heading toward Terran space. The galaxy is holding its breath, waiting to see what happens next.

Zila's expression is as unreadable as ever.

Auri looks like she's going to be sick.

"Well," I say, switching out the feed for my latest calculations, "I have some good news for a change, at least. I've adjusted for drift along our known timeline. If we feed in these course corrections, we should end up exactly where the *Hadfield* incident occurred."

Zila's fingers dance over her console. "Aurora, do you have any premonition as to what we will find?"

"None at all," Auri mumbles, looking down at her hands. One thumb's rubbing across her opposite wrist, where a red patch still marks the place the sedation patch was stuck on. When she looks up, it's to glance back toward the infirmary, where Kal lies. "I don't know what's there," she whispers. "I don't know what it is. I don't know what I am. I don't know what happened." She draws in an unsteady breath. "And I don't know what I'll do next."

Zila and I exchange a long glance. Aurora doesn't look ready for anything, let alone saving the Milky Way. We're putting everything on the line—we've already sacrificed two of our number—for the uncertain chance she represents. But she's all we have.

"Tell you what," I say, making myself cheerful again. "Why don't you and I get some sleep? Zila can watch over us."

Our Brain inclines her head. "I will wake Scarlett when I require rest."

I want to offer to stay up myself, but Zila and I both know

I need the downtime. So instead I stand, and offer Auri my hand to pull her up. She takes hold, and when she's on her feet, I keep her fingers in mine, studying her.

"You look rough," I tell her.

Her tone is dry. "You, on the other hand, look dapper as ever."

I use my free hand to smooth back my hair, which instantly springs up into the disastrous mess it was before. "Hug?"

She hesitates, then nods, just the tiniest jerk of her head. So I pull her in and wrap my arms around her. I'm the kind of leggy you get when you spend too much time in zero gee growing up, and she tucks in under my chin just perfectly. My suit probably sticks into her in a couple of places, but she doesn't seem to mind.

And for a long moment, we just stand there together, her arms around my waist, her cheek on my shoulder, my chin resting on her hair.

When I look up, Zila's watching us. I wonder what she makes of us all sometimes. How long it's been since someone hugged her. If anyone ever has.

As we head down the hallway, Aurora lifts one hand to trail it over the closed door to Ty's room, glancing at it as if she can see right through it, see our missing Alpha inside. She heard it said over and over as we left him behind—*Aurora's the priority, keep her safe.* So she's carrying that with her, as well as the knowledge that everything rests on a power she can't control. A power that scares her.

"Sleep well, Stowaway," I tell her as her door hums closed behind her. And then, with a soft sigh, I turn away from my own quarters and toward the infirmary, where my next challenge waits.

The lights in there are dim, and Kal's resting on a bio-cot, a medi-wrap across one shoulder. He's bare chested, bruises blossoming across his skin, turned black and gray by the Fold. But the sight of Kaliis Idraban Gilwraeth with no shirt on, even all beat up, makes me want to thank my Maker I've lived to see this moment. He's *beautiful*. Those sculpted lines and that solid muscle and—I mean, he's got an *eight-pack*, and that stupid V that leads down to disappear (tragically) below his belt, both of which are meant to be creatures of myth and legend.

Swoon.

Lucky Auri.

"Is something amiss, Finian?"

I startle when I realize he's looking right at me, and snap my mouth shut. "Just checking in," I tell him, sauntering closer and nodding at his biceps. "You got a license for these weapons, sir?"

His brows crowd together in handsome confusion. "I am proficient in weaponry that . . ." But he trails off, because he can tell he's missed the point.

"Never mind," I tell him. "I've got a question."

He somehow knows to be wary, turning to get a better look at me. "Ask."

"Back on the tug," I say, gesturing to the spot over his heart where the bruises are blackest, "once I found out the cigarillo case had blocked that Kill shot, and once I stopped thanking the Maker you were alive, I realized I could open the thing."

Our Tank's interest sharpens. "I take it you did."

"I did," I confirm. "And I still can't figure it out, Kal. There was a note inside it. A note in *my* handwriting. A note I am absolutely positive I have never written."

He returns to the handsome frown. "And what did it say?"

"It said, 'Tell her the truth.'" I'm watching him keenly now. "Do you know what that means?"

He shakes his head a fraction. "I do not," he replies.

"Because we can't afford for anyone to be keeping anything from anyone else right now," I continue. "If there's something you're not telling Auri, or Scar, or Zila, or even your crazy sister, I get it, but now's the time, Kal."

His expression frosts over. "Perhaps the note was for you. You believe you were the one who wrote it. And you were the one who read it."

"But it was *your* gift," I point out.

"And yet I cannot answer your question."

I have absolutely no idea if he's being straight with me. He might as well be Zila, for all I can read of him right now. After a long pause, I sigh.

"You need anything?"

"No."

"Well, Zila has the bridge," I tell him. "Holler if you're in trouble."

"Del'nai, friend."

As I make my way to my quarters, I'm racking my brain for any kind of secret *I* could be keeping. Anything the note might have meant for me. Apart from not telling Scar that I'd crawl over cut glass for a date with her if we both survive this thing, I'm drawing a blank. And the note—however the hells it happened—seems like a huge amount of effort to go to for an unrequited crush.

The door hums closed behind me, and I hit the button for the gravity release. I'm still thinking as the soft countdown completes and the pressure on my body eases. I have no answers.

In fact, as I shed my suit and push off the ground to curl into a ball for sleep, I have nothing but questions.

. . . . .

A soft chime wakes me, and as I stretch slowly, I revel in how much better I feel—my sore muscles have unlocked, and my body likes me again.

Then I remember that Ty's a GIA prisoner, the galaxy's poised on the edge of war, and Squad 312 has no idea what to do to stop it all.

Aaaaaand that brings me down with a thud.

The chime's followed up by Scar's voice over the intercom.

"Good morning, you incredibly good-looking people. It's 08:00 shipboard time; we're sixty minutes from our destination. I'll see you on the bridge when you've risen from sleep and made yourselves even more beautiful. If that's possible."

I shed my uniform and, with a gentle touch against the ceiling, send myself sailing over to the corner where the hydrosonic shower's located. I activate the force field that'll keep the rest of the room dry, close my eyes in pleasure as the nozzles in the wall emit a gentle mist, and let the sonic part of the shower do the rest, the vibrations combining with the moisture to scrub away the dirt, sweat, and panic of the last couple of days. My grandparents had pretty much the same unit on the station where they lived, and though at first I thought it was bizarre—on Trask, water's in no short supply—these days I appreciate the fact that it really gets you clean.

After a few minutes, I reluctantly shut it off, then find a fresh uniform. When I slip into my suit and run a diagnostic, it's in miraculously good condition.

I make my way out to the bridge, feeling the usual settling that comes with full gee—everything protesting a little bit at the extra work. I find my squadmates seated around their consoles, eating breakfast. Auri slides a foil pack down the table to me, and I inspect the label, then wish I hadn't. I don't know what Brunchtime Savory Mix!!™ is, but I'm pretty sure the extra information isn't going to help me feel better about it.

I glance at Scarlett, shaking my breakfast to warm it up. "You shouldn't have let me sleep so long."

She winks. "Some of us need less beauty sleep than others."

"Any news?" I smile.

"There are official statements out from Terra, Trask, and several nearby systems. Nobody wants a war. Everybody knows they might not get a vote. The Unbroken haven't said anything yet, but their fleet is still mobilizing, and it's looking huge."

That adds a grim note to breakfast. Kal in particular looks troubled. We finish eating, and Zila and I settle in to find whatever it is we're actually looking for.

"Compensating for drift over the last century," I report, "we should be on-site now, plus or minus a thousand klicks."

"Scanning now," Zila says to her screen.

"Processing data," I murmur as it begins to flow through to me. It takes less than two minutes before something jumps out from the rest. "Is that . . . ?"

"Confirm," Zila says, turning from her console to the pilot's controls. "Unidentified object detected. Altering course."

I grin at the others. "Picked it to within thirty-seven klicks, my friends!"

This announcement of unmatched prowess is met with polite nods.

"Oh, come *on*," I protest. "This is like finding . . . what do you dirtchildren say? A beetle in a haystack?"

Auri giggles. "A needle."

"Well, even smaller, then. And in this case, whatever a haystack is, it would take about a day to walk across it. And I just led us straight to our destination."

"A commendable effort," Zila says without turning her head.

"High praise," Scarlett says, trying to hide her smile.

"Is it dangerous?" Kal asks.

I shake my head. "It's got almost zero energy signature. Looks totally inert. We were lucky to even find it out here, to be honest."

"Kal, how's your shoulder?" Scarlett asks.

"Well enough," he reports. "You wish me to prepare the docking bay?"

Scar leans back and chews her lip, a small frown on her brow.

"Yeah. Let's bring this thing aboard and see what we can learn."

· · · · ·

We can view the docking bay through a plasteel porthole, and we all cluster around it to peer at the object Kal has tractored inside. It's teardrop-shaped, about half as tall as me. It appears made of . . . crystal, maybe? It's cut like a piece of jewelry, a thousand facets, brilliant light dancing on its surface. There aren't any other markings or details to be seen.

It settles as the rear doors close and the bay starts to equalize, somehow staying upright, floating a few centimeters above the deck.

"That's it?" Aurora asks, saying what at least most of us are thinking.

"That's it," I reply.

"Do you sense anything from it, be'shmai?" Kal asks.

Auri frowns in concentration but finally shakes her head. "Nothing."

"It's kind of small," Scarlett adds, peering at it.

"Your point being . . . ?"

There's a long pause. As one, we all look around, then down. Those words just came from Zila, our smallest squad member. Was that . . .

Did she just make a joke?

"I concur with Legionnaire Madran!" says a tiny, chirpy voice in Aurora's pocket. "Size isn't usually an indicator of performance."

"Hush, Magellan," Auri murmurs.

"You know, I should probably point out again that I'm three times smarter than any of you, and you're constantly telling me to be qu—"

"Silent mode," Scarlett orders.

"Humans," comes a muttered complaint before the uni shuts up.

". . . Can we go in there and take a look at it?" Auri asks.

"That is not advisable," Zila replies, busy at the docking bay enviro controls. "The external temperature is minus 270.45 degrees Celsius."

"Maker's breath," I say, looking over specs. "What is this thing *made of*?"

"It is defying our scanner's ability to analyze its molecular structure," Zila says, eyes roaming the data. "But I am detecting no harmful radiation or microbes. I will attempt to increase the object's temperature. Please stand by."

We all wait impatiently until, eventually, a lifetime later, Zila nods. It looks like everything is okay for us to enter. Kal punches the door control, and we move cautiously inside, crowding around it, pulling out our uniglasses. The thing is giving off *zero* energy. Apart from the fact that it's physically present, there's no way to tell if it's broadcasting, if it has a power source internally, or what it's for. Still, it's a place to start, so we begin our analysis.

Except for Aurora. She doesn't pull out Magellan. Instead, she stares at the thing as if she's in a trance. And then, unblinking, but with a faint hint of a smile, she reaches out to curve her hand across its surface.

"I'm not sure this is such a good idea, boss . . . ," Magellan says.

"Aurora?" Kal asks.

Her fingers touch the surface.

Her uniglass makes a spitting, popping sound.

And she collapses at my feet.

< ERROR >

001!)&#)(0

< FAIL >

< ERROR >

18

AURI

I've never seen a view this beautiful in my life.

Back on Earth, there were no stretches of green like this left. On Octavia, there were endless swaths of wild land, but I never saw them in person—not until they were covered by the creeping Ra'haam. But this place is different to both of them.

Almost as far as the eye can see, it's lush, flawless garden. Waterfalls of flowers tumble down gentle hills. Sprays of red blossoms hang from the trees. It's an endless parade of blooms and plants, each more exquisite than the last, each different from those that went before.

As the landscape stretches—no, *soars*—away from me, my eyes don't know where to settle. This place would make Eden look dull. Everything is brilliantly clear, the air crisp, the temperature perfect. On the horizon is some sort of city, tall spires of crystal stretching up toward a glorious, golden sky.

But the thing that strikes me most is the incredible sense of well-being. It's like I'm drunk on the sunshine, on the purest air I've ever breathed. I don't think I've spent a moment since I woke up on Aurora Station feeling anything less than tired and scared, and the lifting of that weight makes me feel like I could leap one of those distant crystal spires in a single bound.

Lacking anything else to do, I set out toward them. They're a landmark, after all—maybe I'll find something there that will explain to me where I am. I know I should be more worried, but it's somehow impossible to muster any concern.

There are no paths, but the grass is short and easy to walk across. I make my way down into a valley with a spring in my step, walking along a field of waist-high blue flowers. I trail one hand along them as I move past, and they bob and bow, turning their faces to follow me.

It's a little hard to judge time, but it feels like I've been walking for hours when I spot the figure. It's quite close—I wonder how I didn't see it sooner—and although it's human-shaped, it's most certainly not a human.

It doesn't hurt my eyes, but I can't quite look directly at it. It's a creature of light and crystal, a golden glow and a myriad of refracting rainbows inside its shape. It has three fingers on each hand, and I realize that its right eye is white and aglow, just like mine. But though it's one of the strangest creatures I've ever seen—and I've been to a Casseldon Bianchi party—I feel no fear at all. Instead, I continue on my way to meet it, and I'm not surprised when it greets me.

The words are like music, but I don't think I hear them out loud. They just sort of . . . arrive in my head.

Greetings, it says. *Welcome to the Echo. I am the Eshvaren.*

"The Eshvaren?" I parrot back at it, like an idiot. "I thought you were a whole species, not just one, uh . . ." I look its shimmering body up and down. "Person?"

It gives me a tiny bow.

I am a gathering of wisdom. A memory of many. Just as this place is the memory of our homeworld. An echo of a place that once was.

I have no idea of the proper response to that, but I figure I can't go wrong returning the greeting. "It's good to meet you. I'm Aurora Jie-Lin O'Malley."

You are a Trigger, it replies, with a hint of ceremony.

"Yes, that's right!" Eagerness wells up inside me, and I step closer. "And if you're the Eshvaren, you can tell me what that means."

It offers me another one of its little bows. *To be a Trigger means you have choices ahead, Aurora Jie-Lin O'Malley.*

It raises its arms and then simply pushes off, rising above the ground as though it's in zero gravity.

I stare up at it in confusion as it hovers a few meters above my head.

Come, it says patiently. *Join me.*

Nothing ventured, nothing gained, I guess? Feeling ridiculous, I bend at the knees and push off as if I'm about to jump. But instead, completely effortlessly, I rise from the ground. And no sooner do I throw my arms out, wondering how I'm supposed to stop, than I've done exactly that. There's just the faintest texture to the air—nothing as thick as water, but what I'm doing still feels a little like swimming.

With another kick I'm soaring again, arms wide, laughter welling up inside me as the landscape spreads out beneath me. This is like the best part of every flying dream I've ever had. This is, for an instant, like being back at home, back in time, rocketing along the running track and knowing I'm out in front of everyone else.

This is pure joy.

A second quick kick spins me into a somersault, and I tumble through a loop-the-loop, whooping my glee. The Eshvaren hovers in far more dignified style, watching me get it all out of my system.

Follow, it finally tells me.

Together we soar across the beauty that stretches out below us. Great valleys are joined by soft, rolling hills, their golden-green grass giving way to masses of blue and purple flowers that sway in the breeze, to red fields that ripple as we pass overhead. Silver rivers cut through them, twisting and winding, doubling back on themselves, and the crystal city beckons me as we turn toward it.

Once again the Eshvaren speaks, and I can hear it despite the wind.

This place is the Echo of a time long ago. A time when we lived. Before we fought the Ra'haam. You know of the Great Enemy?

"Yes," I say, glancing across at it. "Yeah, we've met."

Then you know it believes in the power of the many as one. In the sacrifice of individuality for the sake of harmony.

"I do."

A question pushes forward in my mind, and though I know this might not be the time or place for it, I have to ask. I'm thinking of my father. Of Cat. Of the other colonists pulled into its embrace, their eyes blooming blue, moss creeping across their skin, hiding themselves inside the uniforms of GIA agents to prevent others from approaching Octavia and disturbing the cradle where the Ra'haam sleeps.

"I've seen the Ra'haam absorb people," I say. "Consume them. Is . . . is there a way to get out once you're a part of it?"

No, says the Eshvaren quietly. The pain in its voice is a match for the sharp hurt in my chest.

"Oh," I whisper, because it's all I can think to say.

Such a little word.

Such a massive thought.

Not *perhaps,* not *maybe.* Just . . .

No.

I'm still trying to wrap my head around it as we cross a wide river, a frothing, quick-moving silver mass that tumbles over itself, crashing into rocks midstream, sending up perfect arcs of spray.

We are unlike the Ra'haam, says the Eshvaren. *We believe in the sanctity of the individual above all else. This is what we fought to defend. It cost us everything, but the war was not won entirely. Though defeated, the Ra'haam did not die. It hid from us, settled into slumber, and we knew we would not live to see its next awakening. So we prepared this place, and this memory, to wait for you.*

"Little bit ironic that the memories of all your species are in one body," I observe. "When you're the ones who believe in individuality."

These individuals consented to this process, it replies solemnly. *The Ra'haam seeks no such permission. But you are our legacy, Aurora. We died to keep alive the hope of defeating the Ra'haam. Now you must complete our work.*

My voice sounds weak, even to my own ears. "But I don't know what to do."

We left a Weapon, it replies. *If deployed before the Ra'haam fully awakens, it will destroy its nursery planets, prevent it from blooming ever again. We did not know where the Enemy slumbered when we made this place. But ages after our passing, our agents still searched for the Ra'haam's seed worlds. They will have left clues—*

"The star map!" I nod, excited. "Yes, we found it."

We also left devices in the Fold. Probes. One of these devices must have sensed your psychic potential and activated you. It knew that in you lay the ability to wield our last weapon against the Ra'haam, and it brought that potential to the fore. Now you must train so you are prepared to use it. You must end the cycle.

All of a sudden, surrounded by perfect beauty, I feel incredibly tiny on a very big planet. The golden sky seems endless, and the crystal towers seem to reach all the way up to it.

"You mean your whole plan hinged on me going somewhere near that probe so it could sense me and activate me? What if I hadn't been selected for the Octavia mission? What if I'd never gone anywhere near that part of space? How did you know I would? Can you see the future? If so, I have Questions."

The Eshvaren shakes its head. *You are special, Aurora, but not unique. We left many probes, suitable for many species, all searching the Fold for potentials.*

"But there's no other Triggers around," I point out. "Or . . . are there?"

You are alone in here, it replies. *But I am not alive. Only* a collection of memories. A recording, if you will. There may have been other Triggers before you. Others who were activated, who came here to train. I do not know. The Echo will reset after you leave this place, and I will forget your passing. But you would not be here, and the Ra'haam would not still exist, if another Trigger had been successful. And if you fail, others will come after you. This task cannot go unfinished.

It's a pretty grim prospect. "You're not much for pep talks, are you?" I say, trying to make myself sound surer than I feel.

The Eshvaren tilts its head slightly to one side. *Please define* pep.

"You're not very encouraging. You're scaring me, is what I'm saying."

Fear is an appropriate response, it replies serenely. *Your training will be arduous. Your testing, dangerous. If you fail, it will cost you your life.*

"Um," I say. "My life?"

This responsibility is yours, it replies. *Like us, you must sacrifice all.*

As if its words cast a shadow, a chill goes through me. All of a sudden, despite the beauty of this place, I want nothing more than to be back on the *Zero.*

"Listen, I've been gone for hours," I say. "My crew will be worrying—they might try something stupid. I should tell them I'm okay."

Time moves differently in the Echo. For those outside, only moments have passed. And in this task, your crew is secondary.

"Well, they're not secondary to me," I reply, and finally I have a real hint of steel in my voice. "Tell me how to wake up."

We will wake you and send you back if you wish. But when

you arise, you must prepare yourself to return here. Take one full cycle of your own time, do what you must, and then touch the probe once more. We will speak again, as we have done now.

It nods.

Then your training will begin.

I open my mouth to reply, but before I can get a word out, I'm suddenly blinking awake. The endless golden sky above is replaced by the ceiling of the *Zero*'s docking bay and the faces of my squad.

They're crowded around me, concern in their eyes. Finian is holding Magellan, and I can see the screen is dark, lifeless. Touching the probe must have—

"Be'shmai, are you well?" Kal asks urgently, cradling my head in his hands.

Zila's running her uniglass over me, presumably conducting some kind of med-scan. "That was unwise, Aurora."

"Seriously, Stowaway," says Fin. "You can't just go around touching every weird probe we find, you know? Who knows where it's been."

"*She's* been somewhere," says Scarlett softly, looking at me intently.

"Have I ever," I reply.

". . . Be'shmai?" Kal asks.

I look into his eyes, see the fear in my own.

"I've just met the Eshvaren."

286

19

TYLER

I wake up with the taste of blood in my mouth.

The walls, the floors, the smudge I wipe off my lips, all of them are different shades of gray, which tells me we're still Folding. I'm lying on a bio-cot, staring up at the ceiling, feeling an engine's low thrum in my aching chest. From the tone, I can immediately tell I'm aboard a Terran carrier. A Mark VII-b, I think, with the new epsilon fusion intakes and 9-Series inertial dampeners.

Hey, I like ships, okay?

Point is, this is a TDF ship. Which means I'm in TDF custody. Which means I'm in every kind of trouble in the galaxy. But I guess I'm not dead?

Could be worse, Jones.

I risk moving, rewarded with stabs of pain all over my body. Looking down at myself, I can see I've received some first aid—the worst of my gouges and cuts are dressed in medi-wraps to stimulate healing, and there's a chill-pack tapped to my bare, bruised chest to kill the swelling. I'm still wearing my Aurora Legion cargo pants and the boots I got in my package from the Dominion Repository, but nobody's seen fit to replace my shirt. For a second I panic, reaching up to my neck . . . but I find the silver chain, my dad's Senate ring still attached to it.

Dad . . .

What would he make of all this? What would he tell me to do? News about the battle between the TDF and the Unbroken has probably gotten out by now. The whole galaxy could be at war. And Scar, Auri, and the others . . . they're out there alone.

I can't protect them anymore.

I sit up, wincing at the pain as I look around the room. In news that surprises nobody, I'm in a detention cell. The door is sealed, the camera above it live, the temperature just lower than comfortable—all as expected.

What I don't expect is that I'm not in here alone.

She's laid out on another bio-cot along the opposite wall. Wearing her Unbroken dress uniform from the waist up and nothing but a pair of black briefs from the waist down. Her thighs are dressed in medi-wraps, bruises darkening the olive skin beneath. At some point she was plugged into an IV drip, but she's torn it out, blood dripping from her wrist, spattered on the floor. She's on her back, black braids, black lips, black heart, staring pure murder at the ceiling.

Saedii.

"Finally awake," she says quietly. "I trust you enjoyed your rest?"

". . . How long was I out?"

"Hours." She shakes her head. "You Terrans are such . . . weaklings."

"You're in Terran custody," I point out. "So what's that make you?"

"A prisoner of war." She turns her head, fixes me with her withering gaze. "One you cannot *hope* to win."

"I warned you," I scowl. "You played right into their hands, Saedii. You gave them exactly what they wanted."

"A conflict in which there can be no victory? The enmity of an Archon who destroys *suns*?" Saedii sits up slow, swings her bare legs around, and places her feet on the floor. There's only the slightest trace of pain in her eyes, despite her injuries. "If your people wanted annihilation, then yes. I have given them that."

"It's not *my* people behind this mess."

"That pathetic Aurora Legion badge you cower beneath will not spare you the Starslayer's vengeance. Caersan will draw no distinction between the TDF and your fellow legionnaires." Her black lips curl, pointed canines glinting. "He will slaughter *all* of you. Your suns will collapse. Your systems will be swallowed. Your entire *race* consigned to the dust of history. *All* of you."

"You sound upset," I say.

Her eyes narrow behind the strip of black paint across her temples. But that infuriating Syldrathi cool slips into place like a well-worn glove.

"You are a fool, Tyler Jones," she says. "And you will die a fool's death."

"I'm not the fool spitting threats for the whole ship to hear." I point to the small black dot above the doorframe. "You realize we're under surveillance, right? That they can hear everything you say? See everything you do?"

"I am a Templar of the Unbroken." She tosses her braids back off her shoulders, pointing to the three blades scribed on her forehead. "Warbreed by birth and troth. Anointed by the blood of Archon Caersan himself. I have *nothing* to fear from your people."

"I keep telling you, the folks running this show aren't *my* people. There's things going on here you can't possibly understand. But believe me when I say, Saedii, birth, troth, blood, whatever. You're in *way* over your head here."

I lie back down on the cot, wincing as I paw at the bruises on my bare chest.

"So be careful you don't run your mouth right off your face."

Placing my hands behind my head, I stare at the ceiling, feeling Saedii's burning gaze roaming my body. I can tell she wants to kill me—I can feel the threat and rage radiating off her in waves. But I know she's not stupid enough to try anything with those cams on her, and besides, her wounds are still far from healed. And so, trying to push thoughts of Templar Saedii Gilwraeth from my mind, I start wondering how on Earth I'm gonna escape this cell.

Aside from what I'm wearing, I've got nothing in the way of gear. I realize they've even taken my uniglass off me, and I feel a sudden pang at losing the last physical object of Cat's I had left.

I guess I'll always have the tattoo we got together. . . .

I find myself thinking about her. Missing her. She was someone who always had my back. For a moment, I find my thoughts drifting to that night on shore leave, running my finger over the ink on my bicep, thinking about the way she felt, the way she shivered as I—

You are pathetic.

I blink. Sitting up carefully, I peer at Saedii, who's still watching me with those narrowed, hateful eyes.

"Did you . . . ?"

Call you pathetic? Yes. Fantasizing about a dead lover at a time like this?

I blink again. Realizing that Saedii is talking to me without moving her lips.

That somehow, she's . . .

Are you . . . in my mind?

She huffs softly in contempt.

If it can be called such.

What . . . how are you doing that?

So very weak.

I frown deeper, trying to figure out what in the Maker's name is going on here. Whether I'm hallucinating or have a concussion or maybe just dreaming this whole thing. But finally, I recall talking with Kal on Emerald City. Remember his warning that Saedii would be able to track him . . . because she could *feel* him.

I look at Saedii. Realization crystalizing in my mind.

Your mother was a Waywalker. . . .

I feel a spark of fury, dark and twisted, crackling like live current between us.

Do not speak of my mother ever again, Terran.

I shake my head. Thoughts racing.

Kal said you inherited some of her . . . some of the Way-walker gifts. I knew Waywalkers were empathic. That they could read moods. Maybe even surface thoughts. But I never knew they could talk to people telepathically?

She looks me over, cool and contemptuous.

291

There is apparently much you do not know, Tyler Jones.

. . . What's that supposed to mean?

She sneers. *That you are indeed your father's son.*

I feel a flash of rage at that, as dark and deep as her own. My hand creeps involuntarily to the chain about my neck, the ring at the end of it.

How about we take mothers and fathers off the table for discussion?

Laughter, echoing in my skull. *You are a fool.*

If you stuck your head into mine just to insult me, you can get out again.

I "stuck my head in," as you so eloquently put it, because I could feel your aphrodisia splashing all over the walls, and I wished to discern the source. She looks pointedly down at her bare legs and briefs. *If I was the focus of your fantasies, I was going to cut your thumbs off.*

I scoff. *Don't flatter yourself.*

I flatter no one. That is what I do to males who seek to woo me, Tyler Jones. Her fingers drift to the cord of severed, desiccated thumbs still strung around her neck. *They are given the opportunity to best me in combat. And if they fail . . .*

I look her over, softly shaking my head.

Great Maker, you really are a psychopath, aren't you?

All the more reason to keep thoughts of me out of your head, little Terran.

I'll try to contain myself.

She places her hands on her knees, bending forward. Her braids tumble around her cheeks as she stretches, languid, running her black fingernails all the way down over her shins to the tips of her toes. Her movements are sensual, almost seductive, but she's obviously just doing it to goad me. As she looks up into my eyes, I can feel the malice in her.

You had best do more than try, boy.

Listen, how about you just—

My thought is cut off by the cell door hissing open. I sit up again, wincing, as half a dozen TDF troopers in light tactical armor march into the cell. Saedii glowers, her hands balling into fists. But the troopers have their eyes on me. I see the ship ident KUSANAGI on their uniforms and realize I must be on the same ship as . . .

The lieutenant leading the posse waves a disruptor in my face.

"Princeps wants to talk to you, Legionnaire Jones."

20

KAL

She is afraid.

I can feel it, like a shadow behind her, looming cold and dark. Like a damp black coat around her shoulders, making her shiver with its chill. I can feel her disappointment in herself.

She knows that the fate of the entire galaxy is at stake.

She knows what will happen if she fails.

And still, she fears.

She is in her quarters, every color around her a shade of gray. She stands at a small viewport, staring out at the colorless tides of the Fold. The space beyond is an infinity, awash with light. A cosmic ballet, billions of years in the making. A beauty as indescribable as any in creation.

And all of it dims to a candle flame beside her.

"Be'shmai?"

She looks over her shoulder at me, the white of her iris catching the light and making my heart stutter. I stand at the doorway, and I watch her wrap her arms around herself as if she were cold. And I know then, deep in my bones, I would do *anything* to take this burden from her.

"Come in," she says, soft.

The door whispers shut behind me as I step inside. Glancing around, I can see there is very little in this room to mark it as Aurora's own. Finian's cabin is equipped to deal with his condition. My own is complete with a small lias flower in a silver urn, and even a siif that I could play if the mood took me. But Aurora's room is bare of adornment, save for a single candle scribed with what I recognize as her father's language. I only know it because the Chinese calligraphy bears no small resemblance to Syldrathi script. I remember the first time I saw it at the academy. It surprised me that humans could produce something approaching the beauty of my own culture.

It does not surprise me now.

The candle sits alone in the room, apart from the girl who must have lit it. It is almost as if Adams and de Stoy knew this place would not be her home for long. And it saddens me to see how adrift she is.

"Finian reports that the damage to Magellan is not critical," I tell her. "Touching the probe did indeed overload its circuits, but with time, he can repair it."

Aurora simply nods, staring out the viewport. I suspect updates about broken electronic devices are not what she needs from me right now.

And so I step up behind her, and I wrap my arms around her. She pushes back against me, closes her eyes, and sighs, as if in my arms she is finally, finally, somewhere close to home.

I look at our reflection in the viewport, me behind, us together. I realize how well we fit. Like two pieces of the strangest puzzle. Like she is the piece that has been missing all my life. The Want in me is almost deafening, but I hold it still, breathing deep and bringing some calm to the tempest inside. Because beyond the adoration reflected in her eyes, I can see the words she wishes to say, long before she finally musters the courage to give them voice.

"I'm scared, Kal," she whispers.

"I know," I reply.

I caress her cheek, and she closes her eyes again, trembling.

"What did the Ancients tell you, to make you so?" I ask.

She sucks her lower lip, uncertain, and I know as she speaks that I am the only one in the galaxy she would admit this to.

"They have to train me," she says. "How to use the Weapon. But they . . ."

She breathes, as if readying herself before a deep plunge.

"They said if I fail, it'll kill me. 'Like us, you must sacrifice all.'"

I feel a thrill of perfect rage at the thought. Before she was mine, I did not know what it was to be complete. Before I found this light, I did not fear the dark. But to have discovered this girl, this missing piece in the puzzle of my life, only to be confronted with the thought that I might lose her so swiftly . . .

"I don't want to go," she whispers. "I know it's selfish. I know after everything we've fought for, everything people have given, Cat, Tyler, all the squad . . ." Tears glitter in her lashes as she shakes her head. "But I don't want to risk this. *Us.*"

She sighs, sinks into my arms, tipping her head back against my chest.

"Tell me this is the right thing to do, Kal," she says.

I smooth back her hair, caressing her cheek.

"You already know that, be'shmai," I murmur.

She pulls my arms around her tighter. "Tell me anyway."

I breathe deep, content for a moment to simply stand with Aurora in my arms. I know she is already aware of what she must do. That she *knows* it, with every atom in her body. She is nothing if not brave. But I know she is also asking me for strength, for certainty, for something she can hold on to as she walks into the fire.

And so I tell her something I have never told another soul.

"My earliest memories are of my parents fighting," I say.

I feel her uncertainty about why I am telling her this. But she trusts me enough not to question and simply lets my words sink in, then holds me just a little tighter still.

"I'm sorry," she whispers. "That's sad."

I nod, staring past our reflection to the Fold beyond.

"My mother and father were young when they met. She was a novice at the Temple of the Void. He a Paladin of the warrior cabal. When they first felt the Pull, their friends and families all tried to talk them out of becoming lifebound."

"Why?" Aurora asks.

"Warbreed and Waywalkers rarely make good pairings. Those who seek answers and those who answer most questions with conflict seldom get along." I shrug, and sigh. "But still, my parents did it anyway. They loved each other dearly in the beginning. So much that it hurt them both."

She manages a small smile. "That sounds romantic. Two people wanting to be together, no matter what anyone else says."

I nod. "Romantic, perhaps. Ill advised, most assuredly.

I think my mother thought she might be able to guide my father's love of conflict into love of family. But Syldra was at war with Terra in those years. And as the rift between my people and yours deepened, he lost himself inside it utterly. The cracks in their lifebond were showing by the time Saedii was born. And they grew deeper still once I arrived."

I sigh again, realizing how bright a blessing it is to be able to speak like this. To simply have someone I trust enough to share with.

"My father was a cruel man. He ruled with a heavy hand, and he brooked no dissent. He commanded that my sister and I be inducted into the Warbreed Cabal, and he oversaw our training personally. When he tutored us in the Aen Suun, he did not hold back. Many were the nights Saedii and I retired to our bedchambers bruised and bloodied by his hand. But he said it would make us strong. Mercy, he told us, was the province of cowards.

"Saedii and I were close at first. When we were young, she was the star in my heavens. But as we grew older, Father began to show me more favor than her, and she became jealous. Saedii loved our father, you see. Loved him with a fierceness that eclipsed my own. Though I was raised Warbreed, in truth I always felt more kinship with my mother. She taught me the value of life, Aurora. The joy of understanding, the justice of an even hand. I loved her dearly, even as my father pressed me to embrace the war within, that I might better fight the war without. Mother would come to me at night, once Father was asleep. The bruises he would lay on her skin were the same shade as my own.

"'There is no love in violence, Kaliis,' she would tell me,

pressing a cool cloth to my wounds. 'There is no love in violence.'"

"That's awful," Aurora whispers. "I'm sorry, Kal."

I shake my head, feeling the old familiar sting.

"The battle lines our parents drew became mine and Saedii's. Saedii sought only our father's praise, cared little for my mother's wisdom." I touch the three blades at my brow. "We were living aboard my father's ship at the time. He wished us close, I think. The better to control my mother, to mold Saedii and me into what he wanted us to be. I grew older. Taller. Stronger. When Saedii could no longer best me in practice, she sought to punish me in other ways. For my eighth nameday, my mother had given me a siif—a stringed instrument, not unlike your Terran violins. It was a gift from her mother before her. And one day, when I was twelve, after I had bested her in practice again, Saedii went to my room and smashed it in retaliation.

"Though I always tried to take my mother's teaching to heart, I was still my father's son. And this was the first time I truly felt the Enemy Within take control. I tasted the hatred on my tongue, Aurora. And I liked it. And so I hunted my sister down. I found her in the sparring courts with her friends. I showed her the broken pieces of my siif and she laughed. And so I hit her with it."

I hang my head in shame. My tongue tastes bitter, dry as ashes. Aurora looks at my reflection, and I can see the question in her eyes. But she can see the guilt in mine clearly, and instead of judgment, she finds compassion. Squeezes my hand, gentle as a whisper.

"You were just a boy, Kal," she says. "You're not the person you were back then. I *know* you. You'd never do something like that now."

"That does not excuse it," I say. "It has been seven years, and still, the contempt I feel for myself has not lessened a drop. She was my sister, Aurora. And I did not hit her for any reason, save to hurt her. When she fell, I hit her again. And again. I could feel my father at my shoulder in that moment. Hear his words in my ear. Cursing weakness. Pity. Remorse. 'Mercy is the province of cowards.'"

I look out into the Fold, at the cosmic ballet beyond the viewport.

"I expected punishment. Instead, Father praised me. He told me that when he heard what I had done, he had never been more proud I was his son."

"Kal," Aurora says softly. "Your father sounds . . ."

"Monstrous," I say. "He was monstrous, Aurora. And my mother saw the monsters he was making of Saedii and me, and finally, she decided to leave him. To break the lifebond and flee back to Syldra. Father told her that he would kill her if she ever left him. In abandoning him, she was leaving behind everything. Her home. What few friends he'd allowed her to have. All of it. Saedii refused to leave, to be parted from our father. So in the end, my mother gave up her whole life for my sake alone. It was the most difficult thing she ever did. But she did it anyway.

"'Mai tu sarie amn, tu hae'si, tu kii'rna dae,' she told me afterward."

Aurora shakes her head. "What does it mean?"

"'There is nothing as painful, or as simple, as doing what is right.'"

She looks to the stars outside, lips pressed thin.

300

"You told me your father . . ."

"Died," I reply, my heart clenching with a strength that surprises me. "He died at Orion, be'shmai. In the same battle that claimed the life of Jericho Jones. Tyler, Scarlett, me, all of us were made orphans that day."

"What . . ." She trails off, meeting my eyes again. "What happened to your mother? I'd like to meet her. . . ."

But Aurora's words falter when she sees the pain in my eyes. I can feel her presence in my mind, just the lightest touch, and in it she sees the reflection of a sun flaring into blinding light, then to bottomless darkness. Enveloping the planets around it, dragging entire systems down to oblivion, ten billion Syldrathi voices screaming as the void opens wide to swallow them whole.

"She died," Aurora whispers. "When your homeworld did."

I hang my head. "The Starslayer took much from me, Aurora. But my mother gave me much more. I would have been on Syldra when it perished had she not instilled her wisdom in me, had she not forced me to see the anger in my blood as something to be used for good, and the safety of the galaxy a cause worth harnessing it for. I joined the Aurora Legion because of her. Even though leaving her and my world behind was the hardest thing I had ever done."

I shrug.

"But that decision brought me to this squad. And you. And your quest. I would have none of that, if not for her."

"What was her name?"

"Laeleth."

She nods, pale hair tumbling about her eyes. "That's beautiful."

"She would have liked you, be'shmai," I say, and she

smiles through her tears, because she can see the truth of what I say in my gaze. "She would have seen the strength in you. The burden you carry, this thing we are a part of, this path we walk . . ." I shake my head in bewilderment. "The fate of the entire galaxy lies in your hands. The courage you have shown to even get this far . . . I know blooded warriors who would have crumbled to dust under such a weight. And yet, here you stand. Strong and beautiful and unconquered."

My hand closes around hers again, and I squeeze softly.

"And though it fills me with joy to have been the one you asked to tell you this truth, I have no doubt you knew it already. Because that is who you are. And just one of the infinite reasons why I love you as I do."

She meets my eyes. "I could die in there, Kal."

My heart seizes again, but I try to show no fear. She needs me to be strong now, and I can give her that, if nothing else.

"You will not die, be'shmai," I tell her. "You are more than you ever imagine."

". . . What will you do out here?" she asks softly. "While I'm in the Echo?"

"Finian says he has managed to isolate a particle trail from the probe. He took *great* pains to explain how difficult it was." She smiles faintly. "He says he can track the device back to its point of origin. Wherever the Eshvaren launched it from. Perhaps we will find the Weapon there. Or more clues to its location."

"The Eshvaren will probably tell me where it is. If I pass their test."

"*When* you pass their test," I say, squeezing her hand.

"But Scarlett says we cannot risk everything on the throw of million-year-old dice. I am inclined to agree. Besides, it will keep us occupied while you are in this . . . Echo of theirs."

"The Eshvaren . . . ," she begins. "They told me that time moves differently in there. That moments out here are hours in there. I was wondering if maybe . . . you might want to come with me? It would be a long time to be in there on my own."

I blink. "Can we do that? I mean to say . . . is it allowed?"

She tilts her head. "They're asking me to risk my life to save the damn galaxy, Kal. I think they can give me a little company on the ride."

I think on it a moment. I do not truly know what this Echo entails, but I feel confident Scarlett and Finian and Zila can conduct the tracking of the probe on their own. And in truth, the thought of being parted from Aurora has been weighing like a stone upon my shoulders. And so I smile at her, nodding agreement. And for a moment, the smile she gifts me in reply is full of the same joy I feel in my heart.

But the shadow soon returns.

I see it lurking with the fear in her eyes.

"There's nothing as painful, or as simple, as doing what's right," she says.

"No. There is not."

We stand there silently for a very long time. Letting it wash over us—the enormity of it all, where she must go, what she must face, what hangs in the balance, resting on so small a point as the two of us. Aurora's eyes are fixed on the dark outside, her thoughts a silent kaleidoscope.

"You know, before I broke him, Magellan used to show

me random science facts every day," she finally murmurs. "I was reading one yesterday about atoms."

The warmth of her, the press of her body against mine, is a drug, and I am conscious of how fierce and loud my heart is pounding on my ribs. With her back pressed into the curve of my chest, surely she must be able to feel it. But I try my best to listen. To be here in this moment for her.

"Atoms," I say.

"Right," Aurora nods. "Every cell in your body is a nucleus surrounded by electrons. And those electrons are negatively charged. So they push away other electrons when they get too close. And this article said that while your brain perceives the force created by electron repulsion as 'touching,' the atoms are actually always hovering some tiny fraction of a millimeter apart."

She runs her thumb across mine and shakes her head.

"So we never *actually* touch anything," she says. "We go through our whole lives totally apart. We never actually get to *touch* another living thing. Ever."

The hunger in me stirs. I can feel it in her as well—the thought that this fire growing between us, this whisper rising into a storm, all of it could be snuffed out tomorrow. Gently, I turn her to face me. Look into her eyes. She shivers as I draw one finger down the arc of her cheek.

Her voice is a whisper as I lean in closer.

"Magellan said if two particles ever actually touched . . ."

Closer.

". . . it'd create a nuclear reaction. . . ."

"That sounds dangerous," I whisper, searching her eyes.

Closest.

"Very," she breathes.

Our lips meet, and our fires collide, and in that instant, all and everything is utterly right. There is no ship. There is no Fold. There is only this girl in my arms, and the Pull in my core, and the press of her mouth her hands her body to mine. She surges against me, breathless, hungry, seeking that same solace I feel, the shelter of oblivion, the everything of us and the nothingness of everything else. Her tongue brushes mine, and she guides my hands to where she wants them to be, and though I know in some part of me that what she said is true, that we are not truly touching at all, for a moment I fear we truly are, that the heat between us has become some nuclear fire that will consume us both.

She pulls away from me after an eon. Looking up into my eyes with something close to the adoration she must see in mine. She presses her fingertips to my face, my ears, my lips, her touch incandescent on my skin.

"You are the fire I long to burn inside," I tell her.

She takes my hand.

She leads me to her bed.

She draws me down with her.

"Let's burn together," she breathes.

21

TYLER

It's cold in this interrogation cell.

The troopers who escorted me from the detention level ignored all my protests, all my challenges to the lunacy of what they're caught up in. Good soldiers don't listen to terrorists, I know. Good soldiers don't think. Instead, they just marched me into this room, bound me to a chair in mag-restraints, and, with a series of crisp salutes, tromped right back out again.

Leaving me with *them*.

I look the three figures over, picked out in the spotlights overhead. Their breath hisses, slow and hollow. They have identical mannerisms, identical mirrormasks, identical charcoal-gray uniforms. Apart from the one leading them, of course, who's clad head to foot in pristine white instead.

"GOOD EVENING, LEGIONNAIRE JONES," Princeps says. "WELCOME ABOARD THE *KUSANAGI*."

I look at the figure where I guess its eyes must be. Imagining the face hidden behind that featureless facade.

"Nice to see you again, Zhang Ji," I say.

The name of Aurora's father. The name of the shell

this thing stole and now wears like a cheap suit. This thing that's slumbered for a million years, wounded, hiding in the shadows, wanting to be unseen, undiscovered, unknown.

But I know its name.

"Or should I call you Ra'haam?"

I look among them, bristling with anger. Waiting for an answer. A reaction. *Something.* But they just stare, silent and still.

"I know what you're doing," I spit. "You're starting a war between Terra and the Unbroken as a smoke screen. Buying yourself time until your nursery planets are ready to bloom. But millions of people are going to die. Maybe *billions.* You know that, right?"

The two gray GIA uniforms take up position on either side of me. The one to my left reaches out with gloved hands and slips a pain collar around my neck. I flinch at the touch of cold metal. I feel the tiny trode slip out and press against my spine.

"Use of pain collars is outlawed under the Madrid Conventions," I say. "They probably should've written something about being possessed by alien parasites in there too, but you get th—"

"WHERE IS AURORA JIE-LIN O'MALLEY?" Princeps asks.

I square my jaw, look into that blank, mirrored face. "Under Aurora Legion protocols, I'm permitted only to give you my name, rank, and squad number."

Princeps tilts its head. "WHERE IS AURORA JIE-LIN O'MALLEY?"

I lick my lips. Brace myself.

"Tyler Jones. Alpha. Aurora Legion, Squad 312."

A bolt of agony rockets up the back of my skull and explodes inside my head. I gasp as every inch of skin bursts into flame, as every nerve is stripped raw and dragged through broken glass, as my eyes burst inside my skull and acid is poured into the sockets, eating through my sinus cavities and dripping down my thr—

It stops. Shut off with a flick of Princeps's finger. I drag a shuddering gasp through my teeth, sweat stinging in my wounds. It only lasted a few seconds, but that was the worst pain I've ever felt in my life, up to and including that time in sixth grade when I caught myself in my zipper.

Princeps opens one white-gloved hand, shows me the pain collar's control. The settings range up to 10. It's currently set to 1.

"WHERE IS AURORA JIE-LIN O'MALLEY?"

"Tyler Jones. Alph—"

The rest of my words are strangled as the collar kicks in again. A groan slips through my teeth. My whole body shakes. I try to think calming thoughts, try to convince myself this isn't real. But though the logical part of my brain knows this is just nerve induction, just the *illusion* of pain, the reptile part is *screaming*. The skin is being flayed off my body with rusted knives, sandpaper is being scraped against raw muscle, blunt chisels are being jammed between my vertebrae, blood and spinal fluid are spilling down m—

The pain stops. A moment of shining, unspeakable relief.

"WHERE IS AURORA JIE-LIN O'MALLEY?"

I breathe deep. Close my eyes. Pray to the Maker for strength.

"T-Tyler J—"

And so we go.

I lose track of time.

I lose count of the flips of that switch.

I know I make it to Level 2 before I start screaming.

I start roaring at them to stop, stop, Maker's breath, stop, at Level 3.

They don't stop till 4.

"WHERE IS AURORA JIE-LIN O'MALLEY?"

"I don't know!"

I thrash weakly against the bonds holding me, just to have something to rage against. I taste copper on my tongue, spit blood on the floor. I realize my screams must have ruptured my vocal cords.

"WHERE IS AURORA JIE-LIN O'MALLEY?" Princeps repeats, maddening.

"I don't KNOW!" I roar, my voice hoarse and broken. "The location we were headed was on the Hephaestus black box! I never saw the data!"

Another impossible lance of pain.

Another bloody, spit-flecked scream.

"THIS CAN ALL END, LEGIONNAIRE JONES."

Again.

"SIMPLY TELL US THE TRUTH."

And again.

"WHERE IS AURORA JIE-LIN O'MALLEY?"

And again.

"I'M TELLING YOU I DON'T KNOW!"

And then it stops. Just like that. I feel vertigo. Delirium. Every second I spend without more of that pain seems like a blessing from the Maker, and I pray for blackness, for

309

sleep, for an end to it all. But then . . . then I feel a gentle hand touching my bare shoulder. Soft lips press against the burning skin of my forehead, cool as ice, relief washing over me like spring rain.

"You always did love being the hero," someone says.

I open my eyes. Blink through the sting of sweat, all the world blurring. And I know I'm dreaming then. That I've lost consciousness, or maybe I'm dead, because the face I see in front of me can't be real, can't be real

can't

be

". . . C-Cat?"

She smiles. Her dark hair is styled in the same undercut fauxhawk. The same phoenix tattoo is at her throat. The same pretty face, sharp chin, bow-shaped lips.

"Oh, Tyler," Cat whispers, caressing my cheek. "My beautiful Tyler."

I feel a sob, strangled, trying to bubble up and out of my bleeding throat. The relief I feel at seeing her, the tumbled crash of emotions, joy, love, disbelief, comfort, all of it threatens to just drag me under and drown me. It's not too late, I realize. The way we ended it . . . all the things I should've said and done . . .

But then I realize she's wearing the charcoal-gray GIA uniform, same as the others. That she has a mirrormask tucked under her arm. Glancing to my left, I realize the agent who stood there a moment ago is missing, and through the blur, through the haze, through the rising despair and anger and fear, I realize that she . . . *she* was the one who slipped the pain collar around my neck. And worse—worse than the pain they've put me through or the agony of seeing her again after I thought she was lost, worst of all is the moment when I focus on her eyes, fixed now on mine. Because the Cat I knew, the Cat I loved . . . that Cat's eyes were brown.

This one's are blue. Faintly luminous.

And her irises are shaped like flowers.

"No," I breathe. "Oh no . . ."

"You don't understand, Tyler."

She's . . .

I look at Princeps. Back at the thing wearing Cat. A wave of horror and fury washes over me, through me, drenching me to the bone.

"You're one of them," I whisper.

"I *am* them," she murmurs, touching my bare chest, right over my breaking heart. "They are me. I am we, Tyler. All of us."

"Maker," I whisper. "Oh Maker, what have they done to you?"

She shakes her head and smiles, looks at me like I'm a child. "It's warm in here, Ty. It's wonderful. It's full and it's complete and it's home. I've never been so loved or accepted. Never felt so real. I *can't wait* for you to feel it, too."

She leans forward, and the horror that washes over me as she presses her mouth to mine is just . . . indescribable. Her skin is cold, like a corpse's. Her breath smells of earth and some cloying sweetness, and her lips still brush mine as she whispers.

"*We* can't wait."

She lowers her chin. Eyes glinting with menace.

"But you need to tell us where Aurora is going, Tyler."

And I look into her eyes.

And I feel the tears spill out of my own.

"Tyler Jones," I say. "Alpha. Aurora Legion, Squad 312."

And the pain hits me again. And again. And again. It feels like forever. And though in the end I can't even scream, in the end I lose any sense of who or what I am, I know that even if I knew where Auri and the others were, I'd never tell them now. Because as much as it hurts, as deep as it cuts, all this pain is nothing compared to the agony of the only thought I cling to.

My Cat's gone.

She's really gone.

And they took her from me.

22

THE ECHO

Aurora

I'm fighting to stay upright, winds ripping through me from every direction. The gale howls around me, snatching at my clothes, trying to push me off balance and send me tumbling helplessly toward the ground.

I'm maybe a hundred meters above the lush grass of the Echo, but I can't see it beneath me. Instead, I'm shrouded by a silver mist that the windstorm constantly snatches apart, then rebuilds. The point of this test—a simple one, according to the Eshvaren—is to keep myself upright, controlling my position by means of mental strength alone. But it's exhausting and terrifying, like drowning in honey.

The Eshvaren's voice sounds in my mind.

You rely too much upon your physicality, it chides gently. *You must focus your mental strength here.*

Right, of course. Mental strength.

Even pausing to think about this creates a crack in my shield, and I'm smashed head over heels, my scream snatched away by the wind. I claw my way back to balance, arms flailing as I stabilize, adrenaline pumping through me as I fight to stay upright a few seconds more.

Then another gust of wind comes from my left, punching me in the ribs and knocking the breath out of me. As I gasp for air, my concentration flickers, and in an instant I'm plummeting, screaming, flapping my arms in a vain attempt to stop myself before I hit the ground. The green below me becomes visible through the cloudy haze, and then it's vivid and alive, and rushing straight at my face. I crash into the earth like a comet, shattering the ground around me.

Above, my own personal storm rages on, but all around, the Echo remains as golden and beautiful as it's always been. The sun shines down gently, wreaths of red and yellow flowers hang from nearby trees. The air smells so good you could eat it. But as I drag myself to my feet in the broken crater, my heart is racing, my face streaked with tears. I turn my head, and there's the crystalline figure of the Eshvaren, rainbows refracted in its shape, watching me as impassively as ever. A light seems to shine from inside it, setting all its colors glittering.

Again? it asks immediately.

"Just g-gimme a minute," I beg, doubled over, hands braced against my knees, "to catch . . . m-my breath."

That is not air in your lungs, it tells me. *That is not sweat on your skin. You have no physical self in this place. Here, your only limitation is your imagination. Your only obstacles are those you place in front of yourself.*

I close my eyes, trying to fight the frustration I feel at another round of psychobabble. It's been going on at me like this for hours now. I realize the Eshvaren knows what it's

314

talking about, but I'm really trying here. And being told every failure is my own fault isn't helping.

"This isn't working," I sigh, straightening slowly. "This isn't working even a little. I'm getting worse, not better."

Your performance does appear to be declining, the Eshvaren agrees.

"Why are we even doing this? What's the point?" I wave my hand at the roiling sky. "Am I going to have to fight my way through a storm to get to the Weapon?"

The Eshvaren shakes its head. *Patience is required in your training. There are two steps in mastering your power. The second is far more difficult. We will begin with the first: you must learn to summon your abilities on command. You apparently find even this simple lesson difficult.*

"Well, it hasn't gone great for me so far," I point out. "I mean, my power has gotten us out of some tough spots, but using it is a lot like unleashing a tiger to fight for you. You're really not sure who's going to get bitten in the process."

As long as the battle is won, what does it matter who the tiger bites?

I blink. "What's that supposed to mean?"

The Eshvaren simply shakes its head, the air around it tinkling like soft laughter. Through the warm glow surrounding it, I know it's smiling at me.

First lesson first, it says simply. *Let us begin again.*

Kal

The golden sky is fading to purple, tiny stars opening like flowers in the heavens overhead, when Aurora finally staggers into our camp. She looks exhausted, her hair snarled, her eyes pouched in shadows, but still, she is beautiful. With a sigh, she walks forward so I can enfold her in my arms. Kiss her brow. Hold her tight.

"How was your first day of training, be'shmai?" I ask.

"Tough day at the office," she replies.

We settle down in our camp. In truth, the place is unworthy of the name—it is simply the spot where we have chosen to sleep. It is situated in a gentle hollow, under a tall, silvered tree with purple leaves that sweep down to the grass. We have no beds. No real shelter. The weather is perfect, and it is not as though we need walls around us. But it still puts me on edge to be sleeping in the open.

"How was *your* day?" she murmurs, cradled and whole in my arms.

"Unproductive," I reply. "I tried walking to the crystal city. I thought to take a closer look at it, to see if perhaps it might be a better place for us to rest. But no matter how far I trekked, it remained forever on the horizon."

"Weird. We could ask the Eshvaren about it?"

I shake my head, pressing my lips thin. "Do not trouble it, be'shmai. I think perhaps the less I deal with our host, the better."

She glances up at me. "Did it say something to you?"

"No," I admit. "But when we first arrived . . . it did not feel pleased to see me. I do not think it wants me here."

"Well, that's tough, Legionnaire Gilwraeth," she says, snuggling further into my arms. "Because *I* do."

I smile, holding her tighter. For a time we simply sit in silence, enjoying each other's warmth, the way our bodies fit together. With her this close, I cannot help but think of our night on the *Zero* before we came here. I long to burn inside that fire again. But for now, it is enough to simply be with her.

"Are you hungry?" I ask.

"No," she replies.

". . . Nor I," I realize.

"The Eshvaren told me this place isn't really physical," she murmurs.

"I suppose it makes sense that we wouldn't feel physical needs?"

She chuckles in my arms, wriggles closer. "Speak for yourself, legionnaire."

I think perhaps Aurora is making . . . what is the Terran word for it . . . innuendo? But then she sits up straighter, calls out into the gathering gloom.

"Hello? Can you hear me?"

The air ripples, and without even a whisper, the image of the Eshvaren is suddenly, soundlessly floating before us. The light within it refracts and shimmers on its crystalline skin. It turns its gaze upon me, and though I am struck again with the sense it does not want me here, I still admire its beauty.

Yes? it says, its voice like music.

"Hi," Aurora says. "Listen, I know this might be a strange request, but could we maybe get some food? I know we technically don't *need* to eat but . . ."

Any refreshment you require can be yours, the Eshvaren replies.

"Oh great," my be'shmai says. "And . . . maybe some furniture or something? It'd be nice to sleep on a blanket and some pillows?"

Any comfort you require can be yours.

"Brilliant," Aurora smiles.

The Eshvaren remains hovering in silence before us. Long moments tick by with no food or blankets making themselves known. Aurora peers at the apparition, her smooth brow slowly creasing into a frown.

". . . Well?" she asks.

All you require can be yours, it says. *You need only will it into being.*

". . . Will it?" Aurora's frown grows darker.

Yes.

"I can't even keep myself upright in a basic training exercise," she says, temper flaring. "You want me to start conjuring things out of thin air?"

I am only a collection of memories, it replies. *I do not want anything.*

And without another word, the Eshvaren shimmers out of existence.

Aurora glances at me, clearly uncertain. I can see how exhausted she is. How much our brief time here has already cost her. But then I see determination flaring in the depths of her mismatched eyes. She breathes deep, sits up straighter in my arms. Leaning into me like I am a rock in a storm.

And, eyes narrowed in concentration, she holds out her hand.

I feel the faintest tingling on my skin. I sense something vast moving beneath her surface. The air around us feels charged with current, and for the tiniest moment, I think perhaps the air before us ripples. Shimmers. Twists.

But only for a moment.

The current fades. The steel in Aurora's muscles wilts, her back bows. I can feel her pulse hammering beneath her skin, hear the strain in her voice as she gasps.

"I c-can't. . . ."

Breathless, she sinks back into my arms, frustrated and angry. I know what it is to train beyond all limit of endurance, to suffer under a relentless taskmaster. I do not know if I can make it easier. But I try, in some small way, to make it better.

"Take courage, be'shmai," I tell her. "All is well."

I kiss her brow.

"We have time."

Hold her tight.

"And we have each other."

Aurora

I'm beginning to hate this rock.

No, scratch that. I *do* hate this rock. I hate it with every fiber of my being. I hate it worse than Mr. Parker from fifth grade, who put *me* in detention for punching Kassandra Lim, even though *she* was the one who cut off a piece of my hair.

I hate it worse than Kassandra Lim.

The rock and I have been in a standoff for seven days now, and by every available measure, the inanimate object is winning. It sits in the middle of a gorgeous blue-green meadow, sprinkled with tiny pink flowers that give the whole scene a rosy hue. The sky is that same rosy color, and there's a perfect little stream to the east, shaded by low-hanging trees with purple leaves.

The task I've been set should be simple for someone with power like mine. All I have to do is pick up the rock and move it to the other side of the meadow.

But of course I can't.

My power still doesn't show up on command like that. And I've never really used it to manipulate objects before. I've just smashed them around and broken them apart.

Are you ready for another attempt? Esh asks.

"Yeah, sure," I mutter, from between gritted teeth. "It's *definitely* going to be the seven millionth time that's the charm."

Self-discipline comes slowly, it replies. *You continue to make small gains.*

I jab a finger in the rock's direction. "That smug son of a biscuit is sitting exactly where it was a week ago. I haven't made *any* gains, large or small."

You have not kicked it in five days, Esh points out.

"This is getting us nowhere, Esh," I snap. "At this rate, I'm going to be an old lady, the entire galaxy will be one giant Ra'haam colony, and I still won't have moved the boulder."

Time is not in short supply, Esh replies. *Though weeks have passed here, little more than an hour has passed from the perception of your crew. Are you ready to begin again?*

I draw breath for another retort, then pause. *My crew.* They're the reason I'm doing this. Saving the entire galaxy and everyone in it sounds ridiculous. It's not the sort of thing you can really get your head around. But saving just a few people . . .

I think of Cat as she slipped away into the Ra'haam. I think of Tyler, dragged off by the TDF. I think of Scarlett, watching her brother get left behind. Of Zila, of Fin, risking everything to protect me. They all have something or someone to lose.

And I think of Kal, of course. Constant, patient, faithful.

When I first understood what the Pull meant, I panicked. Who wouldn't? But he's never expected me to feel what he does. In fact, he's never expected anything of me. He's only ever offered.

And that's *definitely* something worth fighting for.

"All right, Esh," I say, squaring my shoulders. "Let's move this thing."

Your optimism is laudable, it replies, flickering out of the way.

I stride up to the rock and clear my mind. Push aside thought and emotion like it told me, keeping only the sense of purpose I feel when I think about protecting the ones I love. I breathe in. I breathe out.

Then I raise my hands and focus on the rock, visualizing it moving to the other side of the meadow. Sweat beading on my skin. My brows twisting into a frown. I unleash my certainty, my conviction, my will that it's going to move.

It's going to move.

It's going to move.

And absolutely nothing happens.

"Sonofabiscuit!"

With a roar of frustration, I kick the rock. Then I scream and fall on the ground, clutching my foot, tears of agony and frustration in my eyes.

The Eshvaren looms above me, its crystalline face shimmering with every color of the rainbow.

Why do you fail? it asks.

"How should I know?" I shout, eyes stinging.

Why. Do. You. Fail? it asks again.

"You're the one who's supposed to be teaching me!"

What is clouding your mind? it asks. *What stands in your way?*

"I don't—"

You are not merely a vessel for the power, Aurora Jie-Lin O'Malley. You are the power. A power that must shatter planets. This is a place of the mind. The ties that hold you to this—it touches my chest with one shimmering finger—*only hold you back. You must let go of what you were to become what you are.*

It peers at me, eyes shining all the colors of the rainbow.

Burn. It. All. Away.

I hang my head, traitorous tears welling in my eyes.

"And what if I can't do that?" I ask.

The Eshvaren shrugs.

Then you will do nothing.

Kal

Aurora is displeased.

We have been here for weeks, and she seems to be making no progress. As she stomps back to our camp after another day's fruitless labor, I can feel the frustration soaking her through. She sinks into my arms, melts against my lips, and for a moment, all is well. I know she is glad to be back here. With me. Us, together. But still, I can feel how discouraged she is.

"How can I help, be'shmai?" I ask her.

"I don't know," she murmurs. "I don't know what I'm supposed to do."

I hold her close, her cheek pressed to my chest as I smooth back her hair. "What does the Eshvaren say?"

"'Unshackle the strictures of the flesshhhh.'" She adopts a deep voice, mocking that of our host, and wiggles fingers in my face. "'You must let go of what you werrrre to become what you arrrrrre. Burn it all awaaaaay.'"

I chuckle, and the smile she gives me in response makes my heart sing.

Spirits of the Void, she is so beautiful. . . .

"Perhaps it is normal to progress slowly?" I ask. "Perhaps this is just part of the journey all Triggers take?"

"I don't even know if other Triggers came here before me," she sighs. "I don't know anything, other than that I don't *know* anything."

"*I* know you," I say. "You are one of the most courageous, strongest people I have ever met." I turn her away from me to look out into the blue-green clearing around us, my hands at rest on her hips. "Do as it asks you."

"What do you mean?"

"Empty your mind," I urge her. "Think only what you must be, not what you were. And then make us something."

". . . Like what?"

"Something simple?" I offer. "A fire, perhaps?"

She breathes deep. Still uncertain. But finally, she nods. "Okay."

Aurora closes her eyes. Reaches out toward the empty space, the smooth, flawless grass just a few meters away. I can feel the struggle inside her, feel her muscles tense.

"I can't . . . ," she mutters, teeth clenched.

"You *can*," I whisper.

She winces, her hand trembling.

"Burn it," she breathes. "Burn it all away."

I hold her tight. Willing her on. And then, as if some new thought has occurred to her, she pulls my hands away from her waist, steps out from the circle of my arms. Amazement budding in my chest, I see the ground before her shimmer, the air ripple as if it were water with a handful of pebbles cast into it.

"Let it go," she whispers.

And, as if by sorcery, a blaze springs up from the ground before her. Not merely unchecked flame, but a firepit, stacked with burning logs. I can smell woodsmoke, feel heat, hear the timber crackling in the flames.

Aurora turns to me, her eyes shining.

"Kal, I *did* it!"

She squeals and crashes into my arms. Elation on her face, she stands on tiptoe and crushes her lips to mine, and almost all of me is caught up in the joy of her victory. But the smallest part, the part that feels unwelcome when the Eshvaren looks upon me, the part that ached as she pushed my hands away from her hips and stepped out of my embrace, realizes that, yes, she did it. But she did it . . .

Alone?

Burn it, she said.

Burn it all away.

Aurora

It's been a month, and I still feel a thrill of satisfaction every time I move the rock across the meadow. It's light as a feather now, spinning through the air solely under the force of my will.

"How you like *that*," I mutter under my breath.

The stone cannot reply to you, Esh points out, not for the first time. *Not only is it without the ability to think or speak, it is also not a real stone.*

"Then it won't mind if I take a win at its expense," I reply.

I can feel it. All of it. The dozen boulders I have suspended in the air above our heads, twirling and whirling like butterflies on a breeze.

I can feel the power, not just inside me, not just a part of me, but *all* of me. I let go of the feeling of my body, the sun on my skin, the sense that I'm anything at all but this force within me as another boulder rises from the river and joins the others.

I look at Esh, my lips curling. "Not bad, huh?"

"Jie-Lin," says a voice behind me

My heart stops beating. My stomach lurches sideways. Because even though I know the sound of that voice as well as my own, I know it can't be, it can't be, it . . .

I turn and look behind me, and there he is.

He looks like he used to. Before . . . before Octavia. A bright smile and twinkling eyes and the wrinkles in his brow Mom used to tease him about so much. He's standing there in the meadow, surrounded by rippling flowers, smiling at me.

"Daddy?" I whisper.

The ground beside me thunders as one of the boulders above me crashes to the earth. I shriek as another falls, then another, throwing myself aside as the tons of rock I moved around so effortlessly a moment ago all slip away like sand through my fingers. The ground shatters, the flowers are crushed to pulp.

Why do you fail?

Sprawled on the ground, I look up and see the Eshvaren above me, silhouetted against the rose sky, looking down with its rainbow eyes.

What stops you burning? it asks.

I look at the space where my father stood. The broken earth, the shattered rocks. There's no sign of him now. Nothing remains but the tears that the sight of him brought to my eyes. I realize he was nothing but a phantom. A ghost. An echo.

"How did you do that?" I demand, looking up at Esh, anger rising inside me like a flood. "If you're just a collection of million-year-old memories, how do you know what he even looked like?"

We have told you before, Aurora Jie-Lin O'Malley, Esh replies. *Your only obstacles in this place are those you put in front of yourself. You must let them go.*

It leans closer, its voice like a song in my mind.

Burn. It. All. Away.

23

TYLER

I open my eyes, wondering where I am.

I can taste the vaguely metallic tang that Terran oxygen scrubbers leave in the air, and for a moment I wonder if I'm back in my dorm in Aurora Academy. Thinking about the academy puts me in mind of my squad, and of course that makes me think of Cat, and suddenly it's crashing down on me like an avalanche. That detention cell. Those faceless mirrormasks. Cat's new blue eyes, boring deep into my own, dry, cold lips pressed to mine.

It's warm in here, Ty. I can't wait for you to feel it, too.

I jolt upright with a gasp, rewarded with flares of pain: head, chest, throat. My screams have torn my vocal cords up good—it feels like I swallowed broken glass. I wince, pawing at my neck, looking around the cell and finding a pair of cool eyes staring back at me. Black hair. Black lips. Black heart.

Saedii.

You were gone a long time, little Terran.

Her voice rings in my mind, radiating Syldrathi arrogance, a melody of faint disdain. I still find it more than a little frightening that this psychopath can speak inside my head, but given the state of my voice box, it's probably for the best. I don't think the damage is permanent, but I doubt I'll be singing karaoke for a while. . . .

What did they do to you? Saedii asks, looking me over.

What do you care? I shoot back.

I care, little Terran, because they will probably do it to me next.

Frightened?

Know your enemy, boy.

My eyebrows rise slowly.

Are you honestly quoting Terran military strategy at me right now?

She scoffs softly. *Of course not. Do not be a fool.*

Sun Tzu said that. He was a Terran general. "Know your enemy and know yourself, and you will not be imperiled in one hundred battles."

Sarai Rael said that. She was a Syldrathi Templar. "Know your enemy's heart if you wish to feast upon it."

. . . I think Sun Tzu's way of saying it is a little more poetic.

I am Warbreed, Tyler Jones. What need have I of poetry?

Saedii stretches out her long legs in front of her, glaring. I'm painfully conscious of the fact she's still wearing nothing but her underwear from the waist down, but, gentleman that I am, I keep my eyes fixed firmly on hers. Saedii's fingers brush the string of severed thumbs around her neck, and I realize that once again, she's trying to get a reaction from me. She knows how beautiful she is. She knows how that beauty throws people off balance if they let it, and she wants to see what it does to me. Everything about this girl is measured. Strategic. Calculating.

I also realize I'm still not wearing a shirt.

And that those legs of hers go up forever . . .

They want information about my squad, I tell her. *Information you don't have. Torturing prisoners of war is a violation of the Madrid Conventions. So don't worry.*

She arches one perfect brow.

Do I strike you as someone who is particularly worried, Tyler Jones?

If you had any idea what was really happening here, you would be.

I know exactly what is happening here. Your people have consigned themselves to suicide. Who will you mourn most, I wonder, when your world is dragged screaming into the black hole Archon Caersan makes of your sun?

I feel the anger flare inside my head.

You know, you talk about knowing your enemy, I tell her. *Doesn't anything about this situation strike you as suspicious? The Terran government has spent the last two years keeping its nose as far out of Syldrathi affairs as humanly possible. And now we just open fire on an Unbroken flagship for the fun of it?*

The Unbroken never agreed to the Jericho Accord, boy. The war between our people never truly ended. It was only a matter of time before Syldrathi hands once more gleamed with Terran blood. This is a matter of honor.

Can't you see when you're being played?

She looks at me and sneers.

You are afraid of the coming storm.

Of course I'm afraid! Billions of people could die!

You are unworthy of the blood in your veins.

I shake my head and turn away. I know I should be trying

to get her on my side. I know the enemy of my enemy is my friend. But I feel like there's no point in even *talking* to this girl. I understand what it is to be a soldier, to fight for something you truly believe in. But Kal's sister seems like nothing but rage and scorn.

Still, she presses on, looking at me with those black-rimmed eyes.

Jericho Jones had the courage to fight when his world needed him. When the call was sounded at Orion, he at least was honorable enough to answer it.

I glare at her, jaw clenching at the mention of my dad.

You think there's honor in another massacre? We both lost our fathers in that battle, Saedii—isn't that enough?

Saedii's eyes narrow.

Is that what Ka—

The door slides open with a soft whisper. I look up and see half a dozen Terran marines in full tac armor, disruptors cradled in their arms. My heart sinks, my throat constricts, as I remember that pain collar slipping around my neck. The thought of another round of torture fills my stomach with slippery ice.

"Oh Maker," I croak.

The marines file into the room, boots ringing on the floor. But instead of grabbing me, they march over to Saedii's bio-cot, surround her in a small ring.

"Hands, pixiebitch," their lieutenant commands, holding out a set of mag-restraints.

". . . What do you want with her?" I demand, my throat aching.

"Hands," the LT repeats, his comrades punctuating the command by raising their rifles. "Now."

"She doesn't know anything," I protest. "You don't—"

"Shut your mouth, traitor," one of the marines snarls at me.

Saedii's voice rings in my head, that small smile growing a little wider.

This is courage, little Terran. Watch and learn.

She stands slow, languid, extending her arms and offering her slender wrists. She's outnumbered six to one, and already wounded. But as the LT moves to slap on the restraints, Saedii brings up her hand and drives her knuckles into his throat.

The man gasps, flies back three meters into the wall. Despite her injuries, Saedii kicks another's legs out from under him, slaps the third's rifle aside, blindingly quick. But the rest are ready for her, blasting her full in the chest with point-blank disruptor shots. Stun blasts ring out in the cell and Saedii crashes backward, braids flying. I'm half out of my cot before I realize it, face to face with another marine's rifle. He peers down the barrel at me, his laser sight lighting up my bruised and bare chest.

"Give me a reason, traitor," the private says. "I'm begging you."

"This isn't the way we do things," I say, despite the agony in my throat.

"We?" he scoffs, looking at the tattoo on my arm. "Who's 'we,' Legion boy?"

"I'm Terran just like you. I don—"

"Those pixies killed a few thousand Terrans during the *Andarael* attack," the lieutenant growls, picking himself up off the deck. "And *she* was calling their shots. This is *exactly* how we do it. So shut your mouth before we do you, too."

"You're getting played!" I hiss. "The GIA is using the TDF to start a—"

The private steps up and clocks me in the face with the butt of his disruptor. I'm rocked backward, tumbling down onto the cot.

"One more word, traitor," he growls, "and you're gonna be picking up your teeth with broken fingers."

I raise my hands, pressed back onto the bed. I watch as one of the marines slings the semiconscious Saedii onto his shoulders, as the lieutenant shoots me a poison glance and, with a barked order, sends the whole squad marching out of the cell without another word.

I lick the split in my lip, tasting blood, my skull still ringing from the blow.

I have no idea what they want with her, but it can't be good. And then I think of the Ra'haam, wearing those GIA colonists like second skins. I think of Cat with her new blue eyes. All the things I should have said and done.

And I shake my head and sigh.

Maker's breath, none of this is good.

24

THE ECHO

Kal

She has come so far in these last months.

I watch Aurora from our camp, my breath taken clean away by the power she wields. The clearing we sleep in has been transformed. The simple fire she summoned so long ago has been replaced with an ornate stone firepit. The grass we slept on has been crowned with the grandest bed I have ever seen in my life—four-poster, carved wood, silken sheets. My be'shmai even crafted me a siif so I could play during the day while she is about her training.

I sit now beneath our trees, strumming the instrument's strings, watching her. Aurora floats high above me, just a silhouette against a blinding sky. Boulders larger than the *Zero* orbit her in perfect synchronicity, moving in all directions. She floats in the center, sitting as if on the air, her right eye burning. I watch as one boulder shatters into a thousand shards, its fragments forming a perfect sphere around her.

The Eshvaren floats nearby, watching. It does not look

at me. It does not speak to me. As ever, I feel a vague sense of . . . not hostility, but unwelcome, in its presence. But as I strike chords upon the siif my be'shmai made me, I see that the hues within its crystal form change with the music I play.

"May I ask you something?" I call.

It does not look at me. But I feel a fraction of its attention shift.

Ask, it replies.

"A thought has been playing on my mind since we arrived." I strum a minor chord, watch the Eshvaren's hue shift and dance. "Why do you look like us?"

It turns its head then. Regarding me with kaleidoscopic eyes.

I do not fear this thing. A warrior fears only to never taste victory. But I feel the power in it. My people are one of the few species in the galaxy to still hold belief in the Eshvaren. The Ancient Ones were mythical figures to me as a child. And sitting here in the presence of their collected memory, I find its gaze . . . unsettling.

"I mean to say, you do not look *exactly* like us. But you are bipedal. Humanoid. Do you appear this way to make it easier for us to look upon you?"

It is a long time before the Eshvaren replies.

We do not look like you, young one, it finally says. *You look like us.*

". . . I still do not understand," I reply.

Nor do you need to.

"Perhaps not. But I wish to."

Your wishes are irrelevant, young one. You are irrelevant.

I try to ignore the sting to my pride, keep my voice cool.

"Why do we look like you?"

The Eshvaren does not reply, its glowing eye on Aurora in the rose sky above.

"The Terrans, Betraskans, Chellerians, hundreds of other races," I press. "We all wear similar shapes. We are all bipedal. Carbon-based. Oxygen breathers. The odds of that are next to impossible. Many among the milieu take our similarities as final proof of a greater power. As undisputable evidence of a . . . divine will. It is the basis of their United Faith. Of the existence of a god. A Maker."

Again, the Eshvaren says nothing. But I push on.

"Our enemy knows much more than we do. The Ra'haam was there during the last battle. We cannot meet it in ignorance. If there is some knowledge we would benefit from in the coming fight, it might be dangerous to keep it from us."

Finally, the Eshvaren glances at me. I feel a shiver down my spine and my fingers slip on the strings, setting a rainbow loose inside its form.

You would do well not to lecture on the price of keeping secrets.

I blink. "What do you mean by that?"

We have been preparing for eons to win this war. When we first defeated the Great Enemy, through one thousand years of blood and fire, we knew what needed to be done to ensure it did not rise again. And we know now. Better than you. Do not presume to lecture us on the perils of the deceit you so obviously reek of.

It turns its burning eyes back to Aurora.

Do not dare.

The siif is heavy in my hands. The Eshvaren's words heavy in my chest.

I place the instrument aside and sit in silence.

And I am afraid.

Aurora

Esh has brought me somewhere new today. We flew for an hour, soaring over now-familiar landmarks. The meadow, with its pink carpet of flowers. The wide river I must have sunk into hundreds of times before I managed to part it. The tangled jungle where eventually every single leaf held still at the wave of my hand.

We end up on a cliff top, looking out over the broad vista of the Echo, the crystal city on the far horizon. I never thought about this place having an edge, but behind us is a kind of mist that slowly swirls and roils.

This is the end of the world, I guess.

I sit cross-legged on the edge of the cliff, looking out over my training ground, and I wait. Floating beside me, Esh eventually speaks.

You are failing us, Aurora Jie-Lin O'Malley, it tells me.

I blink, looking up into its face and trying to hide the hurt in my own.

You have grown, it says. *But not enough.*

"What do you mean?" I demand. "I'm stronger than I've *ever* been. I can split rivers, shatter boulders—"

Your grip on this power must be enough to shatter not just boulders, but worlds. You know what you must do.

"I don't—"

You do, it replies. *You do know. You are still a prisoner to your old self. You are locked inside the idea of what you were. These affections, these bonds, they tug you backward, when your focus must be on what lies ahead. To truly embrace it, you must burn, Aurora Jie-Lin O'Malley. Or you must leave this place and resign yourself to all that will never be.*

Even though it was months ago, I still remember my failure in the field of flowers. The image of my father. Some part of me knows that what Esh is saying is true—one word from a ghost was enough to make me lose my grip. Reduce me to tears. I can feel them even now, burning in my eyes, welling in my lashes.

"I want to," I say.

Do you?

"Yes!" I shout. "I *hate* feeling this way. But . . . it's hard, Esh. It's *so* hard. When I left for Octavia, I was supposed to wake up a couple of weeks later and start a new life. Instead, I slept two hundred *years.*" I paw at my eyes, angry at the tears, at myself. "And I know there are some things that are more important than one little Earth girl crying over her life, but maybe you could ease off *just* a little." I look up at those rainbow eyes, accusation in my own. "Because everything I've lost is because of *you.*"

It stands there, glittering in the light. I can feel it's almost . . . angry with me.

We understand what we ask you to give up. But the galaxy is at stake.

"I know that!"

Thousands of inhabited worlds. Billions upon billions of souls. All of it shall be consumed if the Ra'haam is allowed to bloom.

"I know that too!" I cry, climbing to my feet. "I'm not an idiot, Esh. I *know!*"

And yet you refuse. To let go. To burn. You are the Trigger,

Aurora Jie-Lin O'Malley. You are the power of the Eshvaren made manifest. And if you do not let go of the obstacles that hold you back, then you will fail.

"But *how*?" I ask.

Do you wish it? Esh asks.

I look up at the rose-colored sky above my head. The billion suns waiting beyond. I think about everything that hangs in the balance. The lives of all those strangers, the lives of all my friends. All that will be lost if I stumble here.

All my life, I wanted to be an explorer. To see and do things most people only dreamed of. To take myself to the very edge. That's why I trained in cartography, why I sacrificed so much to get onto the Octavia mission in the first place, that mission that somehow, two centuries later, has led me right here.

To *this* edge.

"Yes," I hear myself say.

Truly?

"Yes!"

Then close your eyes.

And so I do.

I find myself in a white room, afternoon sun shining through broad glass windows. I realize I'm standing in one of the dozen kitchens my family had as we bounced around the world in preparation for the Octavia mission. And then I feel a flood of sudden pressure in my chest, a rush of joy and heartache and love as I see her, right there, close enough for me to reach out and touch.

"Mom . . . ," I whisper.

She looks up and gives me one of her smiles—the ones

that made me feel like everything was all right in the world. And looking around the room, letting the scene soak into me, I realize that I've been here before. That this isn't just a *place* from my memories—this is a particular night I already lived.

It was my father's birthday. Mom was chopping vegetables for his favorite dish from her side of the family: a thick brown stew full of carrots and potatoes, lamb and barley. I was measuring out tapioca starch for his favorite fresh rice noodles.

I was about thirteen, and she and I didn't always get along by then. I'd already decided I wanted to try out for Octavia. My mom said it was too soon to be making life decisions like that. And I ache at the memory of the fights we had about it, the time we wasted on struggling over something so small.

Now I watch her quick, capable hands as she works, her familiar wedding ring. When this night really happened, all those centuries ago, we just sang and cooked and talked about one of my homework assignments until the others got home. But now, I know, I can divert the vision if I want to, as long as I don't push it too far.

And I *do* want to. Badly.

So I tell the home system to turn down the music, and I lean into Mom's side, rest my head against her shoulder. She wraps an arm around me and gives me a squeeze. It's so familiar, the softness of her so perfect, that I feel tears in my eyes.

"What is it, Auri J?" she asks, pressing a kiss to my hair.

I'm quiet as I consider what it is I want to say to her. I know I can't tell her what's happened—it will break the illusion, the shape of what this place is. But I know I can come close.

"I guess I'm just thinking about some of my friends at my old schools," I say.

"Oh?"

I suck on my lower lip. "I mean, I know we always move, but some of them . . . I think they were planning on having me around a lot longer, you know? I think they felt like they could count on me for things, and now I'm not there anymore."

"Oh, my Aurora." She turns to me, tucks me under her chin. Soon I'll be too tall for that. "You've always taken your responsibilities so seriously. I respect that about you very much. And I know it's hard to move on. But we can't hold ourselves in place forever, darling, not for anyone. Life is for living. The ones you left behind will be all right, I promise. The ones you leave behind in the future will be all right too, even if you make it all the way to another planet."

"But some people depend on us," I say.

"Well, it's true that they do," she says. "But you'll have lots of adventures in the future, and goodbyes will come with lots of them. The ones who love you will take pride in sending you on those adventures, I promise."

I ease back enough to look up at her, my eyes aching.

"I love you, Mom," I say, and she looks down at me with all the love in the world written on her face, in the tender curve of her mouth.

"I love you too, my darling," she says quietly. "And if one day you do set off on all those adventures you imagine for yourself, I'll be proud to have raised a daughter who's brave enough to have followed her dreams. I promise."

"Even if I'm leaving you behind?"

"You'll never do that, baby," she says again. "I'll *always* be with you."

．　．　．　．　．

That night, I cry in Kal's arms.

"I did leave her," I say into his chest, so snotty and muffled that I have no idea if he can understand me. "I left her for an adventure, but for all she knew, I died."

He presses a soft kiss to my hair. "To her, you died pursuing your dream. You were living your life just as she told you to. A life well lived, of any length, is as much as any of us can hope for, be'shmai."

Later, I make us potatoes and carrots and lamb and barley and gravy, and I show Kal how to cook the stew, and my mom's Irish brown bread. And we sit side by side, shoulders pressed together, and I tell him stories about growing up on Earth.

By the time I'm done explaining field hockey to him—he's baffled by the fact that it's *against* the rules to use the sticks to hit your opponents—I'm all cried out, and all laughed out.

I'm lighter, and I'm easier, because the truth is, just being around Kal calms me. His touch, his gaze, the small smiles I draw from him—those especially are something I never could have imagined back when we met. But all of it grounds me, when the pressure of this place might otherwise break me into pieces. Being in the Echo has allowed us months together, to learn each other in the way you only can with time, and I'm so grateful for this gift I don't even know how to tell him.

One thing I've learned about him is that when his gaze slides to my mouth the way it does now, he's thinking about kissing me. And I don't want to wait for him to get around to it, not tonight.

And so I reach across to take hold of the front of his shirt, and he allows me to pull him effortlessly toward me as I lift my chin, a tingle of anticipation starting between my shoulder blades, zipping down to the small of my back as our lips meet.

We're sitting side by side, and as he shifts his weight to lean over me, I curl one hand up around his neck. His hand slides around to support me, and he lowers me down so I can lie back against the soft grass, pulling him with me. His shape blocks out some of the stars, and the soft sound I drag from him when I deepen the kiss makes me forget where we are.

There's an excitement and a familiarity to him that make these moments perfect, and even as I arch my back to press up into him, I'm smiling against his lips all over again.

This is what I needed. Between the lesson from Esh today and now Kal's quiet, solid—and hey, incredibly sexy—comfort, I feel like there's some . . . weight that's been lifted off my shoulders. Some shadow inside me that's been washed away.

I think I'm finally understanding what it is I need to do here. I can feel all of it—the guilt at leaving my family behind, the anger that they were taken from me, the sorrow that I never got to be part of the lives they made when I was gone. But at the same time, I hold on to the knowledge and the realization that they *did* make lives.

Because everyone does.

Here in the present moment I have Kal. He's everything I could ever have wanted, and I don't have to feel the Pull to know that I love him—not suddenly, in a rush, but piece by piece, moment by moment, each new lesson I learn adding another layer to the way I feel about him.

And curling up in Kal's arms later that night, my cheek pressed to his bare chest, I know what I need to do with all this weight that's been dragging me down.

Holding me back.

I need to let go of my past, and focus on my present.

I need to abandon who I was, and embrace who I am.

I just need to burn it all away.

· · · · ·

The next morning, Esh and I return to the cliff top. I feel light as air as we soar over the Echo, all its beauty laid out beneath us. I sit on the edge of the drop, staring out over the edge of the world. And this time, it's my father I see when I close my eyes.

I'm six or seven years old, and he's come in to read me a bedtime story. We have a big book of fairy tales and folktales from around the world. He sits on the bed beside me, and we leaf through the pages together, him reading and me tracing one small finger over the illustrations.

He wraps an arm around me, and in a well-practiced move, I prop my knees next to his so he can shift the book over and I can turn the pages for him.

I let him read for a long while. I breathe in the smell of him, feel the warmth of his skin, remembering the time when his arms felt like the safest place in all the world. But eventually he looks down at me, brow creased in that way I always loved.

"Is there something on your mind, Jie-Lin?" he asks quietly.

He's so tuned in to me, so carefully attentive. All I can think about is our last conversation—or at least, the last conversation we ever had when he was actually himself, instead of part of the Ra'haam.

I shouted at him and Patrice and hung up before he got a chance to reply.

"I'm thinking about someone I left behind," I tell him.

". . . At your last school?"

I nod. "I said something mean. And I didn't get a chance to say I was sorry before we left."

"Ah." He carefully closes the book, sets it on the floor beside the bed. "Well, that's difficult. If you can, it's always good to go back and apologize. But when that's not possible, I think it's very important to remember that no relationship, or friendship, is defined by one moment. It's an accumulation of all the moments we spend together. All the little ways in which we say *I love you* or *I respect you* or *You are important to me* add up. And that cannot be erased with a few careless words."

"How do you know?" I whisper.

"When your grandmother died, I regretted very much that I hadn't called her that week. I had meant to, but I was busy. Over time, though, I realized that one missed call didn't define our relationship. That tens of thousands of *I love you*s did that instead. She knew exactly how I cared for her, and

344

how I respected her. And that was what was important." He gives me a squeeze. "Does that help, Jie-Lin?"

"You're sure last words don't matter?" I close my eyes tightly, soaking up the warmth of his arms. "You're sure she'd forgive you?"

"In an instant. Those who truly know us see the whole, never just a part."

I settle in against his side. Close my eyes and whisper.

"I love you, Daddy."

"I love you too, Jie-Lin."

He kisses the top of my head, and my lips curl in a smile. "Always."

· · · · ·

That evening, Kal and I walk to the meadow and lie back together in the field of pink flowers, their petals all closed against the night. We stare up at the stars that once carpeted the sky above the home planet of the Eshvaren, adrift in each other's arms.

I know I'm making it harder for myself. I'm spending all day pushing things away, and then I come home each night to fall more and more deeply into Kal. And he seems to know it, too. I can feel it growing in him, along with the love he feels for me. A shadow in him. It's heavy tonight, weighing him down even as he looks at the beauty of the stars wheeling overhead.

"Are you okay?" I ask him.

I can feel his mind, the tapestry of golden threads, the faint empathy he inherited from his mother entwined with my own growing strength.

"I am torn, be'shmai," he finally replies.

"About what?"

"I have been thinking." He sighs, looking up at the night sky. "About the gift Adams gave me. The cigarillo box that saved my life aboard the *Totentanz*."

I blink. "Why have you been thinking about it?"

"The case . . . had a note inside it. A note in Finian's handwriting that he does not remember writing. It was he who discovered it. But I wonder if it was for me."

". . . What did it say?" I ask, unsure if I really want to know.

He looks at me, eyes shining. "'Tell her the truth.'"

I remain silent, watching him in the dark. He's beautiful, ethereal, almost magical, and for a moment I can't believe he's mine. But I can see the struggle in him. Feel the torment in his mind.

"There are things about me, be'shmai," he says, and I'm amazed to see tears in his eyes. "About my past. My blood . . ."

"Kal, it's okay," I tell him, touching his face.

He shakes his head. "This thing in me. I fear I will never be rid of him."

I remember the story he told me about Saedii. The pain of his childhood, his father's cruelty to him and his mother, the shadow of his past that always hangs over him. I know he struggles every day. The violence he was raised to, the violence inside him. I can feel it, even now, prowling behind those beautiful eyes.

"You're not your past, Kal." I curl my fingers through his, my eyes on the constellations above. "You're not the things you were raised to be. If being here has taught me anything, it's that. Our regrets, our fears, they hold us back. We have to let them go so we can become what we're supposed to be. We have to burn them all away."

"Our past makes us what we are."

"No," I tell him, remembering the weight lifting from my shoulders as I let go of my mom and dad. "No, it *doesn't*. We choose who we are. Every day. Every minute. The past is gone. Tomorrow is worth a million yesterdays, don't you see?"

Kal looks up at the stars above us, frowning.

"I . . . question this road they make you walk, be'shmai," he says quietly.

". . . What do you mean?" I ask.

"If you cut yourself off from who you were, burn away everything that means something to you as the Ancients bid you to . . ." He shakes his head. "What will give you purpose? What will drive you to fight?"

"Saving the entire galaxy is purpose enough," I say, my voice firm.

"Your fight is honorable," he agrees.

"I can sense a very large *but* approaching."

"But *love* is purpose, be'shmai," he says. "Love is what drives us to great deeds, and greater sacrifices. Without love, what is left?"

I pull my hand away from his. "Kal, I *have* to do this. If the Ra'haam's nursery planets are left alone, everyone in the galaxy, *including* the ones I love, will be taken over. I already lost my father to this thing."

"And now you would lose everything else to stop it?"

"I'm not saying I want to," I sigh. "I'm saying I have to."

I don't know what to say to him. I don't know what to do.

So in the end, hating that I'm doing it, I push to my feet and walk back silently toward camp.

And though I can feel it tearing at him . . .

He lets me go.

. . . . .

I'm expecting to see Callie the next day, but I'm expecting her to be a child like she was when I left her. Instead, as I slip into my vision, I see a woman in her thirties, sleek black hair reaching the small of her back, rippling with her movements as she plays the violin. She's standing by a sunlit window, playing the song from memory.

"Callie," I whisper, my voice sticking in my throat.

Her smile blossoms, and she sets down her violin and bow. "There you are," she says simply, opening her arms to me.

I'm across the room in an instant, smacking into her chest as she folds me up in a hug, holding me tight.

She's older than me, which feels strange, but this is how it must have been almost all her life. I wonder what it felt like for her to reach my age, and then her eighteenth birthday, knowing she was now older than I'd ever been.

"I'm so sorry," I sob, tears soaking through the green silk of her shirt. "I'm so sorry I left you. I never meant to do that."

"Stop it," she chides me gently, one hand smoothing down my hair.

"But I *left* you," I insist.

"Nothing's forever, Auri. Everything has its season. The world keeps turning, and the stars keep dancing after we're gone, just as they all did before we came."

"I was your big sister, Cal. I was supposed to look after you."

She looks me in the eye then, a small smile on her lips.

"Come with me."

One arm around my shoulders, she leads me out through the door. We make our way along the hall in silence, and pause in the doorway to another room. I see a toddler in a crib, curled in a tiny ball. There's just a mop of black hair and a small face, slack with sleep, visible above the quilt.

"This is Jie-Lin," Callie murmurs.

"She's beautiful," I breathe, tears in my eyes.

"I miss you, Auri," my little sister tells me. "But I'm all right. Everything continues without us. The dance carries on."

She's beginning to fade away, and I want to reach out and grab her, hold tight and refuse to leave this moment. But instead, gazing one last time at her face, I let her go.

I let all of it go. Finally. Completely. I look at that little face, that beautiful baby girl who shares my name, and I feel it wash away. The anger and the rage and the pain and the sadness. The thought that I missed all of this. Because I didn't, really. I was here all along. In the hearts of the people I left, but never truly left behind.

I let it all go.

And as I open my eyes, I find the Eshvaren above me. I feel the Echo around me shiver—a ripple that runs through the length and breadth of this whole plane, changing the sound of the horizon and the taste of the sky. And I feel it smile down on me with all the colors in its memory.

At last, it says.

Kal

The world around me trembles.

My fingers fall still; the music coming from the siif in my hands fades into silence. I look to the sky and note that it is a different shade of perfect. For a moment, I sense a shadow at my shoulder, and inexplicably I am put so deeply in mind of my father that I turn, almost prepared to see him standing there.

My fists are clenched.

But there is only the Eshvaren, wearing its crystalline form. It peers at me intently, as if truly looking at me for the first time. I can feel the power in it, in this place, the legacy of the Ancient Ones flowing in this plane's every atom.

Remember what is at stake here, it says. *This is more than you. More than us.*

I blink. "I do not understand."

Only one obstacle remains. Only one hindrance that binds her to what she was, and stands in the way of what she must be.

I feel a scowl at my brow, growing slowly darker. "And that is?"

The Eshvaren tilts its head and smiles a rainbow.

25

ZILA

Finian is leaning in close to Aurora's face, studying the rapid fluttering of her eyelids. "It's been nearly twelve hours since they went under," he says. "Shouldn't something have happened by now?"

"I take comfort in the fact that nothing has," I say. But the truth is, although my tone is calm, I am also concerned. Based on Aurora's account of her first visit to the Echo, it appears that during the two minutes of unconsciousness we observed, she subjectively experienced a period of approximately twelve hours.

This suggests that she would pass a day in four minutes, and so the almost-twelve hours that have now elapsed mean that she and Kal have been in the Echo for nearly six months. Their brain activity is off the charts, which implies they are indeed experiencing the passage of time at astonishing speeds.

The question that troubles me is how long a human or Syldrathi brain can maintain this kind of workload without suffering permanent damage.

"How is the tracking of the probe's particle signature progressing?" I ask.

"We're on the trail," Finian shrugs. "Scar's upstairs on the bridge right now. I'm still trying to fix Aurora's damn uniglass."

I blink, struggling for a moment to identify the feeling in my chest.

Alarm, I realize.

"Scarlett Isobel Jones is flying this ship?"

Finian grins. "She's not that bad. The auto-guidance is helping. Apparently one of her ex-boyfriends gave her some lessons. And she picked up a little from Cat."

I feel a pang of hurt at that. The memory of Cat's face, her smile, her end. The barriers that hold back my responses to these things are not as strong as they once were.

I am not feeling nothing.

"But there's no telling how far across the Fold the probe originated from," Finian continues. "We could be traveling for weeks."

"Let us hope not," I say. "Our brains are not suited for prolonged Fold exposure. Nor should we tempt calamity with Scarlett at the controls that long."

Finian nods. "Yeah. And I don't think the Unbroken are gonna wait long before they let Earth know what they think about the attack on their flagship, either."

I nod. "It is extremely unlikely an attack by Terran forces against a blooded Syldrathi Templar will go unanswered."

Finian looks down at Kal's slumbering figure, chewing gently on his lip. "Pixieboy's big sister was really something, huh?"

"She was . . . most formidable."

Fin checks the bay about us, as if to see if anyone is listening.

". . . Kinda hot, though, right?"

I blink. "I did not know you found psychopathy an attractive quality, Finian."

"Come onnnn," he grins. "Don't tell me you didn't notice. I sure wouldn't say no to a short visit to her torture chamber?"

I purse my lips, picturing Saedii's face. Her form. It is true. The aesthetic qualities of Kal's sister are . . . undeniable, despite her demeanor.

But still . . .

"She is too tall for me," I finally declare.

Finian rolls his eyes and gives me a friendly smile. I feel my cheeks warm a little at the thought of discussing romantic notions with him. I tip my head forward to hide any sign of the vascular response, wondering if this is perhaps what having friends feels like.

I am not feeling nothing.

I nod to Kal and Aurora in an attempt to divert the discussion.

"I will continue to monitor them," I say.

"All right." Finian steps back, his exosuit whispering softly as he stretches his arms. "I'm gonna grab snacks—you want anything?"

I contemplate. "Those cookies Scarlett enjoined me to eat were adequate."

"*Adequate?* You two have practically eaten the entire supply."

"The excess calorie intake will result in an upscaling of my mass, which . . ."

I frown. That is incorrect.

"I mean to say, your affection for me will increase as I also increase in . . ."

No. That is also wrong.

I fall silent. Look up into Finian's blank black eyes.

"Still getting the hang of this humor thing, huh," he says.

I lower my voice to a whisper. "It is *extremely* perplexing."

"Well, keep working on it. I'm off to the galley." His mouth quirks to a crooked smile, and he glances down at Aurora. "I'll see you kids in a month."

26

AURI

I'm gliding home on a storm wind, flying on wings of thunder. I can feel the power rushing inside me like a waterfall. All the shackles holding me back, the guilt, the fear, who I was—all of it is gone.

I roar across the Echo, the earth torn up by the force of my passing. My right eye burns like a newborn star, a midnight-blue tempest crackling in my wake, a tornado of pure psychic force that I can beckon with a wave of my hand.

I can't wait to show Kal.

I think about him waiting for me, like he's always done. The time we've spent here, all he's come to mean to me. I think about Scarlett and Finian and Zila waiting for us outside the Echo, these people who've become my family. All the faith they've placed in me, all they've sacrificed—all of it, *all of it* has been worth it.

I'm not that girl who set out for Octavia anymore. I'm not the girl who woke up two centuries later, cut off from everything I was. I am the vessel they made me to be, the unmaking of an enemy set to consume all life, all light, all hope. And I smile fiercely, almost giddy with the thought of it.

I'm the girl who's going to save the damn galaxy. . . .

Kal sees me coming, the power raging in my wake, his eyes wide with wonder as I drop down to the beautiful green grass around our camp and throw myself into his arms. I kiss him, letting myself flood into his mind, feeling the golden strands of his psyche entwined with mine, the two of us together, complete and perfect.

"I'm ready, Kal," I whisper.

I press my lips to his again, caressing his face, his mind.

"I'm *ready.*"

Not yet.

The voice comes from behind us, soft and melodic. I turn, see the shimmering rainbow form of the Eshvaren watching me. I sense a wrongness in the air—a ripple shivering the trees around us, the golden threads in Kal's mind. And I can suddenly feel something I've never felt in him before.

Kal's afraid.

You have come far, Aurora Jie-Lin O'Malley, the Eshvaren says. *But you cannot yet wield the Weapon.*

I hold out my hand, and a psychic shock, massive, tectonic, flows out across the Echo, shaking every tree, every rock, every blade of grass.

"I'm ready," I say.

Ready, yes, Esh nods. *To cast off the final impediments that hold you to your old self. Your every thought. Your every cell. Your very existence.*

The words hit me like a slap. I glance at Kal, drag myself free of his arms.

"My existence . . . ?"

And looking into the Eshvaren's glowing right eye, I finally realize . . .

"*That's* what you meant," I whisper, my heart twisting a little in my chest. "When you said, 'Like us, you must sacrifice all.'"

I look around the Echo, at its beauty and its splendor, all that remains of a civilization that collapsed eons before mine was ever born.

Esh told me that if I failed in my testing, it would cost me my life.

It didn't say that even if I succeed . . .

"Using the Weapon . . . being the Trigger . . ." I swallow hard as the truth finally sinks in. "It's going to kill me, isn't it?"

In all likelihood, Esh replies. *Yes.*

". . . Mothercustard."

"There must be another way!" Kal spits, his Syldrathi composure fraying.

Look around you, young one, Esh says, its voice a song. *All this, our world, our civilization, our very name, is lost to the sands of time. We gave all we had to destroy the Ra'haam when first it rose. One thousand years of blood and fire from which we never recovered. Our entire race spent itself so that future races might be spared the Great Enemy's hungers.*

Esh looks at me, and I think maybe I feel something close to pity in its mind.

Is one more girl too much to ask?

I can feel Kal's fury. His fear of losing me. But deep down, I know . . .

"No," I say.

I shake my head, and even as I speak, I know it's true.

"No, it's not too much at all."

"Be'shmai . . . ," Kal whispers, reaching for my hand.

"It's okay," I say, smiling as I turn to face him. "I'm not afraid, Kal. I've made peace with who I was. I'm ready to become what I was meant to be."

I think of that little girl, asleep in her cradle, and can't help but smile.

"It's all a cycle, Kal. And if I have to . . . stop for others to go on, it'll be okay. Because here with you, these last few months, I was more alive than I've *ever* been. And even after I'm gone, you'll still have this. You'll still know I loved you."

I rise up on tiptoe and slip my arms around his neck. And I lean in slow, kiss him slower, tears in my eyes, lips brushing his as I pull back far enough to whisper.

"I *love* you," I tell him.

He touches my cheek and kisses my tears away, folds me in his arms and—

No, Esh says.

The world falls still. The spell between Kal and me is broken. Fingers entwined with his, I turn to meet Esh's eyes.

"What do you mean, no?"

You must abandon your past totally. You must surrender your future utterly. There is only the moment you were made for, and you must be ready to act without hesitation when it comes. You must not flinch. You must have nothing that binds you to this place, this self. Nothing at all. You must burn it all away.

It looks at me with its glowing eye, all the way into my heart.

Including him.

"But . . . that's not what humans *do*," I protest. "We fight for ideas, sure, but we fight for people, too."

Esh tilts its head, as though I've said something curious. *Do you truly believe you are a human girl anymore? You must be emptiness if you wish to succeed. When you strike at the Great Enemy, no impediment must remain to stem the power's flow. You must be pure will. No regret. No hurt. No rage. No sorrow. No fear.*

Its words hit me like a punch to my chest.

No love.

I look at Kal, see him looking back at me, agony in his eyes. The sun has sunk beyond the edge of the world, and all the stars, those beautiful, long-dead stars we looked at together, are out above.

And I understand—finally, really understand—what they need me to do.

I have to let him go.

I have to burn him away.

I have to prove to Esh that my ties don't define me or hold me back. That when the moment comes to trigger the Weapon, for the good of all around me, I'll be willing to sacrifice anyone and anything.

My eyes trace out Kal's features in the starlight.

They've become as familiar as my own in the last months.

My mind's a whirlwind of blue and silver, and I know what needs to be done. I have to control it and refine it, shape it into a knife's blade to cut the ties between us. He knows as well as I do. What's at stake here. Everything hanging in the balance.

"Kal," I whisper.

You must, Esh replies.

"Be'shmai?" Kal breathes.

That word.

That beautiful, wonderful, alien word. When we first spoke about it on Octavia, Kal said there wasn't an adequate human translation for it. He looks at me now, silently making me the same offer of his heart that he does every day. And in that moment, I know that although I might not be Syldrathi, and though I'll never know what it's like to feel the Pull, I *do* know what it is to fall in love. I know that I've accepted his heart, and given him mine in return.

"I'm sorry," I say.

And I know that there is no universe in which I'm stronger without him.

"I can't," I declare, turning to Esh.

Silence rings in the Echo. I feel Kal's heart surging behind me, the ripples those two words send spilling across this entire plane.

"I won't," I say.

You MUST, Esh commands.

"No," I say.

No.

Because I won't do what Esh wants.

Not because I refuse to sacrifice myself.

Not because I'm afraid.

But because every moment I've spent here, in training and with Kal, has led me to the same bone-deep truth. Tomorrow might be worth a million yesterdays. But a tomorrow without him isn't worth anything at all.

You will not have the strength, Esh says, something close to fury in its voice. *If you are not emptiness, you will fail.*

"I guess we'll see about that," I say.

You are the Trigger. THE TRIGGER IS YOU.

"Yeah," I nod. "But I'm Aurora Jie-Lin O'Malley, too."

I reach for Kal's hand.

"And I'm willing to fight for what I love."

I take hold of the power. Willing us gone, I feel a severing, a sundering, a tear as wide as the sky and as deep as forever. And in a heartbeat, two heartbeats, mine and his, we blink out of the Echo and back into our bodies aboard the *Zero*.

And the first thing I feel, even before I open my eyes, is his hand in mine.

27

TYLER

They bring Saedii back into our cell a while later.

The door opens and the marines throw her, limp and boneless, to the deck. The sound of her body slapping the floor, the sight of her—it turns my stomach. They've torn the medi-wraps off her legs. The bruises on her thighs are faded, but the ones on her face are fresh. Her lip is split, her eye swollen, one hand pressed to her ribs. The black paint across her eyes and at her lips is smudged, running. Her immaculate braids have come loose, and a curtain of black hair covers her face as she tries to drag herself up.

I rise to my feet, glaring at the marines. Saedii is an officer of the enemy. A Templar of the Unbroken. I saw the kill counts during the battle on the *Andarael*. I know most of these TDF troopers probably lost friends in that attack. But still, there are rules here. There's a line you don't step beyond. That's supposed to be the difference between us and them.

"Maker's breath, what did you do to her?"

The marines don't even look at me. The door slides shut without a sound, leaving Saedii and me alone.

"Here," I murmur, leaning down to help. "Let me—"

"Do not *touch me!*" she roars. Her fingers are curled like claws, black fingernails glinting in the antiseptic light. I back off, out of reach.

Saedii draws a deep breath, steadies herself. I almost don't catch it, but I swear I hear a small, strangled sob in her throat.

"Your sun will b-burn," she whispers. "Your whole . . . wretched r-race . . ."

She hisses, trying to sit up. Her arms, her breath, her whole body shaking with the effort. But it's too much and she collapses. I feel a stab of pity, a wash of shame. These are Terrans treating her this way. My people.

She's the enemy, sure. She threw me into a pit to get devoured by a reptilian killing machine, sure. Her comrades are responsible for the deaths of tens of thousands of Terran troops, including my own father, sure. But I can hear him now in my head if I try. The words Dad instilled in me when I was just a little kid.

To be a leader, you have to set the example. To be a leader, you have to be the kind of person you'd want to follow you.

Know the way.

Show the way.

Go the way.

I know from my time with Kal that physical touch is a big deal among Syldrathi. But I can't just leave her bleeding on the ground. And so I scoop her up in my arms. Saedii comes alive, pointed teeth bared behind a matted curtain of dark hair. I'm afraid she'll hurt herself worse, I hold her tight, the words she spits through clenched teeth echoing along with her thoughts in my mind.

"UNHAND ME!"

"Take it easy!"

"PUT ME DOWN!"

"Maker's breath, I will, relax!"

She bucks again, like a wild thing in my arms, and I stagger over to her bio-cot, holding on for dear life. Saedii spits through split and swollen lips, but I can feel what her rage is costing her, feel the shakes running through her whole body as she tries to fight me off. I lower her gently onto the bed and back away, and she tries to surge up after me. But the effort is too much and she wilts, dragging ragged breaths into her lungs and trembling like a newborn colt.

"You *dare* lay hands on me?" she spits, low and deadly. "I will *skin* you, boy. I will . . . t-tear off both your jewels and w-wear th—"

"Yeah, yeah, you're quite vexed with me, I get it. No need to get graphic."

She tries to speak more, but she can't manage it. I feel sore. Tired. And as I sit back down onto my bio-cot, I'm astonished to realize that the wash of pain, exhaustion . . .

Not all of it is mine.

It's hers?

I'm not sure how. But I can . . . feel it? Bleeding out of Saedii's subconscious into my own. I catch images in her head: Terran military uniforms, bloody fists beating her, a solid hour of pain, silent except for her screams. And she *did* scream. Howled her fury and hurt and demanded to know what they wanted from her. And the whole session, the few times they did speak . . . all they did was insult her.

They never even asked her any questions.

"I'm sorry," I say.

Her bruised eyes flicker open, and she fixes me with a knife-edge stare.

"I'm sorry they did that to you," I tell her.

"They will b-burn," she whispers. "And so will you. . . ."

"Saedii, please—"

"Coward," she spits, voice trembling. "Wretch. Terra will be a mass grave."

I rub my temples, trying to hold my patience, trying to be calm, to be the kind of person I'd want to follow me. "Saedii—"

"We will scatter the Void with y-your ashes, Terran," she vows, rising up on one elbow. "We will drink the blood from your still-beating hearts. The screams of your children will be the song we dan—"

"For the love of the Maker, Saedii, can you just STOP AND THINK FOR A SINGLE *MINUTE*?"

I don't like to lose control. That's why I don't drink. I don't do drugs. I don't even swear. But in that moment, it gets to me. I try to hold it back, but I just can't keep a grip anymore. The weeks of being on the run. The thought of Scarlett, Auri, and the others out there without me. The memory of my dad and the thought of the Unbroken and Terra on a bloody collision course and the Ra'haam just sitting back, silently orchestrating it all, watching through Cat's brand-new eyes. All of it bubbles up and spills over and I rise to my feet, grab my bio-cot, and sling it into the wall, cables spitting current, smartglass screens shattering, metal buckling as I turn on Saedii and roar through my wounded throat.

"And if you won't think, then please SHUT THE *FUCK UP* SO I *CAN*!"

365

Saedii falls silent at that. Clearly taken aback. Sinking down onto her cot, she looks me over, toe to crown. Her lips are slightly parted, her eyes lingering on my clenched jaw, my bare chest, my closed fists. She reaches up to brush one stray lock of ink-black hair from the edge of her mouth. And I can feel it in her then, as surely as if it were written in her eyes. Fascination.

Maker's breath, even *approval*.

She glances at the camera above the door. Spits blood on the floor.

"As you wish."

I sink down onto my haunches, back against the wall. Silence rings in the room, and I'm half expecting the marines to burst back in and kick heads, but nobody does. They're obviously watching us. Waiting to see what happens next. Maybe hoping to learn something they can use? Maybe just to pass the time?

But Saedii's eyes never leave me, her stare lingering, first on my hands and my arms, and then up to my eyes. And finally, I feel her in my mind again.

You have a temper, little Terran.

Not if I can help it.

You saw. The beating they gave me.

I glance at her, then look away. Strange as talking like this is, I don't want to let on to the people observing us that we can communicate. It's one of the few edges we have here, and I need every one if I'm getting out of this. . . .

Yeah. I saw.

Intriguing.

I didn't mean to. Your thoughts just sort of . . . bled into mine.

She scoffs softly, shaking her head and turning her gaze to the wall.

You honestly have no idea, do you?

. . . What's that supposed to mean?

She doesn't reply, eyes glittering as she stares at me.

This is all wrong, Saedii, I tell her. *And you know it. I saw the way you led your troops during the attack on Andarael. You're every bit the strategist I am. They didn't even ask you any questions when they beat you. Why bother doing it at all?*

She sucks her split lip. Her voice echoing in my head.

If the act has no purpose, then the act itself is the purpose.

We've been Folding for almost six hours, I point out. *At full burn, the Earth FoldGate was only about five, maybe five and a half from where Andarael hit us. We should be there by now.*

They are not returning us to Terra, she concludes.

Exactly.

Where are they taking us?

I swallow hard, thinking about Cat's blue eyes.

I don't know. I have my suspicions. But think about it. They pick a fight with an Unbroken flagship, but only after giving you time to alert the Starslayer you're under attack. Against all odds, they manage to capture one of the highest-ranking members of the Unbroken. But they don't use you as a bargaining chip. They don't even interrogate you. Instead, they take you totally off the board and let some testosterone boys beat you to a pulp while we don't fly to Earth.

Her eyes narrow, rage glittering in the violet as I press on.

Think about it. Why would the GIA operatives running this show allow that? Why would they throw that first punch at the Unbroken at all? After two years of TerraGov doing everything they could to stay out of your way?

They want a war, she finally replies.

A war with the Starslayer. A man who can destroy suns. Why would they do that? What could Earth possibly have to gain?

Saedii looks at me, bruised eye and swollen lips.

Nothing.

She breathes deep, and behind the malice and the rage, I can see the intelligence in her eyes. Caersan wouldn't choose a fool to be one of his Templars, and despite her fury, Saedii is far from being a hothead. Now that she's had a while to realize I'm not the enemy she thinks I am . . .

Your GIA would not be goading Caersan if they did not stand to gain.

They're not my GIA.

You said this before. The independence of the Aurora Legion—

Maker's breath, I'm not talking about the Legion. I'm saying the GIA has been infiltrated, Saedii. For all I know, the entire Global Intelligence Agency is working against the interests of Earth. And the whole galaxy. And the TDF personnel aboard this ship are too well trained to question orders. Even suspect ones.

She blinks at that, mistrust plain in her eyes.

Infiltrated? By who?

Not who. What.

I wonder how much I should tell her. Wonder how much she'll believe. The concept of the Ra'haam, its plan for the galaxy, might simply be too much for her to deal with. But from what Kal has said, the Syldrathi *do* still hold some belief in the Ancients, despite most of the rest of the galaxy thinking they're a myth. And Saedii's smart enough to know that *something* insane is going on here. I need this girl to trust me. I need us to start working together.

The enemy of my enemy is my friend.

Or, if not my friend, maybe my ally long enough for us to get out of this.

Because sooner rather than later, we're going to arrive at wherever they're taking us. And if it's one of those nursery planets, like I suspect, the Ra'haam will be able to infect us, just like they infected Cat and the Octavia III colonists. Dragging us into its hive mind, absorbing all we are and all we know.

I'm not sure how those corrupted GIA agents are going to explain it to the TDF crew aboard this ship . . . unless they're planning to infect *everybody* aboard?

Maybe the Ra'haam is that confident.

Maybe it's that *desperate*, with Auri on the loose out there.

Maybe we've tipped its hand.

Maybe they found the Weapon. . . .

I feel my jaw clench, a flood of adrenaline rush through my gut. And, dragging my hand back through my mop of blond, I meet Saedii's eyes.

The enemy of my enemy is my friend.

Okay, you better get comfortable. This is going to be a lot to swallow.

369

28

SCARLETT

"Finian, Zila, are you reading me?"

I'm sitting on the *Zero*'s bridge, looking at the frantic readings and flashy lights on the pilot's console as the whole ship shakes around me. Things cannot be said, by any measure, to be going well. In fact, we're very possibly about to die. The only thing bringing me any sort of calm is the electropop thumping over the chaos—I discovered how to hook my uni into the bridge PA four hours ago, and Brittneee Vox's latest single, "Get It," is playing on repeat and I know I'm an atheist and very possibly about to perish in the middle of an uncharted spatial anomaly, but MAKER'S BREATH I LOVE THIS SONNGGGGG.

Before you get all judgy with me, I just want you to know I am the galaxy's worst pilot. I have no more business sitting in this chair than the Great Ultrasaur of Abraaxis IV has getting a pedicure. Some people are born to fly, is what I'm saying. I was born to be *flown*. Preferably first class, with a criminally handsome flight attendant named Julio waiting on me hand and foot.

The ship shakes again. Harder this time.

Over the PA, Brittneee requests that I come Get It. No points for guessing what *It* is. This song is a lot of things, but subtle isn't one of them.

"Um, Finian?" I ask into comms again. "Zila?"

I mean, I dated an Ace briefly in second year—my first foray into the high-ego, yeah-we-know-we're-hot-but-you-know-it-too world of space pilots that Cat swam in so easily. (Kyle Reznor. Ex-boyfriend #19. Pros: Amazing kisser. Cons: Constant cockpit jokes.) I know enough about flying to apparently have not gotten us killed on the way here, but honestly, I've spent more time in a pilot's chair since escaping the *Andarael* than I have in the rest of my life combined.

Information is scrolling down the screens, disconcerting words like SPATIAL DISTORTION, PROXIMITY ALERT, and EXTREME DANGER. The bridge lights are all gray because we're still Folding, but they're flashing really fast, and the ALERTs popping up on my screens are all helpfully labeled as RED, and I know that any one of these things is usually not *good,* but I'm afraid if I touch anything I'll make it *worse.*

The ship shakes again as if to agree with me.

In sultry tones, Brittneee asks if I *really* Want It.

"Finian?" I ask, tapping comms again. "Zilaaaaa?"

I look up at Shamrock, sitting above the pilot's console. The dragon peers at me with his black button eyes. He says nothing because he's a stuffed toy but . . .

"I can feel you judging me," I tell him.

"Scar?"

I hear the note of panic in Fin's voice, swivel in the chair to face him.

"Hiiiii, Finian."

He looks at the readouts behind me, eyes wide. "What did you do?"

"I flew in the direction of the probe trail like I was supposed to."

"Yeah, but . . ." His eyes grow wider at the sight on the central monitor. "Maker's breath, what is THAT?"

Up on the console, rendered in high-def, is a holographic image of the . . . well, I've got no damn idea what it is, honestly. It's about a thousand kilometers across, which sounds big until you sit through a three-hour astrometrics lecture on how brain-breakingly big space actually is. It sort of looks like a whirlpool—strange, multicolored-gray energy spinning in an endless spiral. It's very pretty. But judging by the fit my controls are throwing, it's also very dangerous.

"Where did that come from?" Fin demands.

"It popped up in front of us, like, five minutes ago."

"Why are we still flying toward it?" he demands, slightly panicked.

"Because we can't stop."

"What?" he asks, abandoning *slightly* panicked for *totally.*

"I tried to turn around. I tried to cut our engines. I even punched the console like Cat used to do when she was annoyed. The flight computer just yelled at me."

The ship shakes again, way more violent this time. Shamrock falls off his perch. Finian blinks around the bridge, frowning up at the PA speakers.

". . . What's with the electropop?"

"Oh, don't pretend you're not a Brittneee fan, de Seel."

"We're getting sucked into a spatial anomaly at hundreds

of thousands of kilometers per second with no engine or nav control. Shouldn't we have a metric buttload of alerts screaming about that? Sirens and whatnot?"

"I turned them off."

". . . *WHAT?*"

I swivel my chair, release the Mute button on my console. Brittneee's sing-along-able tones are drowned out as the bridge is plunged into a deafening cacophony of warnings from the flight computer.

"WARNING: POWER CORE FLUCTUATIO—"

"NAVIGATION SYSTEMS OFFLINE, REP—"

"ENERGY SURGE IN ANOMALY CORE, RECOM—"

I stab the button again.

Brittneee asks Finian if he'd like to Get It.

"See?" I say. "Much more relaxing."

"Great Maker, we're going to die . . . ," Fin declares.

"No, we're not," says a voice.

My carefully cultivated facade of chill in the face of certain death slips away as I look past Fin and catch sight of her standing on the bridge threshold.

"Auri!" I breathe.

I rise to meet her, to throw a hug around her, just overjoyed to see her back on her feet. I have no idea what she went through in the Echo. I know her brain wave activity was off the charts—Zila said she and Kal were living weeks of time in just minutes. But the look on her face, her pose, *everything* about her . . .

She's changed.

I can feel it when I look into her mismatched eyes. When I study her body language. Somehow, even the air around her. She's . . . *alive*. Cracking with purpose, with power, so much so that just the sight of her raises goose bumps on my skin. Kal looms at her shoulder, always just a whisper away. Zila is behind them, eyes fixed on the anomaly we're being rapidly drawn toward.

"You know what this is, Stowaway?" Finian asks.

Aurora stares at the whirlpool, its light reflected in her right iris. For a second, I swear I can see the light inside her, pulsing in response.

"It's a gateway," she whispers.

"To where?" I ask.

"Not where." Auri shakes her head. "What."

"Okay," I say. "I'll bite. A gateway to what?"

She draws a deep breath into her lungs.

Her right eye glimmers like a tiny sun.

"The Weapon," she says.

．　．　．　．　．

We plunged into the anomaly forty seconds later, just as the opening beats of Disasterpiece's drunken-hookup dubpunk classic "Last Heartbeat in the Club" started pulsing through the PA. They're not as good as Brittneee, but hey, no one is.

Anyway, I'm pleased to report we didn't die.

The colorscape of the galaxy shifted from the Fold's monochrome to every shade of the rainbow, crashing right into my head. As we crossed the breach, the *Zero* bucking beneath us, I caught sight of Aurora standing in the center of the bridge—hands held out, eye burning like a beacon—steady as a rock while the rest of us clung on for dear life. I got the distinct feeling that if she hadn't been there with us, we'd have all been ripped into disappointed subatomic pieces by the gateway. As it was, plunging through it felt a little like getting hit in the head with a naked astrophysicist.

Slightly amusing.

Definitely weird.

But mostly painful.

And now we're on the other side. I'm guessing the anomaly was some kind of FoldGate—hidden, semi-sentient, waiting for someone like Aurora to trigger it into opening. The alerts have calmed down to almost normal levels. I've killed the dubpunk—the moment seems to demand a little gravitas. Because as we all gather around the central holographic display, we can finally see the origin point of the probe. The place this journey—Aurora's, all of ours—started, countless millennia ago. The point in space where the Eshvaren made their last, desperate gamble to stop the resurrection of the Ra'haam.

It's a planet.

An *utterly* dead planet.

Lifeless. Waterless. It hangs in space, framed against the soft light of a pulsing red dwarf star, barren and alone.

"What is this place?" I whisper.

"Their home," Aurora says, her eyes on the display. "What's left of it, anyway."

"The Ancients," Kal says reverently.

"Eshvaren," Finian breathes.

Aurora sighs. "I wish you could have seen it like it was."

"I can detect no tectonic activity," Zila says, looking over her scopes. "The core is frozen solid. Atmosphere almost nonexistent. No life signs." She looks around the bridge, dark eyes finally settling on Aurora. "Not even microbial."

"This is the place," Auri says, her voice like steel. "Where they made the probe. Where they made the Weapon. I can . . . see them. Feel them." Her brow creases, and she presses her fingers to her temple. "Their echoes. Their voices."

She looks at Kal, reaches for his hand.

"I know where we need to go."

Kal nods, eyes glittering. "I would follow you to the end of all things, be'shmai."

The rest of us look tired, wired, halfway between shabby and comatose. As usual, Kaliis Idraban Gilwraeth doesn't have a single silver hair out of place on his head. But there's something different about him, too.

Something I can't quite put my finger on.

"What happened in the Echo?" I ask, looking between them.

"Was your training successful?" Zila says. "Can you wield the Weapon?"

Auri looks out on the dead world below us. I can feel fire in her. A heat, burning like a sun. But also . . . uncertainty?

She looks at Kal. Squares her jaw, curls her fists.

"Let's just find it first."

. . . . .

We touch down seventeen minutes later, after a frictionless decent into the atmo-free skies above the Eshvaren world. Zila politely suggested she be allowed to take the controls— well, as polite as Zila gets anyway. After my time at the stick, having somebody who knows what they're doing flying us was a welcome relief.

There are no oceans on this world anymore, no continents, but we touch down somewhere near its south pole. Zila brings us in for a perfect landing: a gentle thump and a soft navcom ping are the only indicators that we've landed at all.

"You're just showing off now," I smile.

"Yes. But do not fall in love with me, Scarlett. I will only break your heart."

I laugh and throw her a wink. "I'm too tall for you, remember?"

Her lips curve in a small smile, and she tucks one dark curl behind her ear. I notice that her stare lingers on me even though she'd usually look away.

Interesting . . .

Soon we're gathered in the docking bay, gearing up. The *Zero* is equipped with enough enviro-suits for the whole squad. They're bulky, ugly, scandalously drab—fitted for us personally and neatly stored in lockers marked with our names. Zila's assisting Fin with pulling his over his exosuit. Auri and Kal are helping each other change with the casual ease of people who are absolutely, definitely, one hundred percent sleeping with each other now.

Lucky girl.

Of course, my musings on the extracurricular activities of Mr. Perfect Hair and Little Miss Trigger are brought to a crashing halt at the sight of Tyler's locker. One glance at his name stenciled on the metal is enough to make my stomach drop and roll inside me. Despite where we are, the scope of all we're doing, I find myself worried sick again. I know we're saving the damn galaxy here, that we're doing exactly what he'd order us to do. But he's my twin brother, and I'm still wondering, hoping, *praying* he's okay.

Fin seems to pick up on it, sliding a little closer, trying to ease the tension.

"Good thing these suits are heavy-duty," he jokes, nodding at the spectrograph beside the bay door. "*Definitely* not bikini weather out there."

"Shame." I smile weakly in response. "I look amazing in a two-piece."

"Hey, what a coincidence, me too."

But it's not his strongest effort, and as he speaks, he glances at Tyler's locker. Swallows hard.

"He's gonna be okay, yeah?"

"Yeah," I sigh.

"Seriously," Fin says, looking around to the others for backup. "After we're done here, we'll get him back, Scar."

Kal bows, which is Syldrathi for a nod. "I vow it on my honor."

"No question," Auri agrees, steel in her voice.

"I know this is difficult, Scarlett," Kal continues, looking at me intently with those picture-pretty eyes. "But we are on the right path here. Of all people, Tyler Jones would understand that."

I buck up a bit, stand a little taller. Buoyed by these people around me, these squaddies who've become my friends, friends who've become my family.

I sniff and nod, drag my helmet down into place. "I know he would."

Fin pats me a little awkwardly on the shoulder.

"Okay," I say. "Let's go find this damn shooter."

We load ourselves into the airlock, and soon enough we're stepping out onto the freezing surface of the Eshvaren planet. I glance at Aurora, remembering the last time we did this, on Octavia III. She was a nervous wreck back then, struggling to come to grips with who she was. But now she takes the lead, marching across the crumbling rock. The landscape is gray and lifeless. The arctic wind is blowing at hundreds of kilometers an hour, but the atmo is so thin, it's barely a breeze.

Even the air in this place is dead.

Kal and Zila carry disruptor rifles, me and Fin walking with hands on our pistols. There's no real sense of danger here as we follow Auri. Nothing close to the strange, otherworldly hostility we met on Octavia III. I'm struck by it then, how unfair that is—that the Ra'haam got to go on, and the race that gave everything to cut them away ended like this. I feel sad. Small. Cold despite my suit.

We march for twenty minutes, up a steady rise, until finally we find ourselves on a bluff overlooking an impact crater: a massive, circular indentation in the skin of this dead world, stretching to the horizon. But in the center of it, I'm astonished to see—

"A doorway," Finian whispers.

At least, that's what it looks like. It's *huge*—at least ten kilometers across. Open like a mouth to the sky, it leads into a vast, dark passage beyond. The surface of this planet is a wasteland, but the tunnel interior is virtually untouched by the elements.

"Should it . . . be open?" I ask, uncertain.

I glance at Aurora sidelong, feel the tension coming off her in waves.

"Be'shmai?" Kal asks, looking at her intently.

"This is where the crystal city was, Kal," she says, her voice not quite her own. "This is . . ."

She shakes her head.

"All of you. Hold on to me, to each other."

She offers her hands, still staring into the abyss below us. Kal takes her right one, and I take her left, holding tight. Zila grabs Kal, and Finian locks fingers with me, giving me a small squeeze of reassurance.

"You okay, Stowaway?" he asks Auri.

"Just hold on," she replies.

I feel it tingling on the back of my neck. A power, a rush, a greasy tang in the air. And without warning, I'm lifted off my feet, up into the colorless sky.

I gasp, tempted to shriek girlishly for a bit. And, looking at Aurora, at her mouth pressed thin, her eye burning with blinding white light, I realize she's the one doing this—moving us with nothing but the power of her mind.

When the Ra'haam attacked us on Octavia III, she lifted us to safety then, too. Kept the Ra'haam at bay. But she was barely in control of it—I got the feeling she wasn't even really herself, just a puppet for the power inside her. But I can see, I can *feel,* she's herself now. This is Aurora, wielding the gift the Eshvaren gave her like a master. Lifting us up like we're kids' toys, over the blasted landscape, down into the crater, and then into that long, dark tunnel beyond.

"Wow," Finian says, watching Aurora's face.

"I concur," Zila murmurs.

We move into the tunnel, accelerating under the force of Auri's will. I can feel that each of us is having a time of it, each reacting to this display of newfound power in a different way. Kal takes it best—he probably got a taste of this in the Echo, after all. I can feel his adoration as he looks at his girl, admiration at how far she's come. But again, I get the feeling he's uncertain somehow. About what, I can only guess.

Zila is looking at Auri with something like fascination. Taking readings on her uniglass. That big brain of hers in overdrive. Fin is a little more gobsmacked, and I'm right there with him. Less than a day ago, Auri was a tiny, frightened kid, afraid of using this thing inside her for fear of hurting the people around her. Now she wields it like she was born to it. Like this is *exactly* what she's supposed to be doing.

We leave the surface behind. The light of the red dwarf we're orbiting fades, but the light from Auri's eye illuminates the tunnel before us. The shaft is kilometers across—so big I can't see all the edges. The stone is perfectly smooth, beautiful patterns woven by the layers of sedimentary rock we're cutting through. My enviro-suit warns me the temperature is falling, gravity decreasing, our speed climbing. I look at Auri, a little worried, but she seems totally in control, determination written in the lines of her face.

The walls change from rock to rainbow-colored crystal. The temperature outside our suits is now a hundred below. I can hear my heart thumping against my ribs, and the tunnel stretches on so long and empty all around us as we float downward into the core of this dead world that I'm almost about to say something, I'm almost about to speak when—

"Great Maker . . . ," Finian breathes.

Before us, the tunnel opens out into a massive chamber. A giant hollow space, carved far beneath the surface of the Eshvaren world, blanketed with the dust of a million years. I can see bizarre structures made out of the same crystal that lines the walls, their purpose totally unknowable. The sense of space in here, the utter *alienness,* is almost frightening.

Each of us looks around in awe and wonder at those impossible shapes, glimmering and shifting in Aurora's light.

"What *is* this place?" I whisper.

"A . . . workshop?" Finian breathes.

"A weapons factory," Zila says.

We fly on toward the center, between the alien machines, the sense of excitement in my chest building. All the time we've spent, all the loss we've suffered, it's all going to be worth it. I can see it in front of us now: a massive scaffold rising out of the darkness. I can feel Aurora's elation spilling into me, the thrill of this discovery, the thought that despite the enemy we're pitting ourselves against, this war can be won, the Ra'haam *can* be beaten, because this girl beside me, this tiny powerhouse thrumming with midnight-blue energy, is the Trigger, and now at last . . .

. . . we have the Weapon.

We reach the crystal scaffold. Tall as skyscrapers. Wide as a city. My eyes straining as I peer into the dark beyond, looking for the key to everything.

"Um . . . ," Finian says.

"Yeah . . ." I frown. "Um."

"Oh no," Aurora whispers.

"Be'shmai?" Kal murmurs.

"No, no, *no* . . ."

We all look to Auri, to her face, and it doesn't take a Legion-trained diplomat to know that something is horribly wrong. We soar on into the dark, weaving through the scaffold, crystal shimmering around us. But it's obvious that this scaffold was built to hold something. And, as alien as it is, we can all of us tell that it's empty.

As I see the tears begin to spill down Auri's cheeks, as I see her face crumple, feel the air around us ripple with her power as her frustration, her horror, her despair comes bubbling to the surface, I know the awful truth.

"It's not here," I whisper.

I look to Finian, to Zila, to Kal, and finally, to Aurora.

My heart sinks in my chest as she speaks.

"The Weapon's gone. . . ."

.   .   .   .   .

We head back to the *Zero*. And from there, back into the Fold.

We don't know what else to do.

I wish Tyler were here. I wish it so badly, it's like a knife in my ribs. We shared a womb together, he and I, we shared *everything,* and to find ourselves without him, leaderless, rudderless, reminds us all just how badly we need him. We stand on the *Zero*'s bridge, the colorscape once more reduced to black and white.

Aurora is pacing back and forth, wearing the darkest scowl I've ever seen. Kal stands to one side, brow creased in thought. Fin sits opposite me at the central station, trawling the news feeds, Zila atop the console, chewing a lock of dark hair.

"How could it be gone?" I ask. "How is that possible?"

"I don't know," Auri replies, voice trembling.

Finian shakes his head. "Crossing into the anomaly would've destroyed any normal ship. And to even know where it was . . . they'd had to have found a probe."

"Or been told of the location by the Ancients," Kal replies.

The answer is obvious.

"Another Trigger," Zila says.

Auri purses her lips. "The Eshvaren said there might have been others before me. The Echo resets when someone leaves it, and this plan has been in place for a million years. But they also said that whoever came before me must have failed, because the Ra'haam is still alive."

She shakes her head, the air about her rippling with her frustration.

"I don't *get* it."

Finian starts spitballing. "Maybe this other Trigger completed their training, claimed the Weapon, then . . . I dunno, fell down the stairs or choked on a creshcake or something?"

"Perhaps they completed their training," Kal says, looking at Aurora, "then balked at the price they would pay to defeat the Ra'haam."

Auri looks at Kal, her voice soft. "Let's not talk about that, okay?"

Zila's eyebrow rises two millimeters, which is practically a scream of alarm as far as she goes. "What price?"

"It doesn't matter," Auri says, temper flaring. "It doesn't *matter,* because the damn Weapon isn't even there!" The air crackles around her, a pale light flaring in her iris. "After all that! After *everything* we've gone through, and someone's stolen it right out from under us! Son of a biscuit, I want to just . . . *scream.*"

I glance at Kal, but, good lad, he's already on the job, folding Auri in those covetable arms of his. He kisses her brow tenderly, smooths back her hair.

"All will be well, be'shmai," he vows. "Trust in this. In us. The sun will rise."

She sinks against him, sighing. I watch the two of them, realizing how deep they're into each other now. I can feel the bond that's grown between them in the time they shared in the Echo, those hours to us that were months to them. The love. And, heartbreaker that I am, slayer of suitors with over fifty confirmed kills in my little black book, I wonder for a moment if I'll ever have anyone who means as much to me as they do to each other.

"Um," Finian says.

I glance at our Gearhead, his big black eyes fixed on his screens.

I do my best Tyler impression, eyebrow raised. "Do you have something you'd like to share with the class, Legionnaire de Seel?"

Wordlessly, he flicks a metal-clad finger, his exosuit humming as he transfers his feed to the holo display above the main console. It's a news feed from TerraNet, the most reliable Earth news source, the words LATEST UPDATE scrolling across the bottom of the screen. It shows footage of a massive Syldrathi armada, thousands upon thousands of ships, all floating like sharks in the Fold.

It's the biggest fleet I've ever seen.

"Amna diir," Kal breathes.

Fin presses another button, arcing the volume of the feed.

"... *Unbroken armada is currently amassing in the Fold near the gateway to Terran space. Terran forces have yet to engage, instead mustering inside the Sol system in defensive posture. This statement was issued from the head of the Terran Defense Force, Admiral Emi Hotep, one hour ago.*"

The feed shifts to a severe, bronze-skinned woman with short dark hair, in a sharp TDF officer's uniform.

"I am sending this message on all channels, addressing the Unbroken fleet: Though we have had differences in our past, the Syldrathi are friends to Earth. We consider you an honorable people, warriors born, and we have no wish to engage in hostilities with Unbroken forces. However, should Syldrathi vessels invade Terran space, they will be met with deadly force."

The feed shifts to a Betraskan man in officer's dress. The label under him reads GREATER CLAN BATTLE LEADER ANALI DE TREN.

"The Betraskan people strive always for peace, in our hearts, in our dens, and in our skies. But should any world or force engage in unwarranted hostilities, Trask will stand with our Terran allies."

My heart sinks in my chest as I look around the bridge. I can see the same despair in the faces of my squad. The galaxy is on the verge of war.

The feed continues.

"Disturbingly, an unknown vessel has been detected within the Unbroken fleet. TDF Command has dismissed claims of a 'superweapon,' but the fate of the Syldrathi homeworld at the hands of Unbroken leader Archon Caersan, aka the Starslayer—an attack in which ten billion Syldrathi lost their lives—cannot be ignored. Moments ago, before our drone was destroyed, TerraNet managed to shoot exclusive footage of this unknown Syldrathi ship."

The feed cuts back to an image of the armada, cruising through the Fold. Again, I'm struck by the size of it—the sheer firepower the Starslayer has brought to bear in retaliation for the attack on *Andarael*.

"This Caersan guy seems to be taking this *real* personal," Finian mutters.

"Yeah," I nod. "I wonder wh—"

"Mothercustard," Auri whispers, eyes widening.

Kal's face is pale and drawn as he watches the feed, a sliver of fear and sorrow appearing in the cracks of his normally ice-cool Syldrathi demeanor. But at the note in Auri's voice, he turns to her.

"Be'shmai?"

I look back at the screen. The footage is blurred, a few frames snatched in the second or two before the TerraNet drone was killed. It shows a glimpse of a vessel between the silhouettes of two Unbroken dreadnoughts. It's absolutely *massive*—easily the biggest ship I've ever seen. Kilometers across, as long as a city. In contrast to the smooth black metal profiles of the Syldrathi ships, it's an odd, conical shape, kinda like an oboe or a clarinet. And it's made of what looks like . . .

Crystal?

"Son of a biscuit, that's *it*," Auri whispers.

Fin blinks. "What?"

"That's *it*," she says, voice rising. "The Weapon! *The Eshvaren Weapon!*"

Silence rings out on the bridge, the shock sinking in slow. My thoughts are racing, my heart pounding, the impossibility of it soaking me through.

"Aurora is supposed to use the Weapon to destroy the Ra'haam seed worlds," Zila says softly. "And the Starslayer somehow destroyed the Syldrathi sun."

"*That's* how he did it!" Aurora breathes. "He used the Weapon on his own world!"

"So, Caersan . . . ," Fin whispers.

"He's another Trigger?" I ask.

Kal's eyes are wide with horror. "Sai'nuit," he whispers, eyes on the screen.

"What's that mean?" Fin asks.

"Starslayer," I murmur in reply.

This just in, TerraNet reports. *We are receiving a transmission from the Unbroken fleet, across all bands. We now cut live to this breaking footage.*

The image of the Weapon disappears, replaced with the figure of a man.

The most stunning man I've ever laid eyes on.

He's tall, wearing a black suit of ornate Syldrathi armor, a long dark cloak flowing over his broad shoulders. His face is pale and smooth, just die-for-me beautiful, razor cheekbones and a piercing violet eye. His silver hair is fashioned into ten braids, curving down over the right side of his face. His ears are tapered to perfect points, the Warbreed glyf etched between his silver brows. He's bright and fey and terrible, gleaming with a dark light. At the simple sight of him, my skin prickles, my belly turns, my heart flutters.

This is the man who led the attack at Orion.

This is the man who *killed my dad.*

And then he speaks, and awful as it is, a part of me almost falls in love at the music of his voice.

"I am Caersan. Archon of the Unbroken. Slayer of Stars."

Glancing around the bridge, I see we're all rocked by the sight of him in some way. Auri bristling with power and rage and fear, Fin sinking down in his chair, Zila turning her head, chewing on a lock of hair. Kal is as pale as death, his hands knotted, a vein throbbing at his neck. Of all of us, he looks the worst—like someone has opened his wrists and bled every drop of him onto the floor. He's clearly horrified, shaken to his core at the sight of the monster who destroyed his planet.

Caersan speaks again. Every word a lightning strike.

"My forces are now massed at the edge of Terran space. Against the Unbroken, there can be no victory. People of Earth, hear me now. I gift you one chance. One choice. One path by which you may spare your people, your world, your sun the annihilation that awaits it beneath my fists."

The Starslayer glares at the camera, and I know it sounds crazy, but I swear I can feel his stare burning in my soul.

"One of my Templars was captured by Terran forces during an altercation in the Fold. I now give you twelve hours to release her."

I glance at Kal and whisper, "Saedii . . ."

"If at the end of this time she is not returned to me, I will destroy your sun. I will consign your entire world to the oblivion of the Void. And should any harm have befallen her while in your keeping, know this: For every second of suffering she endured, I shall repay your species ten-thousand-fold. I will not content myself with the destruction of your planet. I will spend the remaining centuries of my life hunting your kind, until not one human remains alive in this galaxy."

Caersan leans forward, glowering into the lens. And then he speaks five simple words that bring the whole galaxy down on our heads.

"Give me back my daughter."

The feed drops into darkness.

I can't breathe.

I can't see.

I can't speak.

The thought of it washes over me like black icy water. The weight of it hits me in the chest so hard I put my hand to my aching heart.

"Daughter . . . ," I manage.

We all look to Kal, but Kal is staring at Auri, horror in his eyes. The same horror I can see reflected in hers, I feel in mine.

"I'na Sai'nuit," she whispers, voice trembling. "Those Unbroken on the World Ship. *That's* what they called you when Tyler used your name."

"Be'shmai, please," he begs. "Let me explain. . . ."

I'na Sai'nuit.

Son of the Starslayer.

"You're his," I whisper.

I stand slowly, my legs shaking, my face twisting as tears fall from my eyes.

I can't believe it. We've all been so blind.

"You're that bastard's *son*."

PART 4

SHADOW ON THE SUN

29

KAL

Tell her the truth.

That is what the note told me. A message handed to me through an improbable, inexplicable twist of time. The handwriting was not mine. It was not I who discovered it. But still, I knew in my heart that the message was for me. And, looking at the pain in her eyes, she who is my all, my everything, and now perhaps my nothing, I know I should have listened.

"He's your *father*?" Aurora asks me, bewildered.

Why did I not give her the truth, when she gave me so very much?

Because you were afraid.

"Be'shmai . . . ," I whisper.

"You told me he was dead," she says, tears welling in her eyes. "You told me he died at Orion. You *lied* to me."

"I did not lie," I say, heat flushing my ears. "He *is* dead. He is dead to *me*."

Finian shakes his head, aghast. "Maker's breath, Kal—"

"He died the day he chose pride over loyalty," I all but shout. "He died the day he threw honor aside for the sake

393

of victory. He killed tens of thousands of soldiers at Orion under a flag of deceit, and he has remained forever dead in my heart. He is *not* my father." I clench my fists. "And I am *not* his son."

I feel fury in me. Whispering.

You abase yourself before these worms? You are a warrior born. We Syldrathi called the stars our home when these insects were still climbing down from their trees. You owe them nothing, Kaliis.

"Silence," I hiss.

He does not listen. He speaks again, as he has always done.

With my father's voice.

I'na Sai'nuit.

But Scarlett's voice breaks in over his. "He killed my dad."

I look at Scarlett as she speaks, and I see betrayal. Her cheeks are wet with tears, her lower lip trembling. But her voice is hard as iron.

"He killed my dad and you *knew*. You knew what he did. What he took from us. And you looked us in the eyes and didn't breathe a word of it. We had a right to know." She shakes her head, disgusted. "But instead, you had the balls to pretend to be our friend."

"Scarlett, I *am* your friend."

"You put all of us in danger!" she shouts. "Saedii was hunting you for *him*! If not for her, if not for you, we'd never have been aboard the *Andarael*! Tyler would never have been captured by the TDF! And the Ra'haam wouldn't have a way to goad your bastard father into a war that's going to set the *galaxy on fire*!" She glowers at me, fists balled at her sides. "This is your fault, Kal!"

Zila clears her throat softly. "Scarlett, that is overstating somewh—"

"Is it?" Scarlett cries. "You think if he'd told us who he was, he *ever* would have been allowed to join this squad? That he'd have even been allowed to join Aurora Academy?" She whirls on me, eyes narrowed. "I bet you lied on your application, too, right? No way Adams and de Stoy would have accepted the son of the most infamous murderer in the galaxy into the Legion. No *way*."

I meet her gaze, my lips pressed thin. I feel the anger swelling inside me at her challenge, push it down with all my strength.

"Well?" she demands.

"I took my mother's name after Orion," I confess. "I wanted nothing to do with Caersan, or the Unbroken. I joined Aurora Academy because I wished to atone for what he had done! But I knew the commanders would never let me into the Legion if they knew who I truly was."

"So you lied," Scarlett says.

My temper flares, despite myself. "It was none of their business!"

"But it was ours! He killed our *dad*, Kal!" she spits, looking around to the others to register that the blow has landed. "Anything else you wanna confess while you're at it? Your name *is* Kaliis, right? Or did you lie about that, too?"

They all look at me then. Even Aurora, and how my heart aches to see that. I watch as the thought crosses each of their minds—that perhaps *everything* about me is deceit. That they do not know me at all.

"I am Kaliis," I say. "You *know* me, Scarlett."

But she shakes her head, lost in righteous rage. "I don't

know anything about you, you pixieboy bastard. Other than that we can't trust a single word coming out of your mouth."

Zila is chewing furiously on her hair, obviously distressed at the confrontation. Drawing down into herself, hunched small and silent.

Finian speaks, his voice soft. "Did you know your dad . . ." He shakes his head, clearly wounded as he looks at me. "Did you know the Starslayer was a Trigger? That he had the Weapon?"

"*No,*" I insist. "I had no idea. My mother and I left him *years* ago. I was eleven the last time I looked upon him in the flesh, and he was possessed of none of Aurora's gifts then. He has wandered long years since Orion. Perhaps he discovered another probe in the Fold during his travels. Perhaps he stumbled across the gateway or—"

"Or perhaps you're lying about this just like everything else," Scarlett growls.

"I am *not* lying!" I snap.

Finian meets my eyes. "How can we know that, Kal? How can we trust anything you're saying?"

My heart sinks in my chest. I can feel them turning against me, their hurt, their sense of betrayal, all of it blinding them to the person I have been. So I turn to the one who knows me best.

"Aurora . . ."

She looks at me like I have struck her. I remember the same look in my mother's eyes as a child when she looked at my father. When she realized he was not at all the man she had thought him to be.

"Aurora, I am sorry," I say. "Forgive me, please."

"You lied to me, Kal," she says. "That night in my room. The night we first . . ." She shakes her head, arms wrapped tight around herself. "When you told that story about your parents. You looked me in the eyes and you lied."

"He *is* dead to me. My father died at Orion, be'shmai. He died again when he burned my world to cinders. When he took my mother from me. All that remained after that moment was what he'd become." I spit the name, like acid on my tongue. "Sai'nuit. Starslayer."

I take a step toward, and she takes one away, and my heart is bleeding, breaking inside my chest. I should have seen this coming. I have never felt so hopeless, so helpless, as I do right here and now. I can feel her slipping through my fingers with every breath.

"I tried to tell you," I say. "In the Echo. That night in the meadow. I *tried* to speak it, no matter what it would cost me. But you told me I was not the thing I was raised to be. You told me tomorrow is worth a million yesterdays. Remember?"

"I remember," she whispers. "And I remember you said our past makes us what we are. I remember you told me *love* is purpose."

"It is," I breathe.

"But how can you say you love me?" she asks, bewildered. "When you can just lie to my face like that? And how can I say I love you? When I . . ."

She shakes her head. Tears shining in her lashes.

"When I don't even know who you are?"

"You know me," I plead. "You are my moon and my sun, Aurora. You are my *everything*."

Her tears do not fall. They crash, shaking the ship around

me. I look to Finian, to Zila, to Scarlett, desperate for reprieve. For anything.

"I have fought beside you. Bled for you. I have known no home since the Starslayer took mine away, save here among all of *you*." I thump my fist to my heart. "Squad 312. I know I can appear cold. I know I am hard to read, and harder to get along with." I look to each of them. "But I know my friends, and they are few. And those few, I would die for."

Silence rings across the bridge.

And into that silence, Scarlett spits.

"Tell that to Cat."

I feel the words as a blow to my chest.

For a moment, I cannot even breathe.

"Scarlett . . . that is not fair."

"Fair?"

Bristling with fury, she stalks across the deck toward me. Finian rises to his feet, wary, but he does not step closer. Zila hugs her shins, presses her face into her knees. But Scarlett is in my face now, shouting. She only reaches my chin, but her rage makes up for her lack of stature.

"You're talking about *fair*?" she shouts. "My brother's in the hands of the GIA because of you, you son of a *bitch*! How is that fair? What if they took him back to Octavia, huh? Have you even *thought* about that? What if they did to him what they did to C . . . to Ca . . ."

I murmur as her voice fails.

"If I could trade places with him, I would, Scarlett. I am so sorry."

"Fuck your sorry," she snaps, raising her hand. "And fuck *you,* Kal."

She swings. Full of rage. Clumsy. The Enemy Within me

flares, the violence I was born to, the violence in my blood rushing in my veins like thunder. I move, instinct and muscle memory, seizing Scarlett's wrist so hard she cries out in pain.

"Do *not* touch me," I warn her.

"Hey!" Finian shouts, stepping forward. "Get off her!"

"Finian—" Zila begins.

"Let her go!" he shouts.

Our Gearhead plants both hands on my chest and shoves, his exosuit whirring. My whole body bristles, my every instinct aflame with threat.

Break him, Kaliis.

BREAK HIM.

I step aside, smooth as water. Scarlett twists in my grip and I let her go, momentum sending her crashing into Finian and both of them to the deck. Fin cries out, leg twisted, and as I raise my hands, I feel another shove to my chest—iron-hard, midnight-blue power crackling in the air around me.

I look up and see Aurora's hand raised. Aimed at me. Her eye burns like a dying sun, hair whipping around her brow in the breeze of a long-lost world.

"Don't," she says.

"I would never . . ."

And I see it. What everyone who has learned the truth about me has always seen. I was born of a monster, a murderer of billions. And that is what they see when they look at me now. That shadow I will never step out from, no matter how hard I try.

Aurora looks at me, tears glittering like diamonds on her skin. I know what she will say before she says it.

"You need to go, Kal."

"Aurora, no," I plead. "No."

She nods. "Go."

I am torn. Desperate. Searching for anything that might sway her.

"You do not know him, be'shmai," I say, glancing at the screen where the man who made me spoke. "You cannot *begin* to imagine what he is like. He was a monster even before Syldra's fall. If he has somehow become as you are, imbued with the power of the Ancients . . ."

"Are you going to tell me I'll have no chance when I face him?"

My eyes grow hard, my voice like steel. "You do not know him, Aurora."

"I know one thing, Kal," she says softly, wiping the tears from her cheek with the back of one hand. "I know I'm ready now. Truly ready, like the Eshvaren said. I am the Trigger. The Trigger is me. And when I strike at the Great Enemy, there'll be nothing to hold me back anymore. No hurt. No rage. No fear."

She shakes her head.

"No love."

I hear the Eshvaren's words in my head then. That fateful warning it spoke on our last day in the Echo.

Remember what is at stake here. This is more than you. More than us.

Burn.

Burn it all away.

Aurora lowers her hand and breaks my heart.

"Goodbye, Kal."

30

FINIAN

About four hundred light-years from Trask, there's a star called Meridia. The star's core is a diamond the size of Trask's moon, estimated to be about ten decillion carats. My people built a spaceport there—a massive transit hub that's one of the busiest in the galaxy. You can get a ride anywhere in the 'Way out of Meridia. Says a lot about Betraskans that we built a bus station around the galaxy's biggest diamond.

Anyway, that's where we dump Kal.

We're still wanted terrorists and all, so we don't waste time on farewells. Zila brings the *Zero* into one of the tertiary docks, only stopping long enough to let Kal out. Nobody's there to say goodbye. I watch him through the bay cams, stepping out onto the station deck with a rucksack on his back. He's wearing civi clothes—long dark coat, those ridiculous PVC pants Scarlett bought him in Emerald City, pockets stuffed with his share of the credits Adams and de Stoy left for us in the vault.

I think he left his Legion uniform in his room.

Bristling with anger, he squares his shoulders and stalks away.

Nobody speaks for a while after we put Meridia behind us, tearing out of the system and back into the Fold. For my part, I just don't know what to say. I'm scrounging for something—I know I'm meant to be the one who somehow breaks this thick, heavy, hurting silence, but I don't know where to begin.

Everything Betraskans do, everything we believe, everything we *are* is about family. And between losing Cat, leaving Tyler behind, and now Kal's betrayal, it's getting harder and harder to keep my gaze focused on the future. It feels like I've been shot, but I'm still moving. I'm on automatic, but now that the dust has settled, I just don't know what to do next.

The bridge feels too big—it's just the four of us now, with Shamrock on the console and Tyler's and Kal's empty seats to remind us of what we've lost. Which, given that it's our badass pilotry, our tactical genius, and our muscle, is no joke.

Scarlett is hollow eyed. Just as I can't summon up a smart-ass remark to keep us going, she can't find anything in her Face's book of tricks to make this sound better than it is. I know she's blaming herself for not having seen this coming, but though her ability to read everyone she meets is nearly superhuman, there are still limits. For the first time I can remember, she looks . . . I'm not sure what to call it. Beaten? Scared?

Auri's in her own place, her gaze distant. Everything about her has changed—even her posture. She's not the girl we've known anymore. She's utterly focused now. I thought she'd be weaker without Kal's support, but it's as though the heat and fire we've just been through forged her into something stronger.

Something unbreakable.

It's Zila who ends the silence. She has her back to us, piloting the *Zero* through the FoldGate and into black-and-white safety. Now she swings around, her face as blank as it was back when we met. I didn't realize how many small changes I'd seen in it until they went away, along with Kal. She's closed off again, speaking carefully and evenly, her voice flat and gray.

"We must consider our next steps."

Auri's response is immediate and unwavering. "We need to take control of the Weapon."

Scarlett nods. "Ideally, before Caersan uses it to blow up Earth. And we're already three hours into his twelve-hour countdown."

Auri glances at her, gaze burning, chin up.

"And then we have to turn it against the Ra'haam."

"Right," I agree. "So that means we need to get aboard it, yeah? Past a massive Syldrathi war fleet on high alert, ready to unload its many, many guns on anything that looks remotely unfriendly."

Zila inclines her head. "This is an accurate summary."

"Do we have any advantages?" Scar asks. She's reaching for what Tyler would do, I think. Trying desperately to fill the hole her twin has left behind.

"They will certainly not be expecting us."

I wish Zila were making a joke right now, flexing that newfound sense of humor of hers. But she's just stating the obvious. They won't be expecting anybody to do anything this foolhardy, to take on odds this long. Because it's suicide.

"Auri can flatten them with her brain bullets," I offer. "Put that in the advantage column, I guess?"

Aurora doesn't even smile.

"This is true," Zila agrees, equally grave. "However, displays of devastating psychic power would certainly draw attention among the Syldrathi armada. If we wish to maintain our advantage of surprise, we will need to blend in."

Auri's gaze flicks to Zila. "We need a Syldrathi ship."

I frown. "Where are we going to . . ."

My voice fades as I catch the look in Scarlett's eyes. I can see the intelligence behind them, the smarts she keeps hidden behind a mask of sass and indifference. She told me once she never even wanted to join the Legion. That she only signed up to look after Tyler. And she feels her brother's absence worse than any of us, I know. But suddenly she's filling his shoes just fine.

"Raliin Kendare Aminath," she says.

Maker's breath, of course. The Waywalker elder we rescued on *Andarael* told us to find him if there was a way he could repay his debt to us.

Scar looks across at Zila, and our Brain nods, her fingers flying across the pilot's console. "We can be there in four hours," she says. "Shall I set a course?"

Scarlett nods. "Burn as hard as you can."

. . . . .

Each of us finds a way to occupy the next four hours. Zila's at the controls, checking the readings over and over. Auri disappears to her room and closes the door. Scarlett pulls up files in Syldrathi and starts reading.

Me? I got nothing except trying to fix Magellan, and to be frank, hearing a relentlessly chirpy summary of how stupid I am doesn't sound like too much fun right now. Instead, I find something to eat, and I feed Zila and Scar—Auri doesn't answer my knock—then I pace a little. I stare at the closed door to Kal's quarters, trying to figure out what I think of what he did. But though I'm usually a galactic-class champion at dreaming up comebacks an hour or two after the opportunity to say them has passed, this time I draw a blank. I can only be certain of how it feels now that Kal's gone. And honestly, after all we've been through together, it feels like someone reached into the heart of us and ripped out a fistful.

Eventually, on a hunch, I head back to the storage bays. Sure enough, piled in a corner behind the spare fuel cells and replacement parts are drums of thick black paint. Just what we'll need.

This ship really *does* have everything.

Gets me thinking, that. About the note in Kal's cigarillo box. The little metal case itself sure proved useful, and the note inside it proved right.

So, what about the other gifts we were left in the Emerald City storage box? Zila's earrings, Scar's pendant, Tyler's shiny new boots. It's like Adams and de Stoy *knew* what was coming for us—where we'd be, what we'd be doing—and not for the first time, I wonder how.

I reach into my cargoes, find the ballpoint pen they gave me. I frown at it. Wondering what in the Maker's name it's for. I figure if the Legion commanders *did* know about Kal getting shot, if they knew enough to warn him to tell the truth, maybe this thing in my hand has some magic to work in our darkest hour.

I click the button on the end, in and out. Hoping for some kind of miracle.

Nothing.

Absolutely nothing.

"I got robbed," I sigh.

. . . . .

When we arrive at Tiernan Station—Zila did burn it, but the clock's still ticking—we don't know what the reception will be like. So we ease cautiously out through the FoldGate, color restored to the ship once more. The station's structure is beautiful, as all Syldrathi designs are. It's shaped like a large egg, speckled all over with lights. There's a massive Waywalker glyf painted down one side in an elegant script, and close to a hundred fighters and cruisers are swarming around the station in graceful, sweeping arcs.

Every single one of them locks its weapons on us as soon as we appear.

Scar leans forward to speak *very* carefully into the mic. I don't understand Syldrathi, but I can follow along with the translator on my uni, and this encounter is so important that she practiced her script with me before we arrived.

"We are here to see Elder Raliin Kendare Aminath."

There's a pause, and then the reply crackles back.

"For what purpose?"

Scarlett breathes deep and sighs. When you've got no other angle, it's always best to run with the truth, she told me. So she presses the Transmit button and dials her earnestness up to eleven.

"We need his help saving the galaxy."

. . . . .

About half an hour later, I'm standing in one of the landing bays of Tiernan Station, carefully daubing Syldrathi glyfs down the side of an elderly shuttle. The Unbroken sigils are beautiful, elegant . . . but possessed of a savagery somehow. Some hint of the violence the Starslayer's warriors adore so much. I'm following a visual guide Scar sent to my uniglass, watched by a number of very dubious Waywalkers.

Zila's inside the shuttle, having a piloting lesson.

Auri has finally emerged from her quarters and is walking a slow lap of the landing bay. She moves with a kind of grace that I associate more with Kal, and she reminds me of a restless predator. She seems unaware of the rest of us. But the Waywalkers we rescued from their imprisonment on the *Andarael* are fascinated by her, tracking her progress back and forth. All Waywalkers have some kind of low-grade psychic ability. They're empaths. Resonants. I've heard rumor some can even speak telepathically to each other. Maybe they're sensing her new brain muscles.

Scar is talking to the elder, who looks deeply concerned about her life choices. Though his accent is terrible, he's speaking in fractured Terran for Auri's benefit.

"We cannot aid you in this," he tells the girls. "Caersan— Void curse his name—has already destroyed our world. It has taken us many cycles to gather this enclave. We cannot risk his ire, young Terrans."

"I understand," Scarlett says.

Raliin smiles gently. "Your lie is appreciated. And we owe you a debt for our rescue aboard the *Andarael*, no doubt. But we Waywalkers were the smallest cabal among my people, even before our world was destroyed. And since Syldra's fall, Caersan's agents have been hunting us ceaselessly."

Auri's eyes narrow at that. She stops her pacing, looks Raliin in the eye.

"What were they hunting you for?"

Syldrathi nod instead of bowing, so when the elder pauses and nods for a long, slow moment before replying, I realize these people must have *some* small inkling of what she is. What she's about to do.

"We do not pretend to know the designs of a madman," he replies. "We know only that we few have gathered here carefully, secretly. We cannot call attention to ourselves." He gestures to the ship I'm repainting. "But as I said, our rescue from among the Unbroken will not go unrewarded. This is the swiftest vessel we have that is capable of being crewed by four people. And the ident codes we have given you were taken very recently by the few intelligence operatives we still have in the field. With the grace of the Void, the sheer size of the Starslayer's armada, and the thrill of the upcoming attack, the Unbroken may not detect you."

"Thank you, Elder Raliin." Scar nods deeply in respect. "If we haven't contacted you within a day, the *Zero* is yours. No matter what safety you think you have here, I suggest you use her and the rest of your fleet to run. If we don't pull this off, the Unbroken are going to be the least of the galaxy's problems."

To be honest, a day sounds kind of optimistic to me. It's now two and a half hours until the Starslayer drops into the Terran system to rearrange the furniture. And given that we're heading straight toward him to try and stop him, the odds are good it's two and a half hours until Caersan rearranges us as well.

There are a lot of things I wish I'd done or said.

But the truth is, I can't think of anywhere I'd want to be except right here.

31

TYLER

Ra'haam.

Saedii stares at me across the detention cell, her lips pursed. In the time it's taken for me to lay it out for her—Aurora, the Eshvaren, the Ra'haam, Octavia III, Cat, the locker on Emerald City, the GIA, all of it—her blood has dried on her face, on the floor between us. She hasn't thrown a single thought into my mind. Her expression only changed once—a quick flicker, eyes narrowing, when I mentioned the Weapon, which even now I hope the others have found without me.

Scarlett.

Auri.

Great Maker, I hope they're all okay. . . .

Saedii sits there in the aftermath of my confession. I expect her to laugh. To call me a liar and a lunatic, to react the way any normal person might when you tell them that an ancient plant-being that lost a war against a race of ancient psychics is set to wake up after a million-year dirt-nap and nom down on the entire galaxy.

But when she does finally speak into my head, her thoughts are quiet.

This explains the girl you think of constantly.

I blink at that.

. . . What?

Cat, I think? She weighs heavy on your thoughts, Tyler Jones.

I swallow hard. Chest aching.

She was a . . . a friend of mine.

Saedii's eyes narrow. *More than a friend.*

. . . Maybe.

And it took her. This Ra'haam. Turned her. Absorbed her.

I feel anger surge inside me. Welcome and warm.

Yes. It did.

Just as it will absorb the galaxy if we permit it.

Yes, I nod. *It will.*

We must escape this cell, Tyler Jones.

I raise one eyebrow. The scarred one. For extra effect.

I'm glad you're here to tell me these things, Saedii.

Was that sarcasm, little Terran?

I shrug. *My sister inherited most of it. But some rubbed off on me.*

Her eyes narrow again at the word *inherited*. She looks at me long and hard. Glittering eyes framed by dark lashes and dark paint. Her stare lingering maybe a fraction too long on my bare chest.

Listen, I know these pecs could run for president and win, I think to her, more than a little annoyed. *But you could be a touch less obvious about getting an eyeful. In case you missed it, we're in it up to our necks here.*

The Unbroken Templar tilts her head at that. Slowly, slowly leaning back on her bio-cot and stretching those long, bare legs out in front of her. I know what she's doing. I know what she wants. I fill my head with a barrage of unsexy thoughts—my old bunkmate Björkman trimming his toenails with his teeth, that time I caught myself in my zipper, my grandma's underwear, huge cream-colored monstrosities, billowing like sails on the cl—

I can't help it. I glance down for a fraction of a second.

Dammit.

I look up into Saedii's eyes again. Her split lips twist in a small smile.

I am not "getting an eyeful," as you so eloquently put it, Tyler Jones.

She glances back at my chest, thoughtful.

I am wondering what kind of heart beats beneath those ribs of yours.

. . . Meaning what?

Meaning the foe of my foe is my friend. Meaning that despite the enmity and insult between us, I respect the trust you place in me to speak your secrets. And that there are secrets you are perhaps owed in turn. Secrets about me.

She looks into my eyes.

Secrets about you.

I frown.

. . . Me?

She gives a gentle shrug, toying with one black lock of hair as she looks me over once more. *You and your sister, I suppose.*

. . . What's Scar got to do with this?

Twins, are you not?

Yeah, so what?

Jericho Jones escaped Syldrathi captivity before the battle at Kireina IV, yes?

My frown deepens. *How'd you know that?*

She smiles again. *Your father held back a fleet twice the size of his at Kireina. It was the worst defeat we suffered in the entire war. Know your enemy, Tyler Jones.*

I don't—

Jericho Jones was a rear admiral less than a year after his victory. A warrior, born and bred, who fought the best of the Warbreed to a standstill and caused our fall from ascendancy in the Inner Council of Syldra. And yet, he resigned his commission. Became the strongest advocate for peace in your Senate. Why the change of heart?

I have no idea where she's going with this. But something in her eyes urges me to run with it.

He made a speech about it in 2367, I tell her, pride swelling my chest. *It still gets taught today at Aurora Academy. "I can no longer look my children in the eye without seeing the wrong in killing other people's."*

She sniffs. *A pretty lie.*

I bristle. *You watch what you say about my father, Saedii.*

When I first spoke to your mind, you said you were not aware that those who possessed Waywalker gifts could speak to other people telepathically.

I shrug. *I wasn't aware.*

Saedii shakes her head, mild contempt spilling into my mind despite her best effort to hold it in check. *That is because we cannot speak to other people, Tyler Jones. We can only speak to others with the gift.*

My stomach lurches. *I don't . . .*

413

I am Warbreed by birth and troth, Saedii tells me. *But . . . though I loathed her, I did inherit some of my mother's talents.*

She meets my eyes, her own glinting like glass.

It would seem your mother also shared her gift with you.

The thought knocks the breath from my lungs. My heart is thumping, mind spinning. But I'm trying to hold on to the threads in my head, stitch them together into a tapestry that makes some kind of sense, while Saedii looks on, cool and aloof.

We never knew our mom—I always wondered about her, but I could tell how much it hurt Dad to talk about her. I didn't want to push it. And I thought we had a lifetime to ask him about what happened. Where she went.

But Dad *was* missing behind enemy lines for months. I admit it always struck me as kinda strange—for him to have turned from the Syldrathi's greatest enemy into the man who argued strongest for peace. I guess part of me wanted to put him on a pedestal. The noble war hero who came to respect the enemy he fought against. To understand we're all, in some essential way, the same.

But it would make a lot more sense if . . .

While he was captured, if he . . .

It's funny being a twin. Sometimes I feel like I know what my sister will say before she says it. Sometimes I swear she can tell what I'm thinking just by looking at me. Scar and I were inseparable as kids. Dad said we invented our own language before we could talk. And the way my sister instinctively reads people—like books, like she can actually see into their heads sometimes . . .

"Maker's breath," I breathe aloud.

You do not have much of the look about you, Saedii says. *Probably why your mother sent you away. But it is undeniable that you and your sister are possessed of a certain*—her eyes flicker over my body again—*grace. Height. Poise. You saw the images of my torture in your head. You can speak to me in my mind. I feel you in here*—she touches her brow—*as surely as you feel me. There is only one explanation, Tyler Jones.*

Saedii tucks a long black lock behind her ear.

Your mother was a Waywalker.

I swallow hard. Look down at my forearm. My tanned skin. The veins beneath the muscle etched in long scrawls of pale blue.

Scar and me . . . we have Syldrathi blood in our veins?

Saedii's fingertips drift over the string of severed thumbs at her throat. She is looking me up and down, the tip of her tongue pressed against one sharpened canine.

The question is, Are you worthy of it?

My head is spinning, trying to process all this. How did it happen? Why didn't Dad tell us? Who was our mother?

. . . Is she alive?

Gird yourself, boy, Saedii says. *Hold firm.*

The biggest bombshell of my life just got dropped on my head, Saedii. I think I'm gonna need a minute here. . . .

We do not have a minute, Tyler Jones. If what you have told me about this . . . ancient enemy is true, every second we waste in this cell among these insects is another second closer to the galaxy's doom.

I scowl, my temper flaring blood-red across our shared minds.

You think I don't know that?

Saedii watches me for a long, silent moment. I can *feel* her, her emotions, her thoughts, all of her. It's hard to keep straight in my head, to process which parts of all I'm feeling are me, and which are her. It's like we're touching . . . but not.

I think there is much you do not know, she replies.

Maker's breath, what else?

Saedii folds her bare legs up beneath her, leans back against the wall, and crosses her arms over her chest.

You had best get comfortable, boy. This will be a great deal to swallow.

32

KAL

There is a gravity to everything.

I told Aurora that, not so long ago. Looking into her eyes as I finally confessed all I was feeling for her. Every atom in our bodies, every atom in the universe exerts a gravity on the atoms around it. Gravity is one of the forces holding all this together. It is inexorable. Nothing rises without falling. It is not a matter of if, but when.

We Syldrathi believe that everything is a cycle. An endless circle. That one day the expansion of the universe will cease, the force generated by the explosion that began it will be overcome by gravity. And on that day, the universe will begin to contract. No longer spiraling out, but falling inward, every atom in existence dragged backward toward its point of origin, collapsing once more into the singularity that began it all. Only to begin again.

We are all of us gravity's slaves.

All of us pulled by it.

Back to the place it all began and to where we know it must end.

It did not take me long to find transport from Meridia. There is no shortage of folks in the galaxy who fear the Starslayer, who watch the unfolding calamity between Terra and the Unbroken with an absolute certainty of who will triumph. The Chellerian smuggler who agreed to ferry me to the Unbroken armada still took a great deal of convincing, considering the dangers of approaching the largest Unbroken fleet assembled since the fall of Syldra. But my share of the small fortune that Admiral Adams and Battle Leader de Stoy left for us in the Emerald City vault was enough to purchase his peace of mind.

I wonder if our commanders knew what that money would be used for when they left it for us.

If they knew where my path would lead.

I stand in the cockpit beside the smuggler and his copilot—a surly Rikerite with one of his horns snapped off at the root. The smuggler is fond of his rocksmoke, and the cockpit is full of the stink, metallic and thick, drifting from the burner on the console. The gabble of news feeds spills over the cockpit sound system.

The Fold around us is colorless as always, as gray as the storm clouds around my head. I am watching the incoming Unbroken vessels on our scopes—four Ghost-class scouts on intercept course. They cut through the Fold toward us, and beyond them I can see countless ships, sleek and dark and deadly, gathered on the threshold to the Terran system. A force to set fire to the heavens.

And at the heart of it, he waits for me.

The shadow I have never been able to step out from.

A transmission from the lead scout cuts across our news feeds, brought up onscreen with a tap of the smuggler's fingers. I see a young Unbroken adept, the Warbreed glyf on his brow, black war paint across glittering gray eyes.

"*Unidentified vessel,*" he says coolly. "*You are either insane or suicidal. Retreat or be destroyed. This is your first and final warning.*"

The smuggler looks to me. I press one finger to the console and speak.

"I am here to see my father," I reply.

The adept's stare hardens as he takes in the glyf at my brow, the seven braids in my hair. "*We are poised to reclaim the honor the Council of Syldra surrendered so long ago, boy. We are death on black wings, and we shall slay a star this day. This is no place for a family reunion.*"

I press the Transmit button again, my voice soft with threat.

"Archon Caersan may disagree with you, adept."

The adept's eyes narrow, then slowly widen as realization sinks in. He draws one halting breath, his hiss spilling over bloodless lips.

"*T'na Sai'nuit.*"

I press the Transmit button, speak with a voice as gray as the Fold around us.

"Tell my father I wish to speak to him."

· · · · ·

My heart is a war drum, pounding against my ribs.

I am standing aboard the shuttle he sent for me, hands clasped behind my back, surrounded by six of his Paladins. The decor on the Syldrathi ship is black, its crimson light muted to gray by the Fold. The Unbroken warriors around me are clad in ceremonial armor, watching me from beneath silver lashes. None are brave enough to give voice to their thoughts, but in truth none need to. I feel it.

Curiosity. Resentment. Fear.

The lost son, returned.

I watch the shuttle's forward screens as we weave through the Unbroken armada. The sight of it is awe-inspiring, terrifying: the sheer scale of it all, the countless ships ready to unleash chaos at his word. He commands respect, my father. His very name enough to strike fear wherever it is spoken. A man who was prepared to burn his own homeworld rather than sacrifice his honor. A man to whom the murder of billions was preferable to surrender.

I remember him standing behind me beneath the lias trees. His hand on my shoulder. Guiding my strikes as he tutored me in the Wave Way.

I can feel him now, if I try.

My Enemy Within.

And then I see it.

A glimpse between the crescent shapes of two massive carriers. The full scope of it unfolding as the ships part before us like water. The breath is snatched away. I feel like an insect in the presence of a god.

The Weapon.

It is the largest vessel I have ever seen, stretching twenty kilometers from nose to tail and making children's toys of the mightiest ships around it. Its shape is vaguely conical, and a series of massive concave structures are arrayed at what I presume is the bow, like vast lenses—asymmetrical, arcane, and utterly alien. It is carved of the same living crystal that the Eshvaren wore in the Echo, and the rainbow of light playing upon its every surface, hypnotic, melodic, would have been stunning enough were it not for the thought that suddenly occurs to me:

We are in the Fold.

Everything around us should be monochrome. Muted shades of gray. But the Eshvaren Weapon is a song of color, almost heartbreaking in its beauty. This is a device designed to destroy suns, and yet my soul swells to see it.

The war in my blood surges. Something in it calls to me, reaching out across the gulf between us, roiling, rushing, setting my pulse pounding quicker, my fingertips tingling. A power at once alien and familiar. A voice I have not heard in years, and yet have heard every day of my life, echoing now in my head.

Kaliiiiiissssss.

As the shuttle draws closer to the Weapon, we pass through a field of some sort—vaguely glittering, translucent. The ship shudders beneath me. The Paladins around me sway on their feet, and I feel a flood of . . . power in my head. Thick like syrup. Heavy as iron. Blurring my eyes.

The shuttle lands in a strange docking bay, crystalline structures on the ceiling and floors, the colorscape almost blinding in intensity. I glance at the Paladins beside me, but they remain silent. They bay has no doors—no way to keep the cold and the vacuum out. But the warriors march me down to the shuttle's airlock and, without hesitation, cycle it open.

We do not freeze. We do not suffocate.

The Paladin commander fixes me in a gray stare.

"We can go no farther, I'na Sai'nuit," he tells me.

I step out into the bay, the surface humming beneath my feet. I cannot say how, and yet . . . I know the way. Drawn like a needle to north, I walk up winding paths of singing crystal, whispering, thrumming with power.

I feel . . . strange. All the emotions within me seem louder.

I see an image of Aurora standing with her hand raised aboard the *Zero*'s bridge, her power striking me in the chest as she commanded me to stop. I hear the venom in Scarlett's voice as she cursed me, blamed me, hit me. I feel Finian's bewildered pain, Zila's silent acquiescence as they cast me out. I who have fought for them. Bled for them. Risked my all to keep them safe. None of them could understand what it was for me to join the Legion, how much I have given, how much I have suffered, how it feels to be utterly alone, even in a crowded room.

Ever since my mother fled back to Syldra, I have never known a moment's peace. Outcast among my own people for the Warbreed glyf at my brow, the blood in my veins. Outcast among the academy cadets as the former enemy, the pixie-boy, the freak: *Remember Orion, remember Orion.* Among the members of Squad 312, I thought I had found a home. A place to belong. Something worth fighting for.

But I was a fool.

I should have known that the shadow of the past would forever come between us. We cannot deny who and what we truly are.

And Aurora . . .

"Aurora." I whisper the name, as if it is poison on my lips. Pushing thoughts of her aside, the memory of our time in the Echo, the things we shared, locking her and them away in a room inside my head and casting away the key.

I am no one now.

I am only this.

What I have *always* been.

There is not a soul in these vast and glittering halls. Not a single soldier or scientist or servant. The entire ship is empty, save for this *power,* familiar and unknowable all at once. As I walk farther down the crystal way, I feel catatonia, vertigo, perfect clarity. My pulse is rushing, asynchronous, like a drumbeat out of time. My mouth tastes like rust.

This ship is huge. These corridors seem endless. But eventually, the pathways converge, opening out into a vast, spherical chamber.

Power drips from the air, red and thrumming on my skin. The walls are lost in shadow, and my eyes are drawn to the light, the concentric spires of crystal in the center of the room, aglow and radiant. An ever-ascending dais, rising off the floor, crowned with an enormous glittering throne. Branches of crystal reach out toward it from the ceiling, the walls, like the roots of a tree straining toward water. Squinting, putting my hand up against the rainbow light, I see a figure upon it.

A shadow falls upon my sun.

He is clad in black armor with a high collar, and a long cloak is arrayed around his shoulders, spilling down over the steps below him in a crimson train. His hair is silver-bright, woven into ten braids and draped in long, thick waves over one side of his face. And that face is all I remember and more. Beautiful. Terrible. Radiating a dark majesty. He watches, impassive, as I climb the dais, the power around me thickening, my footsteps ringing hollow in the vast crystal sphere, the gravity of him drawing me in. Drawing me back.

Everything is a cycle. An endless circle.

Everything has led to this.

I stand before him.

"Father," I say.

"Son," he replies.

And then, finally, I kneel.

33

TYLER

Kal . . .

Saedii just stares at me. The revelation about her brother, their *father*—who and what he is—it's almost too much for me to wrap my head around. This entire conversation has happened at the speed of thought. It's maybe been ten minutes since it began. But it feels long as a lifetime.

I thought of Kal as a friend. Someone I could trust. Steady and strong and sure. Even when I'd been torn away from the squad, it was easier to deal with—knowing he'd be there to look after them. But to find out he's the son of the man who killed my dad, that he was *lying* to us this whole time . . .

I will follow you, Brother, he told me.

Some brother . . .

But I push the hurt, the betrayal aside. Focusing on the problem I can actually *do* something about. The galaxy is still on the threshold of war. The TDF and the Unbroken could already be tearing each other to pieces. But if everything Saedii just told me is true, if the Weapon the Starslayer used to destroy the Syldrathi sun . . .

What did you call it again? I ask Saedii.

My father named it Neridaa, she replies.

I shake my head.

My Syldrathi isn't as polished as Scar's.

Saedii sneers. *Your boots are better polished than your Syldrathi.*

I peer mournfully down at the kicks I got from the Emerald City vault. They're scuffed, beaten, bloodstained. I'd kill for a tin of polish, honestly.

Wow, that's cold, lady.

Saedii raises one eyebrow ever so slightly. It's kind of amazing how much she can pack into a simple gesture like that. Amusement. Disdain. Arrogance. Smug superiority. Scar could take lessons from this girl.

Neridaa *is a difficult concept to translate into your crude Terran tongue.*

Let's leave my Terran tongue out of this, shall we?

The eyebrow rises higher. *The word describes . . . paradox. A state of beginning and ending. The act of destroying and creating.*

And you're certain this ship is the Eshvaren Weapon?

I feel a tiny sliver of fear, far in the back of her mind.

I am certain of nothing. My father keeps his own counsel. And I was not present when he discovered the first relic.

. . . What relic? I ask.

A probe of some kind. Three years ago. I was already a Templar by then, serving aboard Andarael. *Fighting our war against the traitors on the Council of Syldra. But I was alerted via a panicked transmission from my father's flagship after they discovered an object drifting in the Fold. Apparently, my father*

425

had . . . dreamed of it. He told his science division that it had called to him. And when they brought it aboard, he touched it and fell unmoving to the deck.

Saedii shakes her head.

I had his science staff all thrown to the drakkan for it. The fools. The object they had found was crystal. Denying all analysis of its structure. My father lay on the deck beside it. Nothing we did could rouse him. I thought it was all about to come undone. After everything we had sacrificed, our Archon had been laid low by a freak encounter with some ancient curio in interdimensional space? It seemed a cruel ending to our song.

But eighteen hours later, my father woke, as if from deepest sleep. Crackling with some new power. I was almost weeping with relief. I asked him what had happened, and he looked at me like I was a stranger. Then he commanded the helm to plot a new course. A rift in the Fold, leading us to a long-dead world. And from there to the Weapon that won our war, ended the treachery of the Syldra council forever, and wrote his name, bloody and beautiful, among the stars.

I look at Saedii, utterly bewildered.

You didn't ask him about it? None of you wondered how he knew it was there, or raised an eyebrow that a weapon capable of destroying entire star systems had just been left lying around? Didn't you wonder what it was for?

Saedii sneers.

Of course we wondered. But he was our Archon, Tyler Jones. We his Templars, his Paladins, his adepts. Loyal to the death. The Syldrathi civil war had been raging since the Orion attack. And finally he led us to victory against the curs and cowards who had so shamed us—the Weavers and Watchers and Workers so keen to bend the knee and sign your father's accursed peace.

I shake my head. *Is peace such a horrible thing?*

It is through conflict we attain perfection, Tyler Jones. The blade grows dull when it sleeps in its scabbard. Sharp when pressed against the stone.

Saedii glowers at me, eyes flashing. I can see . . . no, *feel* the conviction in her. The flame burning in her chest. War is more than a way of life for this girl. It's a religion. And the awful thing is, I can see a kind of truth in what she says—it *is* through challenging ourselves that we grow stronger, better, more.

But it's not the *whole* truth.

I'm not afraid to fight, I tell her. *But it's always been for something. Family. Faith. Maker, even peace itself. Fighting for the sake of fighting—*

I was born for war, Tyler Jones, she tells me, those perfect brows drawn together in a perfect frown. *And if you are worthy of the Syldrathi blood within you, you had best become acquainted with that notion. Because we will need to carve our way off this vessel if we mean to escape. We must paint this ship red.*

We're Folding. Everything is black and white.

Her face sours. *Ah. That wonderful Terran sarcasm.*

I shake my head, jaw clenched. *These people are following orders. They're soldiers doing their jobs. The Ra'haam is the enemy here. The GIA, not the TDF.*

They tortured me.

You murdered their friends!

That makes it right in your eyes?

I breathe deep. Looking over the bruises on her face. She knew how I'd answer that question before she ever asked it.

No, it doesn't. But my father taught me that to be a leader, you have to set the example. To be a leader, you have to be the kind of person you'd want to follow you.

Yes, she hisses, sitting up taller. *A warrior. Unconquered and unafraid.*

No. Better. We need to be better than the enemy we fight. The Ra'haam wants us to tear each other to pieces. It wants us at each other's throats. All it needs to do is stall here. To sow chaos and confusion long enough for it to hatch from those seed worlds and then out into the Fold.

Saedii crosses her arms, shaking the hair from her eyes.

I know not if my father understands the purpose of the Weapon he has claimed. But we must get off this ship and warn him of this greater enemy. We are Unbroken. We are no one's pawns. To say he will be displeased at being manipulated is an understatement.

Displeased enough to still blow up my planet even if we get you back to him?

Her stare narrows at that.

If I am returned, Earth will be spared. Believe me when I say, Tyler Jones, my father has no wish to use the Neridaa unless he has to.

He seemed pretty eager to use it on Syldra.

That was a matter of honor. It was also the first time he unleashed the Weapon's full potential. He will not be in a hurry to do so again.

. . . Why not?

Saedii stares at me, cold and calculating. I can see her

suspicion fighting with her instinct. She knows we have to trust each other. And all this is far bigger than she first believed. But still, it's a long time before she answers.

My father paid a price when he used the Weapon, Tyler Jones.

What price?

I was not with him when it fired. . . . She shakes her head. *But even aboard* Andarael, *six thousand kilometers off the* Neridaa's *stern, I felt it. As if the essence were being drawn from me like water into a sponge. And my father stood at the Weapon's heart when it was unleashed.*

You mean it . . . drained him? Like a battery?

She just shrugs. *It took him many cycles to recover.*

So he can't just go around firing this thing on a whim. Are you saying his threat to destroy Earth is just a bluff?

Oh no. My father is as ruthless a man as ever walked the stars. If I am not returned to him, he will make a desolation of your home. He has taken steps to ensure that the next time he is forced to use Neridaa, *the drain will be lessened. A battery of his own, so to speak.*

For a moment, I sense a small shiver run through her.

But he will not waste it unless he is forced to. I must return to him.

I tilt my head and meet her eyes. *Well, you're just as much a tactician as I am. Do you see any way out of this cell? Let alone down to the docking bay?*

When the guards enter to feed us. We overpower them. Take their weapons.

That assumes they're going to feed us at all, I point out.

Then I will pretend my injuries are worse than they are.

Hold my stomach. Collapse. When they send medical person-nel and security, we strike.

Feign weakness, I nod. *Yeah, I thought of that. But they send these boys in packs of six, in case you missed it.*

I most certainly did not, she glowers.

So even presuming we overpower half a dozen fully armed and armored TDF marines, that camera above the door will flag us as soon as we jump them. The whole ship will be locked down before we get off this level.

Perhaps you would care to make a suggestion instead of criticizing mine.

Hey, don't get snippy with me, missy.

Saedii's glower grows hot enough to burn through the cell door.

Do you refer to all females you wish to insult as "missy," boy?

Only the ones who call me "boy," missy.

I look around the cell, sucking my lip. I've studied TDF ships since I was a kid. Good news is, if we can get out of this cell, I know exactly how to get down to the landing bays. Bad news is, I also know exactly how these cells are constructed, and how impossible they are to break out of.

I cast my eyes over the wreckage of the bio-cot I smashed during my little temper tantrum. My stare roams to the sprin-kler system above. The tiny, narrow grilles leading into the ventilation systems. I conjure up plans, then discard them just as quick.

We've got no edge here at all.

Well? Saedii demands. *Impress me.*

I can feel myself getting frustrated again. The thought of everything that could be happening out there while we're stuck in here is derailing me. I feel helpless. Useless. I breathe deep, clenching and unclenching my fists. My mind racing. I know no jail cell is perfect. There's no problem that's unsolvable. Somewhere, somehow, there's a key to be found here. I just need to know where to look.

You are not impressing me, Tyler Jones.

Stop. You're breaking my heart.

I could pluck it from between your ribs and put it back together, if you like?

Shut up and let me think, will you?

Saedii sighs and rises from her cot. Raising her arms above her head, long black hair cascading down her back in waves, she stretches like a cat and begins pacing the cell despite her injuries.

That isn't helping, I tell her.

It helps me to think.

I close my eyes and sigh. *Look, I understand the seriousness of our situation, but you do realize that stalking up and down in front of me in your underwear might not be entirely conducive to clarity of thought?*

Saedii throws me a withering glance and kicks a large chunk of the wrecked bio-cot in my direction. I stop it with my boot heel before it can crash into my legs.

Grow up, she tells me.

I kick the wreckage away from me.

"Up" is exactly the situation I'm trying to avoid.

Saedii rolls her eyes, does one more lap of the cell, then twists on the spot and sinks back down onto her cot. I pout, looking at the wreckage she kicked at me, picking the glass splinters out of the treads of my boot. Scowling at the new scuffs on the leather. Maker's breath, these things *really* need a coat of polish and a—

Click.

I blink. Glance up at the camera lens and away again just as quickly. I shift to sit cross-legged, hunching so the arc of my shoulder hides my feet from the camera. I look down at my boots again. These boots that were waiting for me in that Emerald City deposit box for eight years. These boots Admiral Adams and Battle Leader de Stoy *wanted* me to have. Slow as I can move, I reach down and press the small crack that's appeared in the heel.

I see a metallic glint in the hidden compartment inside.

Saedii catches the shift in my mood. Studiously looks away from me as her voice slips back into my head.

What is it? she asks.

For the first time in a long time, I almost smile.

Something impressive, I tell her.

34

ZILA

The Starslayer's fleet is bigger than any of us dreamed. The black-and-white landscape of the Fold is teeming with Syldrathi ships. They swarm around the mouth of the FoldGate that leads to Terra, crossing each other's paths with only meters to spare. Somewhere between a flawless display of intricate choreography and a battle-fleet-sized game of chicken.

We have arrived at the very edge of the pack as the fleet continues to muster, hiding among the flood of late arrivals and taking stock. I am piloting, and Scarlett and Finian are strapped into their seats at the auxiliary stations behind me. Aurora stands by my side like a hound ready for the hunt, almost quivering as she points in the direction of her prey.

She is nothing like herself, her gaze locked in the direction of the Weapon, obscured despite its size behind the mass of vessels the Archon commands. It's as though the Aurora we know has departed, leaving behind her shell to be inhabited by this new predator, all purpose.

As I begin to weave my way through the fleet, I wonder if it even registers in her mind that the man we are approaching is Kal's father.

Kal, whom she loved.

For my part, I learned my lesson long ago. Open your heart to anyone, and it will end badly. They will betray you, as Miriam did, willing to trade the whereabouts of a six-year-old for her own safety. Or they will leave you, as my parents did, unable to keep our family safe. Cold and dead and left behind, with me thrown into the governmental care system, alone as I had never been.

Open your heart to anyone, and they will betray you, or abandon you.

Now Cat, Tyler, and Kaliis have taught me that lesson all over again.

Soon Aurora will join them.

I know it would be better to withdraw to my former state, but . . . despite my wishes, I do not feel nothing.

It seems I have lost the knack of it.

I ease around the stern of a battle cruiser, and behind me Scarlett murmurs a translation of its name. "*Belzhora.* 'Drinker of Blood.'"

There is something surreal, ghostly, about the fleet we are now a part of. The silence is perfect, broken only by the soft hum of our ship's drives. I have never encountered so much violent potential in one place. Like a coiled spring waiting to unload. Like a warrior watching for the first blink from their opponent.

"What are they all waiting for?" Fin asks.

"Perhaps the Terrans still seek to negotiate," I suggest quietly.

"They're about to run out of time on Caersan's clock," Scarlett replies.

And then the Unbroken ships part, and we see it. A gleaming wonder amid the muted black and white, a rainbow of refracted crystal and endless color. *Impossible* color. It shouldn't be visible in the Fold.

"It looks like a chandelier and a telescope had a baby," Fin says, trying to find some way to cut the tension singing through our small ship. He is whistling in the dark, trying to defy its might. But we are all staring at the vessel, all intimidated by it, except for Aurora. It breaks every rule, it radiates power, and we know it.

The Weapon.

I force myself to make a practical observation. "There is a clear perimeter around it. Approaching it will be difficult. We will be seen."

Aurora shifts her weight beside me. "That won't be a problem for long."

So far she has been quiet, utterly focused, but now I begin to see that silence for what it was—a fuse slowly burning toward the explosives that wait at its end. She crackles with power, with intent, with absolute determination.

I do not want her to be on our shuttle when the spark reaches its destination.

"Options?" asks Scarlett, leaning forward to squint at the ship.

"Two," Fin replies. "If we need to get Auri aboard, then either we make our approach less obvious or we create a distraction."

"A distraction could be fatal," I point out.

There is a short silence. This mission will be fatal anyway, we all know that. But what I mean is that it must not be fatal *too soon.*

"I hate to suggest this," Finian begins. "But if we wait long enough, they're gonna jump into the Terran system and we'll have all the distraction we need."

"That will likely result in a massive loss of Terran and Syldrathi life once the TDF engages the Unbroken fleet," I point out.

"I didn't say it was a perfect plan," Finian shrugs. "I'm not the strategy guy. I have a deep suspicion I only passed first-year tactics because the instructor didn't want me back in class the next . . ."

Finian's joke trails off into silence as he realizes what he has done.

Given us another reminder that Tyler is not with us.

Another reminder of all we have lost.

Scarlett squares her shoulders, jaw clenched.

"Can we listen in on the Unbroken comms?" she asks.

I incline my head. "It will require utilizing the log-in codes the elder gave us, but if they are correct, then yes."

"Do it," Auri instructs me.

I connect to the Unbroken communications network, enter the access codes, and attempt to keep my breathing even as I wait to see whether they will be accepted. A finger of ice trails down my spine, but I do not speak. Abruptly a Syldrathi voice spills out of our speakers.

Scarlett listens a few moments, her brow creased. "Oh *crap.*"

"Bad news?" Fin asks.

"They're getting ready to head through the FoldGate."

A ripple passes through the fleet as it moves into position. A closing of the gaps between ships so the Unbroken can pour through the FoldGate en masse. An immeasurable, unstoppable flow.

Auri grips the back of my seat so hard, I hear the internal structure creak.

"Get us closer to the Weapon! A little more, and I can get myself there."

"You want to spacewalk, Stowaway?" Fin asks. "You're half the size of the average Syldrathi. None of the suits here—"

"I don't need a suit." She meets my eyes. "Zila, just get me close."

I glance at Scarlett, who nods, and so I obey.

Fin curses, hurrying toward the stern of the shuttle and the airlock, Aurora on his heels. She does not say goodbye.

I bank the shuttle sideways, slip between two massive cruisers and ever closer to the rainbow refractions of the Weapon. From behind me, Scarlett puts her hand on my shoulder and squeezes.

I find that her touch unexpectedly eases the tension within me.

"As soon as we're through the gate into Terran space," she says softly, "the TDF will be shooting at us."

"Yes."

"We can't shoot back. We can't fight against our own people."

"I will do my best to avoid combat." The rest of the sentence is unspoken: *For as long as possible.*

A voice spills over the Unbroken communications network. Deep and musical. A voice we all immediately recognize.

"De'na vosh, tellanai," the Starslayer says.

"'Know no fear, my children,'" Scarlett murmurs.

"De'na siir."

"'Know no regret.'"

"Tur, si mai'lesh de'sai."

"'Today, we burn away our shame.'"

"Turae, si aire'na aire no'suut."

"'Tonight, we dance the dance of blood.'"

With a blinding flash of light, the Unbroken fleet begins dropping through the FoldGate. Dreadnoughts and carriers. Wave upon wave of cruisers and destroyers, fighters and drones. Finally, the Weapon itself disappears before our eyes. I steel myself, engage our thrusters, and a moment later we are through it too, with a ripple of sensation I feel in every pore.

We emerge into the utter chaos of battle, missiles and tracer rounds flying past us, the Unbroken fleet spreading out to engage the Terran defenders. Ships are wheeling and turning, dodging and cartwheeling, exploding silently and flying to pieces around us. Syldrathi instructions are snapped and shouted down the comms, broadcasting through our bridge, too quick for me to follow.

"Holy crap!" Scarlett cries.

The Unbroken fleet breaks apart into wings, spreading out across a broad perimeter, lighting the dark on fire. Despite the news feeds disputing the existence of the Unbroken superweapon, it seems TDF Command is taking the claim seriously; a phalanx of Terran vessels is throwing all it can at the wall of Syldrathi ships, hoping to punch its way through the Unbroken defenses.

"Those are Betraskan," Scarlett whispers, pointing at our scopes.

It is true—among the snub-nosed hulks of the Terran fleet, we can see the smooth, beetle-shaped forms of Betraskan destroyers and battleships, locked in combat with the Unbroken force. It seems Earth's allies have kept true to their word, stepping up in defense of Terra. My heart flutters slightly as I realize we are seeing the opening shots of what might become the first true galactic war. I do my best to ignore it, but the biological response to the sight is strong.

Ships explode around us in absolute silence. The cockpit is a cacophony of screaming alarms and warnings from the flight computer, Scarlett shouting unneeded advice, and the thunder of our engines, and among it all I feel so small, so insignificant, that I wonder what I am doing here at all. I fly as best I can, but I know my best will not be enough for much longer, my knuckles white on my controls. I glance up at the stuffed dragon tucked above my seat. Shamrock watches me with beady eyes, supervising in the absence of Cat.

I wish you were here.

Then, as though Cat has given it to me herself, I spot my moment. The carriers protecting the Weapon have unleashed their fighter wings, moving to intercept a storm of inbound TDF cruisers. I stab at my controls, weave beneath the belly of an Unbroken dreadnought bristling with guns. For a brief moment, there is nothing between us and the Weapon. As I swing by for a close pass, spiraling among a burst of inbound railgun fire, a light on my console flickers on—an alarm warns me the rear airlock has opened.

Seven heartbeats later, it closes again.

"Good luck, Auri," Scarlett murmurs.

A spray of missiles from a TDF vessel cuts across our bow, and I stab instinctively at the controls to take evasive action. As I swerve away from the gleaming Weapon, back out into the wider chaos, my vision seems to widen. The battle becomes bigger and bigger, until I'm taking in an ocean of ships thousands strong, stretching as far as I can see.

I cannot see Aurora at all.

I take a deep, slow breath and loosen my hold on the controls, forcing myself to focus on the task ahead—living long enough to render Aurora any assistance we can. Small as I am feeling, I honestly have no idea if it will be enough.

But in the end, what else can I do?

"Scarlett, hold on."

35

AURI

It takes only the smallest corner of my mind to maintain a bubble of air and pressure around me. Only the smallest fraction of my Self to propel me through the ice-cold void of space toward the Weapon. Around me, a thousand ships whirl in a dance of death and destruction, but for me, time slows. I see every move before they make it. I know their fates before they're sealed.

And I am coming closer and closer to my destination.

To my destiny.

I fly through a glittering, translucent field as I approach the Weapon, and within its touch I sense the energy of the Eshvaren. The creators of the thing that hangs before me, radiant in the dark. There's an instant familiarity about that sensation, like an old friend reaching for my hand. For a moment, I'm standing before Esh once more, inside the Echo, hearing that simple instruction.

Your only obstacles are those you put in front of yourself.

You must let them go.

Focus.

And I do.

The man who awaits me inside the Weapon will know that I'm here. I'm sure of it. But I feel no fear, no hesitation. Only certainty about what I must do.

I've burned my loves and my ties all away.

Nothing remains but my purpose.

The docking bay is like a huge, crystalline cave, gleaming and intense. It's completely empty as I soar inside. I set myself down on the floor, and the instant I connect to the crystal structure around me, I'm home, clicking into place, an integral part of this vast refraction of rainbows, power singing through it and into me.

I know the man I've come to find at its center, and it's in that direction that I walk. The pathways seem almost aimless, twisting upon one another, climbing and falling. But I'm patient as I walk them. I feel the way they channel the energy of this place, focus its power and mine, and I revel in the sensation of it flowing beneath my feet.

I crouch to unlace my boots, peel off my socks, abandoning them behind me as I continue on, barefoot. I'm connected to the surface around me fully, utterly. The Eshvaren Weapon sings to me. In me. Through me. I am a part of this place. Like I was always meant to be here. I am the Trigger, and the Trigger is me.

And so I'm not at all surprised when I find him standing ahead of me at a crossroads.

Kal.

He's dressed in the black of the Unbroken, and he stands straight and tall, as beautiful and defiant as the first time I saw him. He was only a vision then, appearing in my room at Aurora Academy before I knew the Syldrathi even existed. Now, with the same arrogant lift of his chin, he greets me.

"You should not have come," he says quietly.

"You knew I would."

"You do not understand what you face, Aurora."

"No, Kal," I return. "*You* don't understand. What I am. What I've become."

"What *they* have done to you."

"*They* were trying to save the galaxy, Kal. *They* were trying to do what's right."

"You do not comprehend," Kal says, his eyes haunted as he glances up the corridor. "But I fear you soon will. *He* will show you."

My lips curl. Those lips that weren't so long ago pressed to his.

"So you're his disciple now, too?" I ask. "Just like the rest of them?"

"I did not want this, Aurora. I did not want any of this to happen. I loved you."

"You can't build love on a lie, Kal."

"Look into my heart, then. Tell me what you feel."

I reach out. Just a moment. Even here, even now, I can't help myself. I feel a touch of familiar gold, a hint of who and what we were. I sever it with a wave of my hand.

"Did you sense deception or devotion?" he asks.

". . . Both," I realize.

"Only one of them is for you, Aurora."

"Just . . ." I look him up and down, then shake my head. Taking all he meant to me, bundling it tight, and with a conscious effort burning it away once more. "If you've come to take me to him, then do it, Kal."

He scowls at me. Shoulders set, jaw clenched tight. I can feel it then. Inside him. The shadow he talked about. His Enemy Within.

And I know, just up that corridor, he waits for me.

"Follow," Kal says.

We walk down the beautiful crystal pathways, him in front and me behind. The power swells around me now, pressing in on my skin, my skull.

The part of me that hurts, that wants, that wishes I could hold Kal's hand as I walk toward the light, is silent. The part of me that regrets, that wishes this could have turned out another way, is gone. There's only the power now, the thing they made me to be, this girl who's going to save the galaxy, as she follows the boy she thought she loved down the shimmering path and finally, finally, out into the heart of the ship.

It's beautiful. Perfect. One massive, spherical chamber, its walls almost lost in shadow, curving up and out from the base and then in again to meet at its apex. Raised up from that lowest point, on spires of crystal, is a throne—huge and jagged, shining with every color of the rainbow.

This is the center of the Weapon, the center of *everything,* and the whole room seems to strain toward it. Shards of crystal emerge from the chamber walls, all turned inward like grasping hands, as if to claim the one who sits atop that throne, or maybe to offer him homage.

I see Kal in his face—the familiar cheekbones, the lift of the chin, the arrogant arch of a brow. He's wearing high-collared black armor, and a blood-red cloak spills down the stairs that lead up to his throne. His silver braids cover one half of his face, and one side of his mouth is curled into the smallest of smiles.

Archon Caersan.

Starslayer.

Father of the boy I loved.

Trigger of the Eshvaren.

Traitor to the Eshvaren.

Kal backs up to stand against the curving wall as I search for words that will test his father, prod him just a little, to see what he does.

"That," I tell him, "is a *very* dramatic costume. Where do you buy a cloak like that? Or did you get it custom made?"

He doesn't reply. But he rises to his feet and slowly makes his way down the stairs toward me, cloak spreading out behind him. I have to admit, it *is* impressive. He doesn't speak at all until he stands before me, towers over me, just a few meters away. He takes his time, looking me up and down as if he's measuring me and finding me wanting.

"I thought," he says eventually, his voice beautiful, musical, utterly mesmerizing, "that you would be taller."

"Sorry to disappoint," I reply, making no effort at all to stand up straighter. I am what I am, and that's short, especially compared to a Syldrathi.

"I have been waiting for you," he continues. "I felt you awaken."

"And now I'm here. And I know what I have to do."

He lifts one silver brow. "Give yourself to the cause of the Eshvaren?"

"Defeat the Ra'haam," I correct him. "Save thousands of worlds."

"Protecting their playground," he muses. "And the dolls they made to live in it."

I blink at him. "What's that supposed to mean?"

"You do not know," he says, "what you are."

"I know I'm the girl who's going to do what you *failed* to."

"Failed?" he smiles. "All I failed to do was kneel as they wished me to."

"The Eshvaren made you what you are. They gave you this power to save the galaxy, and you used it to murder *billions*."

"Is that what you believe?" he asks, his smile thin. "That they wish to save the galaxy? That they actually care a drop for us?"

He huffs a soft, derisive breath.

"We are *things* to them, child. Mere tools. They *created* us."

"Of course they created us," I repeat, flat. "They created us to defend th—"

"Not *us*," he hisses. "Not you and me. *All* of us."

He gestures toward the outside, to the battle I can feel raging even now.

"Everything around you—every race, every individual, from the grayest elder to the youngest babe. We were all created by the Eshvaren in the hope that among those billions, they might find one to continue their fight against the Ra'haam. A vessel capable of wreaking revenge upon the race that bested them." His lips curve into an almost conspiratorial smile. "The Eshvaren are not the noble paragons they'd have you believe. Not selfless martyrs who gave their lives for us. They are demons. Demons who would be gods."

446

I sneer. "I'm supposed to believe that?"

He shakes his head a fraction, as though I'm a slightly dim student. "Have you never wondered why we all resemble one another? Think, child. Every race in the galaxy. We all stand on two feet. Breathe the same air. Speak languages the others can comprehend. The chance of hundreds of races evolving in such similar patterns across so vast a timeline and distance is *nonexistent.*" He folds his arms and scowls. "The Eshvaren *seeded* the galaxy in their own image. We are a virus in a petri dish to them. No better than insects."

The words reverberate in my mind, sending shudders through every part of me. I've heard Tyler and Fin talk about their United Faith. The religion that grew among the galactic races to explain these similarities.

I glance at Kal, pressed against the chamber wall.

"But . . . the Maker," I say.

The Starslayer shakes his head.

"Not a Maker, child," he says. *"Makers."*

The word shakes me, chilling my blood.

"The Eshvaren are our puppeteers," Caersan says, his violet eye flashing. "And we their puppets. Imagine the arrogance it took to seed life in their own image across hundreds of worlds. All for the sake of some petty revenge?" He gestures at the Weapon around us, the rainbows dancing on the crystal. "That is the jest of it, Aurora Jie-Lin O'Malley. That is all we are. There are no gods. There is no grand design. No purpose to *any* of it, beyond the last desperate stab of a fallen empire. A lottery of a million years and countless lives, for one last chance at vengeance."

The thought is almost too much for me to take in. But through the power that links us, binds us, I know Caersan isn't lying. All the religions of all the worlds, all the creation stories, all the beliefs of how and why this began . . .

And really, it was the Eshvaren who made us all?

It's a stone in my chest. A cold hand squeezing my insides. I wonder what Finian might think if he knew. What Tyler would say if I told him.

Makers . . .

But then I push the thought, the weight of it and them, aside. I force my attention back to Caersan as he looks me up and down and sneers.

"You are *nothing* to the Eshvaren. And still, you would die for them?"

"Of course I would," I say. "No matter what you say, the Ra'haam still wants to consume the entire galaxy and every living thing in it. Asking for just one more life to stop it seems like a small enough price to me."

I look him over, taking my time.

"It's a pity you were too cowardly to pay it."

Just for a millisecond, I see anger in his gaze.

Interesting.

"I was strong enough to forge my own destiny," he replies coolly. "To step off the path my would-be masters laid down for me."

I snort. "And your idea of strength was to destroy your own homeworld? To kill billions of your people?"

Out of the corner of my eye, I see Kal shift his weight.

His father simply shrugs. "You speak as though the effort cost me something. But all my ties were long since burned away. Just as they taught us."

Burn it all away.

It makes sense, I suppose. If Caersan cut away all his ties—family, love, honor, loyalty—but didn't replace them with devotion to destroying the Ra'haam, what would be left? Just an empty shell, with all the powers of the Trigger.

But somehow, I'm not sure that's right. There's something in his gaze—that flicker of temper that flashed to the surface like a silvery fish, then disappeared—that tells me that whatever he burned away has begun to slowly creep back in.

That maybe I'm stronger.

I lash out at him with a wave of pure power, quick as a whipcrack. He stumbles back a step, then straightens, radiating disdain.

"What was that, child?"

"Just a hello," I reply, as sweetly as I know how.

Caersan strikes back, but instantly, instinctively, I throw up my hands. My energy is midnight blue, shot through with silver wisps, like nebulas, like starlight. His is a dark, dusty red, like drying blood, threaded with antique gold. There's a depth to it, a richness and a power I'd find frightening if I were still me.

But I'm not. The Eshvaren saw to that, and now I know why.

He comes at me again, unleashing his power like a striking snake, and I meet him, holding the line. Midnight blue and deep russet entwine between us, each trying to choke the other. I lean into my power, impassive, knowing his passion will compromise him. Knowing my purpose will carry me.

I lash out at him again, hard as I can, a crack of psychic force like a slap to his face. Caersan's head whips to one side, a tiny cut opening up on that flawless cheek. The silver braids he keeps draped over one side of his face are thrown aside, showing me the eye that was hidden from the rest of the galaxy.

And of course, like mine, it glows pure white.

But around that glowing eye, I can see scars carved down Caersan's features, like cracks in an old riverbed. The right side of his face is withered, old, as if all the life has been sucked right out of it. The glow from his eye spills out through the cracks in his cheek as he glowers at me, dragging his braids back down over his face as if ashamed. He glances at the Weapon around us, the spears of crystal pointed toward the throne at its heart.

"So now you see. What it cost me to use it. And what it will cost you." His pointed teeth are bared as he snarls. "They bestowed this power upon us, intending for this *thing* to tear it out of us again. To dismantle us piece by piece. No beautiful death. No ultimate sacrifice. They intended us to die in fragments. Twenty-two planets for us to destroy, twenty-two slivers of our souls to be ripped out of us one by one and fed to their vengeance machine."

Even the thought is enough to make me recoil. I can feel the memory inside him, reverberating along the bond between us. I can sense just a hint of the pain he felt as he fired the Weapon, and even that is nearly overwhelming. But given what he used it to do, I know he deserved it, too.

He throws up his hands, his power rolling in the space between us. The Weapon trembles as I force him back, his boots skidding across the crystal. As the power rages around us again, cascading over us in waves of blue and red, the beautiful, powerful man before me takes an unwilling step back. I push outward, crashing into him with everything I have, and he staggers with a grunt of effort. His elegance is crumbling, his poise is fading, and he leans forward like a man battling the wind, those silver braids whipping out behind him. Midnight blue swirls around me in a growing storm, thundering as I harden my voice.

"You've corrupted the gift we've been given, Caersan. You've chosen years of power for yourself, trapped in a dying galaxy, over *millennia* of life for hundreds of species."

My power crashes into him as I summon everything I have. The force of me, the power inside me, pure and unhindered, hits him like a tidal wave. He flails, torn off his feet, and sails back into the wall, smashing into the crystal with a thunderous crack. I strike him again, again, again, as a tiny line of purple blood spills from his nose and down over his lip. My midnight blue begins to consume the old blood it battles, surrounding it, silver twisting over gold. And finally, he collapses to the deck.

"One life isn't too much to pay," I tell him.

I take another step toward him, bathed in glittering midnight.

"Nor are two, Starslayer."

He looks up at me then, braids draped around his face, and I see the pride and hatred crackling in his gaze. I feel his power swell, and I force myself to focus, to keep my hold on him firm. Kal steps forward in the storm, shouting over the roar.

"Aurora!"

But I ignore him, my eyes fixed on his father.

"I can feel it," I tell him. "What you lost when you fired it."

Caersan closes his fists, the air crackling. "What they took from me."

"And once it's gone, it's gone for good."

"Yes."

I smile at that. "Which means you're less than you were, Starslayer."

I reach deep inside myself, ready to finish it.

"Less than me."

"Perhaps," he whispers. "But you are failing to account for one thing."

There's a sudden flicker in his presence that I don't like, that makes me wary.

"And what's that?"

"That I am not alone."

His power flares, like a sun rising over the horizon, and the crystal in the walls around us responds, lighting up from within.

That's when I see them, no longer hidden in the shadows, but lit from behind by blood-red light. Row upon row of Syldrathi, hundreds of them, are pinned against the walls of the chamber above me by some invisible force. Their eyes stare at nothing, their hands stretched out to either side.

"Mothercustard," I breathe.

The glyfs at their brows tell me they're Waywalkers. All of them. And a shudder goes through me as I suddenly realize why the Unbroken have been hunting them across the galaxy.

Every Waywalker cries out, fingers flexing, face contorted. The sudden flow of their power into Caersan is like being caught by a wave, tumbled end over end until there's nothing to do but hold your breath, lungs bursting, fighting to last a second longer, praying to whoever's listening for air.

His eyes—so like his son's—lock onto mine as he speaks again.

"I am a warrior born. I carved my name in blood among the stars while you slumbered in your crib. I am Warbreed. I am Unbroken. I am an eater of worlds and slayer of suns. I am not less than I was before, child. I am *more*."

He stands slowly, arms outstretched. The power around him doubles, triples, a psychic tempest of blood-red and glittering gold. The chamber around us, the whole Weapon, trembles, the screams of those Waywalkers filling my mind.

And I realize with creeping horror that he's been holding himself back.

"You have given me your best, little Terran," he says.

Slowly, the Starslayer curls his hands into fists.

"Now I will give you mine."

36

TYLER

It's called a gremlin.

In the Terran war-propaganda posters I studied for conflict history in fourth year, gremlins were depicted as tiny, malicious humanoids with pointed ears and claws. But they were basically a way for pilots to keep up morale. Equipment failures got blamed on gremlins, so pilots got to avoid pointing the finger at the flight crews they depended on to keep them alive, and the war got won.

Nowadays, *gremlin* is a nickname for any number of portable counter-electronic devices—signal killers, network jammers, or, in the case of the miracle I've just discovered in my boot heel, electromagnetic-pulse generators.

How could they know?

I glance up at Saedii, who appears to be ignoring me for the benefit of the camera above our cell door. But she's caught a glimpse of the gremlin in my heel, and sharp as she is, she knows exactly what it can do for our predicament.

The ones who left that for you, she continues. *How could they know?*

I have no clue, I admit.

How did the Terran marines not discover it? Surely they scanned you?

The heel looks shielded. Whoever put this here knew I'd need to hide it.

How? Saedii demands. *How is this possible?*

Doesn't matter. We need to get out of here. I don't know where we're headed, but there's literally no place the Ra'haam can have chosen that will be good news for us. And the Unbroken and TDF are probably tearing each other to pieces by now.

She glances my way for a brief moment.

Then we are at war once more, little Terran.

You can gouge out my eyes later, okay? From the look of this gremlin, it's got a decent range. But TDF dreadnoughts are huge. When the pulse goes off, we need to move fast. Get to the launch bays and get ourselves off this ship. So be ready.

Saedi sneers.

She's probably always ready for combat, and my warning is a little insulting. Despite the punishment she's suffered, Saedii radiates a steel-cold will, her eyes narrowed and focused. Curling over to hide my boots from the camera, I slip my hand to the gremlin, praying to the Maker that despite all the punishment I've put these boots through over the last few days, it somehow still works.

My finger finds the activation stud. I meet Saedii's eyes.

Go.

I press the button. I feel a slight vibration in my boot, a hum on the edge of hearing. And then every light in the cell dies.

The camera dies.

The magnetic lock dies.

Saedii is on her feet in a heartbeat. The emergency lighting has been knocked out—every electronic device around us that isn't shielded is basically a paperweight now. Without the lights, it's almost pitch-dark in here, but I catch a vague impression of her as she snatches up the wreckage of the biocot I smashed and jams it into the doorframe. I lunge to my feet, grab the twisted strut of metal, and give her a hand. We lean into it, Saedii silent, me grunting softly with the strain. But between the two of us, we pry the cell door open in a few seconds.

The corridor outside is almost pitch-dark too, every terminal fried. But like I said, I've studied Terran ships since I was a kid, and despite the black around us, I know exactly where we need to go.

I reach out in the dark, grab Saedii's hand.

She immediately snatches it free.

"I did *not* give you permission to touch me, Tyler Jones," she snarls. "Do it again at your peril."

I glare at her in the gloom, but I can't see her face.

"Well, how about this," I snap back at her. "I give *you* permission to touch *me*. I know the layout of this ship like I know my own name. So you can stumble about in the dark by yourself, or we can buckle up and run."

I hold out my hand in the black.

"Lady's choice."

The silence stretches between us, broken only by the thrum of the Folding engines. Rising alarms. Running boots. I see laser sights cutting the dark at the end of our corridor. I can see Saedii's silhouette now, black curves against the distant light.

She breathes deep.

She presses her hand into mine.

And, hand in hand, we run off into the dark.

. . . . .

Eight minutes later, Saedii and I are in a supply closet, trying to ignore each other as we strip down to our unmentionables.

The space is small and the lighting is dim, supplied by a flashlight slung under the barrel of a disruptor rifle. The male owner of the rifle, along with a tall female comrade, is in the supply closet across the hall, minus the uniforms we stole. We accosted the two marines in the middle of their security sweep, overpowering them before they could get a shot off. The element of surprise helped. Having a master of the Aen Suun fighting alongside me didn't hurt much either. Both marines got beaten to within inches of their lives—if I hadn't been there to stop her, Saedii would have beaten them all the way.

"Keep your eyes to yourself, Terran," she warns me softly. "Or I will pluck them out."

"We're in a life-or-death situation here. I think I can keep my mind on the job." I fix my eyes on my boots as I drag them off. "Besides, I've seen bras before, and trust me, yours isn't *that* spectacular."

She pauses midway through inspecting the female marine's tac vest. "I wear the garments of an Unbroken Templar, boy. They are not *meant* to be spectacular."

"Well, good," I say, unbuttoning my cargoes. "They're succeeding admirably."

Her glower is almost enough to burn a hole in my chest. I do my best to ignore it and her. And I'm down to my boxers, and she's wearing *very* little in the way of those Unbroken Templar garments, when the first blast strikes the ship.

Hard.

Saedii grabs hold of a supply rack to steady herself, but I'm too slow. Slung across the closet like a kid's toy, I crash right into her. She spits a word I know has a four-letter translation in Terran, and we both go down in a heap. I find myself on my back, Saedii lying on top of me, her long black hair tumbled around us, our faces just a few centimeters apart.

"What was—"

"Silence!" she hisses, her head cocked.

We lie there for a few moments, and Maker's breath, I'm really, *really* trying to ignore it, but there's two meters of Syldrathi warrior princess lying on top of me in nothing but her underwear. And while the Aurora Legion probably doesn't make a medal for it, I still genuinely think I deserve one for what I say next.

"Get off me."

"Be *quiet*, Tyler Jones!"

I lie there in the dark with Saedii stretched out on top of me, staring at the ceiling, hands pressed firmly at my sides.

Think unsexy thoughts.

Think unsexy thoughts.

"I heard that," she whispers, glancing at me.

"Look, I know I gave you permission to touch me, but this is pushing the—"

Another impact strikes the ship. Thunderous. Running through the metal beneath us. Saedii's eyes find mine, lit with triumph.

"There," she smiles.

I frown up at her, mind racing. "That sounded like a—"

"Syldrathi pulse cannon." She presses her tongue to one sharpened canine. "They are here."

"ALERT," cries the shipboard PA, as if on cue. The distant wail of a siren pierces the dark. "ALERT. ALL HANDS, BATTLE STATIONS."

I blink. "Who's 'they'?"

"My lieutenant Erien, I imagine," Saedii replies. "My Paladins. Whatever remained of my adepts. It would be death for them to return to my father without me. I expect they have been tracking us through the Fold since the battle on *Andarael*."

"REPEAT: ALL HANDS TO BATTLE STATIONS," the PA shouts. "SYLDRATHI VESSEL INBOUND. THIS IS NOT A DRILL. THIS IS NOT A DRILL."

I frown at the girl atop me. ". . . You knew they'd come?"

"I suspected."

"And you didn't tell me?"

"I did not trust you, Tyler Jones," she scowls. "I *still* do not trust you. You are Terran. The son of Jericho Jones, our great enemy. Our peoples are at war."

"Our peoples?" I reply. "You just told me I'm half-Syldrathi, Saedii. My people are *your* people."

She pauses at that. Violet eyes searching mine.

"Perhaps," she says.

Goose bumps rise on my skin as Saedii presses her fingertips to my chest, light as feathers. Another blast rocks the ship, more alerts begin screaming, and I wince as her fingernail scratches my skin.

"What blood truly burns in these veins of yours, I wonder?"

"If we don't get off this ship soon," I tell her, "you'll be able to examine my blood up close and personal. Because it's going to be splattered all over the floor."

Her smile comes slowly.

"Mmm."

Another blast rocks the ship as Saedii slides off me, twists into a crouch, and grabs for the stolen tac suit pieces, now jumbled together. I take a deep breath, then pull myself up and separate out the gear I need as the sirens continue to wail. I peek at her once while we get dressed, only to discover that Saedii is already watching me. Both of us immediately look away.

In a few minutes we're geared up, fully armed, and encased in TDF tac armor, faces hidden behind our helmets.

"From the sound of those weapon impacts," Saedii says, her head tilted, "the ship attacking us has four to six pulse cannon batteries."

"Yeah," I nod. "It's Eidolon-class at least. A capital ship."

"In a battle this size, the chaos will be our friend. If we can get to the escape pods, I can set the communications unit to transmit on Unbroken emergency frequencies. With fortune, my crew should be able to retrieve us."

"Unless the TDF blasts our pods to pieces," I say.

Saedii shrugs. "Warrior or worm, Tyler Jones?"

I heft the fallen marine's disruptor rifle, set it to Stun.

"Let's get moving."

37

SCARLETT

The battle raging across our holo displays is the most *insane* thing I've ever been part of in my life. And I say that having once schmoozed my way through six layers of security goons to crash the launch party of multiplatinum interstellar rock band the Envied Dead, an escapade involving twelve cases of Larassian semptar, skinny-dipping on a volcanic planet, sixty-one arrests, and a brief romantic train wreck. (N1kk1 Gunzz. Ex-boyfriend #34. Pros: Rock star. Cons: Drummer.)

The dark all around us is just *swarming* with ships: Syldrathi, Terran, Betraskan. Pulse cannon blasts and railgun fire, missiles snaking through the dark, explosions bursting silently across that big empty. Tens of thousands of people fighting and killing and dying. And I've never been so scared in all my life.

"Look out!" Finian roars.

"Please lower your voice," Zila says, twisting her flight controls. "Increased volume does not equate to increased piloting aptitude."

"Well, pardon me all to—"

"Finian, shut *up*!" I shout.

Zila is hunched over her pilot's console, her fingers moving in a blur. Fin and I are behind her, sitting side by side at the auxiliary stations, with holo displays of the ongoing battle floating above our consoles. Our ship is flying close to the Weapon, far back from the bloody, shooty outer periphery of the battle, but to be honest, it's a miracle we're still flying at all. The air is swarming with fighters, and Zila's flying on the defensive, not shooting back at anyone who opens up on us, hoping the thousands of ships out there will be more interested in killing something that looks remotely dangerous. But our luck is gonna run out sooner or later.

The Weapon sort of . . . flickers. It's done that once or twice now, and none of us are sure why. It's like a flashlight in the dark, like a crystal heart beating amid the carnage. And the carnage is getting worse.

"You think Auri is okay in there?" Finian whispers, gazing at it.

"I hope so," I sigh.

"Please fasten your safety harnesses," Zila says.

"Are you joking?" Fin scoffs, glancing at her sidelong. "Zila, if my harness were on any tighter, I'd be married to—"

Fin shrieks as Zila slams on our thrusters, pinwheeling away from a spray of railgun fire. A missile explodes soundlessly off our wing, another right in front of us, the inertial dampeners that provide the gravity around our little ship struggling to compensate as Zila throws us into a spiraling dive. Glancing at our scopes, I realize we've picked up pursuers—TDF fighters, snub-nosed and angry-looking. I can't blame them for shooting at us—we're wearing Unbroken colors, after all. But still . . .

"Four bad guys coming in fast on our bow," I report.

"Stern!" Fin winces as another missile explodes. "That's the stern, Scar!"

"Dammit, I told you I don't know anything about spaceships!" I shout. "They're on our ass, okay? Four very shooty ships on our very shapely asses, Zila!"

"I see them," Zila replies. "Hold on."

"Shapely asses?" Fin mutters.

"Don't tell me you haven't noticed, de Seel."

We weave and roll through the chaos, the black outside us lit up like fireworks on Federation Day. And Zila is putting on an impressive show, no doubt, but she's not an expert pilot by any stretch, and even with auto-guidance assisting her, I wonder how long all this can go on. Outside our forward blastscreens, the black is red with fire and blood. Earth is throwing everything it can at the Syldrathi fleet, but these Syldrathi are *Unbroken*. Trained every moment of their lives for battle. Fanatically loyal to the psychopath leading them—so much so that they were willing to sit back and applaud as he destroyed their damn sun.

And my heart is slowly sinking in my chest, because the thing of it is, we're part of a moving battle here. Charging right toward the heart of the Terran solar system. We're already past the Kuiper Belt, closing fast on Neptune. And I don't know what the range on the Weapon is, but every minute that goes by, the Unbroken fleet draws closer to my homeworld and the sun it orbits.

The sun they're going to destroy.

The Weapon flickers again, lit from within, as if there's a heart made of pure light pulsing inside it. The glow comes from the rear of the ship, but the whole Weapon responds, lighting up like a length of crystalline optical cable.

"Why is it *doing* that?" Fin whispers.

"I don't know," I reply.

"It's kinda scary—"

I gasp as I'm slammed back in my chair, Zila performing a barrel roll that sends us spiraling up and between two Syldrathi cruisers. The TDF fighters on our tail have picked up pursuers of their own, and two of them break off to engage. But two are still back there, chasing us like we stole their lunch money.

The Weapon pulses again. If I squint at it, the light seems to be gathering at one end. Those strange, abstract shapes at the bow (Ha! See, I *can* be taught!) look like they're glowing brighter with every pulse.

"We need an alternative strategy," Zila declares, twisting us through the firestorm.

"You mean a Plan B?" I ask her.

She glances over her shoulder and nods. "And we need it now."

"What makes you so sure?" I ask.

"I am not. But the Eshvaren Weapon is clearly accumulating power."

"Zila, we have eyes," Fin says. "But that doesn't—"

"Perhaps your eyes noticed the positions of the Unbroken vessels?" she asks. "The way their formation is shifting?"

A near-miss missile blast rocks us, and I nearly swallow my tongue. But squinting at the holo displays, the readouts from our tactical computer, I realize . . .

"The Unbroken fleet is moving out of its way."

"They have been vacating the Weapon's forward firing arc for the past three minutes," Zila reports. "They clearly know it is preparing to fire."

"Shit," I breathe.

I look at our scopes, the holo displays of our little solar system. The gas giants of Neptune and Uranus. Saturn with its beautiful rings of ice, Jupiter with its great red storm, which has been raging for the past seven hundred years. Beyond the asteroid belt is Earth's first planetary colony—the red orb of Mars. Then on to our pale blue dot, Earth, the planet where I grew up, my home, my world. Past that, scorching Venus, where it's so hot the skies rain molten lead. Last of all, Mercury. And at the center of it, of all of this, these billions of lives, this history, this civilization, a small yellow sun. The star at the heart of my solar system.

The star Caersan is going to slay.

"What can we do?" I ask. "How can we stop it?"

"This vessel lacks sufficient firepower to damage the Weapon," Zila says. "But we are flying Unbroken colors. We *can* get close to it."

Fin blinks. "How close?"

Zila glances at him, twists her controls. "*Very* close."

The Weapon pulses again. The light gathering, twisting inside it. It'd be beautiful if it weren't so awful. An ending, all the colors of the rainbow.

"You mean ram it," I breathe.

"This ship weighs over two hundred tons," she says. "It is capable of achieving six-factor velocity with sufficient acceleration time. If we collide with the Weapon at top speed, we will impact with force equivalent to several high-yield thermonuclear devices."

"But we *can't* destroy the Weapon," I frown. "We need it to beat the Ra'haam."

"We cannot hope to destroy it," Zila says. "It is too large. But an impact of that magnitude should hopefully be enough to damage or at least misalign those lenses. Perhaps buy Aurora more time."

Finian looks at me. Back at Zila.

465

"That's some Plan B, Legionnaire Madran."

"If you have a better one, I am willing to entertain it, Legionnaire de Seel."

And then it hits me.

There in that firestorm, with TDF fighters and Syldrathi cruisers and Betraskan dreadnoughts blowing each other to pieces around us, with the fate of my world, my entire civilization, and maybe the whole galaxy besides hanging in the balance . . . I remember.

I remember!

I fumble inside my uniform, Finian watching as I fish around my cleavage.

"Um . . . ," he says.

"Dammit, you could lose the Great Ultrasaur of Abraaxis IV in here," I growl.

". . . Scar?" Fin asks.

"Aha!" I cry, my fingers closing around a length of silver chain. I drag my prize out from my tunic, hold it between thumb and forefinger in triumph.

A silver medallion. A medallion that waited eight years for us in that Dominion Repository vault. A vault that was coded by the commanders of Aurora Academy to open with my DNA, years before I ever joined the Legion or they had a chance to meet me.

On one side, it's inset with a rough chunk of diamond. On the other, engraved in a curling script . . .

"Zila?" I say.

"Yes, Scarlett?"

"Go with Plan B."

38

KAL

"You have given me your best, little Terran. Now I will give you mine."

The chamber shakes.

The Waywalkers above me scream.

My father raises his hand.

A sledgehammer of psychic force slams into Aurora, sending her skidding back across the Weapon's heart. Shards of crystal fall like rain, glittering in her wake. Her face is twisted, mouth open in a silent cry, skeins of midnight blue and burning red crackling in the air around her.

The wall I am pressed against reverberates, the power of their exchange coalescing in the crystal around us. Every time Aurora and my father strike at each other, the Weapon pulses brighter, the air grows thicker. It feels like a coiled spring, like clockwork wound too tight, strained to breaking. I can tell it is almost ready to fire, overflowing with the barrages of energy they throw at each other.

Spirits of the Void help *anything* in its path when it is unleashed.

Aurora strikes out again, a ribbon of force cutting the air, knife-sharp and silver-quick. My father raises his hand, almost lazily, as he would when I was a child striking at him beneath the trees on Syldra. He never failed to press the advantage back then, despite his size, his strength. Punishing every flaw, every misstep, every error, sending me to bed bruised and beaten.

He does the same with Aurora now, and I watch, helpless, as he pierces her defenses and sends her flying. She collides with the wall again, the crystal cracking beneath the force of the blow.

Aurora falls to her knees. But she stands again a moment later, power flowing off her in waves as she drags her knuckles across her bleeding nose.

"Nice shot," she murmurs.

I did not wish it to be this way.

Aurora surges across the room, seeming almost to flicker inside the rising storm. Her eye burns like a sun, matched in intensity only by his own. I can see how hard she struggles, pure and formless. But though my father is less than she is alone, he is *not* alone. He draws on the power of these poor souls imprisoned around us.

He strikes again, again, a crimson blur, moving so swift he leaves an afterimage in the air behind him. Aurora sails upward, shattering the ceiling. She falls among a rain of glittering crystal, and with a flicker of crimson power, he is there beneath her, lashing out again. She is flung across the room, limp and boneless, tumbling across the crystalline floor, rainbow colors crashing like waves on a sunset shore. The Waywalkers scream once more. And though Aurora rises again, fists clenched, she moves a touch slower than she did a moment ago.

They collide like powder and flame. He towers over her, drawing the power of the multitude around us into himself. Her face is a mask of pain and blood, her eye gleaming in the dark. She seems small then. And looking at her, she who was my all and my everything and is now perhaps my nothing, I know the truth.

I told her before she came here, after all.

I cannot fault her for hating me. I never should have lied to her, or to the rest of them. But I warned her not to come here. I wished to deal with this by myself. My shame. My blood. In my veins and on my hands. I thought perhaps to topple the giant. Slay the monster I remembered from my childhood, the man who laid those bruises on me and my sister and my mother alike.

But as soon as I saw my father, I knew he had become so much more, and so much less, than he ever was before. I thought to wait. Perhaps as he prepared to use the Weapon, he would be distracted enough for me to strike at him. Or perhaps after he had fired it, he might become weakened enough for me to cut him down once and for all. I had no real plan, save to spare Aurora this struggle.

My deception and my devotion. Only one of them for her. But now . . .

Now.

I look around me at the Waywalkers, pinned in place against the curving crystal walls like insects upon a board. Their eyes are open, but they do not see. Syldrathi men and women, even children, the Waywalker glyf—an eye, crying five tears—marked upon their brows.

The same glyf my mother wore on her brow.

There is no love in violence, Kaliis, she would tell me.

I reach down to the floor beneath me. My fingers search the shattered crystal broken loose from the wall. I take hold of a shard—long and pointed, like a dagger. And I look at these poor wretches my father draws his power from. The crystal slicing into my palm as I clench it tight.

It would not take much to end them. Cut them loose from this life, and from him. Weakening him. Perhaps enough to topple him?

Mercy is the province of cowards, Kaliis.

But no. That is a choice *he* would make, not me. And if I am to step out from this shadow at last, I cannot do it by walking into darkness. I am not my past. I am not he who made me. I must stand in the light of the sun.

No matter what it will cost me.

I steal across the trembling floor, the crystal dagger in my hand, struggling through the storm of power building around them. My father and my be'shmai are locked together, the Weapon around us trembling now with tectonic violence. Blood drips from Aurora's nose, her ears, her eyes. Her arms shake. Her knees buckle.

She cannot win this alone.

But the truth is?

She was never alone.

I loom up behind my father. Like a shadow. Like the past come back to haunt him. Like the voices of ten billion souls gone to the Void, my mother among them. And I wrap my arm around his throat and plunge the crystal blade toward the sweet spot between his fifth and sixth ribs.

The crystal pierces my father's armor, and for a brief and beautiful moment, I feel the flesh parting beneath, the blade sinking toward the heart I can only assume he still owns.

But then it stops.

I feel his grip on my wrist, though he does not touch me. I feel his hand at my throat, though his own hands are still locked with Aurora's. I struggle, powerless, gasping as his hold on me tightens. He glances over his shoulder at me, his eye burning like cold flame.

"Tsk, tsk," he says.

With a toss of his head, he slams my be'shmai backward, sending her skidding across the floor, bleeding and gasping.

And then he turns to me.

I am held in place. Suspended three feet above the floor, utterly still.

He looks at me, the storm raging all around us. He is so changed now. Severed from the ties that once bound him. But I look deep into his eyes, and I think I see something left of what he was. Something of the man I feared and loved and hated.

"So," he says, disappointed. "You are still your mother's son."

And though I cannot move to strike him, though I can barely muster the strength to breathe, still I draw enough to speak.

"I am n-not yours."

His eyes narrow. The storm wind rises around us, the Waywalkers begin to scream, and I look to the girl who was my all and my everything, watching as she raises her head and looks at me.

"K-Kal . . ."

"Be'shmai," I whisper.

And then I feel my father reach into my mind.

And he tears me apar—

39

TYLER

Auxiliary power has been restored to this section of the ship, and Saedii and I are charging toward the escape pods in the dim glow of the emergency lights. I presume the TDF marine squads are still looking for us back on the detention level, but the Unbroken attack seems to be occupying most of the crew's attention. The decks are a hive of activity: marines, techs, repair crews, pilots all flooding to their battle stations, the ship shaking around us as the conflict rages through the Fold.

The reports we're getting over the headsets in our stolen helmets aren't so good. Turns out Saedii and I were both wrong—it's not an Eidolon hitting us, but four Banshee-class Syldrathi cruisers. The ship we're on, the *Kusanagi,* is a heavy carrier, but Banshees have cloaking tech that makes them almost invisible to conventional radar—probably how they snuck up on us in the first place. That means the *Kusanagi's* gunners have to target visually, which is hard to do when your opponent is moving a couple of thousand klicks a second. All this is to say that even though the Syldrathi ships are smaller, it's still gonna be a brawl.

I honestly have no idea who will come out on top.

Another blast rocks the *Kusanagi*, sending Saedii stumbling into me, and me stumbling into the wall. Half a dozen Terran techs dash past us, and the alarms continue to blare as I haul myself back to my feet.

"Just for future reference," I ask, steadying myself, "if you're falling and I catch you, are you going to knee me in the groin again?"

"Be silent, Tyler Jones," Saedii sighs, staggering forward.

Maybe I should just let you fall right on your arrogant ass, I think to myself.

I heard that, comes her voice inside my head.

"FIRST ENEMY VESSEL DESTROYED," the PA reports. "CRITICAL DAMAGE TO SECOND ENEMY VESSEL. *KUSANAGI* HULL BREACH ON LEVEL 4, PORT BATTERIES DISABLED. TECH CREWS REPORT TO LEVEL 6, CORRIDORS 6 BETA AND EPSILON, IMMEDIATELY."

"The escape pods should be just ahead," I report.

"I see them," Saedii replies, charging on through the gloom.

A TDF carrier has escape pods on every level—one-person units, independently powered in the event of catastrophic reactor damage. I can make out a bunch at the T-junction ahead—a few dozen hatchways set into the wall. Their operating mechanisms are basically big red buttons behind panes of glass marked BREAK IN CASE OF EMERGENCY—they're made to be easy to operate, even in a disaster scenario. If our luck holds, we can b—

The disruptor blast hits Saedii right in her head. The tac helmet she's wearing absorbs the brunt of the blow, but the shot still sends her spinning like a top.

"Contact! Contact!" a marine cries behind us. *"Section A, Level 3!"*

I dive away from the escape pods, dragging Saedii with me into an adjacent corridor as more rifles open up on us. Their shots go wide as *Kusanagi* takes another hit. I can see half a dozen TDF marines behind cover at the end of our corridor. I'm not sure how they zeroed us—maybe the ident numbers on our breastplates—but however they did it, their disruptors are set to Kill. I press back against the corner of the T-junction, cracking off a few haphazard shots. The escape pods are right there, maybe five meters away. But they might as well be five kilometers now.

Are you okay? I yell into Saedii's head.

Lower your voice, Tyler Jones, she says, slinging off her smoking helmet.

Tossing her hair from her eyes, Saedii lifts her rifle and starts shooting around the corner. And suddenly we're in a firefight for our lives. The dim light is punctured by muzzle flashes, screaming alarms are drowned out by disruptor fire. Saedii cries warning in my mind as another group of marines opens up from the opposite end of the corridor. If they maneuver around behind us, we're dead.

The air is filled with the sizzling bursts of disruptor shots, my rifle bucking in my hand. I'm not shooting with much finesse, just trying to get the TDF marines to keep their heads down. But one glance over my shoulder tells me Saedii has already taken out three of them—two with face shots and another with a blast into the fire extinguisher on the wall beside him, which exploded and knocked him senseless. And all this *after* she took a Kill shot to the skull.

Maker's breath, this girl is good. . . .

I heard that.

DAMMIT, STOP IT.

Saedii smirks over her shoulder at me as I crack off a lucky shot, taking out a marine sergeant with a Stun blast right into his visor. He collapses, out cold.

Fine shooting, Tyler Jones.

All the fine shooting in the 'Way isn't gonna help us here—we're outnumbered ten to one!

Another blast rocks the *Kusanagi*, another burst of fire forces me back behind cover. If we stay here much longer, we're finished. I tear off my helmet so I can breathe a little better, pawing the sweat from my eyes as I glance at the escape pods across the corridor from us. They're made to open quick in the event of an emergency; it wouldn't take much time to get inside one. But running across the corridor to reach them, risking the crossfire between us and them . . .

Give me your rifle, I tell Saedii, holding out my hand.

. . . Why?

You go first. I'll cover you.

She scowls. *I do not need your assistance, boy.*

Maker's breath, does everything have to be a fight with you?

Yes, she says, blasting another marine. *I was born for war, Tyler Jones.*

Well, you can't fight a war if you're dead! So get yourself into the escape pod and alert your crew of psychopaths to pick us up instead of blow us up.

And leave you here?

I'll follow you.

475

I duck low as a disruptor blast sizzles over my head, flashes against the wall beside me. I fire off a shot, manage to stun an advancing marine running for cover. Glancing over my shoulder, I find Saedii staring at me.

What? I demand.

Saedii says nothing. Reaching to her tac armor's belt, she grabs the spare power pack for her disruptor, and slings it across the corridor into an escape pod's control panel. Her aim is perfect (why am I not surprised?), the glass does indeed break in the case of this particular emergency, and the panel switches from red to green as the hatchway cycles open. I keep blasting away, but I feel Saedii's hands at my belt, grabbing my rifle's spare power cell. She repeats the procedure—another dead shot, more broken glass, another pod door open, this one for me. The marines are closing in now, and we only have seconds.

Saedii hands me her rifle. Looks me in the eye.

You have courage, Tyler Jones. Your blood is true.

She grabs my breastplate and, leaning in, kisses my cheek.

Spirits of the Void watch over you, she says.

I swallow hard, meeting her stare.

. . . You too, I manage.

If you let me get shot, I will rip your heart from your chest and feed it to you.

I almost laugh. *Go. I've got your back.*

I lean out into the corridor, let loose with a flurry of blasts, one rifle in each hand. The burst is haphazard—there's no way I'm gonna hit anything. But the clumsy spray of fire does force the marines back behind cover long enough for Saedii to make a break. She dashes across the corridor and dives like a spear, black hair streaming out behind her as disruptor blasts cut the air around her, right through the escape pod's open door to safety.

It slams shut behind her. The diode switches from green to blue. And as another blast rocks the *Kusanagi*, Saedii's pod blasts free.

I can taste smoke now, the damage reports spilling thick and fast from the PA as *Kusanagi* takes another hit. I thank the Maker more marines haven't already been scrambled, but I'm guessing they're too busy not getting blown to pieces by those Syldrathi Banshees out there. For a second, I find myself praying Saedii makes it out okay. That her people can pick her up before the TDF blasts her out of space. But then I realize I should really be praying for myself.

My rifle suddenly runs empty. I glance at the power level on the weapon Saedii gave me—it's down to 13 percent. And, looking across the corridor, alive with disruptor fire, I can see my only two spare power cells lying on the floor among shards of broken glass.

Hmm. Maybe she's not a perfect tactician after all.

I stick my head out, rewarded by a spray of disruptor fire from both directions. The marines are advancing quick—it's only a matter of time before they cut around behind me and hit me from all sides.

I'm not sure how I'm gonna pull this off. . . .

"CEASE FIRE," comes a cold, metallic command.

"*Cease fire!*" a marine LT repeats, shouting. "*Corps, cease fire!*"

I press back against the wall. Heart battering against

my ribs. It's one of the GIA operatives out there. Princeps, maybe, come to drag me back to my cell. Or maybe just to finish me once and for—

"Tyler?"

My heart seizes up.

Even under the metal, the mirrormask, I know that voice. I've known it since we were five years old, that first day of kindergarten, when I pushed her over and she smashed a chair over my head.

The voice of my best friend. The girl who always looked out for me. The girl I was supposed to look out for in turn. The girl I loved, and the girl I failed.

I peek out into the corridor, and she's standing right there. Clad head to toe in GIA charcoal gray. That featureless mirrormask over her face.

But still, I know her.

"Tyler, don't go," Cat says.

"Ma'am," growls the marine behind her. "This prisoner escaped his cell and—"

"You're dismissed, Lieutenant," Cat says, not looking at him.

The LT looks unsure. "Ma'am, we have orders to—"

"I am countermanding those orders," Cat snaps. "There are three Syldrathi stealth cruisers outside trying to blow us into component molecules. I am sure there are better ways for you and your men to be spending your time right now, Lieutenant."

"But the prisoner, ma'am . . ."

Cat's still staring at me, head titled.

"He isn't going anywhere. Are you, Tyler?"

My eyes are locked on that mirrormask. My mouth dry as ashes.

"Order your men back, Lieutenant," Cat commands. "I'm sure I don't need to remind you that this operation is under Global Intelligence Agency command."

I can see the conflict in the LT's eyes. The orders don't seem right, and he and his squad know it. But I've said it once and I'll say it again—the Terran military doesn't teach you to think in combat. It teaches you that you follow orders or people die. And right now, given the attack going on out there in the Fold, these marines probably *do* have some better way to spend their time than wrangling me.

"Yes, ma'am," the LT nods, and pulls his crew back.

I listen to the marines retreating. Glancing down at my rifle's power.

Eight percent.

The thing wearing Cat's body waits until we're alone in the smoke-filled, trembling corridor. And then I hear a small, wet hiss. The ship shudders around me.

"Tyler?" it calls with her voice again.

I say nothing. Biting my lip.

"Ty?" it calls again.

"What do you want?" I finally shout.

"I want you to stay."

I risk a glance out, see it standing in the corridor alone. It's still clad neck to toe in GIA charcoal gray. But it's taken off the mirrormask now, and its face, its nose, its lips—they're all *hers*. All except the eyes, glowing soft and poisonous.

"Stay with us, Tyler," the thing wearing Cat's body replies. "Please."

"You're *not* Cat!" I shout. "Don't pretend to be!"

"But I am," it calls. "Don't you understand? I'm more than I used to be, but I'm still in here! I'm still me!"

"You're *nothing like her*! You're orchestrating a war that billions of people could die in, and for what? Just so you can infect the rest of the galaxy?"

"I'm trying to *save* you, Tyler," it pleads. "Don't you get it?"

I hear a crack in its voice. It sounds like it's close to crying. And I risk another glance from behind cover and see it standing there, hands balled by its side, and my stomach twists up like a clenched fist as I see . . . it *is* crying. Tears shining in the glow of those flower-shaped pupils. The *Kusanagi* shakes beneath me, but it's not the motion of the ship that almost brings me to my knees. It's what this thing says next that guts me.

"I love you, Tyler."

I close my eyes. I feel each of those words like bullets in my chest. A part of me knew how she felt about me. A part of me *always* knew it. But Cat never said those words aloud. Not even after the night we spent together. And to hear them now . . .

"I love you," it says. "So the Ra'haam loves you, too."

Cold dread washes over me. My worst fears confirmed.

"I knew it," I breathe. "That's where you're taking us. That's why we're still Folding. You . . . you want to . . ."

"We want you in here with us," it says, tears spilling down its cheeks as it takes one step forward. "We want you to *stay*."

I look out into the corridor again. And I can see her there. The girl who always backed me when I needed her. The girl who sat beside me in that tattoo parlor on shore leave and laughed as she poured me another shot in the bar afterward, who sighed my name as she dragged my shirt up over my head and sank with me down onto the bed. I can see her.

I can see her.

"Cat?" I whisper.

"Yes," she breathes.

"You can . . . hear me?"

"Yes," she whispers. "It's me, Ty. It's *me*."

I thought she was gone. I thought I'd never have another chance to speak to her. To tell her everything I should have told her when she was alive. I know nobody gets a second chance like this. I know I should tell her how I felt about her, how I'd do things differently if I could, how I always loved her and always will. I know she'd want to hear it. I know she'd want to *know*. And my stomach is a knot and my pulse is hammering and I can't deny what my heart is telling me. She *is* in there. Looking out at me with those strange new eyes.

But in the end, that just makes it worse.

"I'm sorry I failed you, Cat."

Because she *is* in there.

"All I can do is promise not to fail you again."

But she's not in there alone.

And I raise the disruptor rifle in my arms. And I see her face twist, and I get a sense of something vast, something ancient, something awful behind the glow of her eyes. And I pull the trigger, spending the last of the rifle's power, and the shot strikes the thing that's Cat and the thing that isn't, sending it sailing back in a spray of gray blood. And then I'm up and moving, running across the corridor and diving through the escape pod hatch. Slamming it shut on its screams.

"Tyler!"

I'm sorry.

"TYLER, DON'T GO!"

I'm so sorry.

And I slap on my safety harness.

And I hit the Eject button.

And I blast out into the burning Fold.

40

SCARLETT

Zila flies like a demon, but she's no Cat Brannock.

Everything around us is chaos. Ships of every shape and size, little one-man fighters all the way up to the biggest that TerraFleet and Betraskan battle command can throw. The whole solar system seems on fire. But crazy as it sounds, I find myself thinking of my bestie. My roomie. My girl. If Cat were behind the stick of this junker, she could've made it dance. There's not a pilot alive who could touch her.

But now she's gone.

Tyler too. And Kal. And Auri.

Fin, Zila, and me are the last ones together.

Three of seven.

The engines are howling, pushed into the redline as we tear across the black toward the Weapon. Zila had to swing out wide, finally throwing off the two TDF fighters on our tail, weaving through a burning storm of bullets and missiles and I don't know what else. Her fingers blurred as she calculated our trajectory, aiming us toward one of the thinner support pillars holding those massive crystal lenses in place.

We're flying right into its face now. One last doomed charge to save our world.

And maybe the entire galaxy.

"Forty-five seconds to impact," Zila reports.

Honestly, I have no idea if this has any chance of working. I have no idea if we're doing the right thing. But the medallion around my neck glints as I look down at it, red alert lights playing on the diamond surface as the alarms around me scream.

Go with Plan B.

I was never a believer. Never bought into the idea of the Maker, or the United Faith. Ty and I used to fight about it all the time—how silly it seemed to me, how obvious it seemed to him. But in the end, he believed hard enough for the both of us. And I don't know exactly how we're going to pull this off, but Aurora Command told us we were on the right path.

Know that we believe in you. And you must believe in each other. We the Legion. We the light. Burning bright against the night.

And as we charge toward our deaths, I find myself looking around at the last few members of Aurora Legion Squad 312. And I realize it's like Tyler says.

Sometimes you just gotta have faith.

"Thirty seconds," Zila says.

I swallow hard. Heart thumping in my chest.

"You okay?" Finian asks softly.

I look at him beside me, the Weapon looming larger in front of us every second. I can tell he's scared. I know what he wants to hear. That this is the right thing to do. That I'm sure. That even though I'm only eighteen years old and I still had my whole life ahead of me, it's okay. Because this is for something bigger than we are. This is for something greater.

But that's bullshit.

I'm scared to death.

"No," I tell him.

I reach out and take his hand.

"But I'm glad you're with me, Fin."

And then it hits us. A missile. A pulse blast. I've got no idea. But we're rocked *hard*, the impact like a fully loaded freighter, smashing me back into my chair and forward into my harness. Stars burst in my eyes. The displays in front of me spew sparks and die, alarms roaring, fire suppressors firing, filling the cockpit with chemical fog. I can taste blood in my mouth, my head is ringing, my—

"Scar, are you okay?" Fin shouts, unbuckling his harness.

"I'm . . . o-okay . . . ," I manage.

He kneels at my side, checks me over. "Zila?"

Our pilot straightens behind her flickering, spitting control panels, dragging a thick curtain of black curls out of her face. For the first time, I realize she's wearing the earrings that were waiting for her in that Dominion Repository vault. The little hawk charms someone left for her, knowing she's never without her golden hoops.

I wonder if there's any chance we're going to live to find out who it was.

"I am alive," she declares.

"What h-hit us?" I demand.

"A stray railgun round, I believe." She shakes her head, a stream of blood dripping from the split in her brow as she stabs at her controls. "Perhaps a fast-moving chunk of debris."

"Damage report?" I cough, looking around the smoking cockpit.

"Engaging secondary guidance systems and auxiliary power. Control should be back online momentarily." Her fingers dance on her consoles. "But the power coil is critically damaged. Engines are offline."

The Weapon pulses again, the brightest it's ever been. The impact hasn't knocked us too far off course—we're still staring down the barrel of those massive crystalline lenses. Still right in its firing line. But we've got no momentum.

We're dead in the water.

Looking into the Weapon, I can see a collision of rainbow-colored energy coalescing like the eye of a storm. I know space is a vacuum, that sound doesn't travel through it, but I swear, I *swear* I can hear a sound. Building slowly. Rushing past the edge of hearing now. Louder and louder.

And all of us know it.

"It's going to fire," Zila says, just a tremor in her voice.

"We're not going to make it," I whisper.

"Yes, we are," Finian growls, dragging on a breather mask.

I raise an eyebrow. "Fin?"

"Engines offline sounds like a job for the best Gearhead in the whole damn Aurora Legion, if you ask me."

"You can fix it?"

"One way to find out." He flicks his wrist, and a multi-tool extends from the arm of his exosuit. All the fear I heard in his voice before has totally evaporated, replaced by his razor grin. "And let's be honest, it's been way too long since I did something incredibly dashing and heroic."

"I'm coming with you," I say, dragging off my harness.

"Be careful," Zila tells us. "Be quick."

Finian grabs my hand, slams open the cockpit door.

I drag the breather over my face.

And we run.

41

THREE ONE TWO

Aurora

Kal crumples to the ground, the familiar violet and gold of his mind overwhelmed by the dark, dried blood of his father's. It's only as darkness descends over him completely that I realize he was still touching my mind, right up to the last second, the lightest of connections.

One he couldn't give up.

One I never completely burned away.

Deception and devotion. I sensed them both in him.

Only one is for you, he said.

The Waywalkers scream above me, their voices rising in a discordant wail.

And as his father leaves Kal lying there like he's nothing, turning back toward me, I remember something else Kal told me.

Love is purpose, be'shmai.

Love is what drives us to great deeds, and greater sacrifices.

Without love, what is left?

Tyler

The Fold is on fire. Flames burning in black and white.

TDF fighter ships swarm through the dark, explosions lighting the night around me. The wreck of a Syldrathi Banshee hangs off the *Kusanagi*'s bow, lifeless and black. Another one is drifting, leaking fuel vapor and thin wisps of fire, spinning away in a slow spiral from the ongoing battle.

But the other two Banshees are cutting the *Kusanagi* to bits.

The tactics nerd in me is totally enthralled by the battle, but honestly, I've got bigger things to worry about than the free-for-all going on around me. Bigger things, even, than the war probably raging around Earth right now.

Problem is, these TDF escape pods are basically missiles, made to fly away from the ship you just ejected from as fast as their little engines will boost them. The Fold around me is *full* of debris—junked fighters, massive tumbling chunks of Banshee, arcs of burning plasma. And while this pod might look like a fish and move like a fish, it steers a lot like a cow.

I wrestle the controls, speaking into comms as I blast farther away from the slaughter.

"Saedii, this is Tyler, over?"

Finian

I grab wildly at the handrail, nearly falling down the companionway in my rush to reach the engines. Everything's built just fractionally too big for me—those tall Syldrathi bastards.

I yelp as my foot slips off the step, and Scarlett grabs me from behind, somehow holding me by one arm until I regain my balance. I don't waste breath on thanks—we make a barely controlled descent to the hallway and break into a run.

A part of me is aware I'm running to try and get my own death back on track, and that's not something I ever saw coming.

But Scarlett hasn't let go of my hand now that we're on level ground. And that's not nothing.

The engine room door is sealed, and I stretch out one hand for the touch panel—then yank it back at the last second, horrified at what I nearly did.

The warning light beside the panel is flashing red.

I lift up on my toes (tall *bastards*) and take a look through the viewport.

Oh.

"What's happening in there?" Scarlett demands.

When I don't answer, she shoulders me aside. And even though she's not our strongest mechanical talent, Scar knows what stole my words away the second she sees it. Inside the engine room, gas and fluids are venting into space.

There's a gaping hole in the side of this piece-of-chakk ship. Its ragged edges are bent inward, and I can see the battle still under way outside. I can see the stars. Whatever hit us punched straight through.

Our engines are in pieces.

I can't fix this.

Zila

The Weapon ahead of us brightens, swirling with color, a thousand rainbows refracted back and forth.

Slowly, I take my hands off the controls. I let my mind rest. My thoughts quiet.

There are no further calculations required of me.

It is strangely peaceful.

I lean into my mic to speak to my squadmates.

"Finian, Scarlett. It has been a privilege to serve in Squad 312 alongside you."

I am not feeling nothing.

Tyler

A Syldrathi Banshee streaks past me, silent as death, black and crescent-shaped. My proximity alarms are shrieking, my palms damp with sweat as I weave past the shattered hulk of a TDF fighter, barely missing a spinning chunk of Banshee hull.

"Unbroken vessels, this is Tyler Jones, do you read me, over?"

I stab at comms again. Wondering if something happened to Saedii. Wondering if her crew managed to scoop her up. Wondering if . . .

. . . if she's decided to leave me here to die.

She wouldn't do that, would she?

"Saedii, do you *copy*?"

"We copy you, Tyler."

The reply rings down my emergency channel, making my pounding heart fall still. It's iron cold. Edged with static. But even still, I know that voice.

I've known it since we were five years old.

". . . Cat."

Scarlett

I hope Tyler's still alive out there somewhere.

I know he'll understand I didn't want to leave him.

I never imagined I'd go out heroically. More at the age of one hundred and fifty-seven, while scandalously making love to the pool boy, you know?

But . . . this is okay too.

I meet Fin's eyes. They're black all over, and the contacts should make it impossible to read his expression. But I've never found it hard.

I realize we're still holding hands.

So I turn toward him and take his other hand in mine too.

Aurora

I stagger to my feet, every muscle screaming, my mind straining to hold back the Starslayer's assaults. The Waywalkers' psychic energy pours into him in a torrent now, and he's so big I can't even find his edges.

He laughs as I barely manage to bat him away, my vision darkening at the edges.

Kal lies still.

But I am on fire.

And I am burning

burning

burning.

Zila

I have always been agnostic. Faith is hard for me. I am not built for it.

But I wonder if my parents will be waiting for me.

We have failed, but I hope they will see how hard we tried.

Tyler

"WE'RE SORRY, TYLER," Cat says.

I frown. "Sorry for what?"

An alert pings on the escape pod's HUD, followed by a sawing alarm from the main computer.

"WARNING: MISSILE LOCK DETECTED."

My stomach drops and rolls. Moments later, another alarm screams through the pod's cockpit, lights flashing as a new dot appears on my HUD.

"WARNING: MISSILE INBOUND. REPEAT: MISSILE IN-BOUND."

Headed right for me.

"Maker, help me," I whisper.

Finian

I can't look away from her.

She squeezes my hands with hers, and somehow, impossibly, she grins. *Maker, but she's luminous.*

And somehow, impossibly, she pulls a grin from me in answer.

Scarlett

I've never seen him just smile before—no cynicism, no guard up.

He's beautiful.

He bites his lip as we gaze at each other, and hey, it's a matter of seconds until the Weapon fires, or a TDF ship blows us out of the sky.

So I use our joined hands to tug him in closer. He's exactly my height.

All I have to do is tilt my head a little.

Finian

Thank you, Maker, thank you, thank you, thank you, thank you.

I can't help dropping my gaze a little—I'm about to close my eyes and go out in style, kissing Scarlett Isobel Jones.

I swear I'm not checking out her cleavage as my lashes lower, but my eyes land on her necklace.

Go with Plan B.

Plan B, my ass. It totally failed. And I never even found out what my pen was for.

But the hells with that. I'm going to . . .

. . . Wait a minute.

Scarlett

He drops my hands, reaching for my b—oh, my necklace.

"Scar," he says, breathless. "This isn't diamond."

He lifts a baffled gaze to meet mine.

"This is Eshvaren crystal."

Tyler

"It's so beautiful in here, Tyler," Cat says. "I wish you could have seen it."

I watch that blip, speeding closer, alarms screaming around me.

"Missile impact in five seconds."

I think about my squad, hoping they'll be okay.

"Four seconds."

I think about my sister, and it hurts, knowing I'm leaving her alone.

"Three seconds."

I reach up to the Senate ring hanging on the chain around my neck.

"Two seconds."

Wondering if he'd have been proud of me.

"One second."

"See you soon, Dad," I whisper.

"Impac—"

Aurora

Everything is pain, and I can't feel Kal anymore.

And the Eshvaren were wrong. I was never meant to burn it all away.

Love is purpose, be'shmai.

Love is what drives us to great deeds, and greater sacrifices.

Without love, what is left?

I don't have to find out the answer to that question.

Because I love him.

I have my strength. I have my purpose.

His father's poisoned mind is in tune with the Weapon now—all around us the crystal is thrumming, singing, screaming as it prepares to destroy my people's sun.

I can't stop it now. It's too far gone, too close to the moment this incredible, impossible surge of power will be released.

But maybe, just maybe . . .

Zila

A beam of pure light ignites ahead of me.

It is the most beautiful thing I have ever seen.

And then everything
                              is
                                        d a r k n e s s
                                        d a r k n e s s
                                        d a r k n e s s
                                        d a r k n e s s
                                        d a r k n e s s

GREETINGS, CADETS!

IT TURNS OUT WE WROTE SUCH A LONG BOOK THAT OUR EDITOR SAYS THERE'S JUST ONE PAGE LEFT FOR OUR ACKNOWLEDGMENTS. OOPS. SO HERE WE GO, AS SHORT AS WE CAN MAKE IT: A LIST OF THE CRIMINALS AND REPROBATES WHO MADE THIS BOOK A REALITY. BE WARNED, THEY'RE DANGEROUS.

THERE'S BARBARA, MELANIE, KAREN, ARTIE, JAKE, JUDITH, JOSH, AMY, DAWN, KATHLEEN, JOHN, ARELY, HEATHER, TRISH, RAY, AND NATALIA, PLUS THE CREWS IN SALES, MARKETING, PUBLICITY, AND MANAGING ED. DEB AND CHARLIE, OF COURSE, PLUS ANNA, NICOLA, SOPHIE, AND THE QUESTIONABLE CHARACTERS THEY ASSOCIATE WITH. THERE'S ALSO JULIET, SHADI, AIMEE, MARK, KATE, MOLLY, BEN, HAYLEY, PAUL, LAURA, AND LUCY. AND LET'S NOT FORGET TO APPORTION SOME BLAME TO OUR INTERNATIONAL PUBLISHERS AND TRANSLATORS.

DON'T LET JOSH, TRACEY, CATHY, OR STEPHEN OFF THE HOOK, AND KEEP ONE BEADY EYE ON OUR FOREIGN AGENTS AND SCOUTS. DON'T TRUST THE CREW OF BOOKSELLERS, LIBRARIANS, READERS, VLOGGERS, BLOGGERS, TWEETERS, AND BOOKSTAGRAMMERS, WHO SPREAD THE WORD, EITHER. THEN THERE'S NICK, OUR AUDIO TEAM, AND OUR SQUAD OF NARRATORS. TOTALLY UNTRUSTWORTHY.

WHATEVER YOU DO, DON'T TURN YOUR BACK ON OUR OWN EXTENSIVE NETWORK OF CRIMINAL ASSOCIATES: MEG, MICHELLE, MARIE, LEIGH, KACEY, THE KATES, SORAYA, ELIZA, DAVE, PETE, KIERSTEN, LT, RYAN, THE CATS, THE ROTI BOTI CREW, THE HOUSE OF PROGRESS, TSANA, NIC, SARAH, MARC, B-MONEY, RAFE, WEEZ, PARIS, BATMAN, SURLY JIM, GLEN, SPIV, ORRSOME, TOVES, SAM, TONY, KATH, KYLIE, NICOLE, KURT, JACK, MAX, POPPY, MARILYN, FLIC, GEORGE, KAY, NEVILLE, SHANNON, ADAM, BODE, AND LUCA. ALSO SAM AND JACK.

AND LAST, MOST, AND ALWAYS, THERE'S AMANDA AND BRENDAN . . . AND NOW PIP.

BUCKLE UP: THIS IS ONE RIDE
YOU CAN'T AFFORD TO MISS!

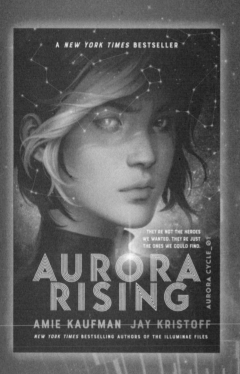

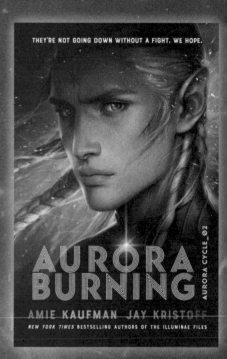

DON'T MISS THE FINALE,
COMING IN 2021!